T0374478

Ready, Set, Action!

Not every desire should
be captured on film.

Ready,
Set,
Action!

Lynne Martin

iUniverse, Inc.
Bloomington

Ready, Set, Action!
Not every desire should be captured on film.

Copyright © 2012 by Lynne Martin

All rights reserved. No part of this book may be used or reproduced by any means, graphic, electronic, or mechanical, including photocopying, recording, taping or by any information storage retrieval system without the written permission of the publisher except in the case of brief quotations embodied in critical articles and reviews.

This is a work of fiction. All of the characters, names, incidents, organizations, and dialogue in this novel are either the products of the author's imagination or are used fictitiously.

iUniverse books may be ordered through booksellers or by contacting:

iUniverse
1663 Liberty Drive
Bloomington, IN 47403
www.iuniverse.com
1-800-Authors (1-800-288-4677)

Because of the dynamic nature of the Internet, any web addresses or links contained in this book may have changed since publication and may no longer be valid. The views expressed in this work are solely those of the author and do not necessarily reflect the views of the publisher, and the publisher hereby disclaims any responsibility for them.

Any people depicted in stock imagery provided by Thinkstock are models, and such images are being used for illustrative purposes only.

Certain stock imagery © Thinkstock.

ISBN: 978-1-4620-8339-8 (sc)
ISBN: 978-1-4620-8340-4 (hc)
ISBN: 978-1-4620-8341-1 (e)

Library of Congress Control Number: 2011962708

Printed in the United States of America

iUniverse rev. date: 1/6/2012

DEDICATION:

I would like to dedicate this work of fiction to my husband. A man who has repeatedly proven that he is much stronger than any of the trials and tribulations we have managed to over come together.

CHAPTER ONE

"Life is not the amount of breaths you take. It's the moments that take your breath away."

—Hitch, 2005

"You sure it's just weed? I thought meth was the drug of choice for all the serious partiers nowadays," Julia mused, dangling a slim packet of grainy white powder in front of her husband's face. "Because you realize, that I had to make a special trip all the way back to the old neighborhood, just to pick this shit up?"

Her husband never looked up, continuing to review his personal notes.

"So you're absolutely positive our girl's not a crankster?"

"You told me to check, so I checked," Boyd finally relented, slamming his Daytimer shut before angrily tossing it down on the seat. "If you don't trust my Intel, then I suggest you do your own damn leg work!" He took a second to straighten his Hermes tie.

"Relax, baby," she attempted to soothe her husband's fragile ego. "You sound like you could use a drink," Julia encouraged from across the limo. Slipping the crystal methamphetamine back into her Gucci bag, she quickly took a moment to check for her alternate stash of pre-rolled joints. Satisfied that she had more than enough, she focused her attention on pouring herself a liberal shot of vodka as the car swung around yet another tight corner. "You know I just want everything to be perfect."

"I know," he grabbed an empty crystal glass from the limo's built-in bar. "But trust me; it's just weed and beer, nothing hard core for our little Indian princess."

"Where we dropping you?" Julia dug out two additional ice cubes and plopped them unceremoniously into her tumbler.

"Back at work. I got shit to do."

"Please take Mr. Giovanni back to the office," Julia repeated to the driver through the car's intercom system.

"I guess it's safe to say that I'm on my own for dinner?"

"Depends," she sipped her drink. "Last girl, I was done in under an hour."

"Yeah, and you remember the one before her? Melanie? You didn't stagger in the door 'til noon the next day?"

Julia generously allowed her prospects as much time they needed for their initial interview. Some opened up quickly. Others, you had to work on for hours. Either way, by the time they both stepped out of the company limo, Julia had definitely decided whether she was going to hire the new prospect to join her stable of contract workers.

Working for Giovanni Films was a job coveted by nearly every porn star in the business. The take home was triple the usual pay, and even when you were busy; you never worked more than seven or eight days out of an entire month.

To her credit, in all her years at the helm, Julia had never thrown a girl out of her stable for being over exposed. She encouraged them to evolve, to change their looks with the passing of time. Develop talents, practice foreign accents, anything that could prolong their life in front of the camera. Julia wasn't naive enough to demand they stay clean and sober while in her employ; she just counteracted their wild ways by monitoring their health with regular checkups and mandatory STD tests.

Her small stable of male talent was treated equally as well. Although men were fewer and far between, *house cock*, as contract males were referred to in the industry, would walk over hot coals for the security of a Giovanni Film Contract.

Only one golden rule existed at Giovanni Films, and that was absolutely, under no circumstances, would there be any moonlighting on any other film projects. During a porn star's days off, they could strip; they could hook. Hell, they could even stay at home and play happy family, but you *could not* work in the film industry. Period.

Only one girl had broken the cardinal rule, and by the time Boyd Giovanni was finished making the rounds, nobody would even hire her on set as a *fluffer*. The last word on the street was that she'd ended up selling her ass for quarters off the strip, in some crack house near Vegas. Whether or not the story was true, it didn't matter. The message had circulated through the industry and the rule was now accepted as law.

"Call me when you're done," Boyd threw the rest of his drink down his throat.

"And don't you forget to call your brother Pete," Julia continued with few last minute instructions. "He was supposed to have arranged for all supplies from the master list that I'd left on his desk two weeks ago. Tell him I wanna go over his purchases before he files the invoice with payroll."

"Why?" Boyd demanded, still a little hot under the collar from having his Intel questioned.

"Cuz last time he paid over a hundred bucks for a cheap case of dollar-store lube, and nearly half the actors got ugly rashes and were ready to walk off the set. I need a little quality here. Right?"

I need, I need; Boyd mimicked his wife's voice in the privacy of his own head.

"Fine, I'll check off your list against Pete's deliveries. But I'm warning you right now Julia; he's not going to be very happy about it. You know what I mean?"

"Screw him. He's just an overpaid errand boy as it is."

"He's my brother."

"Whatever," Julia changed the topic with a wave of her manicured hand. "And one more thing. When you're talking to the Asian clients, you tell them that there's no way in hell one of my girls is going to do that film without some kind of eyewear to protect her vision."

"I don't know. They were pretty fucking picky about the look they wanted."

"Well, how about we throw a little orange juice in their faces? See how they like it?"

"Okay, okay, I'll take care of it. Maybe some sexy black sunglasses or clear lenses with teacher-like horn rims," he began to think aloud. "Just leave it with me; I'm pretty sure I can work something out."

Julia always managed to get what she wanted. But then again, it was in the best interest of the company, as she repeatedly reminded every member of her staff. "Can I have a kiss, doll?"

Boyd obliged, lifting up his Daytimer in the same motion. "You'll need this," he handed her a copy of the address. "She's expecting you by four."

"What's her name again?"

"Stage?"

"Both."

Quickly reopening his book, Boyd shuffled to the appropriate page. "She strips under the tag of Cherry Blossom, but she was born Lillian Anne Cardinal. She's eighteen, and she's never starred in anything other than a high school production of *Our Town*."

"How's she been paying the bills?"

"She's been stripping down at *Cheeks*. That's where I spotted her, remember?" Boyd called out over his shoulder as he turned his body to exit the car.

Julia winced, fully aware of the life on and off the stage. "Well, then I'd better move if I'm going to beat the downtown traffic," she dropped the note next to her bag.

Standing alone on the sidewalk, Boyd shook his head, watching his wife speed off toward another one of her little discovery projects.

———————

Slitting open the cardboard crate of sex toys, Pete Giovanni grabbed the first individual box his fingers could reach and flipped open the top. "Fuck me! This ain't what I ordered." He threw down a handful of cheap plastic nipple clamps, angrily watching them bounce across his desk.

"So what we got?" Boyd strolled unannounced into his brother's office.

"I don't know yet." Pete quickly closed up the lid. "I'll go through it tonight after supper. You know, when everybody's gone home and I'm alone. Last thing I need is people looking over my back and trying to grab a couple freebees."

"I thought you were going home to Ma's for supper?"

"I am. I am," he nervously confirmed.

"Well it doesn't make sense to drive all the way back cross town just to sort the delivery."

"Right, then I'll do it Monday."

"No, I need some of it for a shoot this Saturday. We'll do it now."

Pete could tell by the tone in his older brother's voice that there wasn't going to be any further negotiations. "Fine, we'll do it now," he shrugged. "Roll up your sleeves and lets finish cracking all the boxes."

Hanging his suit coat on the back of his brother's chair, Boyd scanned the desk for the original order. "Where's your paperwork?"

"Filed," he answered. "Hey Boyd, look at this mother," he picked up a gigantic dual-ended dildo and playfully brandished it like a weapon.

"Cute. Now pull your file. I wanna match your order forms with their delivery invoices," he instructed, yanking the company's delivery information off the side of the original box.

"When'd you become such a stickler for paperwork? I remember when we lived off the cash in our pockets, having a good time and not worrying about tomorrow until we sobered up the next day."

"That was a lifetime ago. Now we have accounts payable, a six-figure advertising budget, and a whole stable of contract actors counting on us to pay their goddamn rent. It's just not you and me anymore, bro. Lot of people depend on us, and we can't piss around like we're running this show out of that old diner."

"I liked it when it was just the two of us. Now you've got *her* as the boss, and everything's changing. She's a fucking bitch on wheels."

"Julia's my wife, or you too fucked-up on dope to even remember that?"

"Oh, don't worry about me, bro," Pete threw down the bright pink dildo and walked straight to his office's bar cart. "I don't get a chance to forget for a damn second."

"Look around you," Boyd spread his arms wide. "That little blonde piece of ass you been banging for the last couple months is your secretary. Your... personal... secretary," he drew out the words to emphasize his point. "And this," he continued to wave his arms. "This is your private little office."

"Fuck me, I know. You don't have to rub my face in it!"

"Well, I think I do. Cuz lately, you're starting to forget who's been buttering your bread. You're dropping the ball, buddy, and if you don't pick up your game real fast, you'll be replaced."

"By who?"

"By a fucking monkey. Who cares? Bottom line, you're out of a goddamn job and back on the street, running a couple hoes for cash."

Pete knew his back was up against the wall, and of all the people he could snow in the world; his brother just wasn't one of them. "My job ain't that easy," he said as he dropped back down onto his couch, downing a double shot of whiskey. "You guys hit me with really fucking weird lists of supplies, and barely any time to find them. I'd really like to see somebody else do my job. It's not as easy as you think. You try and find a fucking baby crib that'll support the weight of two grown adults. Don't exist. I know, cuz I've been looking. Don't even know where to look anymore."

"I thought this was going to solve all your problems?" Boyd pointed to the twenty-one inch flat screen monitor sitting on the corner of his brother's cluttered desk. "You wanted state of the art; we got you state of the art. What about your Blackberry, with Internet on the go? Just had to be able to access *on the go*," Boyd continued to rant. "You fuckin' leave that at the track again, too?"

"I hate fucking computers. You ask me, the Internet's for horny teenagers who can't get laid. I'm a man of action. My word is my bond. You shake hands with me, and you've got a deal, bro. That's how I do business, by my word," he slapped his thigh to emphasis his point.

"Well, bro, your word is starting to mean shit in this company."

"Says who?"

"Says me! You got one damn job. Bring in the supplies and props. We hand you a list, and you chase it down. Simple. Cut and dried. How come you gotta make it so fucking hard?"

Pete knew he'd lost the fight; it was now time to surrender and see just what could be salvaged. "You know, ma's really proud that both her sons are working together."

"Don't you dare bring our mother into this," Boyd warned.

"But she *is* so proud. Just last Friday, she was crying and telling me that nothing makes her happier than seeing both her sons working together for the same company."

"So I'm supposed to keep you on payroll cuz it keeps ma happy?"

"No, but I was thinking that maybe I could get out of the office and work more with you. Maybe get into a little of the directing and shit? You know, work with the talent, not the supplies?"

Boyd began pulling more out of the box, angrily dumping the supplies all over his brother's desk. "You know jack shit about directing."

"I know," Pete said, jumped to his feet. "But you could teach me."

"Like I taught you to be a Purchasing Agent?" he laughed. "Cuz I can see how well that worked out." Boyd emphasized his point by yanking a rubber enema bag out of the box and throwing it clear across the room.

"Come on bro, give me another chance? I'm good with people. I'm shit with numbers."

Boyd knew his brother had a point. Pete's computer skills sucked, and he didn't have an eye for details. As far as Boyd was concerned, his brother wasn't good for much, excepting maybe smoking dope and making his life hell. "Julia will never let you direct any of *her* girls. You know how protective she is with all of her projects. But…" he stalled for a second.

"But?"

"But I might have another job for you."

"I'm in."

"You don't even know what it is."

"It ain't this." Pete set his glass down on the coffee table. "Anything's gotta be better than being stuck in this office."

"We'll see," Boyd grumbled. "Now give me the original list so we can go through these damn boxes."

Pete stood up and walked over to his filing cabinet, reluctantly extracting the crumpled order. "Just to warn you, I think they might have made a couple substitutions."

"Well, just let me warn you," Boyd threw back. "Whatever we can't return, it's coming off your pay check."

"Hello," Julia thrust out her hand the minute Lillian had slid into the opposing seat.

"Hi," she smiled back, nervously returning the handshake. "Nice car. Is it yours?"

"Company car," Julia handed the girl a cold beer.

"Cheers," Lillian motioned her bottle toward Julia's glass, a little surprised at just how beautiful the *boss-lady* actually was. She kind of reminded Lillian of a real movie star, with her silky blonde hair and her flawless face, and what looked like a set of killer legs, perfectly crossed at the knee of course. But then Lillian had been fooled by beauty before.

"So, you wanna go for a little ride? I thought we might have a little more privacy in my car rather than at my office."

"Whatever," Lillian nervously shrugged, suddenly uncomfortable with the tone of her *supposed* interview. "I'm not a hooker, you know? I just dance in the pit for tips. I think you might have got yourself the wrong idea."

"Calm down," Julia reached for the vodka bottle to freshen up her own glass. "This ain't *that* kind of interview. We're just gonna talk for awhile."

"Like I said, whatever," Lillian sucked back a good third of the bottle, confident that she'd be able to handle herself should the woman decide to lunge at her across the seat. "So what you wanna know?"

"Would you like one?" Julia opened a designer cigarette case, causally offering her guest a joint as the car pulled away from the curb.

Hesitating, Lillian took a second to soak in her surroundings. "You sure you're not going to try and jump my bones after you get me a little stoned?"

"I'm sure," Julia confidentially smiled, casually taking a second to tuck in an errant lock of hair that had somehow managed to escape her professionally set French knot. Not that she hadn't experienced her fair share of women during her years in front of the camera, but truth be told, Julia had always preferred the strong touch of her *Italian Stallion*, a nickname a few of the girls in the business had bestowed on her husband Boyd, many years before.

A man, not only recognized for his wavy black hair and wide shouldered stance, Boyd had also been touted as a charmer. He was a director, who when push came to shove, had somehow been able to coerce his actresses into performing sexual acts they'd previously refused; an ability that was almost unheard of in the porn industry.

"All right," the young girl slowly reached out, delicately lifting a hand-rolled joint from the case. "You wanna share?"

"No thanks," Julia lit up her own, passing Lillian the tortoise shell lighter once she was sure the tip was sufficiently glowing.

"I hear you're always looking for fresh young faces. That's the word in the pit."

"That's not exactly true," Julia politely corrected her. "I'm always looking for new faces, because fresh and young aren't always what sells."

"Huh?"

"Different clients have different preferences. Some want your typical Barbie Doll look. Others are more interested in something a little more exotic. And some, well, there's a whole range of others who pay for just about any kind of look you can imagine."

"What am I then?

Taking a second to evaluate her guest, Julia was genuinely pleased with what she saw. "You're unique. Your native-American Indian heritage gives you extremely high cheekbones and a lovely amber skin, which photographs really, really well. And of course, naturally beautiful long black hair is an added bonus. The camera will love you, Lillian; we just have to figure out if you will love the camera back."

"I don't understand," she admitted, the dope effectively loosening her inhibitions.

"Let me explain. My clients, the men and women who pay for the filming of their private movies have very specific likes and dislikes. They know exactly what they want, and they'll pay extremely good money to have it captured on film so they can watch it over and over at their leisure."

"Porn to order," Lillian giggled

"Sort of. But my clients aren't willing to pay the big bucks for a faked orgasm and dubbed moans. They want the real thing. We film live," Julia explained. "It's a practice unheard of in the porn industry."

"Isn't all porn filmed… live?" She struggled to understand the implied meaning.

"You ever been on a porn shoot?" Julia asked, motioning for Lillian to pass back the empty beer bottle before she replaced it with a fresh one.

"No, but I know a couple chicks who have."

"Well, there are two basic points that set Giovanni Films apart from the others. First, we give the clients the exact look, positions, and story lines they're asking for. Second, we don't dub a bunch of cheesy music or second rate dialogue over our shots."

Lillian nodded, still unsure what point Julia was attempting to make.

"When other companies film their porn, a director is usually standing off to the side shouting instructions and positions. He'll tell you where to shove your head, and even verbally order when it's time for you to cum. Usually, those directors are just kind of winging a script that only they've read, but they're still in control of the shoot, and do their best to follow some bullshit story line."

"I heard that."

"Well, we do it differently. To start with, you'll get a printed script detailing all the scene set-ups and the character dialogue. Can you read?"

"Yeah, of course."

"Don't be offended, it's nothing to be embarrassed about if you can't. One of my best girls has a study partner who helps her memorize her lines."

"I can read," Lillian firmly reiterated.

"Okay, like I was saying, you'll get a script outlining the action. You'll be expected to memorize the story, and any of the specific dialogue for your character. Then we'll have a run through, a kind of practice shoot and dress rehearsal all rolled into one."

Downing her second beer, Lillian sat quietly, fascinated by the detailed explanation.

"During the practice shoot, all the actors will be present, and we'll run the entire script from front to back. No holding back, full action."

"I get paid for the practice"

"Yes," Julia smiled, not surprised at all by Lillian's standard questions. "During the practice shoot, that's when the director and I will add our input. Don't be alarmed when we stop the cameras and give you detailed instructions, or maybe even call over the costume designer to make a few adjustments. That's exactly what practice shoots and run-throughs are scheduled for."

"I won't," Lillian vowed.

"Then, after reviewing the tapes back at our office, we'll set up a filming date," Julia stopped to grind her roach into an ashtray. "That's the day we pull it all together. That's the day we shoot live."

Lillian was mesmerized. It sounded like a real movie.

"Are you interested in something like that?"

"Sure, why not. Isn't everybody?"

"It's a lot of work. We don't use *jizz balls,* and we don't use *cum inserts.* What you see in our films is the real McCoy."

Lillian had absolutely no idea what a *jizz ball* was, but the fact that they didn't use them sounded just fine with her. "Good stuff. So what ya need from me?"

Leaning back in her seat, Julia re-crossed her legs and leveled a serious look at her new girl. "I need the truth. You can't tell me anything that'll make me think less of you, so I just want the real story. Understood?"

Lillian just nodded, suddenly feeling that old sense of unfamiliarity creep up her spine.

"Let's start with your past. How young were you the first time you were raped?"

"Who told you I was raped?" She couldn't help but bristle.

"No one," Julia lifted her drink up to her lips. But she hadn't met a girl yet who'd worked in the sex industry that hadn't been violated by someone at some point in her past. "Now tell me, Lillian. How old were you?"

"Eleven."

"Who raped you?" she nonchalantly asked, as if filling out blanks on an employment application.

"Some friends of my brother," Lillian began picking at the dampened beer bottle label.

"And was that your worse sexual experience?"

"Can I have another joint?"

Julia nodded, opening her case so Lillian could pluck out a second.

"You know I could lie," she quickly sparked up the weed. "You'd never know if I was telling the truth or just making up a big fat story."

"Maybe, maybe not."

With two more puffs sucked deeply into her lungs, Lillian slowly began to speak, eyes now glued to the limousine's tinted window. "I was four months pregnant, and this guy I was living with was really drunk. He just wouldn't listen, he... he was a fucking asshole."

"What happened?" Julia gently coaxed, her non-judgmental tone successfully drawing out the horrific details.

"When he couldn't get his dick up, he shoved the TV remote all the way up my twat until I miscarried. Then he threw me out of the house, cuz I was bleeding all over his couch."

"You still see him?"

"Sometimes. He's friends with my dad."

Julia evaluated what she'd just heard. "You have any other kids?"

"No, but I've had two abortions since, so I know I can still great pregnant."

"You think you could film a rape scene without losing it?"

"As long as there's no remotes," she laughed, wiping away a falling tear as she worked up the courage to continue with the interview.

Julia appreciated her honesty. But more than her honesty, she appreciated Lillian's strong facial features and well-toned six foot frame. "Well, let me tell you about my latest project. You see, I've got this guy with a Pocahontas fetish. You know who Pocahontas is?"

"I'm Cree Indian," she chuckled. "Of course I know who Pocahontas is."

"Well, are you interested?" Julia offered. "Cuz to be honest, the cowboy and Indian rape scene is pretty much the focal point of the whole thing."

"Sounds good. They didn't have TV's back then, did they?"

"Cheers," Julia lifted her glass. "I think we're gonna be able to work out some kind of deal that'll be mutually beneficial to us both."

"Cheers," Lillian responded, never wanting to leave the warmth and safety of Julia's car.

CHAPTER TWO

"My mother thanks you. My father thanks you. My sister thanks you. And I thank you."
—Yankee Doodle Dandy, 1942

"You want?" a man's voice rang out from the living room as Lillian held her position, slowly stirring the steaming macaroni.

"She's already stoned," a second male answered. "Didn't you see her eyes when she walked in the door? That girl is fucking buzzed."

"Lilly!" her boyfriend barked, the tone of his voice betraying a deep-seated anger threatening to bubble to the surface should she not jump at his next command.

"What? I'm cooking."

"Get your ass in here, bitch."

Pulling the pot off the stove, Lillian slowly sauntered into the living room, exhausted by the apartment's escalating level of filth. "I can't make supper and keep running out here. So you wanna eat, or you wanna bullshit?"

Setting down his glass pipe, Ronnie jerked his head upward, looking directly into his girlfriend's eyes. "Where you been when you was out?"

"I already told you," she crossed her arms at her chest. "I had a job interview with a lady about making a movie."

"Woo hoo. We's got us a movie star making supper," Ronnie's best friend Jerome began to chuckle. "You gonna be working with that Demi Moore? She's so fucking hot! Member her in that Charlie's Angels movie? And she's got marriage trouble now," he added with a knowing grin.

Ignoring his friend's babbling, Ronnie turned his attention back to his girlfriend. "Where you meet that bitch?"

"I told you. Her husband came to Cheeks. Saw me dancing."

"You fuck him?"

"No," she adamantly shook her head. "He bought me a beer and we just talked."

"Just talked," Ronnie repeated in a mocking tone. "I didn't know they paid you to *just talk*."

"I gotta finish with supper," Lillian turned to leave the room.

"Why you wanna leave Cheeks?" Ronnie relit his pipe. "I thought you liked it there?"

"Well, let's see," Lillian spun around, counting her ailments off on one hand. "I'm tired of the ringing in my ears from dancing in front of the speakers. My knees are killing me," she leaned down to rub her left leg. "And you should try crawling around butt-ass naked on those rock-hard floors. And how about my shoulders," she slowly rotated them one by one. "I know it's gotta be my rotator cuff. One of the other girls knows a lady who had to have both shoulders operated on from so much pole work. And you know what else?"

"What?" Ronnie answered, not bothering to raise his eyes up from his pipe.

"I'm tired of this," she whipped up her shirt and exposed her naked breasts.

"More," Jerome whistled as if getting ready for his own private lap dance.

"I'm tired of the bruises and I'm tired of all the scratches," she yanked down her shirt. "I'm just about ready to haul off and nail the next guy who reaches into the pit and grabs my ass."

Leaning his head back into the padding of the threadbare couch, Ronnie closed his eyes and took a minute to soak up the rush from his chemical high. "So you just gonna up and quit? Cuz there's rent, and there's groceries, and diapers, and…"

"That ain't my kid," Lillian motioned toward the back hall. "Your sister had better come by tonight, or I'm calling social services. I ain't spending any more of my money raising her brat!"

"Fuck Lilly, he ain't no trouble. Just shits and eats is all."

"Yeah, and who gets to buy the formula, make all the bottles, and then change all the goddamn diapers?"

"That's what women are for," Jerome howled. "And besides, it's family. I'd take care of it if it was my blood. Or half blood," he smirked, obviously alluding to Tito's dark skin pigment and tight curly hair.

"Like you'd ever have a kid," she nearly spit in his face. "There ain't a fucking hoe alive that's gonna let you drop your seed in her twat. You might as well cut it off and throw it to the dogs for all the goddamn good it's gonna do you!"

Ronnie forced his eyes open, sitting upright to referee the full-blown screaming match that was about to shift into high gear. "Enough with the fucking insults already," he waved his hand as if physically summoning silence. "Lilly, you go make supper. Jerome, you shut the fuck up and go check on the kid."

Returning to the kitchen, Lillian picked up the pot and set the macaroni back down on the burner.

"Fill your boots, Ronnie," she hissed to herself. "Cuz you won't be ordering me round much longer."

———————

As Boyd suspected, the delivery didn't come close to matching the paperwork from his brother's supposed order. "Wanda," he yelled at the top of his lungs.

"Yes, Mr. G.," she promptly appeared, the phone system's headset dangling from her neck. "Is there something you need?"

"Yeah. What do you know about this delivery from…?" He lifted up his brother's crumpled paperwork. "From the *Den of Iniquity*."

Wanda just shook her head; amazed that Pete's shoddy paperwork hadn't landed him in hot water a hell of a lot sooner. "That's not from the Den of Iniquity," she shook her head. "Pete's been getting most of his supplies from some private contact," she couldn't help but smirk. "I kept telling him he should only order from the approved list of suppliers, but he's not gonna listen to me. I'm just his secretary."

"What kind of list?"

Without another word, Wanda disappeared from the office, returning a moment later with a manila folder. "These are the names of fifteen reputable suppliers," she proudly handed over the paperwork.

"What's with the stars?" Boyd flipped over the page as if looking for some further explanation.

Handing Boyd a second sheet, Wanda walked around the desk to explain her work, "Here's the legend. If the company has a star, it that means that dealing in cash will get you a better price. And see the highlighted names? Anybody I've met with in person, I've highlighted."

"Impressive," he nodded. "Why's number eleven got a big question mark with a date beside it?"

"They had a big change in ownership about two weeks ago, and I haven't been able to verify if they're making their deliveries in good faith."

"And the red X on number nineteen?"

"They're off our list. I just haven't had a chance to run a new copy yet."

"Wanda, why don't you close the door and come have a seat?"

"But the phones?"

"Let the service pick up," Boyd ordered, walking around his brother's desk to pour himself a fresh drink."

Closing the door, Wanda reluctantly took a seat. She had felt that a shakeup was coming for a while; she just prayed that when all was said and done, she still had a job and a paycheck.

"Tell me, Wanda, what would make you pull a supplier off the list?"

Taking a deep breath, she began to explain her reasoning for originally organizing the list. How she used her connections from back when she was still working for Unified Transport in the shipping and receiving department to find out whom the other film companies were presently ordering from. Then, after narrowing the names, she would arrange meetings and feel out the owners herself. Sometimes she would just get an invitation for dinner and drinks, other times; she found a reputable business hidden beneath a smutty name.

"So," Boyd picked up her papers. "*The Cum Pit* fell from grace?"

"They were substituting cheaper versions of client's orders and still charging top dollars for their deliveries. And," she raised her hand to make a point. "I've been hearing from a few people around town that it's not an isolated incident. They've been doing it for the last couple of months. I think they're having money problems, but the reason doesn't really matter," Wanda shook her head. "They're off my list."

"You like your job, Wanda?"

"I'm good at it Mr. G. I put in a lot of hours, even working overtime if Pete needs anything after five."

"Yeah, well, that's a whole other issue."

Wanda flushed, realizing just how stupid her last admission must have sounded since everyone in the company knew that they'd been dating.

"You like this office, Wanda?" He slowly sipped his drink, casually strolling around the room's perimeter.

"It's nice," she whispered, totally confused by her boss's line of questioning.

"By the way, what's your last name?" He suddenly turned, realizing that he knew almost nothing about one of his company's full-time employees.

"Finkel, Wanda Finkel."

"Well, Wanda Finkel, how would you feel about your name on that door, instead of Pete's?"

"Where's Pete going?"

"He's taking a more active role in filming. His heart just wasn't in this job."

Wanda nodded her head in agreement.

"You'd be Giovanni Films' new Purchasing Agent. You'd be in charge of all the supplies, props, costuming, and booking of sets. Interested?"

Swallowing hard, Wanda scrambled to organize her thoughts. "That's a really big job for a secretary."

"Oh yeah. And you'd have to hire yourself your own secretary. I suggest you use one of those secretarial services. I think that's where Julia found my girl and her own assistant."

Speechless, Wanda carefully extracted the headset from her mane of blonde curls. "I have to be honest, Mr. G., I'd give my right arm for this job, but just because I made up a supplier's list doesn't mean I'd know what to do."

"You're right," Boyd reasoned. "You're gonna screw-up, I guarantee it. But I have a feeling that the screw-ups will be temporary. You're a smart woman, and you've got the brains and the ambition to learn as you go."

"Thanks, Mr. G." Wanda proudly straightened her spine. "But umh…I was just wondering. Does Pete know about the change?"

"I don't think he truly gives a shit, but don't worry; I'll be the one to tell him. So, is this a yes or a no?"

"It's a yes," she grinned, rising to her feet to shake her boss's hand.

"Before you leave today, I want you to stop by accounting. I think there'll be other forms, shit to do with confidentiality, now that you'll have personal access to our client's information, and crap like that. They'll know what you've gotta sign. I'll phone ahead and tell them you'll be coming by."

Already busy assimilating herself to her new surroundings; Wanda's eyes began soaking up every gaudy ornaments and tacky wall hanging Pete had personally ordered to decorate his office.

"And, you'll be pulling in Pete's old salary."

That was it, Wanda knew she needed to find a chair *tout suite* or she was gonna fall flat on her tight little ass.

———————

"Another cognac Mr. Dubois?"

"Yes. I'll have a second.

"Any appetizers sir?"

"No, I'll just wait for my client. Thank you," he effectively dismissed one of the lounge's numerous waitresses.

"Frank Dubois," a man finally entered from the restaurant's connecting walkway. "I'm sorry to keep you waiting, old buddy, but I just had to strap on the feed bag first, if you know what I mean?"

"Please, take a seat," Francois motioned to the opposing chair.

"May I bring you a drink, sir?" the waitress suddenly reappeared out of thin air.

"Bring me what he's having."

"A cognac, sir?" she confirmed, experience alerting her that her newest patron probably had no idea what Mr. Dubois had been sipping from his stemmed liqueur glass.

"Hell no, little lady. I don't drink perfume," he roared. "Bring me a double shot of Jack, straight up."

Finally settled with their drinks, Francois moved straight to the point. "I agreed to meet you tonight, Henry, because you swore you had a business proposal that would be financially beneficial to us both. You also mentioned that your proposal might help me move the warehouse full of medical supplies I'd been saddled with since repossessing that property."

"I did, I did," he winked at one of the women occupying a padded stool up at the bar.

"Well, I'm listening."

"Stop me if I'm wrong," Henry began his pitch, "but from what I hear, you're sitting on fifty thousand square feet of medical shit you ain't got any use for. You don't have the connections to move it, and don't wanna bother making any, since you never plan to stock that crap again. Am I right?"

Francois nodded his head in agreement.

"Well, I know a broker that moves shit cross the border to Mexico. He buys it cash by the pallet, and then trucks it over himself. All he needs from you is a signed manifest stating that the property was legally yours to sell. It's that simple," he threw back a healthy shot of whiskey.

"Well, Henry, that all sounds doable, but I guess I need to know what's in it for you."

"I want your warehouse, Frank."

"It's priced to sell at two point five. Not a bad price for a ten bay, freeway accessible site. I'm sure you'll agree?"

"Price is good, but it's the terms I'm here to negotiate."

Signaling for the waitress to bring a second drink for his guest, Francois waited for the bomb to drop. "Well Henry, let's hear it."

"I want you to carry the first at four percent, for two years. And I want in with nothing down."

"Well, I wanna be twenty-one again Henry, but I'm not holding my breath."

"Come on, Frankie," the man added an *I* and an *E* onto the end of his already abbreviated name, managing to irritate Francois even further. "You've had that overpriced bitch on the market for six months. You want full asking price, you're gonna have to give something back."

Knowing that Henry was probably right made the situation even that much worse. "Six percent and you're paying all the legal. And should you miss one payment, just one little payment, I'm going to foreclose on your company so fast you won't even have time to move your water cooler out of the hallway. Do we have an understanding, Henry?"

"We're good," he reached across the table to shake Francois's hand. "Now I'm gonna go up to that bar and wrestle me up that little filly that's been eyeballing me."

"Henry," Francois couldn't help but shake his head. "You and I both know that young lady," he cleared his throat, "is a call girl. And we both know she's looking to close her own kind of deal."

Rising up from his chair, Henry brushed off a few of the lingering dinner crumbs stubbornly clinging to his suit pants. "Francois," he struggled to pronounce his name properly for the first time, effectively butchering it with his southern twang. "I've paid millions of dollars to both my ex-wives, and I guarantee neither of them did the things for me that young lady's gonna do tonight."

"Touché," Francois lifted his glass in a silent salute. "You have yourself a pleasant evening."

"I will." Henry grinned, plucking his second glass of Jack Daniels off the waitress's tray before strolling straight toward the bar.

Francois couldn't help but admire a man who had the courage to go after what he wanted. He himself wasn't quite so strong. He'd been battling *certain* urges for years. The pent-up anxiety was becoming a daily weight bearing down on his shoulders. He had been about ready to explode from years of sexual frustration when he heard about a special film studio.

"Giovanni Films," he plucked the business card out of his breast pocket and read the name aloud. *If you can dream it, we can film it,*" was their company motto, and ever since he'd been passed the card, it was all he could manage to think about.

CHAPTER THREE

"Frankly, my dear, I don't give a damn."
—Gone With the Wind, 1939

"I honestly didn't know you could buy pudding in fucking bulk," Pete groaned, grabbing the handle of another five-gallon pail as he prepared to drag it out of the company's delivery van.

"Don't bitch, just work," Boyd ordered, huffing and puffing as he struggled to move his third pail. "We're just damn lucky that Wanda knew enough to call a commercial catering company or we'd have really been up shit creek. Can you imagine having to scoop this shit out of ten thousand little pudding cups?"

"No," Pete huffed, finally able to swing his pail out of the van's cargo bay before dropping it down onto the graveled driveway. "Hey Boyd. Why was Wanda helping you, anyway?"

"Don't worry about it now. You just stay put and watch the van. I'm going inside to see if there's anyone else to help us unload this shit."

Pete nodded, too winded to put up much of a fight.

As Boyd straightened his back, he took a minute to evaluate the surrounding lakefront properties in the immediate neighborhood, actually surprised by the normalcy of it all. Driving by, you'd never have guessed that one of his company's *clients* owned a cabin right in the middle of the development—a man who'd paid dearly for a film crew to invade his very own backyard on a Saturday afternoon while he whisked his family off to visit relatives on the coast. Still shaking his head in bewilderment, Boyd strolled into the large cedar bungalow to check on the status of the preparations.

"Hey there, buddy," a man suddenly called out to Pete from just inside the cabin's front door. "You're supposed to come on in here."

"What about all this crap?" he motioned back toward the open van.

The man turned back toward the house, obviously getting a second earful of instructions.

"Pete! I said get your ass in here now," Boyd stuck his head out of the cabin's open door. "Nobody's gonna touch that shit. We're out in the middle of *God Fuck, USA*."

Trotting up the front walk, Pete was finally able to make his way through all the film crew, equipment, and supplies, before joining his brother as he stood alone in the secluded backyard.

"What going on?"

"We've got a fucking problem. See that hot tub," Boyd nodded his head toward a small bluff of trees. "What's it full of?"

"Water? What's it supposed to be full of?"

"Pudding!"

"Oh," Pete rolled his eyes, wondering just how much of an upgrade working out in the field was actually going to be.

"Find me a fucking hose, and let's get that bitch drained."

"You wanna tell me bro what exactly we're going to be doing with a tub full of lemon...?" Pete stopped mid-sentence, the scope of the film finally hitting home. "So how's this playing out? Gay, straight, combo? What?"

"Just a standard girl-on-girl *Sploshing* gig," Boyd casually laid out the scene, a growing trend introduced to the public after the release of *Splosh Magazine* in the mid-eighties.

"I hate fucking wammers," Pete began to whine. "I hope you brought us some rain gear. Last time I stopped by one of them wam parties, I got a huge gob of greasy butter on one of my favorite shirts, and to this day nobody can get that shit out."

"Wammers?" Boyd repeated.

"You know *W-A-M*, wet and messy?"

"Oh yeah, wammers," Boyd moaned, not as astute when it came to the latest in street slang. "Sploshing, wamming, call it what you like. It's still fucking around in some kind of food or drink product to me."

"So what's the deal with the client?"

"I'll grab the file. You find me a hose," Boyd continued to bark orders.

Pete obeyed, heading off toward the boathouse as his brother left to fetch the client's list of specific instructions.

"Put them right next to the tub," Boyd ordered the two burly men lugging the pails around the side of the cabin.

"I'm running the water right down to the lake through the willows," Pete stepped forward, secretly pleased with himself for rigging up an appropriate drainage system.

"Good," Boyd leaned up against a picnic table and began scanning his wife's notes. "Like I already told you, it's a simple *girl-on-girl*, with limited toys. Seems like he mostly wants a few simple veggie and fruit insertions, and…" Boyd flipped to the next page and continued reading.

"Cunt or ass?" Pete casually inquired.

"Uhmm…" Boyd ran his finger down his wife's checklist. "Vaginal, nothing anal. But," he turned to the last page, "we gotta make sure whatever veggies we use are bagged and thrown in the boathouse's beer fridge."

"What about the pudding?"

"What about it?" Boyd pulled his eyes off the file and turned toward the collection of pails.

"He want a bag of that shit saved, too?"

"Fuck if I know, but I guess we might as well," Boyd laughed. "So it looks like the scene descriptions are pretty specific, but the actual play-by-play mechanics are left to the director's discretion, and that's me." He closed the file with a smile and dropped it down onto the table.

"This ain't a practice shoot? I thought Julia made you always film a run through first?"

"Fuck her! I'm the director," Boyd began to yell. "If I wanna film it live today, then that's exactly what we're gonna do."

"Whatever, bro," Pete shrugged his shoulders. "Any other details we should be worrying about?"

"Uh, yeah, there was," he stopped and mentally ran down the checklist. "No dialogue, just *Stairway to Heaven* by AC/DC in the background. Editing will take care of dubbing in the music after the fact. He wanted it nice and loud."

"The girls are here," a man excitedly announced from the open back door.

"Oh, that's fucking great," Boyd hissed, "Now somebody's gonna have to keep them entertained for the next couple of hours while we prep the set."

Pete twitched his eyebrows, silently volunteering himself for the job.

"Go," his brother waved. "And make sure they're not too fucked up by the time I'm ready to film, or I'll be throwing your naked ass in that tub."

Pete nodded, quickly toddling off toward the house.

"What in the fuck do you mean?" the club's owner continued to shout at Lillian's back. "You're on from midnight to four. There's no way in hell I'm gonna find a replacement for you tonight. None of the fucking girls are gonna answer their cells on a Saturday!"

"I didn't come in to ask you, I just came in to quit and pick up my shit," Lillian continued to shove a few errant pieces of costuming into her duffle bag.

"What's the problem? You get a better offer from Diamonds? I heard they've been checking out a bunch of my girls."

"No, I'm not going to Diamonds," Lillian picked up her bag and moved over to her own patch of real estate at the make-up counter.

"I can take you off the stage. Strictly lap dancing. You'd like that, wouldn't you? Big bucks, and no more pole work down in the main pit."

"Sounds good, but I already got another job."

"I knew it! I knew it!" He began to rant and rave. "And when I find out where you're going, I'll just march right down there and whip their asses. Nobody steals the meat right out of *Big Daddy's* house!"

Lillian zipped up her bag before turning toward her old employer. "Big Daddy, I just wanted to say thanks."

"Thanks for what," he pouted, pissed off at having to watch one of his more popular pieces of ass just stroll out the front door.

"You've fed and clothed me for the last year without making me hook."

"You pissed away a lot of cash. You know that, don't ya?"

"I know," she smiled. "But that just left more for your other girls."

"Where you going?" he asked one last time.

"I'm going to work for Giovanni Films."

"You're gonna shoot porn?"

"Yeah. You think I'll be any good?"

"Hell if I know. You never fucked me."

Lillian stepped over and gently slapped the owner on his shoulder. "Thanks anyway, Big Daddy. So, if it doesn't work out, you think I can come back?"

"Sure, what the fuck," he mused. "We can announce to the floor that…" he stopped to formulate a small plan, "that you were off training to be a nun, but decided to come back cuz you just love to show off your tits to all the hot and horny men."

"Already got the angle worked out, eh?"

"Don't I take care of my girls?" he laughed, already counting the extra cash flow from her returning engagement.

Lillian waved her good-byes to the group of girls entering for the afternoon shift and walked out the door, silently praying she'd never have to step foot inside that strip club again.

Watching one of his cameramen reposition himself for a better angle, Boyd snuck up as close as he could without being in camera range, continuing to guide the action by verbal instructions.

He loved the fact that he was finally able to run a shoot just like he had back in the good old days, with the actors looking to him for direction, and no fucking script hanging around his neck to drag him down. "Now Melanie, lift Cassidy's hips up onto the edge of the hot tub, pull the cucumber out of her pussy, and then *dog-lap* her to clean all the pudding off her cunt."

Turning her back to the camera as she braced her legs to lift Cassidy's weight, Melanie couldn't help but take the opportunity to complain. "This shit is sticky, and I'm getting ready to gag. If I have to swallow another mouthful, I think I'm gonna spew."

"Last scene," Boyd promised his star as she bent down and stuck her tongue into the middle of the Cassidy's crotch. "Now slowly stick two fingers up inside and slowly rotate them. And don't drop the cucumber in the tub this time. I ain't fishing out another one. And Cassidy," he moved around to the other side of the stationary camera. "I want you to free one of your hands and stoke the pudding down the length of Melanie's hair while she goes down on you."

Cassidy did the best she could, considering that she was balancing on the slippery edge of a hot tub and now only had one hand free to stabilize her weight.

"Let's wrap this up with a long and passionate kiss. Make it good, girls," he encouraged them.

"That's a wrap," Boyd finally clapped his hand together, signaling for Pete to step forward with the girl's clean bath towels.

"I laid down the poly," one of the grips pointed to the impromptu path stretching from the tub all the way back to the cabin's shower.

"Follow him, ladies," he pointed toward the back door. "And be careful. Don't want anybody falling flat on their cute little asses."

Pete started to make his way over to his brother's side, very carefully sidestepping the yellow gobs of pudding that had been flung over the edge. "So what now?"

"Shh," Boyd held up his palm. "I've just gotta check something," he quickly explained, leaning in toward the camera.

"Something the matter?"

Boyd never answered; he just cupped both his hands up around his eyes to block the afternoon sunshine from entering the viewfinder. "Oh hell, we've got shadows. We've got shadows!" Boyd barked for a second time.

"Let me see." The cameraman leaned back over his own tripod.

"Top right, check the framing." Boyd stepped back, already tapping his foot in anger.

"Yeah, but it's those goddamn trees." His cameraman pointed

up to the fifteen foot willows planted around the perimeter of the property. "They must have swayed in the wind while we were filming, cuz I checked my frames before we rolled."

Boyd sucked in two deep breaths to calm his nerves.

"Come on, man," the cameraman continued to reason, "You know me, boss. I'm not some amateur. I've been shooting porn since you were a kid jacking off to your daddy's Playboys."

"Look around." Boyd threw both his hand up in the air. "Half the pudding is lying on the ground, and the sun's about to drop behind the trees. We can't re-film shit!"

"I can rig up lights in fifteen minutes." One of the grips quickly threw in his two-cents worth.

"Client wanted natural daylight, not artificial," Boyd reminded his film staff. "How much did you catch?" he quickly spun on his heels.

"I got a solid thirty-five minutes of action, with maybe another ten or fifteen of the girls getting in and out of the tub on each camera."

"That's going to be tight." he turned circles on the grass, his mind whirling as he calculated the usual ten to twenty percent loss rate in the editing room.

Pete finally took another chance and interrupted his brother's train of thought. "Should I go check if the girls found their bags and shit?"

"Yeah, whatever." Boyd folded his arms at his chest to survey the mess. "No, just wait," he suddenly recovered his composure. "You ain't going anywhere little brother. You're in charge of the clean up."

"What, I gotta clean this shit up?"

"I said you're in charge. You've got both grips here to help you, so I suggest you take advantage."

"Where you going?"

"Back to the office. Julia is expecting me. We have dinner plans."

Pete watched his brother pop the tapes from both cameras before turning to leave. "Do I have to refill the hot tub too?"

Snatching the file off the bench, Boyd walked over and slapped it up against his brother's chest. "Original condition. You read the rest." he began to walk away.

"Why me?"

"Cuz you wanted to get out of the office. Remember?"

"Fuck you," Pete laughed.

"And don't forget to bag the cuke, both carrots, and all the lemons. I think there were at least a couple, Boyd held up two fingers without turning back to check for his brother's response.

"You seen Julia?" Boyd popped his head into Wanda's office, surprised to find her working late on a Saturday evening.

"She was around a couple hours ago, but I haven't seen her lately."

"What you doing, doll?"

"Trying to make heads or tails out of Pete's filing system. Figured it would be best to do this on the weekend when the phones weren't ringing and I could make piles all over Pete's office floor."

"You mean your office floor," Boyd teased.

"Yes, my office floor."

"So what have you uncovered in this unholy mess?" He tiptoed through the maze of papers.

"You'd better pray you're never audited, cuz I have a feeling that most of these invoices are all bullshit," she pointed to the largest stack in the middle of the desk. "As far as I can tell," she uncurled the tape from her adding machine, "you've bought nearly six hundred dildos in the last six months."

"What in the hell are we doing? Giving one away with a free coffee to everyone who stops by the office?"

"That's what I mean, Mr. G. As far as I can tell, most of those invoices aren't worth the paper they're written on."

"First, you can drop the "Mister" shit and start calling me Boyd. Then you can you tell me where all the payments have been going to?"

"Alright. As far as I can tell, your brother Pete had been invoicing payroll and requesting that the bulk of the checks be payable to the Purple Orchid Sex Shop."

"I've heard of that place. But I thought it was burned to the ground by some angry neighbors in protest or some other kind of bullshit like that."

"It was." Wanda shook her head. "About this time last year. As far as I know, it was never rebuilt or relocated."

"But we're still ordering all our supplies through their doors. Is that what you're telling me?"

"Yes, that's the way it looks."

"Tell me Wanda. What's your take on this?"

"Oh," she began to stammer. "It's much too early to tell. I'd have to…"

"Enough," he held up his hand. "I know my brother's a weasel, so don't worry about having to enlighten me. This ain't my first ride on the Ferris wheel."

Wanda dug around to extract a specific file before moving around the desk. "You see this column?" She pointed toward a mass of numbers totaling nearly a hundred thousand dollars."

"Yes?"

"Well, in the last six months, your brother had invoiced payroll roughly twice a week for around twenty-two weeks for a grand totally of ninety-six thousand, five hundred, and forty-two dollars."

"And let me guess," Boyd interrupted her. "The checks were all made payable to the Purple Orchid Sex Shop."

Wanda nodded; her words unnecessary at this point.

"That fucking little rat. He's so full of shit. I'll hit him so hard he'll bounce till he starves."

"Boyd, unfortunately, there's more."

"What now?"

Returning to her desk, she picked up yet another file. "This file is full of the invoices for Pete's cash dealings. They total another seventy-five thousand, three hundred, and ten dollars in the last six months all drawn once again through payroll."

"Purple Orchid. Am I right?"

"None other," she closed up her manila folders and braced herself for the explosion.

Boyd began to pace, an old habit he'd inherited from his mother while she waited up, night after night, for his absent father. "How come you've only gone back six months?"

"That's all the records I was able to find in this office. I assume that twice a year, all closed files are moved to storage. Am I right?"

"Yeah, it sounds about right. I just can't remember exactly how often Julia has something like that done."

"Ask her."

"Ask her?" Boyd began to howl. "My wife would love nothing better than to run my brother right out of this company. She thinks he's a total waste of skin and he'd be more useful as a speed bump out in the parking lot."

"That's harsh."

Boyd stopped pacing long enough to offer Wanda a half-hearted smile. "He's family, you know what I mean? You just can't abandon family."

"I understand," she nodded. "I didn't do this to expose anyone; I just wanted to get a feel for how things were running around here, and what I was up against."

Moving back toward the door, Boyd turned around one last time.

"Why don't you start fresh? Don't waste any more time worrying about what Pete did, cuz you and I both know he sucked. From Monday on, just do the best job you can do. I'll take care of Pete in my own way. And as for Julia…"

"If she specifically asks me for copies of the Purple Orchid invoices, I'll have to turn them over. Otherwise…"

Boyd nodded, comforted by the fact that he had at least one ally running up and down the company halls.

CHAPTER FOUR

"Say hello to my little friend!"
—Scarface, 1983

"I don't usually allow food or drinks in my editing room," Martin said with raised eyebrows at the first sight of the coffee cup, clenched firmly in Julia's right hand.

"Well then, we're even. I don't usually allow staff to tell me what to do in my own company."

"I hear ya," he muttered, spinning his chair back toward the screen.

"So, how does it look?" Julia pulled up a stool.

Martin just shook his head, not sure how to put the film into words. "You weren't at the shoot, were you?"

"No. Why? Is it that bad?"

"Let's just say I don't see your fingerprints anywhere on this project."

"Fuck," she hissed, throwing her cup down into the nearest trashcan. "Show me what you've got," she barked; her Monday afternoon off to a fabulous start.

"Well, let's start with the set up. See camera A?" He pointed to one of his screens on their right. "It was set on a pod, and I'm guessing nobody bothered to stabilize or set up absorption cushions under any of the legs. Watch this," he slowly twisted a large black knob, carefully inching the film forward before resting on a desired frame. "Now watch the edge of the tub," Martin pointed to the screen and he continued to crawl forward frame by frame.

"Oh shit," Julia rolled her eyes. "It looks like this was filmed during an earthquake."

"From the looks of Boyd's location, I'd say the tripod was sitting on some kind of a wooden deck, and every time somebody walked by, the camera shook."

"Camera B?"

"Worse," he said as he cued up the other tape. "See the shadows; they're pretty much in every frame. I can't wash them out without overexposing the girls. If I did that, Mel and Cassidy would look like female ghosts, fucking in a giant vat of sour cream."

"Good thing we caught this now. We'll have to take a little more care for the live shoot. Hopefully we can find somewhere else for the tripods to sit when we film this at the client's cabin."

Picking up the packaging envelope, Martin quickly scanned the attached sticker. "Uh, Julia," he said as he nervously handed her the package, "This was the live shoot, and you're actually looking at footage from the client's cabin."

"Fuck me raw," she hissed.

Martin suddenly wished he was back in Bosnia, editing war footage with ground-to-air missiles screaming over his head. *Less chance of being caught in the friendly crossfire*, he began to muse.

"Where's my fucking husband?"

"Where's my fucking wife?" Boyd answered Julia's question with another question.

"What in the hell happened to this Sploshing film? It looks like absolute shit. If I didn't know better, I'd think a couple audio/visual geeks filmed it for a class project."

"Slow down, it's not that bad. Martin can work miracles. Can't you, bud?"

Not willing to be drawn into the marital squabble, Martin quickly rose to his feet and silently slipped out of his own editing room.

"This piece of shit is the exact reason we film a run through. You've just reinforced my case."

"I'm not an amateur, Julia. I have an opinion too, you know?"

"I know," she yelled. "But we both agreed that…"

"You agreed." He pointed his finger directly at his wife's face. "I didn't agree to shit."

"So what?" Julia challenged her husband. "You think your old ways of just winging it is gonna cut it in the big leagues? This isn't the Bay Street Diner, you know?"

"Enough with the fucking diner! I'm so goddamn fed up with your holier than thou attitude. It wasn't more than four years ago that you were down on all fours, taking it up the ass. Or have you conveniently forgotten your own fucking past?"

"I haven't forgotten shit." She jumped up off the stool. "You never let me. You take every opportunity you can find to remind me that I used to fuck for a living!"

"Well it's time to stop thinking like a whore and get up off your knees. This is a business, and your way of filming costs just too damn much money. We need to cut some corners, and filming run-throughs was a stupid idea from day one!"

"Get up off my knees?" She threw Boyd's last statement back into his face. "Me getting down on all fours was what got your sorry ass off the streets. Without me, you'd be filming scat for fucking peanuts, praying that some dumper didn't miss his mark and shit all over your ten dollar Wal-Mart runners."

"You think you made me?"

"Well, you sure as hell think you made me," Julia retaliated back.

"Excuse me, ladies and gentlemen." Martin reluctantly poked his head back into his editing room. "Pete's upstairs, freaking out and all the other staff have already fled the fourth floor. Word is, he has Wanda pinned up against the wall, and is threatening to blow her head off."

Pushing past Martin, Boyd led the charge toward the elevator, holding the door open for his wife as she rounded the corner and threw her body into the waiting car.

———————————

Taking her time, Lillian nervously crossed the clinic's main floor and stood motionless in front of the admitting counter.

"Can I help you?" A nurse smiled, her monotone voice passing through the pre-cut hole in the Plexiglas window.

"This is the Changeroom Clinic, right?"

"Actually, we just call it *The 5th Avenue Community Clinic* now," she alluded to establishment's name change. The previous owners, Tony and Karen DeMarco, having renamed the clinic long before selling off their interest in the business.

"Oh," Lillian suddenly dropped her tone. "I was sent here for some tests."

"I'm sorry, dear," the nurse leaned in a little closer. "You're going to have to speak up."

"I… I work for Giovanni Films. Julia Giovanni sent me down here. She said you'd know what to do."

The lady nodded, turning away from her counter to extract a specific form from the slotted wall file.

"Full spectrum?"

"I don't know," Lillian shrugged. "She never said."

"Have you tested for Giovanni before?"

"No, ma'am."

"Then it's a full spectrum." She pushed the form through a horizontal slot, simultaneously motioning to a plastic cup full of stubby red pencils. "Fill in the top box, and the doctor will complete the rest."

"A hundred and twenty-five dollars?" Lillian nearly dropped the form after reading the printed fee. "I didn't know…"

"See how I circled *no charge*?" The nurse pointed to the bottom of the form. "Giovanni films will be covering all testing fees and lab work for this visit."

"Good," she sighed, reaching over to grab one of the freshly sharpened pencils.

"Bring it up when you're done," the nurse reminded her, turning back to her own stack of files.

———

"You fucking cunt bitch! How could you turn on me? I can't believe you're such a fucking whore." Pete's exact choice of words was not a surprise, but the anger in his delivery was terrifying.

"Hey, bro." Boyd forced himself to walk calmly into his brother's old office. "What ya doing big guy?"

"You see this?" He pulled the gun away from Wanda's temple just long enough to wave it around the room. "You see what this bitch did to my office?"

"I see, but do you really think it's worth shooting her over it?"

Never taking his left hand off Wanda's neck, Pete swung the gun toward Julia's head, as she stood motionless in the doorway. "It was your idea, wasn't it? You've always hated me." He swiveled his eyes back toward his hostage. "Women are shit, man. They'll stomp all over your heart, and then fucking leave you in the ditch to bleed." He decisively pushed the tip of the barrel back against Wanda's skin.

Just as Julia took a step forward, Boyd instinctively reached out for his wife, clamping his fingers down on top of her forearm. "It wasn't Julia, Pete. It was me."

"You're lying. You're just covering for your wife."

"No. I found out how you'd worked a side deal with the guy from the Purple Orchid and I was pissed that you'd been scamming the company for cash."

"Ha!" He threw back his head, Wanda's shallow gasps now echoing throughout the office. "Why wouldn't I? You decide what I'm worth, and that's all I get. I wanted more; I wanted a piece of the big pie."

"I know, and it's all right," Boyd managed to move in a few feet closer. "It's all water under the bridge, bro. Now give me the gun, and we'll forget it all happened."

"You gonna fire me?" Pete asked, dropping his hand from Wanda's neck and turning to face his own brother. "Cuz maybe I don't deserve to work here no more."

Boyd swallowed hard, not so sure of what his next step should be, now that the gun was pointed right in his face. "You're family, I don't fire family."

"But we ain't blood." He shifted his eyes toward Julia. "She could fire me."

"I'm the boss. This is Giovanni Films," Boyd stretched out his arms. "It don't say Meyers on the letterhead, now does it?"

"Hear that, bitch!" Pete swung the gun toward Julia's chest. "It don't say Meyers on any letterhead."

Without thinking, Boyd flung his body full force at Pete's left side, instantly knocking him flat on the floor.

As the gun began sliding across the office carpet, Julia snatched it up and immediately threw it out into the empty hallway.

"I'm sorry." Pete began to cry, his brother's knee jammed down into the middle of his bony back.

"You all right?" Boyd looked first to his wife, then back over his shoulder toward Wanda, as she slowly slid down the filing cabinet, before crumpling into a heap on the office floor.

"I'm so sorry," his younger brother continued to cry, oblivious to the commotion as Julia rushed past his face to Wanda's aid.

"You're fucking killing me, man. You're fucking killing me," Boyd repeated, yanking his brother up off the floor before throwing him roughly down on the couch.

"I'm sorry, bro. I just lost it," Pete wiped his nose on the back of his sleeve. "I... I didn't sleep since Friday, and I guess... well... I just lost it," he surrendered to the exhaustion.

"He's been doing that dope of his all weekend," Wanda cried out from the floor. "He's a meth freak and he tried to kill me!" Her wails began to creep down the company halls.

Julia slowly helped the young woman up to her feet, carefully guiding her out of the office straight toward the executive washrooms.

"This ain't good." Boyd walked away from the couch to look around the room. "You're so fucked up on crystal meth, that you actually could have killed somebody."

"I know." Pete pulled his hands up to his face and began rubbing his eyes. "I'm losing it, man."

Returning with a bottle of red wine and a few of the only glasses not smashed in his brother's tirade, Boyd uncorked the bottle and poured two generous servings. "I should have told you that I gave Wanda your job, but I haven't seen you since the pudding shoot. When exactly was I supposed to tell you?" He looked straight into the enlarged pupils dominating his brother's ragged face, barely recognizing the man who cowered beside him.

Pete never answered; he just concentrated his energies on downing his entire glass of wine.

"You've gotta straighten out, bro. Living like this is gonna kill you."

"I know." Pete reached for the bottle, pouring himself yet another glass. "I just can't seem to find a job that I like."

"Well what do 'ya like?"

"Anything but porn. I fucking hate it all."

"Really?" Boyd turned to have a good look at his brother. "I didn't know that. Why didn't you ever tell me?"

"Cuz all guys love porn. I didn't want you thinking I was some kind of freak."

"But, being a fucking terrorist is a better idea?" Boyd laughed, taking a second to look around the room.

"No." Pete couldn't help but chuckle.

"Well, then you better figure out something else, because I might not be around to cover up your shit next time you lose it!"

"Where you going?" Pete struggled to pull himself to his feet.

"Well, since you tell me you don't like fucking porn, and don't wanna work in this company no more, I'm going to make sure Julia doesn't call the cops. Don't want them dragging your ass off to jail, do you?"

Pete dropped back into the leather couch, watching his brother walk right toward the loaded gun that still lay abandoned in the middle of the carpeted hallway.

"Another one?" Julia stood outside the bathroom stall, offering Wanda a second cup of water underneath the door.

"I... I..." She broke down crying, the trauma of the situation too fresh for her to verbalize.

"Please come out." Julia gently rapped on the metal door.

"Nobody... nobody ever did that to me before." Wanda couldn't help but choke on the revelation as she unlocked the bathroom door.

"Oh sweetie," Julia said and stepped forward to wrap her arms around the terrified young woman. "I'm so sorry that happened to you."

"You know he, said he loved me one time—why'd he do that?"

"Crystal meth." Julia pulled back far enough to wipe the tears gently from Wanda's face. "That's gotta be one of the *dirtiest dopes* out there. Fuck, you cook it with kerosene and filter it through red phosphorous." She shook her head in disgust. "Honey, there ain't nothing natural about shit like that."

"I like him. Well, I used to like him," Wanda suddenly corrected herself. "But I can't be around him no more. Not when he's smoking meth."

"Don't worry." Julia made a mental note to handle the situation herself. "He ain't gonna be hanging around the office no more. I promise you that."

"Excuse me. Can I come in?" Boyd hesitantly poked his head around the ladies room door.

Wanda nervously nodded her head—terrified that Pete might just be a few steps behind his brother's back.

"We're not ready yet." Julia rushed over, shooing him back out the door.

"Is she all right?" he whispered.

"That fucking asshole scared the living shit out of her. How in the hell do you think she is?"

"I mean, is she physically hurt?" Boyd angrily whispered at his wife's face.

"Is she bleeding? Does she have any broken bones? No!"

"Good," Boyd sighed with relief, slowly shifting his weight to lean against the doorframe.

"Just cuz you can't see the damage doesn't mean it ain't there,"

Julia reminded her husband. "That woman's gonna need some serious therapy to get over all the shit she just went through."

"I know, and we'll cover it," Boyd looked down at his shoes.

"Damn right, we will. Where's Pete?" she suddenly stretched her neck to look over her husband's shoulder.

"He's still in the office. I just came to check on you. Make sure you girls weren't doing anything really rash."

"Like calling the cops?" Julia quickly turned her head to check on Wanda's condition before taking a second to step out of the bathroom.

"What a night." Boyd backed up to allow his wife access.

"What a night?" she screeched, unable to fathom Boyd's cool response. "Your brother is a ticking time bomb and this was bound to happen. You know he just as easily could have attacked me? Don't you?"

"You think I'm not ripped up inside? Cuz I am," he began to shout back. "I thought I might lose you today, and I was scared shitless."

"Good." Julia wiped tears from her own eyes as her voice began to break. "I... I thought I might lose you, too."

"Come here, baby." He pulled his wife into his arms, holding her so tight her breath caught in the chest. "I'm so sorry I let him roam free. I knew he was fucked, I shouldn't have let him do whatever he wanted for so long."

"Thank you," Julia broke down, weeping freely in her husband's arms. "That's all I needed to hear."

"So now what?" He shook his head. "I honestly don't have a fucking clue what I'm supposed to do."

"Well, I think you're right about the cops. They ain't gonna do shit for this family. They'd just be interested in locking him up for attempted... whatever," she said and threw her hands in the air."

"And ripping this whole place apart looking for dope."

"Yeah, you're right."

"So what should we do?" Boyd looked to his wife for direction, a habit he'd unconsciously developed over the last few years of their marriage.

"I don't know about tomorrow, but right now I need to get Wanda outta here to somewhere she feels safe. I think I'm gonna check her into the Carlton downtown."

"Good idea. I'll take Pete home, and try to straighten him out before he wigs out again."

"Call me later?"

"I will," Boyd promised, throwing his arms around his wife and tenderly kissing her one last time.

CHAPTER FIVE

"Greed, for lack of a better word, is good."
—*Wall Street, 1987*

Applying what felt like two pounds of stage make-up and then topping it all off with a cropped brunette wig, Julia finally settled on a pair of corduroy pants and a nondescript cable knit sweater.

"I look all right?" She threw over her shoulder at her husband, as he stood motionless in front of his dressing mirror.

"You look fine," Boyd answered, without even bothering to hazard a glance.

"Well, I'm a little nervous. I've never checked any family into a Psychiatric Treatment and Rehab Center before. I thought a little discretion might be in order." She took another minute to secure the wig cap carefully to her skull. "Last thing we need today is some guy recognizing me from one of my old films and then following us around the center like a horny old dog."

"You're probably right," Boyd agreed, finally turning to reach into his closet and pull out the first articles his hands were able to grasp. "I just can't believe Pete agreed to go."

"Why?"

"Why?" Boyd threw an outfit down on the bed. "Because he's gonna have to *own* his addictions, and he's gonna have to *own* his temper tantrums, too."

"I think a temper tantrum is a rather mild description of his freaking out last night at the office."

"How is Wanda?"

Julia stepped back from her wall mirror, holding up two pairs of leather boots. "Wanda's really messed up and she's taking the rest of the week off... with pay." She swung her head toward her husband, just waiting for him to even consider arguing the point.

"How'd you talk her out of going to the cops?"

"I didn't. She realized on her own that nothing would be gained, and the company would probably take the biggest hit if the police were brought in. Quite the show of loyalty from just a secretary, don't you think?"

Boyd never spoke—he just nodded.

"Is Pete ready?"

"I don't know. As soon as I'm dressed, I'll go check."

"Don't bother." Julia snapped on a single gold bracelet watch. "I'll check on him, you hurry up. Our appointment is for ten o'clock, and after that, I have a really busy afternoon."

"Fine." Boyd continued to dress, looking forward to carting his brother off to rehab about as much as driving a wooden stake through his own heart.

"Pete, you ready? Pete?" Julia moved down the house's main staircase.

"Please quit yelling," he barked from the kitchen's doorway. "My head's splitting, I'm about five seconds from puking out my guts, and... and that's enough of a fucking reason. Don't you think?"

"Did you eat anything?"

"No. Did you?"

Julia walked straight over to Pete and looked him square in the eye.

"I think you're doing the right thing by checking yourself into rehab. I'm really proud of you, and as soon as your twenty-eight days are up, I'll be waiting with the limo to pick you up."

"Twenty-eight days of freedom for ya both." Pete quickly turned away, secretly touched by Julia's proclamation. "What ya gonna do without good old Pete around?"

"Work," she laughed. "I'm bringing on a new girl by the name of Lillian Cardinal. I think she could possibly evolve into our new number one.

"Why? What's so special about her?" Pete made his way back toward the kitchen's center island.

"Attitude mainly. What you see is what you get, no pretense. The perfect lump of clay to mold into a *Giovanni Girl*."

"Still think you're gonna find another *you*?"

"I'm not looking for another me. I'm looking for an original look with an adventurous spirit to match. A girl with a strong work ethic and good sense of self; someone who won't be damaged by the business. A girl who can benefit from the money, yet leave her scenes on the cutting room floor."

"Like you," Pete continued to drive home his point.

"I'm ready." Boyd finally made his entrance.

Pete reached for his cigarettes and shoved them deep into his pants pocket, checking the kitchen counters as if afraid he might forget something terribly important. "Well," he nervously sighed. "I guess it's time to make tracks."

Throwing his arms around his brother's shoulder, Boyd gently walked Pete out the same front door he'd dragged him in less than twenty-four hours before.

Julia prepared to follow, unable to reconcile Pete's take on her talent search.

———————

Enjoying a steaming plate of three-cheese manicotti, with a nice glass of Italian red would have been a great lunch. The paper plate he'd been handed, filled with supermarket-quality crab puffs, and a disposable glass of room temperature house white was not.

"Amazing, isn't it?" Francois Dubois's date leaned over, and excitedly whispered into his ear. "I've heard a lot about *Outsider Artists* for the last year. But this is the first time I've been able to stumble across a decent showing."

"It's amazing, all right." Francois set his plate down on an empty stand, or maybe the top of a flat sculpture. At this stage, he just wasn't sure.

"Come with me, please?" she begged, linking her fingers through his, gently attempting to drag her date across the gallery's main floor. "What do you think of this?" Monique stopped in front of a landscape.

A trained businessman, Francois's eye shifted directly to the purchase price. "Well, it looks like a steal for only eight hundred dollars."

"I'm not asking about the price, darling. I'm asking about the painting. What do you think? How does it speak to you?"

Francois liked Monique. She was an attractive, well-educated, inspiring young woman. But he was much too old, and far too calloused, to spend his afternoons indulging her whimsical love of the arts.

"Let me tell you what it says to me," she brushed off his indifference. "This painting by *Helen Broms* is the work of a woman fighting her way out of debilitating depression. See the trees? We always seem to be standing in the shadows and yearning for a position in the light. It's like she's reaching for the warmth, fighting to step out of the darkness."

Francois nodded, wondering just how many more gallery openings and dinner dates he'd have to endure before Monique would finally grant him access to her own *work of art.*

"It just continues to amaze me that none of these Outsider Artists have any traditional training. She's been painting for years, and this is her first public showing."

"Yes, it's hard to believe," Francois smirked, not the least bit impressed with the additional collection of hand carved facemasks adorning a neighboring display.

"Non-traditional is the true meaning of an Outsider, an artist who's tired of hawking his wares in established galleries. Spending all his time and energy selling *himself* to an unappreciative public... well... it's exhausting." Monique shook her head for emphasis. "These artists, and practicing artists, are the true embodiment of pure creation. You know what? I think I'm going to buy a piece for my office. I want to support this show."

Francois nodded his approval, before wandering off in search of a *properly* chilled glass of wine.

"It's just not appropriate," another woman's voice rang out above the crowd. "How dare they show something of this... this caliber in such a respected gallery?"

"I know," another faceless voice joined in the protest from within the inner circle. "It's almost pornographic. Maybe a couple years of professional training wouldn't have been such a bad idea after all?"

Curiosity piqued, Francois carefully jockeyed for a closer position.

"I'm going to find the artistic director," one of the women announced, turning on her heels and pushing her way back out through the perimeter of the crowd.

Taking the remaining two steps toward the center, Francois was finally face to face with the wooden sculpture.

"Oh, my God," his own voice caught in his throat, his sexual urges immediately beginning to stir.

"Isn't it just horrific?" a lady exclaimed.

He was speechless. Never in his wildest dreams had he expected to run into a three dimensional representation of his inner most sexual fantasy. It was truly unbelievable.

"Excuse me, ladies and gentlemen." Francois pushed his way out of the crowd. "I also need to see the gallery owner," he announced, reaching down into his breast pocket to extract his personal checkbook.

Carefully timing her arrival with the lunch hour exodus, Wanda quietly entered the rear of the building and made her way up the back stairwell. Slinking around Giovanni Films wasn't that difficult, especially since she'd been the one staff member responsible for organizing, and then implementing the evacuation plan, in case of fire or natural disaster. A necessary evil since the tragedy of 9-11 had caught nearly every man and woman in the US with their pants down.

Grabbing the day's mail delivery deposited at her old secretarial desk, Wanda quickly tucked it under her left arm, and rushed over to her new office door. Fumbling with her set of keys, it was a good minute before she finally realized the door wasn't even locked and someone was already waiting inside.

"Boyd!" she exclaimed in absolute shock, the bundle of mail falling straight to the floor.

"Oh, Wanda," he set down a cardboard box. "I'm sorry if I scared you, but I just wanted to get this done before you came back. And hey, what exactly are you doing here anyway? Julia said you were taking the week off."

Finally collecting her composure, she dropped to her knees and quickly scooped up the envelopes and flyers before rising to face her boss. "Please tell me. Am I still the Purchasing Agent for Giovanni Films?"

"Absolutely," he vigorously nodded his head.

"Well then, I'm aware there's no back up for my job, and I think I'd feel better working, than if I was sitting at home, relieving last night's attack."

Every time the woman opened her mouth, Boyd couldn't help feeling more and more impressed with her sense of professionalism.

"I think you should know that Julia and I checked Pete into a twenty-eight day rehab."

"Lock down?" she inquired with raised eyebrows.

"No, he's free to check himself out at anytime. But, the center will call us immediately, should he do so against the doctors' recommendations."

Wanda slowly moved toward her desk, gently setting the mail on the far corner.

"And you'll call me?"

"Absolutely. Day or night," he swore.

"You know, Julia was amazing." Wanda's voice suddenly cracked, the emotional pain still simmering right under the surface.

"I know," Boyd smiled, clearing his supplies off the main desk. "Why don't you have a seat? I'll just finish with this last box and get out of your hair."

"No, no," she argued. "Don't run just because of me. I came to work to get my mind off of everything, not to add to anybody's stress."

"I know what you mean. I'm here cleaning out my brother's stuff cuz I don't want to deal with any new clients or Martin down in editing."

"Martin, huh?" Wanda smiled as if she was the keeper of an inside joke.

"Yeah, Martin. What you hiding?"

"Nothing."

"Fuck nothing. Now spill." Boyd walked over toward where she was standing and gently poked her in the arm.

"Well, when he was dating the company receptionist, she told me that Martin would only have sex with her if he was blindfolded the entire time."

"Kinky."

"Twisted," Wanda shook her head in response. "Do you think he was maybe fantasizing about other women? Well, I'm not going to have sex with a man who won't even acknowledge I'm there, no matter how big he is."

"Are you saying he's hung?"

"Like King Kong." she covered her mouth with her hand.

"Well, well. That just might fall under TMI."

"TMI?"

"Too much information."

Wanda finally felt comfortable enough to slip her arms out of her jacket, setting it down on the couch before taking a minute to survey the damage. "Doesn't look like that much was broken?"

"No, just some crystal glasses and a picture frame. But I'm packing up all Pete's shit and sending it to storage. The way I figure it, he doesn't need any excuse to come back up here. And the locks," Boyd pointed to the door. "I called a locksmith. He's gonna stop by and fix you up."

"Thank you, Mister... I mean Boyd," she immediately caught herself.

"You're welcome."

"And..." Wanda handed him another empty box. "I was just wondering how your shoot went on that sploshing flick. You know; the one with the lemon pudding?"

"That's why I'm hiding out from Martin." He quickly reached for the packing tape and sealed up the last box.

"Sounds to me like the finished project didn't exactly turn out like you'd planned?"

Plopping down onto the couch, Boyd relaxed his shoulders and let his head fall back into the pillows. "Actually, it didn't turn out the way *Julia* planned," he whined, heavy emphasis on the word Julia.

"But I saw the script. She'd already signed off on the scenes. Her initials were on every page."

"It wasn't the set ups, it was the actual filming. She's bitching about a couple of corner shadows and a few frames of tripod tremors. Suddenly we're making Masterpiece Theatre, or some kind of highbrow shit."

"That was your sploshing video you're talking about?"

"*Was,* seems to be the operative word. Julia is now talking about refunding the client and eating all the pre-production costs."

Wanda took a second to collect her thoughts, slowly walking across the office to join Boyd on the far end of the couch. "Well, let's look at the options," she rationalized. "First off, can you re-film?"

"Impossible. Client had specific setting requirements, and we can't access the location again."

"All right then," Wanda moved on. "What about some special effects techniques? I know that guys like Martin can do miracles with their computer editing programs."

"Yeah, but there's only so much you can do with an hour worth of TTs."

"Are the tripod tremors that bad?"

"Julia thinks so." Boyd sat up and turned to face his new protégé. "Say, I have an idea. Since I gotta go see Martin anyway, how about you come down with me, and we can look through the film together?"

"I'd like that." She rose from her seat, not bothering to pick up her jacket. "But maybe you should clear it with Julia first?"

Boyd's reaction was swift. "Look Wanda, I'm the filmmaker here at Giovanni Films. My wife may be good with the clients, but I'm the brains behind the camera. And don't you, or anyone else, every forget that! Have I made myself clear?"

"Yes, sir," she said, repeatedly nodding her head in acknowledgement.

"Good, then let's go." He turned and led the way out the door.

"Hey Boyd," a man called out as they both exited the basement elevator. "It's me Lenny. You know where I can find your brother Pete? He'd ordered some stuff for me, and I'm still waiting for my payment."

"What kind of stuff?"

"Oh, you know. Just stuff," he winked, unwilling to explain any further.

"Well, don't hold your breath," Boyd smirked. "Cuz he won't be back for at least a month."

"What?" the guy stood motionless, his mouth dropping straight to the floor.

"And how the hell did you get into the basement anyway?"

Flashing a maintenance pass that Pete had previously given him, the visitor was a little surprised when Boyd leaned over and snatched it right out of his hand.

"Now beat it," Boyd started to move, steering Wanda straight down the hall, and directly into the basement's editing room "Do me a favor and find out exactly how many more of those passes are floating around," he muttered under his breath, simultaneously checking over his shoulder to make sure the guy had turned around and left.

"Consider it done," she vowed, as Boyd continued on with his tour.

"Now I think it's time you got a sense of exactly what I do around here. Especially since you are the company's purchasing agent."

Wanda nodded, amazed by the four solid walls of computerized equipment. "I… I never knew," she muttered, genuinely surprised that the editing process was such a complicated procedure.

"Well, this *is* Giovanni Films, you know."

Martin pulled over a rolling stool, patting the leather top, and signaling Wanda to take a seat in front of his bank of monitors.

"Welcome to my world," he smiled, excited to have a visitor other than Boyd or Julia down in his editing room.

"Pull up the sploshing video and show us the corner shadows."

"Hold on." he carefully cued up the footage, consciously selecting the worst frames possible. "And here we go, ladies and gentlemen." Martin leaned in closer to inspect the film for what felt like the hundredth time.

Wanda shifted her eyes toward the monitor, surprised to see two beautiful young girls covered in lemon pudding, sucking and stoking each other's naked bodies.

"Well, what do 'ya think?" Boyd straightened his back and crossed his arms at his chest.

"I don't think I'll ever eat lemon pudding again," Wanda wrinkled her nose and unconsciously swallowed.

Impressed with the woman's sense of humor, Martin couldn't help but snicker to himself.

"I meant, what do you think of the shadows and the TT?" Boyd shot Martin a dirty look.

"I guess I didn't notice them," Wanda shrugged her shoulders.

"See," Boyd playfully slapped his edit man on his back. "It's not such a fucking big deal. This is porn. Not Shakespeare."

Wanda turned her face back toward the screen. But this time, now that the initial shock of the nakedness had passed; all she could focus on were the looming shadows through the jittery filming.

CHAPTER SIX

"I am big! It's the pictures that got small."
—Sunset Boulevard, 1950

Struggling to make his way through the knee-high growth, Boyd raised his right hand to shield his face from the early morning sunshine. "I prefer my grass in a baggie, dried, and ready to be rolled."

"I hear ya," Wanda smiled, struggling to keep up as her boss lead the trek through the farmer's back pasture.

"He said a quarter of a mile, right?"

"That's what... he said," Wanda breath came in short gasps, sweat beginning to dot her forehead. "But... if he's anything like my uncle... a quarter mile... might be three."

"Fuck me." Boyd stopped dead in his tracks.

Plowing straight into her boss's back, Wanda threw her arms around Boyd's chest as she instinctively fought to stay on her feet without propelling him face first into the hay field. "I'm so sorry," she blurted out an apology.

Laughing to himself, he slowly turned around to face his attacker. "If you wanted to play leap frog, why didn't you just say so."

"I'm really sorry, Boyd," she immediately took two steps backward. "I was just looking down and…"

"Wanna remind me again why we couldn't drive out here?" he yanked out his pack of smokes and lit a fresh cigarette.

"Cuz your gas guzzler wouldn't fit through the gate. That's why."

"Oh… so we don't like the new hummer?"

"I *like* the hummer." Wanda smiled. "But I *love* the ozone layer."

Forced to answer his ringing cell phone before continuing with their verbal joust, Boyd reluctantly turned his attention to his call. "Hello."

"Mr. Giovanni, please hold for your wife," his secretary announced before connecting the call.

"Boyd, where the hell are you?"

"Working. Where the hell are you?" He took a second to quickly stow his lighter in his pant pocket.

"Well, I'm just sitting at your desk, reading your Daytimer. Know what it says?"

"What?" he rolled his eyes and stuck out his tongue to Wanda's delight.

"Wednesday, ten a.m., Francois Dubois."

"Oh shit, sorry babe," he instinctively stepped away from Wanda in a bid for the smallest measure of privacy. "I'm out in the middle of some damn hay field, scouting locations for that fucking cowboy and Indian flick."

"But this guy sounded so… educated. So high class, when he was talking on the phone. I'd sure feel better if you were here with me. Maybe I should reschedule?"

"It's your call." Boyd turned back around to find that Wanda had respectfully wandered off toward the tree line.

"Why? You think I won't be able to relate to him?" Julia nervously ran her hands through her hair.

He knew where this conversation was heading and the part he was expected to play. It was going to be one round of *woe is me,* followed by a second round of *you can do it,* unless he could condense the call and wrap it up in one brief statement.

"Actually Julia, on second thought, I think it would be a good idea if you took the meeting yourself. You might not have a college education, but you know more about the business than anyone I've ever met. And don't forget, he's the one coming to you. That Dubois guy is willing to pay good money for the services of Giovanni Films."

"Okay, I'll take it," she said, slamming her husband's Daytimer closed in response.

"Good. I'll see you later, maybe we can grab an early dinner." Boyd carefully ground out his cigarette among the tufts of grass.

Julia quickly agreed before disconnecting the line.

Snapping his phone back onto his belt, Boyd began trotting toward Wanda's figure, thrilled to see that she'd already located the barb-wired fence.

"It's perfect," she shouted out the minute Boyd was in earshot. "It's got double barbs all over it"

"Yup, just like the client ordered." He walked up and leaned down to appraise the potential prop.

"I think we've got at least ten or twenty clear yards of fencing to film against." Wanda stepped back to evaluate the site. "No power lines, no out-buildings, and no corn silos in sight. I think we could make this look like the old Wild West."

"You sure this is the right kind of wire?"

"Absolutely. I spent a couple hours researching everything from the razor wire used in penitentiaries, to the home-made twisted barbs of the eighteen hundreds."

"Not scared of the computer, are we?"

"Not at all," she grinned, having already logged countless hours acquainting herself with the world of sex toys and their care and maintenance

"So, little miss fix it. What we gonna do about the gates? I'll tell you right now that I ain't packing a couple hundred pounds of gear on my back through this damn grass."

Wanda took a second to evaluate the problem. "Well, we probably have two options. We can pay the farmer a fair price to move it."

"What's fair?"

"I guess that'd be up to the farmer."

"Number two?" He brushed away debris from his palms.

"We could invite the old bachelor down to view the shoot. I have a funny feeling that once he gets a peek at some naked skin, he'll be quite accommodating when it comes to negotiating the price of his damaged fencing."

"Smart girl," he winked.

Wanda found herself blushing, thrilled to have her boss's approval.

———————

Carefully opening the delivery box, Francois suddenly realized he was unconsciously holding his breath, absolutely thrilled to finally be in possession of his latest sculpture.

"Francois, you lucky bugger," a man shouted from his doorway. "I hear you found some goof to take that piece of shit warehouse off your hands."

Snapping closed his cardboard box; Francois Dubois quickly returned the playful banter. "So bored with your own life that you've started living vicariously through mine?"

"Yep," his ex-brother-in-law rolled into the room, instantly flopping down into the first available chair.

"So Andy, why don't you take a seat," Francois sarcastically offered.

"So, what's new in our corner of the world?"

When Francois had finally admitted to himself that his marriage was not going to work, he'd sat down and systematically listed all the pros and cons of separating from his wife. Unbelievably, Andy had been considered an ally, a friend that Francois hadn't been prepared to lose.

Carefully planning his next statement, Francois decided it was as good a time as ever to break the news of his personal dating exploits to his ex-wife through the conduit of her own brother. "Actually, I'm seeing this professional psychologist by day and art lover by night. Her name is Monique."

"Monique," Andy repeated, as if tasting the word before digesting the information. "She sounds French. Is she?"

"Yes," Francois nodded, fully aware that cultural barriers had been one of his marriage's unfortunate hot spots.

"Does my sister know?"

"No," he shook his head.

"Is it a secret?"

"No, it's not a secret. But calling up my ex-wife just to make an announcement seemed a little, how would you say... cruel?"

"Cruel works," Andy agreed.

"So," Francois nervously tapped the top of his delivery box. "You wanted to see me about something?"

"Yeah. I need some bridge financing for one of my deals. You interested in floating a half a mil for about two, maybe three weeks?"

"Who's the client?" Francois demanded, not interested no matter what the percentage was, should the client's name match one of the players from his personal black list.

"New guy." Andy leaned forward in his chair, grabbing the untouched muffin balancing on the edge of his brother-in-law's desk. "He's fronting a small group of businessmen looking to get their feet wet in the commercial market."

"I need a name," Francois reluctantly pushed his parcel to the side.

"Here's his bio." Andy whipped a two-page report out of his breast pocket. "Pretty basic shit. The only thing of interest is his family."

"Eleven children?" Francois repeated the line.

"Yup, eleven children. I assume we're talking about a good old Catholic boy?" Andy mockingly crossed himself, his right hand moving first to his forehead, then his chest, before finally taping his left, then right shoulders.

"You sure this isn't a blended family?"

"Nope," he stuffed half the muffin straight down his throat. "Same wife, same husband."

"So where'd he make his money?"

Andy waved his right hand toward the *bio*, unable to speak as he desperately attempted to force the dry baked goods down his throat.

Francois took advantage of the silence, taking a final minute to complete his evaluation of the information. "All right, what are you offering for a half a mil on a thirty day bridge?"

"Twelve percent."

"Get out of my office." Francois threw the papers back toward Andy's position.

"Weekly." He crossed his arms over his chest.

"Compounded every seven days?"

Andy threw his head back and laughed. "What are you fucking nuts? There'll be no compounding. A flat twelve points a week, for a total return of two hundred and forty thousand dollars."

"Let me get this straight. Your guy is offering forty-eight percent for a one month bridge?'

"Absolutely."

"Get out." Francois rose to his feet, ushering his guest toward his office door.

"No really, it's a good deal. The guy's straight up. And he reserves the right to payout at anytime within the thirty days without penalty."

"Out!" he barked.

Andy scrambled to make a final pitch. "Can I bring him by tomorrow? That way, you can see he's for real."

"Good bye." He shook his head, giving Andy a gentle push before locking the door behind his back.

Checking his watch, Francois realized that he had exactly thirty minutes to head across town if he was going to keep his appointment at Giovanni Films.

"Please have my car ready," he quickly buzzed his secretary, before taping up the folded lid on his cardboard box.

———————

"Hope you don't mind," Boyd began to apologize. "But I just need to take a minute to call Pete. You're not pissed, are you?"

Wanda shrugged her shoulders, turning back toward the window and watching the grain fields flash by from the passenger's seat in her boss's hummer. "He's your brother. You can't abandon him when he needs you most." She always managed to understand.

"And besides," Boyd said as he gently nudged Wanda's right shoulder. "I'd like to just check in, know he's still there."

"Dial away," she encouraged.

"Hello, this is Mr. Boyd Giovanni calling. I'd just thought I'd check in to see how my brother, Pete Giovanni, is doing."

"Hold please," a voice answered on the line.

"Mr. Giovanni," a second voice returned to the line. "We have a slight problem here."

"What kind of a problem?"

"Pete is unwilling to come to the phone at the present time."

Boyd was unsure what to say.

"We here at the center feel it might be a good idea for you to give your brother a little space. He's presently dealing with some fairly deep family issues of alienation."

"And that means what?"

"Pete feels like he has been abandoned by those closest to him, and is dealing with the concept of finally taking responsibility for his own actions."

"That's good, right?" Boyd unconsciously nodded his head in agreement.

"It's a process, Mr. Giovanni. Severing unhealthy dependencies and then accepting one's own personal failures can be extremely liberating, however, very painful."

God, how he hated all them fucking shrinks. They talked in circles, and seemed to take great pleasure out of making everyone around them feel absolutely stupid. "You know, all that sounds good. But can you tell me if he's getting any better? Is he ready to give up the dope?"

"Drugs are not the cause of your brother's problems; they are just an outlet that he's used to mask the pain. We must first deal with his personal demons before focusing our attention back on his chemical dependencies. No use applying band-aids if we haven't treated the underlying emotional wounds."

"Thanks. You have my number if anything changes, right?"

The counselor said his goodbyes and hung up the phone.

"Is everything all right?" Wanda couldn't help but ask.

"Why?" He abruptly turned his head toward her.

"Cuz you look like you're about to rip the steering wheel right off the column," she said, pointing to his glaring white knuckles.

Boyd first lifted his left hand, and then his right, taking turns shaking the tension from his muscles. "Pete's still at rehab, but he's pouting and doesn't wanna talk to me. He's being a goddamn pussy."

Wanda evaluated the information, secretly grateful for the confirmation of her attacker's whereabouts. "So you want me to drive?" she suddenly offered.

"Can you drive a stick?"

She just smiled and shook her head no.

"I'm fine."

"So," Wanda quickly decided to try to change the topic. "I think I might have found an authentic Indian tepee for the shoot."

"And where in the hell did you find that? Tepees Are Us."

"No such website. But, I did remember seeing one set up behind a daycare on the south side of the city, a few months ago. When I stopped by, the director told me he was planning on revamping the playground theme anyway, so he sold it to me for seventy-five bucks."

"Nice find," Boyd smiled. "And the leather costuming?"

"I'm working with a seamstress who beads for traditional native Powwow ceremonies, so I'll keep you informed when we've settled on an exact price. But I'm warning you right now. It won't be cheap for that level of artistic talent."

Boyd just nodded his head in agreement, so thankful that he'd found a competent Purchasing Agent to lessen his workload. In less than a week, Wanda had suddenly become one of the strongest links in the company chain, and Boyd couldn't help but wonder if Julia was going to take the credit for her development too.

CHAPTER SEVEN

"Well, houses don't kill people. People kill people."
—The Amityville Horror, 2005

"**W**ell, Mr. Giovanni, I see from your counselor's notes that you're not very impressed with our group sessions here," the staff administrator reported as he scanned the notations in Pete's personal file.

Silently nodding, Pete slumped back against the chair, allowing his boredom free rein over his posture.

"You haven't even completed the first quarter of your twenty-eight day stay. Group sessions are an integral part of your rehabilitation therapy."

"I could give a fuck about everyone's bullshit problems. I'm here for myself, not them," he barked back in response.

"Sharing events from our past experiences can sometimes be cathartic. Even though everyone here comes from varying backgrounds, you'd be surprised at the common ground, when we all let down our walls and share."

Crossing his arms at his chest, Pete mentally calculated the remaining days of his stay, doubled by the two daily mandatory group sessions. "I'll log the time with my counselor, but I'm not going to group."

"Group is vital, Mr. Giovanni. I don't think I'll be able to sign your graduation certificate without verification of your fifty group hours."

Since he'd been a child, Pete had managed to hustle up a living. At the tender age of eleven, he'd learned to snatch boxes of plastic grocery bags from the big food chains and sell them by the handfuls to the Korean grocers, in exchange for leftovers from their deli counters. During those years, experience had taught him that money wasn't the only viable currency when it came to getting what you wanted.

Twenty years later, Pete had returned to his childhood lessons, forced to bargain for what he wanted. Before the month was over, he'd need the administrator to sign his graduation papers, and the administrator obviously needed some semblance of Pete's co-operation for patient and staff morale. It was time to make a deal.

"I'll attend your group, but as a silent observer. Nobody forces me to speak, or try to share. I'll listen to everybody's stories, but I ain't gonna spill my guts for nobody."

"That's a fair proposal, Mr. Giovanni. But I must insist that you maintain a hundred percent attendance record with your own one-on-one counselor for me to consider signing your graduation certificate. And no more giving the shift nurses grief over taking your medications. Deal?"

"That'll work," he nodded, pleased that the negotiations had gone so well in such a short period.

"And on behalf of our group counselors, I do want to extend the invitation for you to rejoin group discussions whenever you feel ready."

"Fine," Pete agreed, rising up from his chair to shake the man's outstretched hand. "I think I can live with our arrangement."

"One more thing, Mr. Giovanni," the administrator rose up from behind his desk. "You came here because you recognized that you needed to make changes within yourself, to change your perception of life and its purpose. You won't be able to embrace those changes without opening your arms, and welcoming in new ideas. A closed heart is…"

"An empty heart," Pete abruptly completed the clinic's one line mantra.

"That's right. And unless you open up, you're not going to reap the full rewards of our treatment. You know, graduation is only the first step in the healing process. You're going to have to carry those lessons…"

As Pete politely held his ground, waiting for the man to conclude his little pep talk, he found his mind wandering to his evening plans. It had taken nearly forty-eight hours, but he'd finally been able to sniff out *the supplier*. Every rehab clinic had one, and with very little effort, and only a flash of a few bucks, he'd made the man's acquaintance. A staff nurse who went by the moniker of Poppy Jones was the guy to know. Hired for his brawn as much as his medical education, the six foot seven, three hundred pound nurse was an underground pipeline for anyone willing to spare a little cash for a few of life's special conveniences.

Chocolate for the fatties, vodka for the drunks, and of course… there were always the drugs for the addicts. Sure, the cost was almost triple the normal street value, but who could argue when you were living in near lock-down conditions and Poppy Jones was your only connection to the outside world.

"I'll be looking for you at group tonight," the administrator called back to Pete, as he finally was able to make his escape into the common hall.

Strolling back to his room, he flopped down on his bed and reluctantly closed his eyes, anxiously counting the hours until Poppy

Jones made his rounds, his legs and chest wrapped tightly with taped bundles of contraband.

Boyd and Julia might have been able to force him into rehab, but nobody was going to tell him that he was a junkie, and couldn't handle his dope. He knew what he could handle, and a couple puffs of meth weren't going to kill him. He was just so relieved that he'd had the peace of mind to mule in a decent wad of cash.

Checking his watch, Boyd poured himself a second shot of vodka while waiting for Julia to join him in the back of the company limo.

"Sorry, baby," she began to apologize the minute the driver pulled open the door and she was able to slide down the leather seat. "I've had a fuck of a week, and I just wanted to wrap everything up properly so we could enjoy our weekend together."

Without speaking, Boyd handed Julia a glass, ice cubes already clattering within the crystal tumbler. "Where you wanna go for supper? Mario's, maybe the Harvest Grill? Or how about sharing a pizza in front of the fireplace at home? How does that sound?"

"But it's Friday night. You always like to go out for supper on a Friday night," Julia reminded her husband.

"Pepperoni, double cheese, and plenty of mushrooms," he tempted his wife. "Sound appetizing?"

Sliding even closer across the seat, Julia nestled into the crook of her husband's arm. "It sounds like heaven. I can't remember the last time we had supper at home alone, just the two of us. No guests, no interruptions, and no reason to put on a show."

Arriving home at the same time as the pizza, Julia rushed ahead into the house to prepare for their little picnic, just as Boyd intercepted the delivery boy and graciously tipped him for the prompt delivery.

"I can smell it," she laughed, mouth suddenly watering at the thought of the spicy pepperoni and gooey cheese all piled on top of the crispy cornmeal crust. "Just put it on the coffee table. I'm bringing napkins and wine glasses. You wanna grab a bottle of red from the cellar?"

Boyd never answered.

"Fine, then white," Julia conceded, misreading her husband's silence for disagreement. "I'm so hungry; I don't care what we drink it with. Grab whatever you like," she called back over her shoulder before returning to the kitchen to grab a bottle opener, and a jar of deli grated parmesan cheese. "You wanna change your clothes before we eat?"

Boyd suddenly appeared in the kitchen, still looking down at the illuminated screen on his I-phone.

"Where's the wine, honey? I'm ready to eat."

Boyd never answered. He just raised his face and stared directly into his wife's eyes. "When Pete never showed up for afternoon group, the administrator went to his room and found him passed out on the floor." Boyd slumped down onto the nearest kitchen stool. "Then when he tried to wake him, he couldn't get any response, so he called a code."

Julia instantly set down the grated cheese jar, walking over to where her husband sat near the granite island. "Did he... did he have a heart attack?"

"No. He overdosed."

"Is Pete alive?"

"Yeah," Boyd shook his head, once again gravely disappointed with his brother's conduct.

"What did he overdose on?" Julia pulled up a stool, gently intertwining her fingers into her husband's icy hands.

"According to the clinic, crystal methamphetamine."

"What? He was smoking meth in rehab? How'd he get it?"

"Dr. Grant, the administrator guy that called me. He said Pete must have smuggled it in."

"But I read somewhere that they strip searched all their patients before admittance." Julia suddenly jumped up to her feet, scrambling through a pile of papers to locate the clinic's glossy brochure. "He couldn't have been packing, could he?

Boyd threw his hands in the air. "That's what I was thinking, and Dr. Grant confirmed that sometimes hard core addicts will carry in small quantities of street drugs in their body cavities."

"You think your brother Pete muled meth into rehab? He was packing a stall?"

"Fucked if I know," Boyd threw his I-phone down onto the nearest counter top. "But they've moved him to the hospital ward, so I think I'm going to head on over. You coming?"

Julia just nodded her head up and down. "You wanna throw on some jeans first?"

Boyd shrugged, turning to follow his wife up toward their master bedroom. He was suddenly exhausted, drained by the mere thought of nursing his brother through yet another overdose. At least this time he'd partied alone, and Boyd wasn't looking at picking up a five-digit hospital bill or the cost of another funeral.

It all had started what seemed like a lifetime ago when Boyd had picked up his first tab for Julia's friend Serena. A *wanna be* actress who'd committed suicide by a heroin overdose, the girl had no one, and Julia was unwilling to stand by and watch her be cremated as a Jane Doe.

"How serious was it this time?" his wife spurred him back to reality.

"Pretty serious." Boyd threw his sports jacket down onto the bed. "They think it might have been a half-hearted suicide attempt."

"You believe that?"

"Fuck no." He stood at the foot of their bed, dressed in only his black dress socks and plaid boxer shorts.

"Well, then maybe it was the place. That rehab might have driven Pete crazy. Made him do something he normally wouldn't have considered."

Boyd shook his head in disagreement. "You can't blame that clinic for the damage Pete has chosen to inflict on himself for the last twenty years of his life. That place didn't hurt him. He hurt himself. He knows how much is too much, and he still chose to smoke the shit anyway. He fucked himself. Again!"

"Well, we better go then, and see if he's going to be all right," Julia conceded. "You want me to call for the car?"

"No, I'll drive. It might help me blow off a little steam."

Julia turned toward her nightstand, and reached for a bottle of prescription tranquilizers, choosing to put her own faith in a little chemical remedy.

———

Scanning the contract, Francois Dubois took his time, carefully perusing each paragraph of the three-page agreement. It wasn't by any means one of his more complicated deals, however it was a business arrangement he was preparing to enter into without his solicitor's approval; and this demanded a second look.

"Mr. Dubois," his assistant interrupted him through the crack in his office door. "I'm ready to leave for the night, sir. Is there anything else I can get you before I lock up?"

"No," he raised his head to address one of his company's most senior employees. "I'll be fine."

Confident that he was finally alone with his own thoughts, Francois leaned back in his chair and began to read the final page aloud. *"Section 14A. Upon selecting the final cast of actors from the Giovanni Company files, the client will be responsible for any additional financial costs incurred from changing the said cast list or cast requirements anytime after the final notarization of the above mentioned contract. Section 14B. No actor, amateur or professional, will appear in a Giovanni Production unless previously sanctioned by the company's director and hired through the Giovanni Company files. Section 14C. All cast members hired from the Giovanni catalogue are contract employees of Giovanni Films and will not be starring in any like projects during the duration of their employment at Giovanni Films or any Giovanni subsidiaries."*

Francois couldn't help but smile, strangely comforted by the formality of the document. He was a businessman at heart, and from a legal standpoint, he was doing nothing more than finalizing the details of yet another purchase. However, on a more personal note, Francis Dubois was actually ordering customized pornography.

"Section 15A," he continued down the final page. *"Should the purchaser be unsatisfied with the finished product, or pieces thereof, all mediation and possible refund of the purchase price will be determined by a third party mediator, other than the film's director. Note: Should the client at any time refuse to answer any of the fifty mandatory questions from the company questionnaire, he/she automatically voids any chance of monetary refund due to an unsatisfactory finished product."*

Grabbing his pen, Francois signed his full name on the bottom of both copies, quickly folding one set into three, before shoving it back into the provided envelope.

"Francois," a woman's voice purred from the darkened hall.

"Monique, my dear. Why are you hiding in the shadows? With a face as lovely as yours, I wouldn't be afraid of the light."

"What makes you think I'm hiding?" she teased, slowly pushing open the large oak door. "I'm not hiding. I was just taking my time making an entrance."

Never taking his eyes off the young woman strolling toward his desk, Francois quickly scooped both the signed original and his personal copy of the film contract from the top of his desk and unceremoniously dropped them into a side drawer.

"Tsk, tsk," the woman teased. "Always working. Always wheeling and dealing. You never afford yourself any time for the simpler things in life."

"Such as?"

"Such as carnal pleasures." She dropped her satin wrap on the back of an empty chair. "You seem to believe that physical pleasure is just a vice of the down-trodden. Well, Mr. Dubois," she purred, slowly slipping one spaghetti strap off her bare shoulder. "I'm here to convince you otherwise."

Rising from his seat, Francois slowly loosened his gold tie, amused by Monique's impromptu attempt at *le grande séduction*. "Why don't you tell me how you were able to access what I had previously believed to be a secure building?"

Running her hands along the fitted sides of her red satin dress, the young woman slowed her movements, paying special attention to the cinched material hugging her waist. "I was having coffee in the mezzanine downstairs, and when I spotted your assistant leaving for the night, I walked over and convinced her to bring me back up through your private elevator."

"Resourceful."

"I'm really going to have to send her a fruit basket."

"So now that you've managed to gain entrance, what do you plan to do with this privilege?"

Carefully reaching behind her back, Monique slowly unzipped the hidden zipper, simultaneously allowing the material to flutter to her feet. Within a single breath, she had shed all her clothing and was standing totally naked in the middle of his private office.

"Well, well," he strolled up to where Monique stood, stopping just short of her reach. "Looks like you're starting to feel the effects of the building's air conditioning," he smirked at the appearance of goose bumps.

Determined not to lose her composure under the scrutiny,

Monique slowly rubbed her left forearm with the fingers of her right hand. "Maybe I wouldn't be so cold if you'd hold me," she teased, hoping that he would end the uncomfortable situation and pull her forcefully into his arms.

Francois responded by moving around toward her back, carefully maintaining his two foot perimeter as her circled her stationary position. "Quite the sight you are, my dear, for anyone walking by my door."

Clamping her eyes closed, Monique silently cursed herself for not taking the time to lock up his office. Anybody walking down the hall would certainly be treated to quite the spectacle as a naked woman continued to stand motionless in the middle of the boss's office. Her entire seduction scene was suddenly escalating into a world-class farce, and she didn't know how much longer she'd be capable of playing along.

"Maybe you'd be more comfortable wearing this," Francois quickly slid his arms out of his suit coat and gently draped the satin lined jacket over her vibrating shoulders.

His kindness and obvious modesty was more than she could handle, and within seconds, Monique had tears streaming down the front of her face. "I'm so sorry," she apologized, still frozen in place, head now buried in both her open palms. "I just wanted to... to surprise you," she choked out the words through broken sobs.

Francois quickly spun on his heels and locked the office door, returning to Monique's side before gently guiding her to a velvet loveseat. "Why don't you just sit down and relax," he said, attempting to soothe her, his heart beginning to pound in his chest as he watched her nervously wrap the suit coat around her heaving breasts.

"It's all right," he rubbed her back, dropping down to join her as she fought to regain some semblance of her previous composure.

"I... I'm so... sorry," she finally forced herself to raise her head, simultaneously wiping the teardrops as they escaped down her cheeks.

Once again in control of the situation, Francois was turned on by Monique's absolute helplessness. Her willingness to accept total responsibility for the failure of her own seduction was exhilarating. He could barely contain his excitement, and the more she apologized, the harder he had to fight to control his urge to rip off the jacket and once again expose her nakedness.

"Maybe I should go? You looked like you were busy before I interrupted you… and I should have called. I'm sorry," she sniffled.

"Come here," he pulled her body snugly into his chest, feeling the warmth slowly radiate from her cheeks as her face pressed against the skin of his neck.

"I'm so embarrassed," the young woman continued to whimper, misreading Francois's attempt at comfort as nothing more than friendly concern.

"Don't fret, my little *cheri*," his right hand reached up under the satin fabric of the suit jacket, his fingers slowly making their way up the vertical line of her spine. "Let's just relax and enjoy our time together. All right?"

Monique pulled back just far enough from Francois to stare up into his eyes, slowly offering herself up for his sexual pleasure.

He excitedly accepted her offer, bending down to taste the salty tears still painted on every curve of her face.

Monique was now totally submissive to his deepest desires.

Francois knew this, and took the opportunity to enjoy her body as if it was nothing more than a play toy, gifted to him for his personal enjoyment.

CHAPTER EIGHT

"We said we'd play like we had nothing to lose."
—*Ocean's Eleven, 2002*

Clothes strewn all over the bed in jumbled piles, Lillian searched for something appropriate to wear. Anything that looked a little more professional than her usual attire of faded jeans and skin-tight tank tops would do the trick.

"Too short," she threw a brown leatherette miniskirt down on the bed, turning away from the closet to continue her search through a beat up old dresser.

"What the fuck's going on?" Ronnie demanded from the bedroom door. "Don't tell me you got fucking lice again? Cuz this time, I'll go down to that goddamn strip club and beat the shit out of any guy that's spreading it around. I ain't shaving my head and I ain't gonna sit back and watch you fry your hair with that chemical shampoo crap. Ya hear me?" he continued to yell.

"I don't work there anymore," she shook her head, not bothering to even turn and face her boyfriend. "I quit! Remember?"

"Then where'd you get the lice?"

"Who said anything about lice?" Lillian finally yanked a simple cotton blouse out from the bottom of a drawer.

"Well, what the fuck?" Ronnie suddenly decided that it was safe enough to enter.

"I need something to wear. Something a little bit classy."

Scanning the bed, Ronnie pointed to his favorite neon-pink spandex dress, each hip adorned with gold-colored buckles.

"I said classy," she repeated for a second time, irritated with her boyfriend's ignorance. "I have a business meeting. I'm not dressing for a lap dance."

Walking over to a corner chair, he sucked in a deep breath before dropping down, not bothering to move a single stitch of clothing before crushing them with his body weight. "Meeting with that lady from the film company again?"

"No," she vigorously attempted to shake out a few of the worst wrinkles. "I just gotta go in and see a lady named Wanda for measuring and photos."

"Nude?" his interest piqued. "Cuz I'd like a set if they're printing you up. I know a couple guys who'd pay good money for some, too. Why don't you see what you can get?"

"Sure, whatever." She turned back toward her boyfriend to search for another skirt, preferably something that covered more than the cheeks of her ass.

"You know, I was thinking. I ain't got nothing to do tonight, how's about I come to your meeting with ya?"

"Why?" she asked, suddenly suspicious of his ulterior motives.

"I'd go back to Cheeks and straighten shit out when you got into trouble, didn't I?"

Lillian just nodded her head, carefully holding another black skirt up to her waist to measure the length.

"Well, maybe I could be your manager or something. Help negotiate your contract and shit like that. You know, baby," he casually waved his right hand. "Take care of you, and make sure nobody walks over your ass."

Finally choosing her longest black skirt and the only white blouse she owned, Lillian quickly began shoving clothes back into her dresser drawers. "It's Friday. I thought you and Jerome were taking a road trip with some guys or something. He's been babbling about it for the last couple of days."

"Fuck Jerome," Ronnie laughed. "He ain't got enough money for gas, never mind his share of the beer for a road trip. Besides, I think you might need me tonight."

Returning to her closet, Lillian busied herself returning articles she had removed from the hangers, quickly arranging them in their former positions. "I'm just going to meet a lady named Wanda. She said to be there by seven, and it wouldn't take more than an hour. I think you'd be pretty bored, to tell you the truth."

Looking around the room, as he debated his next statement, Ronnie searched for just the right words to make his point without sounding desperate. "Tell you what. I'll walk you in, and if that Wanda doesn't want me there, then I'll leave. I promise."

"You promise?"

"I fucking said I would. Want me to write it in blood?"

She did, but Lillian knew she would have to settle for a verbal confirmation.

———

"He looks like hell," Boyd stepped out of the private recovery room and whispered under his breath.

"I know," Julia echoed her husband's opinion, unsure of what else to say.

"Let's go see the doc that worked on him. You still got the directions to his office?"

Julia pulled the paper out of her pocket and began to read what the nurse had jotted down. "Dr. Mason. He's on the sixth floor. You see an elevator? Cuz I'm not in the mood for any stairs."

Boyd took the lead as they reluctantly began making their way down the hall.

Settled in the doctor's office, Boyd and Julia nervously listened while the man went into great detail, regarding Pete's self-inflicted overdose.

"He's not in a coma. Your brother is sleeping as if heavily sedated. Presently, his body is working to rid itself of the remaining chemicals still polluting his system. He was lucky, Mr. and Mrs. Giovanni. Pete very easily could have slipped into a non-responsive coma, eventually leading to brain death."

"I have to tell you," Boyd first looked to his wife and then back at the clinic's administrator. "My brother Pete really knows his dope. I'm actually a little surprised that he'd overdose in a place like this."

"I don't understand, Mr. Giovanni. What do you mean by *a place like this*?"

"I think my husband means that there's nothing here to make Pete lose control." Julia took the opportunity to intercede, leaning forward in her chair to make her point. "You said he wasn't drinking alcohol, or partying with any other of your patients. Isn't that right?"

"Yes," the doctor nodded, still unable to grasp the woman's point.

"Well then, what we can't understand," Julia motioned toward her husband, "is why he smoked enough meth to nearly kill himself. Pete isn't suicidal, and he knows what he can handle."

"It just doesn't make sense," Boyd jumped up from his chair. "He wouldn't smoke, and smoke, until he nearly died. I gotta tell you, doc, something just ain't sitting right with me."

Nodding her head in agreement, Julia crossed her arms at her chest and slowly leaned back into her chair.

Gently closing the patient's file previously splayed across his desktop, Dr. Mason finally realized the source of the Giovanni's confusion. "Have either of you taken the opportunity to read the information package you signed upon your brother's admittance into the clinic?"

Both shook their heads no, embarrassed that they hadn't even bothered to take a cursory glance.

"Well, I think the information inside might have been a benefit. Either way," he pulled a leaflet of the top of his desk, "I'll brief you now."

Returning to his seat, Boyd silently waited for the explanation.

"I assume neither of you have ever heard of *GBR 12909*?"

Both Julia and Boyd shook their head no.

"How about *Vanoxerine*?"

Again, they shook their heads side to side.

Standing up from behind his desk, Dr. Mason pulled down a multi-colored wall chart adorned with a cross section of the human brain. "Vanoxerine is a selective dopamine reuptake inhibitor. Basically, in layman's terms, it reduces cocaine's effect on the brain. We here at the clinic are attempting similar clinical trials on another drug to see if it is a viable option for treating crystal methamphetamine addiction too."

Julia unfolded her arms, slowly wetting her lips in an attempt to search for just the right words.

"So what in the hell does this have to do with my brother?" her husband beat her to the punch.

"Well, as part of his treatment, your brother Pete was administered our clinical drug."

"So when he took the meth, he didn't get any of his usual effects. Is that right?" Boyd struggled to understand.

"Absolutely," the doctor nodded. "In addition, I must add that Pete never ingested his drug by way of smoke. The slightest spark from a disposable lighter or flare-up of paper matches would have set off the patient's room sensors. Even the smallest wisp of smoke would have activated all the bells and whistles."

"He injected it?" Julia demanded, worried that her brother-in-law had suddenly progressed to intravenous drug abuse.

Without verbally answering, the doctor reached into his desk and pulled out a plastic syringe. "See how this has been altered?" he motioned toward the absent needle that had already been plucked out and discarded. "Well, this is used by patients for what's known as a *Booty Bump*."

Boyd reached over the doctor's desk, curious to examine what he was holding in his hand. "What good is this without the needle?" he asked as he turned the plastic tube over in the palm of his hand, quickly depressing the plunger with his right thumb.

"It's the newest method of administering crystal meth. It's becoming more and more popular with the young men and women who don't want to be plagued with *meth mouth*."

Nodding their heads in agreement, Boyd and Julia had both seen junkies with rotten teeth poking through the open sores in their mouth. The toxic smoke eventually dissolving all the tooth enamel and eating at the gum line as the addicts continually gnashed their crumbling molars together.

"You see," the doctor continued to explain, "The methamphetamine crystals are mixed with water, poured into the syringe, and then after the needle is removed, the plastic tube is inserted into the anus, and the plunger is depressed to flood the rectum with the mixture."

Boyd dropped his eyes down to the syringe cradled in his hand, immediately flinging it back onto the doctor's desk.

"By way of insertion, it might take a few minutes longer to reach the desired high than if the drug was injected or inhaled, but ultimately, the addict will achieve his desired effect without the visible damage to his teeth or surrounding facial tissue. It's much faster than swallowing the crystals and waiting fifteen minutes for them to make their way through the stomach lining."

Rising from his chair, Boyd walked over to the office window and stared down into the adjoining parking lot. "You trying to tell me that my brother was shoving crank up his ass with that… that syringe?"

"Yes. And unfortunately, when he did not achieve the desired effect due to the *trial drug blockers*, he injected himself anally with a second and possibly third dose."

Shifting her back against her leather chair, Julia nervously watched her husband's shoulders began to vibrate with anger, his fists balling up at the end of his sleeves.

"How'd he get the dope? You got another fancy explanation for that?" Boyd demanded from his standing position. "I thought you searched him and his belongings before he even got to his room?"

"As I mentioned on the telephone, we don't have the right to insist on cavity searches, Mr. Giovanni, so unfortunately, some of our patients have been known to smuggle in small amounts of illegal substances in their vaginal or anal cavities."

"And this," Boyd marched across the room and snatched the plastic syringe off the top of the desk. "Don't try and tell me that my brother brought this through your door in his ass. This came from you guys. Ain't that right?"

It was the doctor's turn to cross his arms at his chest and lean back in his chair, momentarily out of answers.

Watching Ronnie peel off singles to pay for the cab ride, Lillian nervously tapped her toe on the sidewalk, anxious to rush inside the building and keep her seven o'clock appointment. "Come on," she muttered under her breath.

"Let's go babe," he said as he finally straightened his back, slinking his arm around her waist, and roughly pulling her to his side. "What'd you say this woman's name was?'

"Wanda."

"Well, let's go. Time to lay a little Wanda on ya," he laughed at his own joke.

Lillian wasn't amused in the least. She was nervous, and her boyfriend's lame attempt at humor was doing little to appease her jitters.

"I'll need to see some photo identification," the building security guard announced, unwilling even to consider allowing them access to the building's main bank of elevators without establishing their identities and confirming an appointment.

Digging into her purse, Lillian whipped out her wallet, passing the guard her entire cache of identification.

"And you?" he turned toward Ronnie. "Let's see yours."

Ronnie quickly ran his hands down the sides of his baggy jeans, knowing full well that each of his pockets were empty. "Uh, sorry man. I… I…," he stammered, looking toward Lillian for a rescue. "Did you grab my wallet off the kitchen table?"

Shaking her head, Lillian's eyes never left the security guard's outstretched hand as he slowly handed her back her wallet. "Sorry, it must still be on the kitchen counter."

"Fuck," her boyfriend cursed. "Well, you know who she is," Ronnie shrugged his shoulders. "Can't you just write me up as her escort or something like that?"

"No," the guard shook his head, spinning the guest book for Lillian to sign her name beside the notation of her appointment.

"But she knows who I am," Ronnie pointed an accusing finger at his girlfriend as she busied herself with signing on the appropriate line.

"You can wait there," the guard motioned to a group of leather chairs.

"I'll be quick," Lillian promised, clutching her purse to her chest and desperately praying that her boyfriend wouldn't spot his wallet protruding from the side pocket of her small bag.

"Whatever," he groaned, as the guard handed Lillian a laminated pass and pointed to the elevator doors.

Rising up through the floors, Lillian took a deep breath and tried to shake off the nervousness. She couldn't put her finger on it, but somehow she knew this was a big step and if she played her cards right, everything in her world was about to change.

"Lillian Cardinal?" a voice called out from down the darkened hall.

"Yes." She squinted, fighting to distinguish the figure making its way toward the vacated reception area.

"Sorry, but I just had to step out to the washroom. My name is Wanda Finkel." The woman thrust out her right hand.

"Oh, hi. I'm Lillian Cardinal," she said, and shook Wanda's offered hand. "Sorry if I'm late, but the security guard took an extra ten minutes."

"He's thorough, isn't he?"

Following Wanda into her office, Lillian was immediately impressed with the classy decorating and the fresh smell. No lingering stale smoke, no stench of sweaty socks, or soiled carpet—her private space was almost a breath of fresh air. "This is really, super nice."

"Thank you, but I'm still in the process of redecorating. The guy before me liked to lay it on a little thick." Wanda nodded toward the two naked sculptures waiting by the far wall for transportation to the basement storage room.

Accepting an offered chair, Lillian took a seat and crossed her legs, not sure exactly where the appointment was heading.

"Julia Giovanni told me that you were a dancer down at *Cheeks*. Is that correct?"

Sighing, Lillian cleared her throat and struggled to find just the right words. "I stripped under the stage name of Cherry Blossom. I never hooked, and I was the lead dancer down in the pit. I did seventy-five percent pole work, with twenty-five percent on the floor serving drinks and kitchen orders."

"How'd you do?" Wanda looked up from her papers.

"I did good," she nervously smiled. "But my shoulders were starting to ache, and I've got permanent knee damage from trying to seductively crawl around on the laminate floors to pick up my tips," Lillian shrugged her shoulders.

"How was the money?"

"Money's good, but there's a lot of hands in the pot, if you know what I mean."

"Tell me," Wanda grabbed a bottle of water off the corner of her desk and took a sip.

"You got the doorman. He needs to be *tipped out* to make sure that only paying clients get in the club and the chairs don't fill up with squatters looking for a comfortable place to blow the afternoon. And of course, there's the bartender. He gets a cut from the waitresses and the dancers. And you better tip him good, cuz he's responsible for keeping his eye on the pit and sending in a cleaner to wipe up any spills or clutter that hits the floor between sets."

"That's a lot of people," Wanda laughed.

"That's only the half of it. There's the DJ, the house mom who sets up the lap dances, the cook who runs the kitchen, and of course the floor manager."

"What does the floor manager do?"

"Schedules the dancers, hires and fires the waitresses, and generally gives the rest of the staff a hard time."

"I see. Sounds like a lot of backs to scratch."

"Ya. It's a bit of a juggle. You gotta figure out really fast who deserves a good chunk and who you just flip a couple of bucks to. Do it wrong, and you could be dancing on a dirty floor littered with pennies, trying not to fall on your ass, while the speakers are blaring the wrong music. Hell, I've seen girls' personal costumes just up and disappear after they snubbed the floor manager."

"Well, let me assure you, Lillian. Giovanni Films does not work that way. Your paycheck is all your own, and tipping is strictly forbidden. Everybody here earns a good wage, and if anyone ever approaches you for a kickback, I wanna hear about it. All right?"

"All right," she smiled, feeling a little more comfortable. "Wanda, can I ask one question?"

"Sure, anything."

"Well, I was just wondering. If Giovanni Films pays so well, then exactly how much do they charge the guys that order these special kinds of films?"

Reaching for a bound manual sitting on the credenza behind her desk, Wanda swung back around and began quoting directly from Julia's fee schedule. "A minimum of one-hundred thousand US dollars per film."

"A hundred thousand dollars cash money?" Lillian repeated.

"Well, for a hundred, you get two actors, your choice of gender, age, and look. Two set-ups, but neither can be any further than fifty miles from city center. Two costume changes per actor, and eight hours of script conference with a Giovanni house script writer."

"A hundred thousand dollars?" Lillian repeated, still unable to grasp the notion that anybody had that level of disposable income to blow on porn.

"Hey, guess what extras they'll throw in for another fifty-thousand dollars?"

"I can't imagine. Maybe my first born?"

"No," Wanda flipped to Schedule B in the company manual. "For another fifty grand, they allow you to keep all the costuming, bondage equipment, sex toys, and objects of insertion in authentic condition."

Unable to stop now, Lillian felt she had to ask. "What exactly does authentic condition mean?"

"Well, nothing's dry-cleaned or washed. It's all still covered with the actor's cum shots, lube smears, blood stains, sweat rings, salvia trails, and of course, urine and feces marks. And that's authentic condition," she folded her hands and set them down on top of the manual.

"Well, I asked."

"Now," Wanda returned to her original stack of papers. "If you don't mind, I need to take about a thousand measurements for our costuming department, starting with your height," she pointed to a wall chart discretely tucked behind a towering hibiscus tree.

Planter rolled to the side, Lillian gladly stepped out of her heels and pressed her back against the wall for Wanda to record her height, secretly grateful for the chance to stand up and digest all the previous information.

"Have you been at this present weight for awhile?"

"Since tenth grade," she proudly announced, always worried about the ever-expanding waistlines common to many of the women in her family. Skinny legs and *muffin top* bellies was definitely a family look in the Cardinal clan.

"Only reason I ask is that many of the costumes you'll be expected to wear are form fitting, and if you're the type to yo-yo up and down, we'd have to make adjustments for that and work in extra large seam allowances."

"No, don't worry about me," she smiled. "And I think it's safe to say that I've stopped growing, too."

Within an hour, Wanda had filled in all the blanks on her forms and had added an extra page of personal feedback. "I like your attitude, Lillian. I think you're going to find your experience here at Giovanni Films to be a positive step in your life. But I do have to warn you that Boyd and Julia Giovanni do not take the *non-*

competition clause lightly. I can't stress the fact enough that you're not allowed to work anywhere else in the film industry while employed with us. Do you understand me?"

"No moonlighting for another company, no matter the money or the part. I got it," Lillian confirmed.

"Good," Wanda flipped over the last page of the contract for Lillian to sign. "This contract is month to month. So should you at anytime decide the grass is greener on the other side of the fence, you're free to go with only thirty days written notice."

Reaching for the offered pen, Lillian was eager to sign, anxious for her new career to begin.

"One more thing," Wanda suddenly snatched back the contract. "I don't care if you're gay, straight, or bisexual, or something in between. But take some advice from me. Never mix bedroll with payroll. In other words, don't sleep with your boss. Either of them," she said and winked with an all-knowing smile.

"Are you trying to warn me that Julia Giovanni or her husband, Boyd, might expect me to have sex with them?"

"No, not at all. I'm just warning you never to make a move yourself. It'd be the quickest way to get your ass tossed out of this company."

"I hear you," she nodded in agreement, watching Wanda point to the blank line she was expected to sign. "You don't have to worry about me. I've already got one useless boyfriend, and if the truth be told, I'm just about ready to be single."

"Welcome to Giovanni Films." Wanda rose from her chair and reached across the desk to shake the girl's hand. "I hope you find your experience here to be a positive one."

Lillian vigorously nodded in agreement.

CHAPTER NINE

"We're all in this for one thing: money. I make it when the guys come in. You doctors, you make it when they go out."

—And the Band Played On, 1993

"Saw you drinking root beer in the cafeteria once, so I brought you a can," the orderly whipped the soda out of his uniform's front pocket. "Straw or glass?"

Struggling to focus his line of sight, Pete Giovanni continued to blink his eyes, fighting to connect a face to the male voice hovering at the foot of his bed. "Who... who are you?" he nervously demanded, his voice little more than a hoarse whisper.

"It's me, Poppy Jones," the orderly moved up to Pete's left side. "Figured it was about time you woke up and joined the living," he chuckled to himself. "Plenty of time for being alone when you're gone and dead."

Attempting to reach for the tepid drinking water to lubricate his throat, Pete's trembling hand moved over the bed frame and up toward the nightstand.

"Let me get that," Poppy Jones snatched up the plastic water jug, simultaneously flipping over the cup shaped lid that doubled as a water glass. "You sip it slow," he warned Pete, having seen more than one patient throw up after gulping down high volumes of drinking water.

"What time is it?" Pete slowly set the cup down on his bed, twisting his head side to side, as he worked the invisible knots out of his neck.

"I think you should be more concerned with what day it is."

Looking first to the window and then back toward the orderly, Pete suddenly realized he wasn't in his usual room. "Why, what day is it? And what the fuck happened to me?"

"You overdosed, bud. They've got you in the hospital wing."

"Fuck me. I overdosed?" he repeated, not quite able to grasp the gist of the conversation. "What happened cuz…"

"A nurse found you on the floor with your fucking pants around your ankles and foam streaming out of your mouth. She was sure you were dead."

Rubbing his forehead with his left hand, Pete pressed his eyelids shut as his fingers made their way down to his temples. "I remember that nothing was working, I wasn't getting any kind of fucking buzz, so…"

"So you took a little more. Right?"

"Yeah, that's right," he pulled down his hand, once again attempting to focus his eyes on the orderly's face. "But that didn't work either, so I got really mad, and I just swallowed it all."

"Figured," Poppy Jones shook his head in disgust. "You fucking junkies have the patience of a three year old."

"Fuck you," Pete flipped off the orderly. "You sold me some bad shit, probably cut with too much sulfate. Fucking amateurs," he angrily hissed. "Nobody knows how to cook a decent batch of meth anymore."

"It wasn't the dope, man. My meth is just fine. It's that shit they've been pumping into your system."

"What shit?" Pete's vision finally began to clear.

"I don't know what it's called, but they're giving it to all you guys. I hear it stops you from enjoying your dope. Don't matter if you shoot it or smoke it, either way, you don't get no buzz."

"I never heard of nothing like that. I think you just hosed me and you're making up a bullshit story to cover your tracks."

Realizing that it was time to mend a few fences, Poppy Jones dug down into his uniform pants pocket and retrieved a handful of pills. "How about a little pick-me-up?"

Checking over the orderly's cache, Pete recognized two of the dark green painkillers in the middle of his palm. One side of a tablet stamped with an *OC*, the other with the number *80*, his interest was suddenly piqued. "I ain't exactly flush right now," he shrugged his shoulders. "I assume all my cash is back in my room with my stuff."

"On the house, just to show you that I ain't pulling your chain, man."

"How I know these pills will get by those meds they've pumped into my veins? If your shit couldn't get past, what makes you think a couple hits of Oxycontin will do the trick?"

"They're treating you for crystal meth addiction, not pain killers. And besides, it's free. What you got to lose?"

The logic was undeniable to the uneducated pair. "Give them to me," Pete held out his hand while the orderly dug down into his other pocket to retrieve a coveted metal knife to crush the tablets, and a plastic drinking straw so Pete could snort the powder up his nose.

————————

"Three slices of the lemon cake and a half dozen white crusty rolls, please," Wanda announced with a smile to the bakery's counter girl.

"Paper or plastic?" the young girl routinely questioned while removing the cake from the display case.

"Better use paper, my brother hates plastic."

"Four and a quarter," she called out, continuing to wrap up the cake before filling a bag with their freshly baked buns.

Stopping to dig for a five-dollar bill in her purse, Wanda took a second to answer her ringing cell phone. "Good morning, Wanda speaking."

"Wanda, it's your brother, Warren calling," the man plainly stated as if she might confuse him with another one of her male callers. "I thought you were going to be here by noon for lunch?"

"I will. I just stopped off at the bakery for some fresh buns and a little treat."

"Well, unless you can snap your fingers and magically transport yourself to my doorstep, you're still at least fifteen minutes away. Why didn't you call me and tell me you were going to be late?"

"Warren," Wanda couldn't help but moan, "I'm on my way, and I'll be there as soon as possible. See you in a jiff." She disconnected the line, attempting to leave the conversation on the cheeriest note she could muster.

Warren Finkel was Wanda's fraternal twin. Not only had they shared the confines of their mother's womb, but until puberty struck, they'd even shared a bedroom. As siblings, they couldn't have been closer, and until the day of Warren's wedding, they'd never even spent an entire week apart.

Since the miserable failure of his marriage, Warren yearned to step back into that very routine. Unfortunately, during the fourteen years he'd been absent, Wanda had reluctantly been forced to build a life of her own. She'd managed to buy a small apartment-styled condo, had worked her way up to a position of trust in Giovanni Films, and developed a small circle of friends independent of her twin brother.

Recently divorced with primary custody of his precocious thirteen-year-old daughter Amber, Warren was still struggling with the obligations of his custodial agreement. Suddenly a full-time father and mother, he found himself looking to Wanda for the additional emotional support he was going to need to adjust to his new role.

"Anybody home?" Wanda called out from the house's front porch, setting her bags down on the oak bench before slipping her arms out of her coat and making her way inside.

"I'm stuck here at the stove," her niece shouted aloud. "Dad said not to dare take my eyes off the soup and to consider finding a new place to live if it boils over," Amber sarcastically repeated.

Lifting the lid, Wanda leaned over and inhaled a deep breath of the rising steam. "Yup, it smells like soup. Let me guess," she pressed a finger to her lips. "Your dad made a pot of homemade minestrone?"

"It's the only kind he knows how to make," Amber snickered, covering her mouth with the garishly painted nails on her left hand.

"Well then, minestrone it is," Wanda opened up her bag of buns and unceremoniously dumped them down into a waiting breadbasket.

"Twelve twenty-two," Warren announced from the back hall. "Good thing we weren't having quiche. It would have been as hard as rubber by now."

"I brought lemon cake," she waved the wrapped package as if it was a white cotton flag.

"Fine then, let's eat," he finally relented, marching past his guest to turn off the heat and serve his main course.

"I gotta run," Amber suddenly announced a few minutes later, pushing her empty bowl and half-eaten bun toward the center of the table.

"What about your cake?" her father demanded. "Aunt Wanda brought it special for you."

"I'll eat it when I get home. I gotta run; my hair appointment's in half an hour."

Warren silently nodded his head as his daughter leapt up from the table and disappeared into the depths of the back hall.

"*When she gets home,*" Warren hissed, yanking his linen napkin up off his lap and throwing it angrily down onto the tablecloth. "That girl's just like her mother. She's got wings on her feet. Can't sit still for an hour."

"Where's Amber going?"

"She's getting ready for some kind of kiddy party. Seems like the parents of one of her little friends is throwing some kind of lavish *bat mitzvah* and invited half the junior high. We're talking floor length gowns and hundred dollar presents. You ever heard of anything so stupid?"

"That's important stuff when you're in eighth grade," Wanda gently explained as she stood up and began clearing the table. "It's kind of liberating when you actually think about it. A party to celebrate a young girl's passage into womanhood, similar to the traditional all male *bar mitzvahs*."

"Yeah, but she's only thirteen, and we're not even Jewish," he audibly sighed. "You want to tell me what happened to teenage girls wanting a horse and listening to records in their parent's basement?"

"Amber's not interested in the same things we were. Our generation was a thousand years ago to her. The stuff we enjoyed as teenagers is so outdated; I half expect to see the game *Trivial Pursuit* on display in the Smithsonian. "

"Smart ass." Warren reached across the table and snatched up the cake packet.

"Dad, I need twenty bucks," Amber's voice echoed from the back recesses of the house.

"In my wallet," he called out. "And make sure you only take one twenty."

"I will," Amber replied as the thump of her departing boot heels met with hardwood floors.

"You know, her mother's being such a witch lately."

"Why?"

"I'll tell you why," Warren took a second to shove another piece of cake into his mouth. "It was Jody's decision to move out of the city, and now all of a sudden, she's blaming me for keeping her from her daughter. I can't win with that woman. She's the one who moved away, and now she's ranting and raving that she feels alienated and is losing touch with her own flesh and blood."

Preparing to return to her chair, Wanda refilled her coffee cup from the carafe before taking her seat at the table. "I have to be honest with you Warren. I kinda empathize with Jody. She must feel like her daughter's growing up without her."

"Hell, Wanda. She's the one who needed to move away and commune with nature. I didn't tell her to pick a place an hour from Amber's school."

"There're many families separated by distances far greater than an hour, and they still manage to survive."

"It's not the distance," he finally admitted.

"Then what is it?"

"It's her attitude. She's suddenly trying to force a bond with a teenager. You can't do that. Amber's bucking her, every step of the way."

"Maybe I could talk to my niece. Explain to Amber that her mother is just trying to carve a niche for herself in her life?"

"Maybe, but you said you're going to be a lot busier at work now that your job has been revamped. How are you going to manage that?"

"I can move my schedule around and maybe take Amber for a couple of lunches now that I've had that promotion."

"A promotion? Wow. You finally managed to claw your way out of the secretarial pool?"

"Purchasing Agent," she announced with a flourish. "My hours are a lot more flexible now that I'm not tied to the phones."

"What's the name of your company again?"

"Giovanni Films."

"Sounds like another Public Service Corporation. Let me guess. Its' government funded for making documentaries on weird little topics like cockroach fertility rates and the life of bread mold. Am I right?" Warren knowingly shook his head.

She'd somehow managed to evade the question for months. But this was shaping up to be totally different scenario. Her brother was suddenly taking a direct interest in her employment.

"We're not government funded, and we're not a non-profit organization."

"Oh. So what are you then? I've never heard of Giovanni Films?"

"We're a... an independent film company. We make... customized films. And television commercials," Wanda quickly remembered to add. "We do a lot of advertisements for local business owners."

Warren never moved an inch, his brain digesting the information. "What exactly do you mean by customized? Are you talking about Indie Projects?"

"Well," she took a second to organize her thoughts. "Should a client be inclined, they can order a customized film project; laying out the characters, scene requests, and the specific plot lines for a pre-determined fee," she nervously quoted the company's development manual.

"Who in the hell would do that?"

"Eccentrics with a lot of money to spend?"

"Eccentrics? I think we're talking about social deviants, aren't we?" His voice began to rise. "You're candy coating everything, aren't you? Your company makes pornography. Right? Am I right?" her brother suddenly jumped out of his chair.

"It's not for mass consumption. It's for private enjoyment."

"So that makes it right? Well, pornography is pornography. You're working in the sleaze trade and I don't care who orders it. It's still reprehensible!"

"Warren, I just order props and costumes and book the locations for the shoots. I don't sell it and I don't star in it. I'm just trying to pay my bills and keep my head above water. Can't you understand that?"

"No!" he barked. "That's the exact attitude that is going to be the ruination of our society. You don't think you're to blame because you're not directly touching the product. Well you're wrong, missy. If you contribute to the production, then you're to blame, too. There's no ifs, ands, or buts about it. Do you understand me?" He dramatically pointed his finger toward her face.

"I understand your point. It's not the first time I've heard that position before. But let me tell you…" she took a swig of coffee in an attempt to screw up her courage. "An adult's sexual fantasies are their personal business. And if they're interested in paying cash money to have another consenting adult act out those fantasies on film—well, Warren, that's their business, and I don't think we have the right to judge."

"You're wrong," he slammed his chair into the table as he shouted down into his sister's face. "Pornography is the rot at the center of our society. If we don't cut it out and destroy it, it will spread and contaminate even the purest members of our community!"

"Rhetoric," she shouted back.

Warren took a deep breath, willing himself an ounce of control. "Do you know what John Wayne Gacy, the serial killer said, when he was finally caught?"

"John Wayne who?"

"You know, *The Killer Clown*, the guy who murdered thirty-three young boys and men."

"Oh yeah, I remember hearing about that freak," Wanda shook her head in disgust.

"Well, Gacy said that instead of banning the classics like *Catcher in the Rye* and other great works of literature, we should be worrying about banning magazines like Hustler and Penthouse."

"Well… that's not really the same," Wanda struggled to defend her position.

"Oh really? Well maybe if you had a family, if you had a daughter, then you'd understand. The thought of some social miscreant running around with a briefcase full of twisted pornographic images only fuels my fear that he might one-day act out his twisted fetishes with my daughter, or some other innocent child. You're just fueling his fire, keeping the sickness alive with your disgusting little movies, until he gets the chance to experience it in person."

"You're wrong," Wanda argued. "That's just an old wife's tale that pornographic images will entice men and women to act out their sexual urges on innocent children. Yes, it's true that sexuality is sometimes youth driven. But come on, Warren, not everybody gets a woody from watching an adolescent girl suck on a lollipop. Ninety-five percent of our clients' fetishes have nothing to do with underage boys or girls."

"Well then," he waved his arms in the air. "What about the five percent who do?"

"Giovanni films only hires actors eighteen years or older. We'd be shut down in a minute if we even thought of doing anything else, and I for one, wouldn't even consider working there if they did."

"I'm ready to go," Amber announced, two fashion magazines tagged with examples tightly clutched in her arms.

"You just don't understand," Warren reached out and grabbed his daughter, pulling her tightly in toward his chest. "Until you have a child of your own to protect, you'll just never understand."

"Raspberries and what else?" Boyd stood with his head still positioned inside the refrigerator door.

"Whipped cream," Julia shouted back, eyes never leaving the Teflon griddle as she carefully flipped over the second batch of buttermilk pancakes.

It had been ages since Boyd had seen his wife standing in her housecoat, cooking anything for him. Surprisingly, the sight was very appealing, and he was amazed at just how much he'd obviously longed for a little domesticity.

"Put it on the table, and then bring me both plates from the plate warmer," she continued to instruct her reluctant helper.

"A plate warmer. We have a warmer?"

"God," she cursed, quickly turning on her heels to extract both stoneware plates from the metal drawer below the built-in wall oven. "You're totally lost in here, aren't you?"

"Potato chips there," he pointed to one of the cupboards, "and beer there," his arm swung back toward the refrigerator. "I know where everything important is."

Smirking to herself, Julia loaded up the plates and set them gently on the kitchen nook, motioning for her husband to dig in.

"This is really good," he shoved a second mouthful into his face even before he'd finished swallowing the first.

"I see that," she laughed, liberally spooning a mound of fresh berries onto her own stack. "Took me a second to get my bearings, but it looks like I can still feed my husband when I want to."

Nodding his agreement, Boyd grabbed the tub of freshly whipped cream and gave his pancakes another liberal glob.

"Are you thinking of maybe heading out to the clinic to check on your brother this afternoon?"

"I don't know. He makes me so damn mad. Why can't he just stop taking that shit for even a week?"

"Cuz he's an addict, pure and simple."

"So what do I do? Lock him in the wine cellar 'til he's clean. Or maybe I should just give up on him and let him slowly kill himself back on the streets."

"Relax," Julia leaned over and gently stroked her husband on the cheek. "Pete had a bad week. I don't think you have to make any life altering decisions right here and right now."

"A bad week? That little shit has had a bad fucking life. He doesn't seem to care, Julia. It's all about the dope. Always has been since we were kids still living at home with ma."

"I know."

"Hell, I love letting loose—drinking beer, smoking a little weed—you know what I mean. It's just that we're not eighteen anymore. We can't party like a couple of fuckin' teenagers every night of the week."

"So what now?"

"I don't know for sure. But I have to tell you something that's been gnawing on me for a long time."

"What is it?" she gently laid her fork down on the edge of her plate.

"What if it's impossible? What if it turns out that junkies hooked on crystal meth can't be rehabilitated? What then?" Boyd demanded.

"Everybody can be rehabilitated. You just have to want it bad enough. You know, hit rock bottom and all that stuff," Julia repeated the general public's concept of addiction.

"But what if this meth shit is something different? What if the high is so fucking amazing that you can't imagine a life without it? Look at this," he jumped up from his chair and snatched a brochure off the far counter. "Listen," Boyd said as he began to read from one of the clinic's brochures. *"A person's first hit of crystal meth is the equivalent of ten orgasms, all on top of each other, each lasting for thirty minutes to an hour, with a feeling of arousal that lasts for another day and a half."*

"Really," Julia walked over to where her husband was standing. "That's absolutely amazing. No wonder people get hooked after their first hit."

"Hang on, there's more. It also says," he flipped to a second page and scanned down the paragraphs for the specific quote. "It says that... *the initial effect does not last long. After you've been using meth about six months or so, you can't have sex unless you're high. After you've been using it a little longer, you can't have sex even when you're high. Nothing happens, your penis doesn't work in males, and you're unable to reach any level of arousal in females."*

"I didn't know that," she stood motionless, a puzzled look on her face.

"Hold on, there's one more line I think you should hear."

Julia locked eyes with her husband.

"A single dose of meth lasts for six to eight hours. The identical portion of cocaine would get you high for maybe twenty minutes."

She didn't even have a reply, never mind an answer to Boyd's initial question. Julia had never stopped to consider that one day, humanity might actually invent a drug so powerful and so destructive, traditional rehab would be rendered useless. That thought just hadn't occurred to her before, and if that day was actually here, everything she'd accepted as truth was about to change.

The streets of her city and the people of her county were about to be divided into two groups. Those who were not using, and those who were addicted to meth would be forced to opposite sides of the fence. She couldn't imagine living in a society where a portion of the citizenry was instantly deemed hopeless, without any chance of rehabilitation.

How would the world cope with the men and women who had no future and were labeled as nothing more than a drain on the country's resources and health care? Only one word came to Julia's mind and the mere thought of it scared the hell out of her. *Segregation!*

CHAPTER TEN

"I started fooling around. Then I started screwing around, which is fooling around without dinner."
                                                    —Chicago, 2002

Filing complete, phone messages sorted, and the week's photo shoots already organized by date and location, Wanda stopped working long enough to grab her empty coffee cup and head down the hall to the floor's lunchroom.

"Wanda," a young mail boy called out from the far end of the hall. "I got another truck trying to unload at the front door. What should I do?"

"Again?" she moaned. "Why do those guys always screw up and try to bring their stuff down here. Do we look like we're shooting a movie in the parking lot?"

"I don't know," the agitated young kid tapped his right sneaker, anxious for a solution to the problem that inadvertently been dropped in his lap.

"Let's go," she said, setting down her mug and marching toward the elevators doors.

"I don't know why security always calls me," the kid continued to whine. "I don't order the stuff. Why call me? They should call you."

"You're in charge of shipping and receiving, so security calls you when anything bigger than a letter arrives," Wanda laughed. "But don't worry; I'll take care of this… again."

"Good," he nodded, nearly leaping out the elevators doors the minute they opened on the main floor.

"Gentlemen," Wanda called out, "we seem to have a problem. Can I please see your delivery order?"

Without speaking, one of the coverall-clad men thrust a tattered clipboard in her face. "Deliver to Giovanni Films," he grunted as she scanned the document. "This is Giovanni Films, right?"

"Sure is, boys," she stepped forward, shoving the clipboard back into his hand. "But just because we've ordered the delivery, and we're paying for the delivery, doesn't mean we want it delivered to our offices. Now does it?"

"No, I guess not," two of the men chimed in together, disappointed to realize that they wouldn't be unloading their freight deep inside the building's private sanctum.

"See the address clearly printed in the delivery box. Well, this isn't it, now is it?" Wanda pointed up toward the office tower.

"Ah shit," the man with the clipboard double-checked his paperwork. "That's clear across town. We'll never make it before five."

"Yeah," the other chirped up. "We're supposed to clock out at five."

"Looks like we have a problem, boys," she crossed her arms at her chest. "This is the second time your company has messed up with my delivery. So here's what I'm gonna do. I'm gonna call my drop off and make sure they wait for you guys. You're gonna have to put in an extra hour of your time for free, but if you have it there by six p.m., I won't call your dispatcher and complain. You think you guys can live with that?"

They nodded in silence, the driver climbing back into his cab while the other man ran around the back to secure the rear of the truck.

Returning to her desk to make her call, Wanda suddenly realized that she'd still forgotten to retrieve her coffee cup. Damn, was she ever going to be able to get her head screwed on straight? Every since her brunch with her brother Warren, she hadn't been able to shake his accusations. Maybe he was right, maybe she was deluding herself? How could you work in the porn industry and kid yourself into thinking that you weren't contributing to... what were her brother's words? Oh yes... *the decay of society.*

"Wanda," a woman's voice called out over the intercom. "Julia was wondering if you'd mind stopping by her office. She'd like to have a quick little meeting with you."

"That's fine. Tell her I'll be there in a minute."

"Good, love," the elderly secretary answered back. "And she asks that you please bring the personnel file for a Miss Lillian Cardinal."

Papers discreetly tucked under her arm, Wanda made her way to Julia's private office.

"...Then, please tell Mr. Dubois that I'll be in and out of my office today, and he can reach me at his convenience," Julia instructed the receptionist before disconnecting her line. "Oh Wanda," she noticed her standing by the door. "Thanks for coming right over." She walked around her desk while motioning for her guest to take a seat on her couch. "I just wanted to go over Lillian's file with you."

"Its right here," Wanda set it down on the coffee table. "She's quite a girl. I can see why you're anxious to get her into production."

"You're right." Julia generously poured two shots of sherry and carried them over to the couch. "Not only is she strikingly beautiful, but she's got a good head on her shoulders."

"I agree," Wanda smiled, accepting the delicate stemware.

"During my interview, I found her to be honest, and straightforward. She's really looking for a change; a chance to make something out of her life."

"Well then, she's come to the right place. She'll make some decent money, and she'll have a chance to save up for her future, should she ever decide to leave us."

Downing her entire glass, Wanda carefully set it down on the table, mindful to hit a leather coaster and not leave a dampened ring.

"Something the matter?" Julia couldn't help but notice. "You look a little bothered. Is it Pete, or are you worried about Lillian? Is there something not right with the new girl that you want to tell me?"

"Absolutely not. So far, everything checks out, including her age. She's legal. And by this afternoon, I'll have the results of her medical."

Shooting back her own glass, Julia returned to grab the bottle before moving to the couch, kicking off her three inch Jimmy Choo's before plopping down on the heavy upholstery. "Now spill," she ordered, quickly refilling both their glasses.

"Well, I was just wondering about our girls?"

"What about them?"

"What's left after we're all done with them?"

"I don't know," Julia leaned back, resting comfortably against the padded back. "Why the sudden interest?"

"Well, after you've starred in a handful of porn's and had your face and body exposed all over a bunch of x-rated films, what's left for you? Certainly not the white picket fence; or the local community college."

"I walked away from the camera," Julia reminded Wanda. "It can be done. Look how successful I am."

"Well, you didn't really walk away from the camera," she

respectfully reminded her boss. "You just kind of changed positions and moved around the back."

"True. So what's going on with you? What's with all the questions?"

She'd never counted Julia Giovanni as a friend, their relationship was little more than business. But she needed to talk, and the woman seemed to be genuinely concerned.

"You having trouble with someone here at the company," her boss continued to question.

"Julia, if you could turn back the clock, maybe have three magic wishes, what would you do with your life?"

"You mean instead of porn?"

"Yeah, instead of porn. What interests you?"

"Hell, I don't know," she tucked both her bare legs underneath herself. "I've been on the streets since I was a kid. I don't know what else I could do, you know what I mean?"

Nodding, Wanda pointed to Lillian's personnel file. "She's been a stripper, but until now she's never sold her body for sex. Starring in porn is a whole new venture for this girl. I… I was… well… I was just wondering if you think it's really worth it. The money and all, you know what I mean?"

"That's up to the girl, or the guy," Julia suddenly remember her old friend Tony DeMarco. He'd managed to walk away from starring roles in porn, find himself a girl to marry, and then train for some kind of medical license. Or so she'd heard, having lost contact with him once he'd relocated to another city.

"I'm just trying to decide if we're the problem or the solution."

Julia shook her head, forcing the past from her mind as she turned her attention back to the conversation at hand. "Lillian has to decide if it's worth it for herself. For some, this is a step up from their previous lives. For others, it can be a whole new set of problems. We all have our personal reasons." She shrugged her shoulders.

"But what about us?" Wanda waved her hand back and forth between herself and her boss. "If it wasn't for us, maybe some of the women would go back to school, or find other jobs. Who knows? Maybe without us, they'd have found husbands and lived happily ever after, with kids and house mortgages?"

Nearly choking on her drink, it was Julia's turn to set down her glass. "What, are you fucking kidding? You ready to take all the blame for these girls' lots in life?"

"No, not the blame for their pasts. But do you maybe think that maybe we're screwing up their futures?"

"What in the hell happened to you this weekend? You find religion or something?"

"No," Wanda laughed, her turn to pick up the sherry bottle and refill their glasses. "I kinda took an emotional beating from my twin brother, Warren. He thinks I work in the sleaze trade, and that people like me are the downfall of our community."

"And?" Julia pushed, knowing there was more to the story.

"And he said I couldn't understand because I wasn't a parent. Without a child to protect, I'd never appreciate the dangers."

"That's a big crock of bull."

"I don't know, maybe my brother has a point. We are fueling the fires for a lot of these guys."

"These are guys with means," Julia quickly reminded her. "They could afford to hire a hundred of the city's best prostitutes to fulfill their deepest desires every night of the week. We just offer something a little different, a chance to put it down on tape. We're not corrupting them; we're just giving them another outlet for their specific fetishes."

"You really believe that?"

"Well, what in the hell do you want me to believe?" Julia sat straight up on the edge of her couch. "You think that if we didn't make these films, the guys would start fantasizing about their boring little wives and forget that they dream of spanking some little blonde wearing a rubber pig suit with a curly little plastic tail sticking out of her ass?"

"No."

"Well, we're just filling a void, Wanda. If we didn't do it, these so called *clients* of ours would just look for another outlet for their fantasies."

"But I'm not talking about the clients and their padded wallets. I'm talking about our girls. The women who allow us to film them in some of the most degrading and unusual situations you could ever imagine."

"Well, sweetie," Julia said and lifted her glass in a mock toast, "Either you can handle the job or you can't. It's up to you."

"It's up to me," Wanda repeated aloud.

"Miss Julia is still in a meeting," the secretary repeated to Boyd. "She must have her phone switched to *do not disturb*. Would you like me to go in there and tell her you're waiting on the line?"

"No," he shook his head in anger. "Just tell her I'm on my way out to the rehab center and I'll be back in the city by supper. You got that?"

"Yes sir," the woman confirmed. "Anything else?"

"No," he disconnected his cellular and tromped down on the gas.

Within another half an hour, Boyd was once again parked in front of the center's main doors.

Identifying himself to the security guard stationed at the front desk, Boyd reluctantly accepted his visitor's pass and made his way directly toward Dr. Mason's private office.

"Thank you for once again making the trip on such short

notice," the doctor began their meeting. "I see that your wife will not be joining us here today."

"She was busy," he cut the pleasantries short. "What's happened to my brother now?"

"Pete is presently packing his belongings Mr. Giovanni."

"What?"

"I'm sorry, but after meeting with your brother's personal counselor and the staff nurse he attacked, we've decided that he is no longer welcome at our facility."

"Hold on there. What are you talking about? Some kind of attack?"

"Your brother Pete was under the influence of an extremely potent narcotic this weekend, and during one of his few mobile states, he wrestled one of our nurses to the ground in an attempt to steal her computerized hall pass."

"Hold on, just back up a damn minute," Boyd began to shout, simultaneously rising to his feet. "You're talking about something different from when my brother overdosed?"

"Please retake your seat," the doctor attempted to coax Boyd back to his chair. "I have all the information you need here," he gently patted the paper file.

"All right," he forced himself to swallow two deep breaths. "What in the fuck happened after Julia and I left?"

"After the overdose, you're aware that your brother was initially transferred to the hospital wing?"

"Yeah, I know that. We visited him there."

"Well, it was later determined after that move, an additional forty-eight hours of observation would be a good idea before returning your brother to his private room. However, during his observational stay, he was able to procure somewhere between one hundred and two hundred milligrams of Oxycontin. This drug is one of the most powerful medications for pain control that can be ingested orally. It's so powerful, that back in May of 2001, the one hundred and sixty milligram tablets were discontinued."

"Where'd he get it?" Boyd waived his hand, annoyed with the doctor's pharmaceutical lecture.

"We haven't established that. However, members of my staff have positively confirmed that he did not enter the hospital wing with the narcotic in his possession."

"I see," Boyd crossed his arms at his chest. "You're finally admitting that someone on the inside passed it to him."

"Yes, your brother has sparked an internal investigation. We are trying to figure out how he gained access to one of our most controlled substances."

"Oxycontin," Boyd repeated the name. "You're talking about *hillbilly heroin?*"

"That's correct," the doctor shook his head in agreement. "Abusers crush the tablets and then snort the powder, defeating the time-release mechanism set up for patients who swallow the medication orally as per their doctor's orders."

"So my brother attacked a nurse?"

"Yes, and he was brandishing a kitchen knife."

"Ah fuck," Boyd cursed, realizing that assault with a weapon was a serious offence any way you looked at it.

"He was manic, looking for a way out of the clinic. You have to realize how powerful this drug actually is, Mr. Giovanni. Under the inappropriate influence of this narcotic, a man's actions are totally unpredictable. And we here at the clinic are not prepared to deal with those kinds of patients. We are a rehabilitation facility. We're not set up for violent detox. And for those reasons, Mr. Giovanni, I'm going to have to ask you to remove your brother from our facility."

"Well, what the hell am I supposed to do with him now? He ain't better yet, he needs more rehabilitation."

"Mr. Giovanni, I'd love to be able to help your brother, but

I have to think of my staff and the other patients first, and their personal safety seems to be in jeopardy."

Rising from his chair, Boyd stopped for a brief second before walking out the door. "Can I ask you an honest question, doc?"

"Yes," he nodded.

"Have you ever run up against an addict that you couldn't clean up, no matter what?"

"Yes, I have," he bravely admitted. "I can't help a patient if they're not interested in being helped."

"One more question. Do you think crystal meth might turn normal people into just those kinds of patients? People who'd rather die on the drug than live a life without it, no matter how much it'll cost them?"

"Ask me in ten years from now," the doctor closed the patient file and carefully handed the collection of papers over to Boyd. "We don't have enough information yet to make that kind of determination."

"So anything's possible?" Boyd sighed.

"The medical community just doesn't have any long term studies to draw on when it comes to the damage inflicted by crystal methamphetamine use. We're still operating on a learning curve."

"Meaning what?" Boyd prompted the doctor to explain his last statement in layman's terms.

"What I mean is...that we might be facing a social and financial epidemic. We all may be left with a friend or a family member who, through their addiction, has become no more than *a shell of the person they used to be*—men and women who seemingly are unable to ever function again in a positive community setting. Just a shell," the doctor reiterated with palpable sadness.

Boyd signed his brother's *release to-care-of* papers and left the doctor's office without muttering another word.

CHAPTER ELEVEN

"It seems that destiny may have caught up with us."
—The Core, 2003

"Thanks again, bro." Pete nervously scratched the skin on his upper forearms, a common practice when he was *jonesing* for a hit. "I had about all I could take of that fuckin' place."

"Funny, that's exactly what they had to say about you."

"So, where you taking me, man?"

"I don't know," Boyd admitted as he slammed his Corvette into fifth gear. "You know I'm about at the end of my fuckin' rope?"

"Sorry, bro. It's just that... well you know rehab, man. All that sharing and letting your feelings out kind of shit..., well..., it just ain't for me."

"So what the fuck is going to work for you? You can't just come home and pretend like nothing ever happened. Julia will slit my throat if I just let you waltz into work tomorrow, acting like you're all cured and all drug free."

"I know, I know," he waved his left arm to silence his brother. "I got a plan of my own."

"Really? Well, this I gotta hear. What you gonna do to fix this big pile of shit?"

"I'm gonna rehab myself."

"What?" Boyd gunned his engine to pass a slow moving motorist. "What the fuck is self-rehab?"

"It's kinda like a cooling off period. You lay low, no heavy partying, and just like...kick back and relax."

"Relax, that's all you do? Who do you think you are? Fucking Charlie Sheen?

"No," he sarcastically replied. "You just spend a lot of time thinking, kind of evaluating all your options and what you plan to do with the rest of your life. You know, life decisions and shit like that. And who's this guy, Charlie Sheen? We know him from the diner?"

"Life decisions?" Boyd repeated, ignoring his brother's total ignorance of the latest celebrity gossip. Where the fuck did you learn that from?" He couldn't help but tease. "You're starting to sound like you did log a few hours with some of those rehab shrinks."

"Well, you got a better idea?"

"Actually I do. I was thinking that maybe a trip to this place that I found up state might be a good move for you."

"Are you fucking kidding me?"

Boyd expected his brother's response—actually, anything else would have been a shock. "Well then bro, I'm at a loss, cuz I don't have a fucking clue what to do next."

"Just take me home. I'll be fine, I promise."

"Can you be honest with me for one damn minute," he pulled his eyes off the road to gauge his brother's reaction.

"Sure man. What's the deal?"

"How important is the dope to you?"

"It's fun, it's a party. You know what it's like. We've snorted more than a couple rails together in our days."

Boyd was definitely not a puritan himself, but somehow he'd managed to survive the wave that was threatening to crash down onto his brother's head.

"It's kinda like your vodka," Pete reasoned. "You like to sit down and enjoy a couple shots after work. Well, I like to kick back with a hit of meth. Nothing really that different when you think about it."

"You don't actually believe that shit, do you, man? Cuz if you do, you're really fucked up," Boyd countered back, the doctor's words still ringing through his head.

"Who in the hell do you think you are?" Pete began to yell at his brother. "Getting all high and mighty and coming down on me like your all superior and shit. You're no fucking better than I am. You know how many times I've picked your coked-up ass off the floor and thrown it in the back of my car. How dare you look down your nose at me, you fucking jerk wad!"

"It's the meth, man," Boyd yelled in an attempt to make his point. "It's dangerous shit. When you take it, you change. I can't have you around the office or around me and Julia when you're high on that crap. Its poison, man, and you gotta give it up."

"Says who?" Pete argued as if suddenly transported straight back to their neighborhood playground. "You're not my fucking father, so quit trying to tell me what to do."

Boyd was about ready to explode. All he wanted was to get his brother out of his car as fast as humanly possible, before he drove them both head first into a speeding semi-trailer. "Just tell me where to drop you," he growled, no longer interested in getting to the heart of Pete's addiction.

"The bank. I need to pull out a little cash before I head home, if that's fine with you?" he growled back.

"Fine by me," Boyd wound his car around the curve of the highway, silently praying his passenger door would fling open, and his brother would be sucked right out into the oncoming traffic.

———————

"Where's my wife?" Boyd demanded the second his foot stepped off the elevator.

"She's at the hairdresser, Mr. Giovanni," Julia's personal assistant quickly stepped forward. "Her appointment was for two this afternoon, so I assume she'll be back by five."

"I'll just wait in her office." He marched straight through his wife's doorway and plunked down on the couch.

Drink in hand, feet up on the coffee table, Boyd ran a succession of plans through his head. Maybe he didn't need to tell Julia that his brother had been tossed out of rehab and was out roaming the streets? Maybe he could just stash him in a motel for a couple of days until he decided exactly what he needed to do? Maybe...

"Oh, I'm so sorry," Wanda immediately apologized upon walking in unannounced to Julia's office. "I didn't know you were in here. I was just dropping off papers," she rushed over to the desk and deposited her delivery.

"Don't worry. I'm just squatting myself," he said as he rose up to his feet.

"I'm sorry," she apologized for a second time, turning to exit the room.

"Wait, I need to talk to you." Boyd rubbed the muscles at the back of his neck. "Can you please take a seat?" He continued to stretch by rolling both his shoulders.

"Is something wrong?" Wanda slowly lowered herself into the closest chair.

"I don't know how to say this, so I'm just going to spit it out. Pete is out of rehab and running loose."

Jumping to her feet, Wanda nervously began to pace the room. "Do you know where he is? He isn't here, is he?" she spun around to watch the office door.

"No, no. Just sit," Boyd shook his head side to side in a frustrated rush of anger. "I don't know where the little fucker is hanging out, but I can promise you that he's not here."

"He's fixed; he's done his rehab already? It just seems like he went in," she continued to ramble, her voice taking on a nervous edge. "How come they released him, can't you take him back and check him in for a little while longer?"

"Slow down a minute," Boyd walked over and threw his right arm around Wanda's shoulders as she nervously stood up from her chair; gently squeezing her in what he hoped would feel like a brotherly embrace. "Building security has been alerted, and he won't be allowed on the premises. His pass for the parking garage and the freight elevator have also been cancelled and red flagged. Even an attempted entry will register. And to tell you the truth, Wanda, I can't think of any reason he'd even want to stop by. He hates this place and everyone who works here."

"Especially me," she said, slowly turning out of her boss's embrace and making her way toward the office window. "Not only did I take your brother's job, but because of me, he was forced into rehab. I'll be lucky if he doesn't hunt me down with a machete."

"That's enough!" Boyd switched gears and took a firm stand. "I told you you're safe here, so you're gonna have to trust me on that. All right?"

"Sure," she shook her head, fighting to control the river of tears threatening to make their escape down her face. "But... but there's only one problem."

"What's that?"

"I don't live here, do I?"

"We clock enough hours around this joint that you'd think we all did live here," Boyd tried to lighten the mood.

"Ain't that the truth," Julia walked in unannounced just as

Wanda turned away to blot her tears, unsure if she should stay put or flee to the privacy of her own office.

"Oh, hi hon," Boyd blurted out, walking over and giving his wife a quick peck on the cheek as she stopped dead in the middle of her office.

"What's the matter?" Her eyes darted back and forth between her husband and her purchasing agent. "What in the hell is going on here?"

Wanda turned, eyes shifting around the room and finally locking on Boyd's face as she unconsciously withdrew from the spotlight, waiting for him to step forward with an explanation.

"Dr. Mason called from the clinic," Boyd opened his mouth and let the words begin to spill out. "They had no choice but to kick Pete out of rehab."

"That little fucker!" Julia threw her beaded clutch down onto the couch. "I'm ready to grab his hairy little sac and twist until he screams for bloody mercy. So tell me," she demanded in an angry tone. "What kind of crap did that piece of shit pull this weekend?"

"He…"

"Don't tell me," Julia spun on her heels, suddenly interrupting her husband's train of thought. "That son of a bitch couldn't keep his fucking mitts off the dope. Am I right? Am I right?" she continued to demand, snatching a liquor bottle off the moveable cart.

"As I was trying to say," Boyd threw his hands up in the air, "he never overdosed again, but he did wig out and attack one of the nurses after swallowing a bunch of pain killers."

"What kind of pain killers?" Wanda surprised everyone by jumping back into the conversation.

"They said Oxycontin. The doctor figures somewhere around two hundred milligrams."

Wanda just crossed her arms at her chest, threw her head back, and then let out a huge rush of air. "He hates pills, says they're for women. Pete must have been really desperate for a high to swallow that stuff."

"Sounds like he was out of his fucking mind, is what that sounds like to me," Boyd agreed with Wanda. "The file said Pete even made a grab for the nurse's floor pass when she was checking his vitals," he alluded to the paperwork still sitting on his desk. "She fought back, of course, and the scuffle was picked up on some kind of hidden security camera out in the hallway."

"Was the nurse hurt?" Wanda reluctantly whispered, almost too afraid to ask the question aloud.

"No," he answered, deliberately omitting the existence of the knife.

Lifting the first bottle to eye level, Julia quickly scanned the label before pouring three generous portions of brandy into crystal snifters. "Where is he now?" she demanded, passing Boyd and Wanda their glasses before returning to the bar cart to take a large swig from her own.

Passing his drink under his nose, Boyd shook his head in disgust before turning and walking over to Julia's side. Without saying a word, he dumped the sweetened liqueur directly into his wife's glass. "You know I don't drink that shit," he growled, grabbing a fresh tumbler and splashing a good three ounces of vodka down into the bottom.

"Fine," Julia stomped around her desk before plopping down into the leather chair. "Drink your fill. But before you get polluted, I need to know where he is and what the fuck you plan to do about him. We," she pointed at Wanda and then back at herself, "we ain't going to put up with any shit from that mother fucker! I'm one step from going down to the cops and filing a restraining order against him. You get me, *bro*?" she sarcastically snapped. "And," she stalled momentarily for effect, "I have no qualms about hiring some outside muscle to patrol this building and guard our asses, one on one."

Topping up his glass after just one sip, Boyd ground his teeth together in an attempt to control his temper. "I'm mad too, but this shit ain't my fault," he angrily reminded everyone.

Forcing down her own drink, Wanda decided that it was time to slip out of the room and let Boyd and Julia fight it out between themselves. Besides, she needed to pack a few things and find somewhere safe to hide out until Pete got himself under control.

"Where you going?" Julia cried out the minute Wanda turned her back and began making her escape.

"It's time to go home," she said with a forced smile, hoping she'd been able to mask her fear.

"I don't think so," Julia looked toward Boyd.

"You heard the woman," he shrugged his shoulders. "Might as well take a load off," he rose to pull out the nearest guest chair in front of Julia's desk.

"I'll be fine," Wanda argued back. "He's not gonna hurt me again. He knows that you'd kick his ass," she nodded toward Boyd. "Besides, I wasn't planning on going home, anyway. I think I'll just camp out at my brother's tonight."

"Does Pete know where your brother lives?" Boyd began to question her.

"No."

"Does he know his name?"

"Maybe. I don't know. I might have mentioned Warren's name."

"Your brother has a kid living in the house. Isn't that right?" It was Julia's turn to throw in her two cents.

"Yes," Wanda dropped her head in defeat. "I guess it wouldn't be a good idea to go there," she finally gave up the fight.

"Guess not," Julia looked straight at her husband. "She needs a safe place to crash. Something with solid security in a good neighborhood. You know what I mean?"

Boyd just nodded, fully aware of where his wife was heading.

"Okay, Wanda," Julia scribbled eight numerical digits on a pink piece of paper. "Here's the security code for our main gate. I'm gonna phone my housekeeper and tell her to expect you. I don't want you to go home; I want you to head straight to our house. Do you understand?"

Wanda looked down at her skirt and blouse.

"Don't worry. I have three closets full of clothes. You'll be fine."

"Thank you both, but I think we're jumping to conclusions here. Aren't we?"

Neither Boyd nor Julia answered, both taking their time evaluating their possible responses.

"Besides," Wanda finally thought of a positive point. "He's just come out of rehab. All Pete's gonna be worried about is getting high and hooking up with some chick. He'll be too busy letting loose to worry about settling any scores with me. Right?"

"Right," Boyd nodded in agreement. "But just to be safe, spend the night with us. We'll have a few beers, order a little Chinese. Trust me, it won't be that bad."

Julia leaned back in her chair, evaluating her newest houseguest as she kept another eye trained on her husband. He was looking really sad, almost like he'd been physically beaten and left for dead. Boyd's relationship with his brother was beginning to take a serious toll on his inner reserves, and Julia began to question just how much energy her husband had left to expend on that useless piece of shit.

———————

For the first time in his life, Pete was unsure just how much dope his body could handle. Was the clinic's medicine still cursing through his veins, or was he finally free of their chemical hold? He couldn't be sure, and he wasn't in the mood for another overdose.

"Is there a problem," the store's clerk gently rapped on the change room door. "Do you need another size? Maybe I could bring you another style?"

"No, I think…"

"Do you wanna try a button fly?" the teenage kid continued to harp. "Oh, how about a new pair of Diesel's? Everyone I know loves the new black denim. They're the jeans in the front window. Did you see them on your way in?"

"I'll take these," Pete finally burst out of the small wooden cubicle.

"They do look good," the kid rushed over, preparing to fawn over the two hundred dollar denim pants. "I have the perfect shirt. Wanna try it on?"

"No, I'm good," Pete roughly yanked the price tag off his hip and handed it over with a piece of plastic.

"You sure? I have a nice blue button-down that would look great with your hair. And the entire line is on sale for an extra twenty percent off. Let me get you a couple to try on."

Pete had enough. He just wanted a clean pair of jeans, not an entire fucking wardrobe. "Look, you little squeak," he began to yell at the kid. "Either you ring up these god damned jeans right now, or I'm gonna walk out of here and you can pay for them yourself."

The clerk never answered, he just ran straight for the till, almost mowing down another shopper who inadvertently stepped in his way.

"Hey Petey, my boy," a man poked his head into the store. "You just about done in here? We got somewhere to be."

"Your card," the kid suddenly reappeared at his side, handing over the computer receipt for Pete to sign.

"Thank you for shopping with us here at *Seams like Denim*. Should you ever…"

Pete shoved his card and receipt into his wallet.

"Your original jeans," the kid attempted to hand him a store bag.

"Keep em'. You could always stuff the crotch and wear them yourself," he sneered, strolling straight out the building's front door.

Finally settled in the front seat of his friend's Porsche, Pete was ready to get down to business. "All right, let's get to it," he reached backward toward the young girl sitting quietly in the backseat.

Without speaking a word, her fingers slowly reached down into the leather folds of her purse and carefully withdrew a 9mm Glock. Gently setting the gun in Pete's outstretched palm, the girl's face broke into a smile, watching as he lifted the weapon up toward his face and seductively planted a single kiss on the polished barrel.

CHAPTER TWELVE

"Distance is not a factor. Women have testicle telepathy, man."

—*The Fog, 2005*

Arms laden with groceries and disposable diapers, Lillian somehow managed to unlock the apartment door and haul everything over the narrow threshold without dropping a single item.

"Where the fuck you been?" Ronnie barked, barely taking his eyes off the television screen as his fingers continued to manipulate the wireless controller.

"Grocery shopping?" she stumbled over the empty beer cans on her way to the kitchen table. "What you guys doing?"

"Just checking out a few of these games," Jerome chirped up. "Wanna challenge?"

Lillian just shook her head, retreating to the kitchen to stow away the week's food supplies before any of the guys hanging out in their living room decided to help themselves to their limited rations.

"Where'd you get the games?"

"A guy we know owed Ronnie for an eight ball of crack but couldn't pay, so instead of taking a beating, he turned his back at the video store he works at and Ronnie grinched a Play Station and a couple of rental games. Not bad, eh?"

"Too bad the guy didn't work at a butcher shop."

"Hang on," Jerome ran from the room. "See this," he returned from the bedroom waving three plastic cases under her nose. "*Grand Theft Auto, Vice City,* and *The Punisher.* Top rentals, and now they're ours."

"Great," she muttered, hiding the sandwich meat and the bread in the plastic crispers at the bottom of the fridge.

"That fucking Tommy Vercetti is one guy who's got it going on. You should see this mother, he's fucking amazing," Jerome continued to babble about a character in one of the games. "He kills who he wants—mows down any piece of shit that stands in his way. It's the best set-up ever."

Catching another glimpse of the crowd assembled in the living room, Lillian turned her attention back to her task at hand. "Did you guys just get here?"

"Why?" Jerome began snooping in the brown paper bags for something he could snack on.

"Cuz I was wondering if all those guys will be leaving soon. I was going to make some supper, but I don't wanna have to cook for all those deadbeats."

"What's going on in here? Having a little Powwow?" Ronnie teased Lillian.

"Who are they?" she nodded her head toward the living room.

"Just guys. Don't worry; it's none of your fucking business anyway."

Shaking her head, Lillian began folding up the empty paper bags. "I bought diapers, but the store was out of razor blades, so you're gonna have to use your old electric until they get more."

"Oh yeah, I forgot to tell you. The kid's gone," Ronnie pushed past his girlfriend and began making his way to the apartment's only bathroom.

"Gone where?' she hurried after him, suddenly afraid that he might have sold the helpless toddler for a case of beer and a bag of cheap weed.

"Gloria picked him up. Took him home," he unzipped his fly and began to urinate down into the toilet bowl without even bothering to lift up the seat.

Rushing out of the bathroom, Lillian ran straight to their bedroom, shocked to see an empty corner where a makeshift playpen and two cardboard boxes of baby clothes had recently sat.

"Is Gloria back staying at your mom's house?" she shouted from the bedroom.

"Don't know. Maybe he said something about some kind of friend."

"You didn't ask," Lillian rushed up to her boyfriend's side. "You let her take the kid out of here without even knowing if she had a place to stay?"

Digging in his pocket for his cigarettes, Ronnie took a second to light a smoke before even bothering to answer his girlfriend. "Why you suddenly all jacked up about the little brat? You was fixing to call welfare a week ago. Now all of a sudden, you're worried whether or not he's got a warm bed. What's with you, you on your fucking moon?"

Not bothering to answer, Lillian turned and marched back to their bedroom, slamming the door closed in her wake. "Fucking asshole," she cursed, dropping down on the bed in a frustrated huff.

"Give it here, it's my turn," one of the male voices demanded from down the hall, followed by the unmistakable shatter of breaking glass.

"Straighten up bud," Ronnie roared in laughter, obviously not the least bit concerned that one of his girlfriend's personal belongings had just been trashed.

Falling back onto the mattress, Lillian slung her right arm over her eyes, wanting to cry, yet unwilling to surrender to the ugliness of her present life.

"This is fucked," she muttered to herself. Their relationship was a total disaster, and realistically, it was never going to change.

Ronnie had started pursuing her a little over a year and a half ago down at the strip club, asking her out and hanging around the exit door after the club was closed. She'd given him the same answer every stripper used when a client found the balls to cross the floor. Lillian had told him she had a boyfriend, a *patched* member of the Hell's Angels biker gang.

For a month, Ronnie had backed off, amusing himself with a couple of the club's cocktail waitresses. Then one night, when ten or twelve drunks from a bachelor party were giving the girls down in the pit a really hard time, he'd jumped up and interceded. With two quick punches, he'd laid out the asshole who'd been heating quarters with his lighter and flicking them at Lillian's bare skin.

For the first time in her life, that she could remember, a man had actually stood up and protected her for no other reason than it was the right thing to do. She'd thanked him that night with two hours of wild sex, a home cooked omelet come morning, and eventually, a key to her apartment.

In her heart, from the minute they met, Lillian had known that Ronnie wasn't marriage material. But somehow, she'd fooled herself into thinking that with enough support; he might at least turn into a decent boyfriend.

She'd been dead wrong.

As the weeks had evolved into months, he had settled into her life and begun to suck up whatever financial support she could spare.

His menial jobs or *lack luster* attempts to hold them soon evaporated, and by the end of the first year, Ronnie was living off Lillian fulltime and tunneling his limited interest into the world of street drugs.

"Hey Lilly," Jerome shouted from somewhere down the hall. "Someone's here to see you," he continued to bellow, successfully ending her trip down memory lane.

Reluctantly rising, Lillian plodded down the hall, shocked when she strolled into the living room and saw Ronnie's sister, Gloria standing motionless at the front door.

"He won't sleep without Boo-Boo," she shouted, hands on her hips, her eyes burning with anger. "You wanna tell me what the fuck a Boo-Boo is?"

"I thought you packed everything?" Lillian turned toward Ronnie as he stumbled out of the bathroom.

"It's mine. Why the fuck am I gonna give her my shit?"

Shaking her head, Lillian felt the disgust welling up in the back of her throat. "The first night you dropped Tito off at my door, he was crying and scared shitless. So I made him a stupid little sock puppet out of one of Ronnie's white gym socks. I don't know," she shrugged her shoulders. "I guess it stayed in his playpen and he slept with it after that."

Running her fingers through her greasy black hair, Gloria's eyes swept the room for a familiar face. Unable to find a friend, she turned her attention back to Lillian. "You telling me that I took a twenty-dollar cab ride to pick up some fucking dirty socks?" she screamed across the room—Ronnie's friends barely aware of her presence.

"You ain't picking up jack shit!" her brother stood up and marched into the kitchen. "Member this bitch?" he shoved a rumpled piece of paper at her face. "You still owe me three hundred and fifty bucks for diapers, bottles, and everything else that Lilly bought to take care of your whining little brat."

"Oh, fuck me!" she grabbed the paper and began shredding it into dime-sized pieces. "You wanna charge me for that shit. How about I charge you for two years rent, you cum wad? The two fucking years you and your loser friend lay on my fucking couch and sucked every piece of groceries I had right out of my house?"

"Your house? I don't think that was..."

Lillian turned and walked back down the hall, once again slamming the bedroom door firmly behind her. Without wasting another moment of her day, or even her life, she dropped to her knees and leaned against the bed. To an observer, it would have appeared she was praying, but they'd have been wrong. With a little effort, she was finally able to locate the duffle bag she'd stashed, quickly yanking it out from underneath the bed frame.

She could always come back for more of her personal shit later, but right now, she just set her mind on packing a few of her treasured keepsakes. Stuff that Ronnie might get pissed off and destroy when he finally realized she wasn't coming back. Like her mom's photograph, a ceramic cross her *cookum* had given her before her death, and all the cash she'd been secretly hoarding behind the bedroom's light switch.

Unscrewing the wall plate with a metal nail file, Lillian carefully extracted the small roll of tip money she'd tightly wrapped in an elastic band and stashed over the last few months. Silently praying that it'd be enough to tide her over until she got her first pay check from Giovanni Films, she shoved the roll down the front of her jeans.

Stopping to fill up the duffle bag with a few basic toiletries and a couple changes of underwear, Lillian consciously topped it all off with an armful of her own soiled laundry. In less than two minutes, she had effectively decided to change the course of her life and immediately began taking all the necessary steps.

Taking one final look around her bedroom, she realized that she wasn't leaving anything behind that she couldn't live without. Her clothes were all wrong, drawers filled with outfits that only a stripper would wear. The dishes, the bedding, and furniture, were all beat to shit or threadbare. Her once cute little apartment had turned into a flophouse frequented by Ronnie's posse of junkies, looking for their next hit and a dry place to crash. Nothing even slightly resembled its original condition.

With her next breath, Lillian knew in her heart that she was ready to walk away from it all. She'd let Ronnie have everything she owned if he'd just let her go—an almost impossible dream but definitely something worth fighting for.

Duffle bag slung over her shoulder, she slipped on a new pair of sneakers hidden in the back of her closet, shoved a simple pair of black heels into the side pouch of her bag, and turned to walk out the bedroom door.

"Yo there, pussy cat," Ronnie called out from his seat on the couch. "The boys was wondering if you'd do us a little dance?"

"I'll dance with ya," Jerome jumped up to his feet and began swinging his hips from side to side.

"Sit your ass down!" Ronnie barked; leveling an empty beer can straight at Jerome's recently shaved head. "So how 'bout it, girllllll? Just pretend we're down at Cheekssss," he grinned, his speech beginning to slur as the dope continued pulsing through his system.

"Let me put in the laundry, and I'll be right back," she reached down into the front closet and snatched up the open box of laundry detergent.

"Take my coat," Ronnie barked. "It smells like shittttt."

"Good idea," she reasoned aloud. "Mine could use a wash too. And Ronnie," she screwed up her courage and she forced herself to walk into the middle of the living room. "I need some change for the machines. You got anything in your pockets?"

Digging down, he came up with his *gansta roll* of twenty-dollar bills, money she'd never see for food or rent. "Got no coins, but I'll give you a few bucks," he peeled forty dollars off his roll. "You run down to the corner, grab me a pack of smokes and... and a roll of quarters. Now you bring me back the change, bitch," he warned, shoving the remainder of the roll back down into his jeans.

"One pack," she confirmed the order. "Can I get a milk? I didn't have enough money when I bought groceries?"

"Kid's gone," he laughed. "We don't need no fucking milk. Now hurry your ass up," Ronnie moved back toward the couch, simultaneously losing his footing and nearly falling directly into Jerome's lap.

Lillian took one last look around her apartment before turning her back and walking straight out the front door.

––––––––––––

"I smell ravioli," Pete called out the minute his boot hit the creaky front step.

"Peter," his mother called out. "Come, come," she stepped aside to beckon him in the door. "Time for supper." Watching her son move up front steps, Pete's mother was struck by just how thin he'd become, still confident that all his ailments could be cured by a good plate of pasta and the right woman to serve it to him.

"How ya doing, mama?"

"You know," she said with a shrug of her shoulders, slowly stirring the meat sauce that would smother the freshly boiled ravioli. "Some days they're bad, and some days they're not." She alluded to the throbbing arthritis that continually plagued her twisted joints. "Today they were good, so I made pasta, and did the laundry."

"You seen Boyd today?" he casually inquired, walking over to pour himself a glass of red wine from the open bottle on the corner hutch.

"No, no Boyd. He's so busy, making those movies." She shook her head.

"What kind of movies?" He couldn't help but ask, surprised that his mother even entertained the idea that her sons were involved in the adult entertainment industry.

"Sex movies," she said as she began straining the fresh pasta out of the boiling water.

"Mama," he chuckled in complete shock. "Where did you hear that?"

"Rosa's son, Antonio, left boxes in her basement when he moved his family across the city. She cleaned for him, and found... found your movies." She shook her head. "I'm not smart like you," she said, alluding to her son's grade ten education, "but I know the name of your company from when you both still lived in the neighborhood, and it was there. I saw it with my own eyes," she repeatedly nodded her head.

"So," Pete threw back nearly an entire glass of wine. "You and Rosa watch any of those movies."

"Stupid boy." She stepped across the floor and gently slapped the back of his head. "Movies are for men without wives, not women who've buried their husbands."

"You're right, mama," he smiled, turning to take a quick peek out the kitchen window to make sure his friends were still waiting in the Porsche.

"Now eat," she said and sat a steaming plate down in front of his usual seat at the table.

"Thanks." Pete pulled out the chair and quickly dove in, reluctantly forcing himself to chew and then swallow what had once been his favorite meal.

"You need a wife. A good woman to make you supper, then you won't have to eat at your mama's table." She waved an accusing finger. "It's time."

"Mama, I don't wanna get married," he argued for the hundredth time.

"Yes, you do," she corrected him, not the least bit interested in discussing the possibility that her baby might be a confirmed bachelor. "Rosa knows a girl who cuts hair. She's nice, has her own car..."

"Stop, please stop." Pete held up his right hand. "I know lots of girls, Mama. I don't need you to fix me up."

"*Manga, manga*," she encouraged him to eat up and finish his plate. "You know girls, but not nice girls," she said and cursed under her breath. "Why you not take Rosa's hairdresser for supper? Show her your smile." She reached over and patted her son's face.

"Mama," he said as he shoved the last cheese ravioli into his mouth. "I just stopped by to tell you that I'm going away for a little while."

"Where?" She reached for his empty bowl.

"Somewhere warm," he answered, intentionally vague. "I just stopped in to say goodbye for awhile."

"Why? How long you be gone? What about your job? Don't Boyd need you at the company?"

"Boyd don't need me." He looked down at his shoes. "He's got Julia. He don't need me no more."

Teresa Giovanni silently nodded her head in agreement, fully aware of the hurt feelings between her sons ever since Boyd had married Julia, ignoring his brother's protests. "Will you call me?"

"I'll call you, Mama." He unconsciously began scratching his right arm.

"Then come here," she beckoned. "Give your mama a big hug."

Stepping forward, Pete allowed himself to be wrapped up in his mother's embrace. "I love you, Mama."

"I know. And mama loves you, too." She reached up and planted a succession of warm kisses on both his cheeks.

Walking out his mother's front door, Pete wouldn't allow himself to turn back and look, even though he knew in his heart that his mother would be firmly planted on the step to wave her goodbyes.

CHAPTER THIRTEEN

"There are only two tragedies in life. One is not getting what you want. The other is getting it."
                                    —Lord of War, 2005

D ressed in casual clothes and carting two dozen crates jammed
     with all their supplies, the crew from Giovanni Films made
their way toward the practice shoot.

"Don't put anything in the circles I've marked with spray paint,"
Boyd yelled out. "That's where the tepee is going to sit."

"And the fire," Wanda pointed to a smaller circle. "Nothing
should be closer than three or four feet from that fire pit."

Everyone continued to set up the location, doing their best to
transform the farmer's grassy field into an Indian camping ground.

"Sure got a lot of people here to make one little old picture," the
farmer muttered aloud, standing off to the side, sipping his second
cup of coffee.

"Mr. Jacobs," Boyd stepped up and shook the man's hand. "We
really appreciate you tearing down your fence so we could drive our
vehicles in here."

"You can call me Noah. And I didn't tear down no fence, I just pulled up a handful of my corner posts and laid down the wire so you's could all drive over it without having to cut the line."

"Smart thinking," Boyd stepped forward and patted him firmly on the back. "Now, I was wondering if we could possibly talk about renting a few of your horses for this Friday."

As her husband busied himself, negotiating a deal with the farmer, Julia turned all of her attention to her newest star. "How's the costume?"

"Gorgeous," Lillian continued to fawn over the intricate beading adorning the length of her bodice. "And a little tight," she admitted, sucking in another deep breath. "But from what I understand, I won't be wearing it all that long anyway."

"It's snug," Julia corrected the young girl. "But it's supposed to be form fitting. I've never heard any stories about Pocahontas running around in a baggy sweatshirt and rolled up sweatpants."

"Well, it's form fitting all right. That's for sure." She sucked in her abdomen muscles, "And what about these?" Lillian gently tugged at the leather strapping limply hanging from behind her back.

"Turn. I'll lace them for you."

As Lillian braced herself against the hood of the nearest truck, Julia began threading the leather strips though the metal grommets, carefully creating the desired crisscross pattern down the center of her back.

"How's the cowboy supposed to get me undressed?" she snickered, wondering if he was going to take the same amount of time unthreading her laces as her boss was taking to thread them up.

"He's going to use a knife to slit open the front of your costume. The lacing in the back is just for show."

"What?"

"Relax." Julia's nimble fingers continued to tug at the leather. "The actor playing the cowboy will be carrying a retractable dummy knife. Look down at the front of your costume."

Upon closer inspection, Lillian was very pleased to see that only small strips of Velcro held the front bodice together. Easily pulled apart by any blunt object, the costume had been constructed with the prop knife in mind.

"We're bringing in Malcolm to work with you on this picture. He's an old pro who's worked for us the last couple of years. He knows what he's doing, and he'll be able to walk you through the set ups. But listen to me, Lillian," she knotted the laces before gently swinging the young girl around. "You're going to have to be able to play this right up to the edge. Do you know what that means?"

"If she's brand new, she won't have a clue," Malcolm strolled up behind the women. "I think we're going to have to educate this fine young thing."

"Well, there you are. Welcome to the set," Julia leaned over and kissed her leading man firmly on the lips. "We worked together a couple of times, before I..."

"Before she ran off and got herself all married and stuff," he teased his old friend. "Now, what's this I hear that you want me to grow a pencil-thin moustache for your little picture. I can't stand having a *crumb catcher* hanging down below my nose. It'll just cover my beautiful lips," he puckered up in a mock pose.

"Malcolm, I thought I could smell you clear across the set," Boyd waltzed over and shook his hand. "Still buying your Old Spice by the gallon?"

"On what you pay, I'd be lucky to afford anything else," he answered back, easily slipping into the friendly banter.

Watching the men get reacquainted, Lillian felt like she had stumbled into the midst of a high school reunion, not the set of a pornographic movie.

"Excuse me, Malcolm," Wanda suddenly interrupted the group. "I have your costume ready. You want to come over and change?"

"I'm all yours," he answered with a wink.

Once again alone with Julia, Lillian couldn't help but express her gratitude. "I don't even know where to start. You've given me such a great opportunity here. Everyone seems so nice."

"Of course they do. It's just a run through, today. But you wait 'til the day we actually film—Malcolm will be so stressed, you best just keep out of his way. He's all bubbles and sunshine now, but come Friday, he'll be yelling for better lighting, or bitching about the props. Trust me dear, in three days from now, you'll get to see a whole new side to our *little star* that you could have never imagined."

"Oh," she muttered, suddenly afraid of what was to come.

"All right people," Boyd yelled from behind one of the stationary cameras. "I wanna try the chase scene where Pocahontas is picking wild berries in the grass and our lonely old cowboy chases her down, mounts her for the first time, and then ties her up. Malcolm," he cupped his hands and shouted across the grassy field. "You got the rope?"

Lifting the two lengths up over his head, the male lead continued to move off toward his first mark.

Boyd suddenly turned his attention back to Lillian. "See this?" he walked over and thrust a makeshift drawing of the set plan into the girl's hands. "I want you to run in a figure eight just like I've drawn here. See the X?"

She nodded, pointing to the obvious mark on the map.

"That's where I want you to slow down so Malcolm can catch you. Did Julia explain everything?"

"Yeah, but what does *playing it to the edge* mean?"

"Well, you're gonna have to tell us when he's going too far."

"How will I know?"

"Well, the ropes gotta be tight, but if they're cutting off your circulation or really pinching your skin, then you speak up. Shit like that. I know it's kind of tough, but this rape has to look as realistic as possible, so you're going to have to take the brunt of his attack until you feel he's crossing the line. We'll do as many shots of *air thrusting* as we can, but there's gonna have to be some skin shots of him actually penetrating you. You understand?"

Lillian nodded, her stomach beginning to churn. "Mr. Giovanni, I was just wondering... well... what's *air thrusting*?"

"Wanda," he lifted his head and shouted at the top of his lungs.

"What you need?" she asked, suddenly appearing from behind their backs.

"Ask her," he nodded his head toward his purchasing agent before turning back to adjust the angle on a camera.

Double-checking his Daytimer, Francois Dubois was genuinely surprised to find that his afternoon's schedule was blank. Granted it was midweek, but he still couldn't remember the last time he'd been able to kick back in the middle of the workday.

Taking the opportunity to jump in his car and head downtown, Francois strolled unannounced, straight into the manager's office at his local bank.

"Mr. Dubois." The man instantly rose from behind his desk. "How nice to see you. Why don't you take a seat. Can I offer you a beverage?"

"No, thank you," he said as he chose one of the opposing chairs, waiting for the bank's manager to close his door and retake his position behind his desk.

"Why don't you let me inform my staff that I'm in a meeting so we won't be disturbed?"

As Francois debated which account he'd pull his funds from, the bank manager quickly ordered his secretary to rebook any appointments previously scheduled for the following hour.

"Well, Mr. Dubois, you have my undivided attention, so why don't you tell me what it is that I can do for you today."

"I need one-hundred and fifty thousand dollars."

"That's absolutely no problem," the manager pulled open one of his side desk drawers to pluck out a withdrawal slip. "I assume you're referring to US Funds?"

Francois nodded in agreement.

"And which account would you prefer to withdraw the funds from?"

"I think I'll just use my personal savings. Unfortunately, I don't have my account number handy."

"That's no problem. Why don't you let me get that for you?" He quickly picked up his phone and instructed his secretary to locate the appropriate information. "So tell me, Mr. Dubois, would you like a bank draft or would you prefer to directly wire your funds to another account?"

"I'd like cash."

"Cash?" the manager repeated, unsure that he'd heard his client correctly.

"Yes. I want a hundred thousand dollars in one hundred dollar bills, and an additional fifty thousand in smaller denominations."

As the small beads of sweat began to form on the manager's upper lip, he pulled a monogrammed hankie from his suit pocket and nervously mopped the skin above his brow. "Uh, Mr. Dubois. We... well... that's a big order, sir. We..."

"Is there a problem?" Francois demanded, sensing that his personal request had somehow sent the manager careening toward a cardiac arrest. "You're familiar with my business and personal accounts here at this branch, are you not?"

"I am very familiar with your business," the manager said, beginning to recover some of his senses. "Please understand that it's not a matter of whether or not you can cover the withdrawal Mr.

Dubois. It's the idea of one hundred and fifty thousand dollars in cash. We just don't do that," he tried to explain.

"Are you trying to tell me that this branch does not hold more than one-hundred and fifty thousand dollars in reserve at any given time?"

"Oh, we do," he rushed to defend the bank. "But please understand that at least fifty percent of our liquid funds are in five, ten, and twenty dollar denominations, for our cash machines located in the bank's lobby for after-hour access."

"So order it for me," Francois said and crossed his arms. "I'm sure if you wanted to; you could easily bring it in from your main branch or even treasury. Isn't that correct?

"Mr. Dubois, have you ever heard of the BSA, the MCLA, or the OCC?"

"BSA?" he ran the acronym through his head and still came up empty.

"I'm talking about the *Bank Secrecy Act*, the *Money Laundering Control Act of 1986*, and of course, the *Office of the Comptroller of the Currency*," he finished, heaving a giant sigh, the color instantly beginning to drain from his face.

"And what exactly do those government offices have to do with me?"

Frantically digging through the top drawer of his desk, the manager suddenly yanked out a laminated file, reluctantly opening it to its introductory page before beginning to read aloud. "*The reporting and record keeping requirements of the BSA regulations create a paper trail for law enforcement to investigate money laundering schemes and other illegal activities. This paper trail operates to deter illegal activity and provides a means to trace movements of money through the financial system.*"

"What are you reading from?" Francoise demanded, not the least bit daunted by the legal terminology.

"*My Comptroller's Handbook*," he lifted up the pages to flash the letterhead. "It sets out the procedures I have to follow for dealing with *Placements, Layering,* and *Integration,* terms all dealing with money laundering schemes."

"Listen," Francois rose to his feet. "I'm not trying to launder money; I just want to withdraw some of my own personal funds for my own private use. Is that too much to ask from an institution I have dealt with for the past nine years?"

"I'd be more than happy to cut you a bank draft, free of charge," the manager offered as a token incentive.

"What in the hell is going on here? I've moved millions of dollars around this country with nothing more than a simple phone call. Now, when I come down here in person to withdraw a measly hundred and fifty thousand, you're actually trying to tell me that I can't have it? I think it's time that I called my solicitor."

"No, sir. That's not it. I just wanted you to understand that with a cash transaction of that magnitude, there are some very serious consequences."

"Such as?"

"Well, for one, we'll have to fill out the appropriate forms. Any cash transaction over ten-thousand dollars in a business day will have to be documented. That document will have to be filed with the government so they can track the movement of the funds. And in the case of ordering specific denominations, well, that's just another set of paperwork all together."

"This is quite the situation," Francois walked around the back of his chair, slowly adjusting the furniture to return the legs to their original positions in the rug.

"Mr. Dubois," the manager pleaded. "Please understand, sir. If there was anything that I could possibly do to circumvent these unfortunate and unnecessary regulations for such an upstanding businessman as yourself; please rest assured that I would."

"I understand, and thank you for your time." Francois turned to leave the manager's office.

"I hope this doesn't affect any of our future business dealings." He frantically swabbed at the rivulets of sweat beginning to run down the back of his neck.

"Good day." Francoise exited the bank, making a mental note to send his solicitor by to close all his accounts and transfer his business to another institution.

———————

Cell phone vibrating at her hip, Julia stepped away from the action long enough to answer the ringing phone. "Julia speaking, can I help you?"

"Julia, this is Francois Dubois," a deeply masculine voice announced from the other end of her line.

"Francois," she purred, unable to help herself as she unabashedly flirted with the company's potential client. "You just couldn't stay away from me, could you?"

"No ma'am," he responded in kind. "I was wondering if it would be possible to speak with you in person regarding our financial arrangement."

"Well, I'm a little tied up at a shoot for the remainder of the afternoon, but if you don't mind meeting me after business hours, I'll probably be done by seven or eight."

"Eight would be perfect," he quickly agreed. "Do you have a meeting place in mind?"

"Any lounge that serves a lady a nice stiff drink will be fine with me."

Francois named his favorite Scotch bar and they agreed to meet later that evening.

By the time the sun had begun to set behind the trees, Julia had long since disappeared from the shoot, leaving early to freshen up and change her clothes for her meeting with Francois.

Boyd too had made a run for it, packing up the early tapes and heading straight to his editing room, curious to sit down with Martin and see just how Lillian had performed in her first screen test.

Left behind to wrap up the shoot, Wanda began by checking on her actors, the most important asset of any film.

"Malcolm, what did you think of the leather chaps?" she called out, waiting for him to exit the portable dressing room that had been set up inside a lopsided hexagon.

"You tell me," he strolled out from behind the privacy screen, butt naked except for the tanned hides wrapped around each of his muscular legs with the matching cowboy hat perched on the top of his sun-bleached hair.

"Looks good." She had to be honest, having learned early on that porn stars had an extremely high embarrassment factor, and losing your cool around their nakedness was considered totally gauche. "You okay with the boots?" She glanced down at the discarded clothing piled up on the grass. "Cuz if they're too tight, I can have them stretched at a shoemaker's."

"Nah, they're fine." He looked down at his own growing erection. "You sure you're not interested in working part time as my fluffer?" he teased.

"No, I think I'm better off behind my desk pushing papers, than down on my knees pulling you."

He liked her. She wasn't like one of the usual bimbos who hung around some of the shoots, flirting with the actors as they tried to set up dates to trade sexual favors for personal introductions into the business. "You heading back to the office, my dear?"

"Well, after I check with Lillian, pack up the props, and pay..." she flipped through her note pad, "...pay Noah Jacobs his land rent, then I'll be ready to go. So if you wanna wait that long, I'll give you a ride."

"I'll see," he said as he leaned over, gently setting his cowboy hat down on top of Wanda's head.

"Wanda!" a voice yelled from the other side of the parked vehicles.

"Gotta run." She plucked the hat off her curls and reached up to drop it back down on top of Malcolm's head. "Please find me as soon as you're done changing, then I can have the guys tear down the screens and get them folded up for transport."

"Yes, ma'am," he winked, turning and sashaying out of her line of sight just as a few angry voices began to ring through the air.

"What's the problem?" Wanda demanded, rushing over to find one of the grips dropping the used rope and slimy ball gag down into an open box of sex toys.

"I told him not to," the senior cameraman announced, as he took a moment to relax, lighting a fresh cigarette before continuing with the breakdown of his equipment.

"What's the big fucking deal?" the grip complained. "It's just a bunch rope and a couple gags."

"They're dirty," Wanda reached in the box and pulled out the soiled articles. "The toys in that box are brand new. They *were* sterile," she tried to explain.

"Whatever," the kid wandered off, not the least bit concerned with the woman's hygiene issues.

Grabbing the cardboard flaps, she closed the box, whipping out a felt marker to label the lid with a giant black X.

"I think I'm done," Lillian announced, her costume carefully draped over her outstretched arms. "I didn't know where you wanted me to put it."

"See the garment bags hanging off the back of the pick-up truck?" Lillian just nodded her head.

"Well, you find the one that that's marked Pocahontas, and you'll have the right bag."

As Lillian scurried off to stow her costume, Wanda made sure each of the boxes were loaded, instructing the grip to set the marked box in her own car.

"Can I help?" Lillian reappeared, her pumping adrenaline manifesting itself into nervous energy.

"In the backseat of my red Corolla, you'll find a bunch of garbage bags. Grab one, and hunt down any Styrofoam cups, cigarette packs, or soda cans. Got it?"

"Consider it done," she took off in the direction of the parked cars.

Within another twenty minutes, the site was clean, and except for a large patch of trampled grass, you'd have never known it had been the practice site of a movie shoot.

"Guess we're ready to hit the bricks," Wanda announced, waving everyone off and moving toward her own car.

"Excuse me," Lillian rushed up to her side. "Do you think I can have a ride back to the city? I came out with Julia, but I don't think she's coming back to get me."

"Hop in honey," she motioned to the back seat. "Just slide some of that shit over," she pointed to the prop box.

"Malcolm," Wanda called out. "Anybody see Malcolm?"

"He took off with one of the camera guys about fifteen minutes ago."

"Then you've just been promoted to the front," she waved Lillian forward. "Let's get out of here before its pitch black and we spend the rest of our night driving up and down the gravel roads."

"I'm with you," Lillian tenderly lowered herself into the bucket seat, already starting to feel the stiffness creep into the muscles of her lower back.

CHAPTER FOURTEEN

"A lawyer's not supposed to become personally involved with his client, but there's all kinds of lawyers and all kinds of clients, too."

—The Rainmaker, 1997

Armed with industrial strength antibacterial soap, a hand sponge, and a second pan of hot rinse water, Wanda pulled on a set of rubber gloves and carefully began cleaning the shoot's cache of sex toys. Starting with the rubber dildos, she dipped them one by one in the hot water before applying the soap, careful not to immerse any of the housing units in an attempt to protect the battery packs.

"Do you want me to dry them?" Lillian offered her services.

"Awe, just pack up and head home, girl. This definitely ain't part of your job."

"I'm kinda avoiding home right now. Had a fight with the old man," she summed up her situation in a flourish. "So, should I dry?"

"No, I found that cotton towels just leave lint balls all over the shafts. If you really wanna help, grab some gloves, and then lay them all down on a clean towel and let them air dry. It really works the best."

Following her instructions, Lillian unconsciously began lining up the dildos by size while Wanda reached back into the box for second handful of sex toys.

"You do this after every shoot?"

"Hell no," Wanda chuckled. "The sex toys are only used twice; once for the run through and then again on the main shoot with the same cast of actors. After that, they're discarded. Except for the ball gags. We chuck those each and every time."

"Makes sense."

"Was this a good size for you?" Wanda inspected the two-inch ball gag Lillian had worn before unsnapping it from the leather head-strap and dropping it down into the wastebasket. "Because we stock em' in all different sizes."

"It seemed fine," she shrugged her shoulders. "But you know; I really don't have much experience with all this kind of stuff. Even though I was a stripper, my sex life was pretty normal, kinda boring when you actually think about it."

"Well then, come over here," Wanda beckoned; eager to share her accumulated wealth of researched knowledge "You see; a ball gag should fit securely inside the pocket of your mouth without you having to overly stretching your lips to get it inside. When the ball is positioned halfway inside your mouth, it's supposed to sit on top of your tongue with your teeth held open by the center width of the ball. But even then, you should still be able to slightly shift the ball side to side before the strap is tightened around your head."

Lillian nodded her head, concentrating to remember every detail.

"Cuz if the balls' stuffed in so tight that you can't shift it around your mouth, then it's too big a gag for you. And if you're closing your lips around the entire ball when it's sitting inside your mouth, then it's definitely too small. Understand? Half the ball should effectively pry open your mouth but still leave a little wiggle room."

Lillian nodded, gingerly picking up the two different gags. "What's the difference," she examined the two different styles. "One looks kinda solid and the other one looks kinda like a shrunken floor hockey ball."

"That's a wiffle-ball style," Wanda stated as a matter of fact, "Complete with small air holes that allow you to still suck or blow through your mouth. The other is solid rubber. Admittedly easier on your teeth, but it can be a little claustrophobic if you're never worn any kind of gag before."

"Which kind do you like?" Lillian passed both to Wanda, genuinely interested in her opinion.

"Oh no," she laughed, "not me. I've never tried any of this stuff. I'm just responsible for ordering the film props and maintaining our stock."

"But then how do you know so much?" Lillian glanced back down at the gag straps dangling down off her palms.

"It's my job to find out. I have to know everything I can about my props, and the more I know, the safer and more comfortable performing will be for you. Anymore questions?"

"Well... I did hear people talking about *Jizz Balls*, and even though I've seen the porn my ex-boyfriend used to rent, I've never even heard of them."

"Don't worry, we don't use those," Julia leaned over to pluck a small piece of cotton fluff off the tip of a dildos.

"I know, but what are they? Fake balls or something?"

Reaching into another box, Wanda pulled out an enema bulb. "You know what this is, right?" she held up a red rubber ball with a pointy tip.

"Yeah," Lillian blushed, having just flushed out her vaginal and anal cavities earlier that day at Julia's request.

"Well, many directors will fill this rubber ball with a mixture of water thickened with cornstarch, and a couple teaspoons of milk to simulate a man's ejaculate." Dropping the ball to her side, Wanda threw her head back and let out a fake moan, squeezing the balls at the exact second to simulate the squirting motion.

"Oh, I get it, I get it!" Lillian giggled.

"See, when the camera's *not* focused on the head of the cock, the guys squeezes the jizz ball and squirts the liquid all over his partner's back, stomach, or face. It's used a lot in the industry for cheap porn. But it's really a total fake out if you ask me."

Lillian nodded her agreement, unconsciously beginning to rub her lower arms.

"Your wrists still burning?"

"They're not bad," she pulled down the sleeves on her sweatshirt. "I guess the rope was a little tighter than I realized."

"You're lucky I had Malcolm use Japanese bondage rope instead of that crappy baling twine Boyd had originally wanted to use for your wrists."

"Really," Lillian reached down into the bottom of the box and pulled out a coiled mass of black rope. "What's the difference?"

"About fifteen bucks for twelve feet," she smirked. "Actually, that cotton restraint rope won't chafe or irritate your skin as long as the knots aren't tied too tight. Baling twine, on the other hand, will literally rip your skin to shreds every time you twist or turn. It's made for dried hay, not for human skin."

"Shit, I'm really glad that you're in charge of all this stuff," Lillian nodded her head.

"Well, it is up to me to make sure we have the most suitable product for each and every film shoot. Can you imagine what kind of mood Boyd and Julia would be in if, during filming, none of the vibrators had fresh batteries, or I'd brought the wrong size ball gags? Let me tell you, the shit would surely hit the fan."

Lillian nodded, already having witnessed a small sample of Boyd's temper earlier that afternoon when Malcolm had thrown a hissy fit about some kind of sting nettles mixed in with the field grass. By the time Boyd had set him straight, Malcolm was not only willing to kneel down on the stuff, he'd have shoved it right up his ass if Boyd had asked him to.

"So Lillian, what'd you think of your first day of work on a Giovanni Film shoot?"

"Fine." She couldn't help but feel the heat flushing up toward her cheeks. "It's just kind of weird having sex with so many people watching and all. I kinda thought it would be a little more private, you know, with music and stuff."

"No, our customized porn has to be a little more staged that your usual run of the mill gang bangs. When you have a client willing to pay money in the six figure range for a specific plot line, you owe it to them to stick to *their* script."

"I just can't understand why they pay it?" Lillian had to admit. "There are hundreds of sleazy strip bars, and entire blocks full of peep shows. I can't even guess how many hookers there are running up and down the streets of this city. For that kind of money, you could have a fresh piece of tail three hundred and sixty-five days of the year. It just doesn't make any sense to me."

"I'm not sure I can explain it, but for some of the people who hire Giovanni Films, money isn't really the issue. Privacy is more important, and so is getting exactly what they want."

"I know girls that'll do whatever, and I mean whatever," she rolled her eyes, "For two hundred bucks, the options are open. So why pay to have a film made when you can have it for real?"

"You know what fetishes are?" Wanda pulled off her gloves and walked away from the washtubs.

"Like stiletto heels and rubber underwear?"

"Those are a couple of the basics, but many of our client's fetishes are really quite unique. And you have to realize that having a fetish doesn't necessarily mean that you want to experience it in person. Many of our clients are more than content to witness their deepest desires on film, not actually wanting to experience their fetish in person for a multitude of reasons."

"Give me an example," Lillian pressed, "something really weird that you hadn't seen before you worked here."

Hands on her hips, Wanda stopped to think for a second, throwing the enema bulb back into a box while she scanned her own memory banks. "I don't know. Nothing really stands out anymore."

"So watching a cowboy run through a grass field and then tie up an Indian princess after raping her repeatedly on the ground beside her tepee isn't strange."

"Truth be told, your little screen test was actually one of the more mainstream pieces of tape that we've put out since I've been here."

"Oh come," Lillian continued to beg, "tell me something juicy."

"We did have that one really big fat guy who paid big money for a special film."

"Like…" she encouraged her to go on.

"Well, he actually wanted to star in the production himself, which truly is kind of unusual. Anyway, it was kind of half sploshing, and half anal insertion. A combo film."

Lillian's attention was a hundred percent focused on Wanda, and as they delved deeper into the impromptu lesson, neither noticed a man quietly lurking outside the office door.

"I can't remember exactly what Julia charged the guy," she mused, "but we had to pay big bucks for the set design on that one."

"Why?"

"First off, we had to build a special wooden dining room table from scratch. You should have seen it," she laughed, "it was really, really huge. This table had holes in it like an outdoor toilet, except the girls never sat on it; they crawled underneath the table and shoved their naked butts up through the holes from the bottom as they leaned their stomachs over padded stools."

"What are you talking about?" Lillian struggled to form a mental picture.

Grabbing the stool from in front of her computer desk, Wanda leaned her stomach over the seat and pushed her butt up toward the ceiling. "Get the jest?" she snickered. "All six girls' asses poking up through the holes in the table while their heads and bodies were tucked unseen underneath the framework."

Lillian silently nodded, unsure whether she actually wanted to hear the rest.

"Well, our client requested that each girl's rectum be inserted with an empty cylinder that we'd hired a machinist to mill out of stainless steel."

"I'm lost again," Lillian shook her head in disgust. "Why the empty cylinders?"

"No, no," Wanda teased, pushing her stool back under her computer desk. "Don't ask why the cylinders? Ask, why the dining table? That's a better clue."

"All right," she played along. "Why are six women's naked butts poking through a dining table with empty cylinders stuffed in their asses?"

"So we could fill them up with food and then our client could sit down to enjoy a lovely six course dinner," Wanda pretended to tuck a linen napkin in at the nape of her neck.

"No fucking way! You've gotta be pulling my chain," she couldn't help but shout. "Nobody is that twisted."

"That's just one project, and last count, Giovanni's had filmed over a hundred and fifty of these special little films."

"Nobody's eating dinner out of my ass," Lillian stubbornly crossed her arms at her chest. "I don't care how much they're willing to pay me."

Wanda laughed, beginning to enjoy Lillian's spark just an unseen man suddenly took advantage of the break in the tutorial to announce his presence.

"Guess that gives a whole new meaning to the phrase *eating in*," Warren couldn't help but sneer at his sister Wanda.

———————

Dropping the dried leaves into dime sized sandwich bags, Jerome continued on with his task, always aware of Ronnie's whereabouts as he continued to pace up and down the apartment's back hall.

"I think this is really a fucking dumb idea. Nobody's gonna believe this *bunk* is the real thing. Anybody with two cents for brains is gonna know that it's just some old mixture of kitchen spices and chopped up leaves. There's no way in hell that anybody's gonna believe that it's actual dope."

Jerome sealed up the plastic zipper on his baggie and dropped it down into his ratty old knapsack. "I ain't gonna take this down to the strip and try and sell it to a bunch of hard cores, you know. I'm gonna head down to the amusement park and pawn it off on a couple of tourists. They don't have a fucking clue what they're actually buying, and before they have a chance to spark up a joint, I'll be so long gone that they wouldn't even be able to find me with one of them police tracking dogs."

"Selling *bunk*," Ronnie moaned. "What in the fuck has happened to us? We should be peddling Grade A Shit, not bags of fucking oregano to some god damned tourists stopping over on their way to Vegas."

"We need to set ourselves up," Jerome attempted to reason

with his friend, "and without at least a few bucks in our pockets, nobody is going to front us any of their dope. Ain't that what you always tell me? We gotta have at least ten percent. Right Ronnie, ten percent?"

"That fucking bitch," Ronnie began to rant, slamming his right fist into the nearest wall. "Where in the hell could she be hiding?"

Jerome ignored his best friend, having witnessed the same tirade every hour on the hour since Ronnie had figured out that Lillian had split. "Too bad you spent all your cash on other shit. We could have really used a couple hundred for our front."

"The bitch always had money coming in. And she could've pulled a couple more shifts dancing down at Cheeks if I really needed her to. You know, I wouldn't be suffering so fucking bad if she hadn't been such a whore and ran off on her responsibilities. She owes me," he continued to shout as if raising his voice would somehow make the situation better.

"She'll come back. She's just a little pissed about the Play Station is all. We got games and beer, and you wouldn't let her have no money for milk. When she calms down, she'll come wandering back home. You'll see."

"She better have both my twenties or I'll tan her ass. That fucking squaw is begging for it," he leered at the front door, his hands balled up into fists as if waiting for her to stroll back into the apartment.

"What's today?" Jerome suddenly looked up from behind his collection of baggies.

"Tuesday, Monday. Fucked if I know."

"No. What day of the month is it?" Jerome suddenly stood up and walked to the kitchen.

Shaking the cramps out of his fingers, Ronnie shook off his anger and followed his friend. "What ya doing?" he demanded, watching him run his fingers up and down the wall calendar.

"I think today's the twenty-ninth. If Lilly doesn't show, we've got two days to come up with some cash for rent. How much you pay here?"

Ronnie opened his mouth but quickly closed it when he realized that he didn't have the slightest clue.

"Well, don't worry," Jerome walked over and patted his buddy on the back. "I'm sure that she'll show. She's not the type to leave a guy high and dry, is she? Lilly's your woman, she wouldn't do that to you. Right?"

Suddenly, Ronnie wasn't quite so sure.

By the time Julia had been able to leave the *run through*, it had been almost four in the afternoon. Having left herself her precious little time to run home and spruce up before meeting with Francois Dubois at eight, she chose to skip her usual hot bath and jumped straight into the shower.

"Do you wanna join us?" she'd taken a minute to call her husband from the limo.

"No babe, that's fine," he said and continued scrolling through the footage. "I've got Martin down here working overtime and we're going to wade our way through the rest of these tapes before we call it a night."

"Well, my cell will be on should you change your mind."

Boyd wished her goodnight and hung up the phone, anxious to return to the job at hand.

"We can leave," she called out to her driver. "Mr. Giovanni will not be coming with us."

As the car pulled out of her driveway, Julia found herself checking her appearance for the fifth time since she'd showered and dressed.

"Excuse me, ma'am," the driver politely inquired. "Would you like me to wait for you outside the lounge?"

"No, that's fine. I don't really have any idea how long I'm going to be, so you might as well call it a night. If Mr. Giovanni does not join me later, I'll just call a cab and head back home."

Plans solidified, Julia rode the remainder of the way in silence.

Already seated in a corner table near the bar's dual-sided fireplace, Francois took the opportunity to relax, take a deep breath, and wait for his guest. He'd had a hell of a day, and after his unsuccessful meeting with the bank, he'd spent the remainder of the afternoon exploring alternative options.

One potential source had actually been presumptuous enough to pull him aside and inquire whether he required their assistance in alerting the authorities regarding a possible kidnapping.

He'd immediately set them straight and decided once again to take his business elsewhere.

The third source had seemed less concerned with his personal safety as he was with his personal fees. A hundred and fifty thousand cash was going to cost Francois ten points, which they'd scoop off the top. Should he need to order specific denominations, it would cost him another two points across the board. Eighteen-thousand dollars seemed awfully steep for changing a personal bank draft into liquid cash.

The one man who was willing to complete the transaction for a more reasonable rate didn't seem to worry about anything at all, and the longer they negotiated the finer points of the deal, the more Francois realized that it probably would be best not to associate with this level of business man at all.

"Good evening." Julia had walked up unnoticed; forced to pull out her own chair as Francois scrambled to his feet.

"Julia, I'm sorry," he reached forward and gently shook her hand. "I honestly never saw you arrive."

"You looked like you were lost in thought." She smiled to herself. "Dreaming about your little movie, are we?"

"Actually," he raised his hand to summon the waitress to their table, "I was thinking of you."

Flattered that he even bothered delivering such a transparent compliment, Julia ordered a vodka tonic and settled back into her chair. "So now that you have me here, Mr. Dubois, what would you like to speak about?"

"Your pronunciation of my French surname, although rusty, is quite pleasing."

"Thank you," she smiled. "I guess I just have a way with my tongue."

He smiled, any other response would have been considered tasteless.

"So, when you called this afternoon, you mentioned that you'd like a meeting regarding your finances. What exactly is the problem?"

Waiting until after their drinks had been deposited by their waitress, Francois took a quick sip before recounting the day's escapades, beginning with his visit to the bank, and ending with his back alley liquidator.

"Everyone knows that cash is golden, but very few have the ability to raise it," Julia laughed. "To tell you the truth, I was a little surprised when you informed me that you were interested in taking advantage of our cash discount and would have no problem delivering a hundred and fifty large."

"Well, I'm here with hat in hand to apologize. It's not as easy as I initially believed, but then, I guess you already knew that, didn't you?"

Reaching over and lightly patting Francois's hand, Julia couldn't help but softly giggle. "You're a well-respected business man in the world of high finance, correct?"

"Correct," he answered, a smile now spreading across his face.

"Well sir, I'm a well-respected business woman in the world of underground finance. We're both professionals, but we operate on two different planes."

"Such as?" he prompted her, hoping for a further explanation.

"Well, you operate in the white zone. Accountants balance your books, lawyers review your business contracts, and a publicist manages your personal life. All your money and assets are either held, or are transferred back and forth, by one or another of the major banks. Am I correct?"

"Yes."

"Now let me tell you about the people who live in the black zone." Julia lifted her glass for a long pull on her straw. "These people have never set foot in a bank in their life. They live month to month in a perpetual state of feast or famine. Instead of any accountant, they have a right hand man who carries their stake. Lawyers are replaced by their personal muscle, and the thought of a publicist is absolutely absurd since very little in their life is ever planned or worthy of a public announcement."

"You speak very eloquently when you so desire."

"I speak eloquently when I'm passionate about the subject. And trust me, Francois; nothing makes me more passionate than money."

"So Julia, you're trying to tell me that the world is comprised of black or white?"

"No, not at all. Actually, some of the most successful people that I know live in the grey zone."

"Tell me of the grey zone," he encouraged. "This I would like to understand."

"The grey zone, or my area of expertise, is the best of both worlds. I don't have a bank governing my every move, yet I hold my money in a place a little more secure than an old mattress. You've got to learn to be a little more creative, Francois, to expand your circle of friends."

"You mean with someone like yourself?"

"I mean, there's more to the world than just the prime rate," she teased. "Besides, I didn't think you were the kind of man who liked hearing how and when you could withdraw your own funds."

She was good. If the woman hadn't already been involved in her own successful business, Francois would have stolen her for his. She was a closer, that was a given, and with what he figured was probably little more than a high school education; she had cultivated the ability to manipulate six figure deals.

"I think I'm ready to meet with some of your people. I'm sure our two ventures would mesh well together."

Julia nodded her head in agreement. "And I promise not to charge you twelve points for the privilege."

CHAPTER FIFTEEN

"Sometimes, you can beat the odds with the careful choice of where to fight."

—*Sin City, 2005*

A s the blows continued to rain down on the back of Jerome's bloody skull, he struggled to tuck his face in behind the limited protection of his upper arms.

"You fucking piece of shit! You cum-sucking faggot! You think you can sell us this crap?" One of the guys crouched down over Jerome's body, yelling into his ear as he lay helpless, curled up on his side in a fetal position on the rock hard asphalt.

"Thasss enufff," Ronnie spat through a mouthful of blood and broken teeth. "Yous got yourrr cassss."

"You're right!" Both suddenly turned their wrath back to Ronnie, pummeling his kidneys and stomach as he fought to roll away from their repeated assault.

Just before he lost consciousness, Jerome remembered hearing Ronnie cry out in one final protest. He tried to answer back, but his breath was in short supply, so he did the only thing left at his disposal… he passed out.

———————

"Get up! I said, get the fuck up," the voice kept repeating, over and over in Jerome's ear.

"Go away," he moaned; wanting nothing more than to slip back into the pain free world of unconsciousness.

Ronnie knew that he had to get Jerome up and on his feet, because if they were still lying in the back alley when darkness fell, they'd probably never make it out of there alive. He'd be damned if he was going to be used as target practice by some local gang bangers or possibly even far worse at the hands of some gay tweakers cruising back and forth through the shadows.

"Cops are coming," Ronnie shouted one last time into Jerome's ear.

"Coppsss?" he finally muttered back through swollen lips and broken teeth.

"We gotta blow man, so you gotta get up."

With Ronnie's assistance, Jerome finally pulled himself up off the asphalt, struggling to remain upright as the world around him began to spin. "I'm fuc… fucked…" he began to cough, the loosened blood clots threatening to block his swollen airway.

"Lean on me," Ronnie offered, his own footing precarious at best.

Half stumbling and half dragging each other down the pavement, both Ronnie and Jerome somehow managed to make their way out of the back alley. By staying off the main streets and avoiding other pedestrians wherever possible, they miraculously were able to cross the three excruciating blocks to Ronnie's apartment building. Blood soaked hoodies pulled down over their faces, arms slung around each other's shoulders for support; they managed one last feat, literally clawing their way up the two flights of stairs, only to collapse in tears outside the apartment's front door after realizing the apartment key had been lost during their beatings.

"I give up. I can't... I can't take it," Jerome began to wail, his unleashed cries of desperation drifting down the halls and frightening even the most hardened of tenants.

"Shut up, or I'll come out there and shut your ass up for you," a door cracked open just wide enough to release the verbal threat.

Forcing himself to drag his entire weight up to his feet, Ronnie slowly turned his body sideways, carefully positioning his good side to the door as he dangled his severely beaten arm on the other.

"Jerome, count to three for me, bud," he tried to calm down his best friend.

"One, t... t... twooo..."

And before Jerome was able to mouth the word three, Ronnie rushed over, throwing his entire body weight against the door.

Having only locked the bottom knob and not the upper deadbolt, his desperate strike had been successful, and upon impact, the door gave way and finally swung open.

———————

With one last stop at a local bulk grocer, Pete had effectively managed to spend the remainder of his available cash on survival supplies. Having finished stacking the six flats of bottled water next to the packaged trail mix, oatmeal bars, and fruit cups, he took a second to scratch at the scabs crisscrossing his entire right arm.

"This enough?" his friend Rico held up a twenty-four pack of toilet paper.

"Two dozen rolls for twenty-eight days, sounds like enough to me," Pete smirked, motioning toward the far wall.

"What about a TV? Don't tell me you're actually thinking of doing this without any games or movies to watch? That's just brutal, man. You're gonna go fucking nuts."

"Well, I think the *boob tube* might be the one fucking things that actually drives me nuts. See this," he opened a cardboard box and pulled out a handful of well-thumbed brochures. "Listen to this. It says that: *some types of music, or the repetitive voice patterns common in television sitcoms can sometimes drive detox patients to bouts of rage.*"

"What the fuck does that mean?"

"It means I'll be doing a lot of reading, is what it means."

Rico helped Pete unload the remainder of the truck, watching him carefully mark the packages of linens and textbooks before deciding which wall they were to be piled up against.

"Are you sure about this, man? It seems pretty drastic. Why don't you just go back to that rehab your brother Boyd had all lined up for you? Good food, comfy beds, and good looking nurses."

"What makes you say that? You never even saw any of those women."

"They're nurses," he held up his palms. "They're all hot."

Pete nodded his head as he pulled the master list out of his back pocket and quickly ran down the page. "Did you bring the ammo?"

Reaching down into his coat pocket, Rico reluctantly handed his friend the ammunition. "Are you sure this is enough to protect you from robbers or some cracked out junkies?"

"If this doesn't do the trick, nothing will," he scooped up the plastic box and dropped it directly into his pocket.

"So you really want me to chain up the door and lock you in here for twenty-eight days... nobody visiting you or nothing?"

"No contact. Period," he attempted to reinforce. "Cuz if you think you're gonna do me any favors and stop by for a visit, I'll blow your fucking head off."

"No matter what you say?" Rico took a minute to confirm his instructions.

"No matter. I don't care if I'm begging for my life and shitting all over the floor. You just look through that peephole, and if I'm breathing, you stay the fuck away."

"I'm worried, man," his childhood friend admitted, turning his head side to side to make sure no one else had heard his admission of weakness.

"About what?"

"About you."

Pete clenched a bag of toiletries between his hands in an attempt to calm his nerves. "Look Rico. We've been buds since we were kids. Our families still live on the same street. I trust you, cuz I know you won't fuck this up."

"But, what if…"

"But what if—nothing!" He interrupted the questioning before his friend had even a chance to wind it up. "I'll be fine. But if something does go wrong, you just go and find Boyd. He'll take care of everything from there."

"You mean if you die, don't you?"

Walking over, Pete threw his arm around Rico's shoulder. "I'm not gonna die, man. I'm just taking a month off to straighten up a little. You understand, don't you?"

Rico nodded, not willing to trust his voice, should it fail him and betray his worry.

"So, let's recap?"

It was Rico's turn to pull the handwritten instructions out of his pocket. "Once a day, I stop by and look through the peep hole. If you're breathing," he stopped to take a deep breath of his own, "then I write the day number on a piece of paper and slide it under the door. No matter how much you scream or beg, I don't open the door, not even a crack."

"And," Pete prompted him.

"You're gonna scream a lot. You're gonna puke, you're gonna shit, and you're gonna beg and cry for me to let you out."

"That's right, man." Pete patted him on the back. "I'm gonna beg and cry, but you're not gonna open that door as long as I'm breathing. Right?"

"Right." Rico wiped the cold sweat from his brow.

"Well, then I guess this is it."

"I guess so," he turned to leave the room. "Can I ask you one question Pete?"

"Shoot."

"Why the gun? Why the ammo? It ain't just for protection, is it?

"That's my business, Rico." He patted the coat pocket holding the 9mm Glock. "So then," he attempted to brighten the tone of his voice, "it's time to lock her up, buddy. I'll see you in a month."

Rico never turned around; he just locked the metal door as per his instructions and without even raising an eye to the peephole, he turned and began climbing the basement stairs.

———

By the time Warren had dropped Lillian off at her motel room, Wanda had yet to utter a word from the backseat. She'd spent her precious time working out a plan, any way of explaining her career choice to her brother without coming off as harsh, insensitive, or oversexed. She couldn't be sure it would work; she could only be sure that she'd have to try.

"Thanks again," Lillian leaned her head back through the car's open door. "I really appreciate the lift."

"You're welcome," Warren curtly nodded his head.

"I'll… I'll call you tomorrow?" Lillian slowly spun her face toward Wanda, her voice taking on a questioning tone.

Wanda never said a word, sitting motionless in the shadows of the backseat.

"Well goodnight," Lillian reluctantly withdrew herself from the car's interior, careful not to appear ungrateful by slamming the front passenger's door.

With the car idling in park, Warren sat outside the motel and waited while Lillian dug in her purse for a key.

"You don't have to sit here," Wanda finally screwed up the courage to speak. "She's a big girl. She can take care of herself."

"Just because she makes her living on her back doesn't mean she's mature enough to take care of herself," Warren snapped at his sister. "I think it's time you stopped equating promiscuous sex with maturity. They don't necessarily go hand in hand, you know."

She shouldn't have bothered to speak. Her brother was still too angry to be rational, he was...

Slamming his car into drive, Warren's foot tromped down on the gas, immediately sending a small spray of rocks into one of the motel's trampled flowerbed.

"I've been staying at a friend's house," she suddenly found the courage to admit from the back seat. "I haven't been sleeping at my apartment."

"I know, I've been calling," he sneered. "Your niece Amber, you remember your niece, don't you?" he snapped.

"Is something the matter? Is she hurt?"

"No," the car careened around a sharp corner before Warren exited the main stream of traffic and pulled off on a darkened side street. "Amber is fine," he shouted up into the rear view mirror. "She just wanted to invite you to a mother/daughter tea at her school this Friday. Nothing really important, surely not as exciting as one of your fake rubber cocks," he waved his hands in the air.

"Warren, it's just a job," she tried to make her brother understand. "You've got to realize that just because I work for a company that films pornography, it doesn't mean that I'm directly involved in the action. I'm not one of the actors; I'm just the purchasing agent. I've already tried to explain this to you before," Wanda found herself shouting. "Why can't you at least try to understand me?"

"I didn't draw the plans. I didn't build the bomb. All I did was fly the plane that dropped the bomb, so I know I can't be responsible for all the people lying dead in the rubble."

"How dare you," Wanda hissed, "comparing me to some kind of terrorist or something. I don't think it's fair, at all. I'm not killing people."

Warren grabbed the wheel and squeezed, his fingers turning white as the blood drained from his hands. "You're so sure that you *ain't getting nothin' on ya*. Aren't you?" he continued to yell.

"I told you," Wanda began to cry. "I just buy the supplies and book the locations. I don't star in…"

"You don't star in any of the movies," Warren jumped in and finished his sister's sentence while yanking the car's gearshift down into drive.

"Where are we going?"

"I think you need a little reality check, little miss *ain't getting nothin' on ya.*"

Wanda knew it was useless to try to argue. Her brother needed to make some kind of point and he'd be hell bent until he did, the exact reason he had insisted on driving her home

"Now have a good look around you," he suddenly slowed the car to a crawl. "This is the kind of neighborhood your company feeds.

Turning toward the window, Wanda took a moment to gauge her surroundings. Obviously, they'd driven onto some downtown side street and now sat in the midst of the late night action.

"See those girls?" Warren pointed to the group of prostitutes strolling up and down the darkened streets. "Movies like yours make deviant sex acts acceptable, something sick, and twisted, that people yearn for."

"We just make the movies," Wanda muttered in frustration. "We didn't invent the stuff you heard me talking about," she bowed her head at the thought of their lemon pudding themed sex tapes.

"That's where it starts. Men buy the movies and take them home. Then when their wives, the mothers of their children, don't want to take part in their twisted fantasies, they go looking elsewhere. These hookers," he pointed at the sixteen and seventeen-year-old girls, "fill that void. Society has convinced them that even if they drop out of school, have no training, and no job experience, it's still all right. Cuz no matter what; they can always sell their bodies to the men looking to fulfill some warp need they learned from your porn."

Wanda didn't know how to argue back. Warren was her brother, her protector, her rock. How was she supposed to debate something that he believed was the ruination of society?

"People like you," he said as he spun around in his seat, "make life a nightmare for people like that. Just look at those girls." He pointed. "They're lost; they're our community's biggest failures. Even the mayor doesn't give a damn what happens, as long as it's kept in the shadows and off the front steps of his office. Everyone down here is disposable, treated like garbage, and you and your company—you're part of the reason. Can't you see what I mean, Wanda? Can't you tell in your heart that what you're doing is absolutely wrong?"

"It's just my job," she muttered, tears beginning to wet the flushed skin on her cheeks.

"Look," Warren pointed as another hooker crawled into the front seat of a pick-up truck. "It's just her job, Wanda. She's not the cause of the sexual disease creeping through our society, or the rampant drug abuse spreading throughout the kids in our schools, cuz she's just doing her job."

"I didn't mean to hurt anybody," Wanda began to wail, fingers scrambling to open the rear door of her brother's sedan. "I just tried to find a job where I could support myself and not have to ask Mom and Uncle Mike for any more money," she begged him to understand, still unsure why she'd even consented to a lift in his car.

"But that's the problem," Warren yelled as his twin sister suddenly jumped out of the backseat of his car. "It's not enough to just find a job to pay the rent," he rolled down the passenger's window. "You have to be accountable for the kind of work you do. You have to be accountable for your company. You have to..." his voice faded off into the background.

Wanda never heard her brother's last statement. She was running down the street in a vain attempt to clear the hateful words from her mind and put as much distance between herself and Warren as physically possible.

"Where's the fire?" an old man yelled after Wanda as she fled past the steps of his stoop.

She never stopped to answer. Her sudden flight was draining all her energy, and it would be another ten minutes before she was finally exhausted, forced to drop down to her knees, and pant for breath behind a festering mound of restaurant garbage.

CHAPTER SIXTEEN

"It can't stop at once; because it's in you, and you can't stop something that's inside of you."

—Pleasantville, 1998

Wednesday had been a haze of painkillers, tequila shots, and fistfuls of ice cubes wrapped in soiled bath towels. But by the time daylight broke on Thursday morning, Ronnie and Jerome had somehow managed to weather the worst of the storm.

"I gotta eat something or my stomach's gonna rot out," Ronnie forced himself to rise up off the recliner. "What's in the kitchen?"

"Don't know man," Jerome painfully twisted his back as he attempted to bury his face deeper into the upholstery of the couch.

First rummaging through the empty cupboards, Ronnie suddenly remembered how Lillian liked to stash their food down in the vegetable crispers. Out of sight is usually out of mind, she'd claimed, forced to protect her groceries from his buddies who'd stop by night and day to hang out. Maybe they had been pigs, eating everything in the apartment, but it was his place too, and he needed to get some kind of food in his gut right now. His stomach ached for a sandwich or a bowl of soup before he began another uncontrollable round of dry heaving.

"What'd you find?" Jerome managed to stumble into the kitchen, still rubbing off encrusted blood from the bottom of his nose.

"Canned soup, a loaf of bread, and some…" he stopped to rip open the cellophane, "bologna."

"You make the sandwiches, I'll open the soup," Jerome announced, aware that Ronnie's bum arm wouldn't work well with a can opener.

Working together, they bumbled their way through the preparations, finally dropping into the kitchen chairs to consume their meal.

"I think you gotta go see a doctor about your arm, Ronnie, it looks broke."

"Maybe," Ronnie cradled his right wrist in his lap while shoveling soup into his mouth with his left.

"Not maybe—for sure. We should walk down to that clinic; you know the one that Lilly took Tito to when he got that flu bug. Member?"

Ronnie just nodded, swallowing hard to try to keep the tomato soup in his belly and off the kitchen floor.

Digging in his pocket, Jerome managed to pull out a handful of rumpled one-dollar bills. "Looks like those fucking bastards got the rest."

"You just about fucking killed us. You know that?"

"Sorry, man." Jerome grabbed another piece of bologna and stuffed it down his throat. "I thought it would work. Fuck, it almost did." he snatched up the mustard bottle and squirted it directly into his open mouth.

"The sandwich bags were sweating you asshole. Dried dope don't sweat none, no matter how hot it gets. Now does it?"

"Guess not," he shrugged, picking up his bowl to pour the remaining soup down his throat. "How'd I know they'd sweat?"

"Cuz you shoved grass clippings in the bag, you fucking moron. The spices were dry, but the lawn grass was damp. You're such a goof."

"Hey." He stood up, shaking with the sudden effort. "At least I was trying. You gotta pay rent tomorrow morning, and unless you've got some cash hiding that I don't know about, you're fucked!"

As the realization of the situation washed over Ronnie, he dropped his spoon and stared blankly at his empty bowl.

"What we gonna do man?" Jerome continued to babble, turning to pace the floor. "My mom's changed the locks on me, too. If I don't stay with you, I'm on the street. You know I've been on the street, Ronnie, and it really sucks. I don't wanna have to be out there again, especially now that I've been beat. They can smell it, Ronnie—they'll know I'm weak and they'll beat me more. I can't go back to…"

"Shut the fuck up!" Ronnie finally forced himself to his feet and shuffled off to the living room. "I think I have an idea, but I gotta make a call first."

"Call who?"

"Just clean up the kitchen and let me think for awhile."

Jerome began clearing the table, tossing the leftover bread and mustard in the fridge and then throwing the dirty dishes into the kitchen sink. "Should I wash the bowls and plates?"

"Don't bother." Ronnie picked up his cell and dialed a number. "I got an idea."

Within half an hour, both boys had managed to stuff pillowcases full of clean clothes, and whatever other personal belongings they deemed valuable. Twenty minutes after that, a thunderous knock vibrated the apartment's only door.

"That's our guys." Ronnie walked over and invited his guests inside. "Now, look around boys and tell me what you think."

"We talking appliances too?"

"Why the fuck not? It's not like my names on the lease."

As the two guys walked room to room, appraising the furniture and personal belongings, Jerome scuttled up to Ronnie's side.

"You selling all of Lilly's stuff?"

"It ain't Lilly's," he argued back, "cuz she gone and ran out. All this is mine to do with it what I please. And sure, I'm getting ready to sell it."

"Hey guys. Those closets are full of women's clothes. Some of them like new," one of the men announced, holding up a purple leather skirt with a price tag still dangling from the waist.

"Everything," Ronnie repeated. "The furniture, the fridge and stove, the clothes, the dishes. Fucking anything you see is up for sale."

"I'll give you two-hundred for the lot," one of the men stepped forward to make his offer.

"Two hundred ain't enough to even get me a month's rent and groceries. I'm gonna need a little more."

"Well, how about you just sit on my offer for a couple of days, think it over awhile? And then when you can't pay the rent and the sheriff is called to lock down your apartment, then you can try and sell it for a better price."

"Two fifty?" He nervously smiled, knowing that they had him by the short hairs.

"Two twenty-five," the man countered, pulling a wad of cash out of his pocket while silently signaling for his partner to call in the trucks.

Standing alone in the kitchen, Wanda cradled a fresh cup of coffee between her two hands, slowly willing herself to wake up and face the day. She hadn't slept well the night before after her fight with her brother, yet she owed a cheerful disposition and a positive attitude to her hosts.

"Any left?" Boyd strolled into the room.

"A good half a pot," she confirmed, reaching for a clean cup. "Double double?"

"You know, I was only eleven when I started drinking my coffee like that. Always figured that if a restaurant was giving away the cream and sugar for free, I'd better take advantage of it."

Wanda continued to stir Boyd's coffee before handing him the cup. "We all did weird little things when we were kids. I'll tell you a secret if you promise not to repeat it to another soul."

"I promise," he accepted the cup from her outstretched hand as he simultaneously reached back to locate a wooden stool.

"Let's see," she began to delve into her past, desperate to vent her feelings but unsure of where to start. "My brother Warren and I are twins, and all my life I've adored him. My mom said I've worshiped the ground he walked on since I could talk and would have readily laid down my life to save his in a heartbeat."

"And this is your secret?"

"No," Wanda shook her head, needing to dredge up some positive memories in an attempt to wash away her hurt feelings. "When Warren and I were both in eleventh grade, he had his first serious girlfriend. You should have seen them, always holding hands, and staring into each other's eyes. He was so happy for about a month, and then without warning, she just up and dumped him. I thought my brother was going to die."

"Puppy love." Boyd took another sip of his coffee, mildly amused with her childhood story.

"Well, like I said, Warren was crushed. He wouldn't talk to anyone and had to be dragged downstairs for every meal. Every night he hid out in his room, and eventually, he even stopped going to baseball practice. I was desperate to help my brother. I couldn't stand to see him in so much pain."

"So what'd ya do?"

"That's the problem. What's a teenage girl supposed to do? I tried talking to him, begging my brother to tell me what happened, but whenever I mentioned his girlfriend's name, he just buried his head in his pillow and started to cry. I was absolutely worried sick, my own health starting to fail, especially when words like *suicide* and *psychiatrist* were whispered throughout the house."

"What's going on in here?" Julia suddenly waltzed into the kitchen.

"Nothing much." Boyd stood up to refill his cup. "We were just comparing old war stories from our childhood. Wanna join in?"

"No, thanks," Julia buried her head in the refrigerator, rummaging through the waxed boxes as she looked for any appetizing leftovers.

"So go on then," Boyd prompted his guest. "I wanna hear the rest of your story."

Wanda suddenly closed her eyes to search for her place in the story, slowly continuing to dredge up the emotional details. "Well, after about two weeks of crying and moping in his room, Warren finally started to open up. It was kinda like pulling teeth at first, but eventually, he let me into the painful events of his teenage world."

"Your brother was crying last night?" Julia interrupted their conversation, stepping over to the silverware drawer to grab a fork.

"No, this was back when they were kids," Boyd barked, annoyed at his wife's repeated interruptions.

"Fine," Julia rolled her eyes before shoveling in a mouthful of special fried rice.

"As I was saying," Wanda turned her attention back to Boyd, "he finally started to talk after a couple of weeks. It seems that his girlfriend broke up with him because he kissed like the inexperienced virgin he was. A young excitable teenager with no history and very little skill, he slobbered all over her lips and neck, his tongue lapping at her face as if he was a horny neighborhood dog. She eventually had enough, and told him not to call her again until he knew what he was doing."

"What a bitch," Julia set down her box of rice and leaned in across the counter. "That's just awful. What did he do?"

"Warren was devastated," Wanda reminded them both, "and I loved him so much. I just wanted him to be happy, to stop crying, and get back to his normal way of life."

"So?" both Julia and her husband prompted her to continue the story.

"Well, we came up with a plan. Warren and I both decided that the only way for him to get his girlfriend back was for him to prove to her that he was not a *virgin kisser*."

"No way," Boyd interrupted, the stirrings in his groin proving that his interest in the story was more than just casual.

"So we practiced," Wanda admitted, blushing beneath their undivided attention.

"Practiced sex?"

"Hell no," she laughed. "We're brother and sister, and this wasn't the Ozark Mountains. We just practice kissing, and boy, did he need practice. Somewhere, somehow, my brother got the idea in his head that girls liked having a boy's tongue shoved as deep down her throat as humanly possible. Well, even though I was only seventeen, I cleared that up in about thirty seconds."

"Really?" Boyd shifted on his stool, trying to alleviate the uncomfortable pressure as the front seam in his cotton pajama pants strained against his growing erection.

"I still couldn't kiss my brother," Julia shuddered, "no matter what the reason."

"The truth is, it was kinda weird the first time I closed my eyes and Warren leaned across his bed. But after a few seconds, I just thought of it as practice. Remember, I was already in eleventh grade and hoped to have a boyfriend, too. I didn't want to be dumped and told that I kissed like a virgin either."

Boyd and Julia were speechless, mesmerized as they listened to the woman's tale of teenage angst.

"After a couple of days of practicing, so to speak, we both decided that he was ready, so Warren got on the phone and called his ex-girlfriend. They made a date and promptly headed off to the movies. Well," Wanda sighed, "as you probably guessed, I waited up for my brother, dying to know if it had worked out or if all the chapped lips had been in vain."

"And was he any good?" Julia anxiously stepped forward.

"He was great! His girlfriend Jodie said that she loved him, and do you know that four and a half years later, they got married as soon as they both turned twenty-one?"

"You win," Boyd spun away from the counter before getting off his stool. "You've got the weirdest childhood secret I've ever heard of," he threw over his shoulder, shielding his erection from public view.

"Hey Wanda," Julia called her over in a whisper. "I thought you told me that your brother was divorced and raising his daughter as a single parent?"

"He is," she opened the dishwasher and gently set in her empty cup.

Pete had already forced himself to eat a container of cold soup and two granola bars, desperate to regain a few of the pounds he'd dropped over the last couple months. Straightening the sheets on his floor mat had only taken another couple of minutes, so unless he was interested in crawling around the concrete floor practicing a few Pilates moves from one of his *how to books*, he was going to have to find some other way to pass the time.

"You could always jerk off," he laughed at the thought, having recently started the practice of talking to himself.

Deciding that it was probably best just to change the dressings on his upper arms, Pete pushed up his sleeve and was peeling back the blood spotted gauze when the initial stomach cramp brought him right to his knees.

"Holy fuck," he cried, the salvia from his open mouth falling in stringy droplets toward the concrete floor. "Oh god," he continued to moan, the sweat beginning to run down his forehead as he painfully crawled toward the mattress, suddenly grateful that he'd chosen to forgo any sort of off-the-floor framework.

Rocking back and forth, as the pending storm began to churn deep in his bowels, Pete's watering eyes somehow managed to catch an unexpected movement.

"You've got mail," he moaned, having picked up the saying from some old movie a girlfriend had played day in and day out until he'd tossed her ass out the door.

Crawling on all fours, with his stomach beginning to give off dire warnings of things to come, Pete still forced himself to make it to the scrap of paper.

"*Day 3*," he moaned, the fingers of his right hand starting to crinkle the page just as his stomach exploded, the vomit not only splattering the paper, but also shooting a good twelve inches up the bottom of the basement door.

CHAPTER SEVENTEEN

*"You call me evil. But unfortunately for you, I'm a
necessary evil."*

—Lord of War, 2005

The day was slightly overcast, the high bank of clouds light and
puffy, unable to threaten any serious measure of rain. With
all the crew assembled and each of the starring actors accounted
for, Boyd was suddenly struck with the notion that filming might
actually go off without a hitch. Elated with the sudden revelation,
he rushed off to look for Julia as she took a few minutes to inspect
Lillian's final hairstyle and make-up.

"You really make a beautiful Pocahontas," he announced the
minute he was in earshot of the group.

Everyone stopped what they were doing, not surprised by
Lillian's natural good looks, but shocked by the mere fact that the
compliment had originated from their director.

"What's the fucking problem?" He suddenly stopped dead in his
own tracks to survey Julia's crew.

"Nothing, sweetie," she said and stepped over to gently nudge her husband in the ribs. "Glad to see you in a good mood. You're usually just a little growly come filming."

"That's not true."

"Like fuck it isn't," the make-up lady muttered under her breath before bending down to check one of her kits for a lighter shade of eyeliner.

"Anyway, let's talk about Malcolm," Julia quickly steered the conversation back to the matters at hand. "He's come up with some idea for a scene change. Something about hog tying."

Lillian stopped breathing at the mere mention of the word.

"Hog tying? I don't think so," Boyd shook his head as Lillian released an audible sigh of relief.

"Well, then you'd better go talk to him, because he's been busy playing with the ropes ever since he was finished with hair and make-up."

As Boyd tromped off to deal with Malcolm, Julia turned her full attention back to their female lead. "You did excellent at the run through on Wednesday, but as you know, today's going to be a little different. We're shooting live action, so neither Boyd nor I will be prompting you with instructions from the sidelines."

"Just follow the boards," the make-up lady whispered in Lillian's ear.

Smiling, Julia patted the woman's stooped shoulders. "She's right. Before the camera rolls on each scene, Boyd will review the storyboards with you. He'll set the mood for the scene, remind you and Malcolm which sexual positions you'll be expected to achieve, and roughly how long you'll be expected to roll tape. Since we've already filmed the run-through, I really don't believe you're going to have any problem with today's shoot. But should you forget what to do, for God's sake, please don't open your mouth and ask. Take a second and look at the storyboards. They're really big, and they'll be positioned just out of camera range.

Really handy should you suddenly forget what's next and just need a little reminder."

It all sounded so simple; yet every nerve in Lillian's body vibrated on alert. She was well aware that the crew had arrived before at dawn to get everything ready for the day's shoot, and she had no intention of being the one screw-up who brought their production to a grinding halt.

"Do you have any more questions?" Julia bent down to look directly into the girl's face.

Lillian just shook her head no, her hand unconsciously dropping down to rub her stomach.

"Upset tummy? You feel nauseated?"

"No, I'm fine," she reassured her boss. "I think it's just nerves," she moved her hand back onto her lap, "and too much fast food. I'm really sick of deep fried everything."

"Well, tomorrow you can come by the office and pick up your pay check for this film, and then you'll be able to eat whatever in the hell you want."

Lillian kept that thought firmly planted in her head as she marched out toward her first mark in the grassy field. Unconsciously rubbing her stomach, she turned and looked across the field at Malcolm, too busy preening to take a second and return her little wave.

"All right people," Boyd shouted into his bullhorn. "I want everyone to take positions. We're gonna roll tape in about five minutes and I don't wanna have anybody crawling through the grass at the last minute trying to scramble out of camera range. You got that?" he turned his back and nodded at one of his grips.

The man silently nodded in return.

"All right everybody," Boyd turned back to the action. "Call if off."

"Ready," Malcolm shouted at the top of his lungs.

"Ready," Lillian croaked in a nervous voice.

"Ready camera A. Ready camera B..." the voices continued to callout from their surrounding positions until all twelve posts were accounted for.

"Then we're ready to roll," Boyd turned and walked out of camera range. "Now let's get this shit on film," he continued to bark orders.

"Scene one, take one," a grip snapped the clapper board, slowly turning sideways so each camera could catch the scene numbers on film.

"Ready, set, action!" Boyd picked up the whistle slung around his neck and gave it a hearty blow, alerting Lillian and Malcolm that it was time to make their moves.

———————————

It wasn't his usual kind of place, but truth be told, the country and western music vibrating through the wall-mounted speakers wasn't all that bad. However, the wooden bar stools and hand-cut tables were another issue all together.

"Mr. Dubois?" a man sauntered up to his table.

"Mr. Foster," Francois stood up to shake the man's hand.

"Call me Jake. Mr. Foster's my dad," he chuckled at his own lame joke. "So hows about a few beers?"

"Beers will be fine," Francois returned to his seat as Jake held up two fingers for the waitress.

"So Julia said you were looking to turn a little of your personal paper into some liquid cash. That right?" he jumped right to the heart of their meeting.

"Yes, that's exactly why I'm here," he looked around the room, a little uncomfortable to be conducting such sensitive business in an obviously foreign environment.

"Don't worry about these good old boys," Jake pulled his elbows off the table so the waitress could set down their mugs of draft.

"Six fifty," she smiled at the table, not exactly sure who'd be picking up the tab.

Pulling one of the neatly folded twenty-dollar bills out of his suit pocket that he kept handy for tipping doormen and seating hostesses, Francois paid the waitress, graciously tipping her three dollars and fifty cents. A healthy fifty-three percent tip that he was able to instantly calculate in his head.

"Thanks," Jake picked up his glass mug and downed a good third of the iced liquid in his first swig. "Next rounds on me."

"What exactly did Julia Giovanni tell you about my particular situation?"

"About as much as she told you about mine, I figure."

Francois took a moment to taste his drink, unable to remember the last time he'd indulged in any yeast-brewed ale.

"How much you looking to turn over?"

"A hundred and fifty thousand," he set his glass down, still working on adjusting to the overly chilled assault on his taste buds. He'd never understand why the average patron insisted on nullifying the personality of their beverages with excess refrigeration, or for that matter, the texture of their main courses with searing heat. Too much of anything was definitely a bad habit that was repeatedly indulged in by the masses.

"What kind of paper are we turning?"

"That's negotiable," Francois moved his beer mug off to the side of the table. "I can write a personal or a company check, or I can draw a bank draft. Or, if you prefer, I can transfer funds directly to a specified account of your choosing."

"Well, that's a real set of options, now ain't it"

Pulling out a pocket sized Daytimer; Francois extracted

a pen and prepared to make a few notes. "Before we go any further, I was wondering if we could take the time to discuss your fee?"

"Sure, no problem," Jake signaled the waitress to bring them a second round. "All right," he looked up to the ceiling as if pulling down an invisible wall chart. "With a bank draft, anything under fifty will cost you four points. Fifty to two hundred, four and a half, and anything over two hundred will cost you five."

"Specific denominations?"

"No problem, as long as you don't get crazy on us and want a lunch sack full of tens. And boy, you got a thing about consecutive serial numbers, you let me know right now, cuz if I bring you a brick and everything runs together, I ain't returning it at the last minute cuz you want it mixed."

"Consecutive serial numbers are not a concern, as long as the money is legitimate."

"That's an insult," he slammed down his beer and glared across the table. "I'll let it go this once, cuz we ain't never danced before, but if you bring it up again, we won't be doing business. No matter what the points. Got it?"

Francois nodded his acknowledgment. "So can you tell me what your rates are for personal checks?"

"Add a point to everything and that's my rate," Jake whipped out a five and two singles for the waitress.

"Do you mind if I ask you how it's done. How you're able to turn a hundred and fifty thousand dollar bank draft into a briefcase of cash?"

"Whoa there, my man. You're jumping the gun. Let's do a little business before we spill all the company secrets. Okay?" he laughed.

"All right," Francois smiled, snatching up his mug to force down yet another swallow.

Finally waking after another round of violent shivers, Pete slowly reached up to rub his eyes, accidentally loosening a patch of crusted vomit glued to the side of his cheek. Stomach still queasy from the repeated bouts of nausea, the mere smell of his own breath was nearly enough to send him once again reeling with convulsions.

Forcing himself to his knees, he slowly crawled on all fours straight toward the toilet, muscles shaking with the effort. Aware of the fact that he probably didn't have the physical strength to rise up and twist open the sink's taps, never mind reaching the open flat of bottled water still piled up high in a vertical tower, Pete focused his limited energies on struggling to reach up and trip the flush lever.

Praying that the porcelain toilet now contained a fresh bowl of clear water, he thrust his chin over the edge and began splashing mouthfuls of the cooled liquid down his throat with the cupped palm of his right hand.

The realization that he had just deliberately drank from a toilet bowl would have been enough to activate most people's gag reflexes to the point of uncontrolled retching, but somehow, it wasn't really a concern at the present moment. Pete viewed his renewed hydration as a dire necessity and refused to give in to the obvious disgust factor. With his head throbbing and his heart threatening to burst through the walls of his chest, he was well aware that he didn't have the luxury of worrying about the origin of his fluids.

Resting for a few minutes before attempting to crawl back toward his corner mattress, Pete's line of sight suddenly wandered toward the locked door. A new piece of paper with the words *day 4* lay beside a dried mound of puke, silently announcing that he'd made it through one seventh of his self-imposed detox.

"Well fuck me," he groaned, forcing himself to crawl back over to his soiled bedding.

Malcolm had chased Lillian through the grassy field and round the tepee twice before finally overtaking her at the predetermined mark beside the fire. Squatting on top of her chest, he'd provocatively flicked the leather lacing with his prop knife while waiting for the camera to move in for the desired close-up.

Satisfied that everyone was in position, Malcolm leaned toward Lillian's shoulder as he pretended to bite the tender folds of her skin. It was a well-practiced move designed to disguise his search for the concealed lube pot.

"You should be able to reach it with your left hand," he whispered into her ear. "It's sitting right behind the woven baskets."

Lillian never uttered a word of acknowledgment, other than thrashing her head side to side as ordered by the script.

"Now hold still, you savage squaw," Malcolm threw back his head and began reciting his lines. "I'm going to show you what it's like to have sex with a civilized man," he roared, prompting Lillian with a verbal cue to dip her fingers into the lube pot and secretly lubricate herself before he peeled back her costume and plunged his Viagra fueled penis deep inside her vagina.

"How's it look?" Julia leaned over and whispered into her husband's ear the minute he strolled over and joined her behind the action line.

"Good. So far, it looks really good. We've lucked out with the weather," he motioned, his chin up toward the overcast skies. "No trouble with shadows or sunspots today."

"Hey, what's she doing now?" Julia leaned closer toward the action.

"Fuck me," Boyd cursed under his breath. "She's fumbling around. I think she's looking for the lube."

"Where is it?"

"She's got it now," he took a deep breath as the finger's on Lillian's left hand moved back to her side, silently reaching up underneath her leather skirt to apply the clear jelly to her own genitals.

Readjusting his position, Malcolm raised himself up on his haunches before ripping the plaid material off his own shoulders. Continuing on by thrusting his pelvis toward Lillian's face, he made a grand show of unbuttoning his fly and releasing his cock from inside the white-cotton britches.

Responding to the action, Lillian had raised her hands up to her partner's naked chest, tentatively stroking the waves of his sculpted muscles just as her eyes suddenly locked on a series of red streaks. Following her fingers down the vertical length of Malcolm's chest, she realized that the fresh blood trail had originated near his pecs and abruptly ended just before his pubic line.

"What the hell," Boyd's eyes caught the discoloration, pushing one of his own cameramen aside to check the action through a viewfinder.

"What's going on now?" Julia instantly picked up on the problem.

"Cut," Boyd yelled, marching toward the campfire just as Malcolm jumped up to his feet.

"You hurt?" he looked down at Lillian at she stared in shock at her bloody fingertips.

"No."

"Well, then what's the matter?" Boyd thrust out his hand to pull Lillian upright.

The minute she rose up to her feet, Lillian felt the first rivulets of blood run down the skin of her inner thighs. As her stomach began to cramp in protest, she spun on her heels and ran as fast as she could toward the portable washroom positioned behind a small grouping of poplar trees.

"She's on her fucking rag," Malcolm hissed, angrily dabbing at the blood streaks still adorning his naked chest.

"Holy fuck! Now what are we supposed to do?" Boyd yelled up at the sky, his angry voice vibrating off each of the crewmembers as they nervously mulled in a circle around the edge of the shoot.

CHAPTER EIGHTEEN

"There's no problem leading a double life. It's the triple
and quadruple lives that will get you in the end."
—Lord of War, 2005

S he didn't have any of her old costumes, and very little of her
own make up, but Lillian still marched into *Cheeks* and asked
Big Daddy if she could pick up a couple of shifts.

"Your film career over already?" He couldn't help but tease.

"No. I've already done some work, I just haven't been paid yet,"
she nervously looked out of his office toward the main pit. "I'll take
afternoons if it's all you got."

"Afternoons? You're too good for that. Afternoon's are for fat
housewives with stretch marks and saggy tits. I'll give you eight to
midnight. You think you can handle that?"

"I'll handle it fine," Lillian reached over and patted her old
boss on the shoulder. "You think I can dig through your box of
house costumes and old make-up? I moved, and all my shit is still
packed."

"Packed, huh?" he shot her an accusing look. "Never met a

dancer yet who'd let her costumes and make-up cases out of her sight."

"Well, to be honest," she picked a loose hair off her own sleeve. "I moved out of my apartment in a real hurry and I haven't actually been around to pick up my stuff yet."

"No problem. Fill your boots," he motioned toward the closet off to the left of his desk. "I was wondering when you'd smarten up and leave that asshole behind. He was a leech honey, sucking the life right out of your ass."

"Speaking of Ronnie," Lillian began, as she thumbed through a few of the well-worn pieces. "If he drops by, please don't let him pick up my pay, no matter what he says. All right?"

Having worked in the industry for a good twenty-five years, Big Daddy had seen his share of *suitcase pimps*. The business was flooded with men who latched on to young, working strippers and sucked them dry, emotionally and financially. Sure, they might carry the girl's luggage in and out of the dressing rooms, but that was the end of their contribution. Over time, they promoted themselves from boyfriend, to advisor, and finally manager. Handling all the money and negotiating with the house owners, the suitcase pimp eventually worked himself to a position of absolute authority and the working girl found she had little or no say in her own career. They were no better than a common pimp, and the sooner the girls realized these guys were bleeding them dry, the better off they'd all be.

"Don't worry sweetie, I wouldn't let that fucker lick the sweat off my balls. Actually," he leaned back in his chair. "I think I'm gonna ban the little piss ant."

Grinning to herself, Lillian plucked a yellow skirt up out of the box, pleased to see that at least ninety percent of the sequins were still intact. "It's your club, Big Daddy, and I'm just one of the girls. But you've always told me you wouldn't bitch about how I danced

down in the pits just as long as I don't try to tell you how to make
your business decisions up on your floor."

"God, I missed you," he laughed.

————————————

Slowly stuffing his dried bedding into another of the black garbage
bags, Pete took his time to make sure he didn't rip the plastic and
jeopardize the seal. He was still weak and extremely irritable, but
at least the nausea had passed and he was confident he wouldn't be
puking all over his second set of sheets.

Having forced a granola bar and a bottle of water into his
stomach earlier that morning, he stumbled over and picked up the
piece of paper citing the fifth day, gratefully realizing he'd made it
to the weekend.

"Party time," he muttered to himself, laughing at the absurdity
of the idea, as he glanced around his basement quarters. They might
have been primitive, but a twenty-eight day stay in his buddy's
basement had cost him his gold Rolex and two hundred bucks cash,
upfront. Seems like even the slums were trying to take a serious bite
out of his ass.

Suddenly feeling lightheaded, Pete decided he'd better sit down
and rest for a while before he continued on with his clean up, but on
the way to his corner mattress, he reminded himself to stop and grab
a couple bottles of water off the top of the stack. He did not intend
to drink out of a toilet bowl again as long as he lived, and this time
if he got really sick and was confined to all fours, he wanted to be a
little more prepared.

"What to read?" He found himself straightening his back before
shuffling over toward a box of textbooks. "*Recognizing the Three
Triggers*," he mumbled to himself, tucking the self-help book under
his right arm while slowly lowering himself onto his bed.

Settled, he flipped past the opening pages to the beginning of the first chapter. *"Entertain, medicate, and celebrate,"* he read the subheadings aloud. *"Whenever an addict is bored or lonely, many entertain themselves by consuming too much food, too much alcohol, or too many recreational drugs. It's a common habit, leading to obesity, alcoholism, and drug abuse."*

Silently nodding his agreement, Pete continued to read aloud, a habit he'd also developed from spending the last five days in a state of solitary confinement.

"When not feeling at the top of their game, instead of increasing their exercise regimen, or adjusting a deficient nutrient intake, many addicts also choose to medicate themselves by once again consuming large quantities of food, alcohol, or drugs. Unfortunately, these overindulgences usually lead to a mir... mirade," he stumbled over the word, *"of additional health concerns such as heart problems, liver disease, and serious bouts of depression and paranoia."*

"No shit," Pete sat up, readjusting the rolled blanket behind his back before returning to the printed page. *"Finally, should they find themselves faced with a genuine occasion to celebrate; once again, addicts tend to pounce on the idea of over consumption. Hence, the celebration becomes an excuse to pollute their bodies and long before the celebration is over, they've lost track of the moment, and are totally obsessed with ingesting as much food, alcohol, or drugs as humanly possible."*

Pete set down the book and reached for a bottle of water, forcing down a couple of small sips while he debated the three triggers. Deciding that he'd at least finish the remainder of the first chapter, he once again picked up the text and began to read aloud.

―――――――――

Sneaking up the back stairwell of her old apartment building, Lillian stopped to take a deep cleansing breath before slowly creeping down the hall, ready to bolt should either Ronnie or Jerome suddenly show their face.

"Where you been?" a kid from across the hall suddenly poked his head out of his mother's apartment, nearly scaring her right out of her skin.

"I've been busy," Lillian smiled down at the young boy. "How ya doing?"

"Me, bored. Where's Tito. I been knocking, but he don't ever want to play," he shrugged his shoulders. "Mama said Tito must be sick in the stomach. Is he sick?" the four year old continued to pepper his old neighbor with questions.

"No sweetie. Tito moved home to his mama's house."

Confused, he shook his head and stepped back toward his apartment door. "You his mama," he muttered.

"No, I'm his aunty."

"Tell Tito I got new toys," he waved the small plastic figurine clutched tightly in the palm of his right hand.

"I will," she smiled as the child turned and disappeared behind his apartment's door.

Turning toward her own apartment, Lillian leaned in against the frame, listening for any sign of her ex-boyfriend or his group of moochers. Confident that no one was home, since neither the television nor the stereo were blaring, she grabbed the doorknob, shocked when it turned even before she'd pulled her key out of her pocket. "Holy fuck," the words instantly tumbled out of her mouth and bounced off the empty walls.

Her one-bedroom apartment was totally empty. Not a single stick of furniture or a solitary ornament existed anywhere in the three rooms. The place had been stripped, top to bottom, but it wasn't until Lillian noticed that the fridge and stove were missing that her heart really began to pound.

"You idiot," she turned and ran out of the small kitchen before the landlord got word she was in the building and came flying upstairs, trying to hunt her down.

Not only had Ronnie taken every stitch of clothing and all of her pots and pans, the asshole had been stupid enough to steal the landlord's appliances. She was fucked, and she knew it. The lease had been in her name with her social security number, her date of birth, and her *cookum's* old address for a reference. That was enough information to track her back and forth across the city until she was caught. Lillian knew she was screwed. It wouldn't be long now before the landlord pressed charges and she was carted off to rot in the city jail.

Frantically running the twenty-one blocks back to her motel room, Lillian burst through her door, exhausted and struggling to catch her breath. She needed to make a plan, to think of some way to fix this up before she was charged with theft. But first she needed to pack up her shit and move.

"Nancy Smith," she began to try out new names as her hands flew from her dresser to the duffle bag laying empty beside the bed. "Carol, Carol Brown," she finally settled on, worried that she wouldn't make it out in time before a cop checked the motel's book and found her registered under her real name.

Men were always trouble, and she damn well knew better. Allowing Ronnie to move into her apartment had been her first mistake, then running off without calling the landlord and making other arrangements had been her second. Together, they were going to add up to Petty Larceny and a permanent criminal record if she wasn't careful.

Checking her cash, Lillian made a mental note to rent a place with some kind of kitchenette. She needed to be able to cook, cuz spending her hard-earned money in restaurants was going to kill her budget, and if she continued to eat cheap take out, either her face or her hips were gonna explode.

Her limited possessions haphazardly stuffed back in her duffle bag; she quickly checked the room for any scraps of paper that might tie her to Giovanni Films. Making a mental note to change her mailing address with Wanda the minute she checked in with work, Lillian threw her key on the bed and closed the door gently behind her back.

———

Malcolm continued to pace the reception area, waiting for Boyd to finish his phone call before rushing into his office.

"All right Malcolm," his boss finally beckoned from his doorway.

"Thanks, man." he strolled in, nervously looking around the room to see if anything had changed since the last time he'd stopped by.

"So, what's the big emergency," Boyd leaned back in his chair, feet resting comfortably on a side drawer of his desk.

"Well, we were supposed to get paid today, right?"

"Right. Day after filming."

"But we didn't."

"That's right, too. Cuz we didn't finish the film."

"Well," Malcolm stretched his arms over his head as if stalling for time. "I uh… I uh… I have commitments," he suddenly blurted out as if revealing some deep dark secret.

"We all do."

"No, you don't understand." He leaned forward in his chair as if their close proximity would somehow lend creditability to his argument. "I have… *commitments*," he heavily stressed the word.

Boyd wasn't insensitive to the financial heat that his actor's were subjected to when they weren't paid on schedule, but if Malcolm wanted an advance, he was going to have to climb down off his high horse and ask for it.

"What kind of commitments?"

"You know," he waved his hand as if swatting an errant fly. "Commitments."

"No, I don't know," Boyd just smiled and shook his head, still a little pissed about the way his star had reacted to Lillian's *woman problems* during their Friday shoot. "Will a hundred bucks help?" he reached into his pocket and threw two fifty dollar bills down onto his desk.

"Fuck man, I need at least a thousand."

"A thousand? What for?" Boyd demanded, as if it was really any of his business.

Malcolm stood up and quickly closed the office door. "You know I'm still paying for my plugs and the lipo. Well, I'm already two months behind. If I don't give the guys at least five bills, they're gonna come looking for me. You know, *looking... for me!*" he nervously stressed.

"You really think a couple of plastic surgeons are gonna kick your ass over a late bill?"

"No, but their goons sure as fuck will. How you think they collect? With a mean letter or a nasty phone call?"

He'd heard enough, so before Malcolm bored him with any further details, he pulled open his top drawer and took out a large company checkbook. "I can't give you the whole thousand bucks, cuz our petty cash account is only set up for a thousand and I'm already holding a check for Lillian's advance."

"Pocahontas?" he yelled. "She fucking killed the shoot. Why the hell you wanna advance that bitch?"

"She got her period, man," he reminded his actor. "She didn't come in hung-over and throw up all over her co-star. She didn't forget we were shooting and fly off to Vegas. She didn't..."

"Fine, I'll take the five bills," he finally conceded, knowing full well that his boss was alluding to a couple of his antics from the early days. "But she could have warned me. You know how much I hate blood," he shivered at the thought.

Boyd shook his head and began writing out the check.

"Gentlemen," Julia swung open the door and marched directly into her husband's office. "Sorry to interrupt, but I need to steal my husband for a few minutes."

"We're done," Boyd reached across the desk and handed Malcolm his advance. "Don't forget we've rebooked the shoot for next Friday. All right?"

"Friday," he repeated, already one foot out the door.

"Honey, your mom just called." Julia dropped down into the recently vacated chair. "She's worried about your brother Pete, and she's wondering if you knew where he's hiding out?"

"Don't know, don't care," he summed up in a simple statement.

"I know, but don't you think it's kind of strange. He just up and disappeared. I haven't heard a word for a week. Have you?"

"Nope." He stuffed his checkbook back into the top drawer. "So you wanna tell me why we're suddenly looking for trouble?"

"Don't shoot the messenger," she as she turned to leave. "I just didn't want you saying that you didn't get the message."

Boyd casually saluted his wife's back as she marched out his door and back down the empty hall.

CHAPTER NINETEEN

"That's the secret to survival. Never go to war. Especially with yourself."

—*Lord of War*, 2005

The last time Lillian had crawled out of the pit at *Cheeks*, she'd vowed never to step foot on a stripper's stage again. Now here she was, only two weeks later, prepping to head back down onto the same floor.

"Sure I'd never see your ass again," one of the dancers shook her head as she carefully adjusted her nipples, gingerly tucking them inside the leather cups of her bikini top. "But you know what they say?" Brandy teased.

"No. What'd they say?" Lillian never bothered to shift her eyes off her own reflection.

"Shake it for cash once, and you'll shake it as long as somebody pays."

"Piss off," she answered back, grabbing the eyeliner to carefully rim her upper and lower lids.

"Don't bite my head off." Brandy leaned closer toward the mirror to check her own reflection. "I think you're a good stripper. The guys really get hot for your legs and your hair and you can actually dance. You know; if its money you're looking for, the pit is just a steppingstone. The real action is on the floor. How come you won't step out after your show and work it a little? You'd damn well clean up. You know that?"

Dropping the black charcoal pencil down into the Tupperware bowl of abandoned make-up, Lillian plucked out the only case of pressed eye shadow, rolling her eyes at the limited selection of colors.

"It ain't sex; it's just *rubs and tugs*. Nothing too special. And you don't have to worry about condoms or getting busted by any overzealous vice."

"Thanks, I'll give it some thought." She applied the shadow, praying Brandy would give the sales pitch a rest.

"It's Saturday. I got a regular coming in with his buddy. They both like double straddles and I think you're legs are long enough to work."

"I don't think…"

"Oh, come on. I'll take the front and face the guy, all you gotta do is sit on his knees behind me and wrap your legs around mine. We'll bounce around, grind to a song or two, and you'll make a hundred bucks."

"A hundred?" she stopped to confirm the amount.

"A hundred bucks each. Two guys, that's two hundred cash in your jeans for half an hour of your time. Not bad, eh?"

"I still don't know," she hesitated, walking over to the wall sink with her disposable razor. "I've seen the girls do double-straddles before, and it looks kinda tricky." She raised one arm and quickly swiped at a few of the fine hairs protruding from her left armpit.

"Sure, if the rear bitch is too short. But you're really tall and you'll have no trouble wrapping around me with plenty of leg to spare."

Rinsing the double blades under a running tap, Lillian switched hands and quickly touched up her right armpit.

"Come on. I heard you're in a bit of a jam. I'll let you use my makeup and hair case for the rest of the week?"

Standing to strip off her jeans and tee shirt, Lillian picked up a white tank top and quickly pulled it down over her head. Stepping into the yellow sequined skirt, she wiggled the material up and over her hips until it was snugly fastened around her waist. A fresh pair of white cotton panties with little pink bows purchased that morning, and she was almost ready to head out. "What size are your shoes?"

"Nines."

"Close enough," Lillian gave in; bending down to grab Brandy's open-toed black stilettos. "I'll also need to share your heels."

"Fuck, you lose everything in a fire?"

"Worse. I was robbed." She bent to buckle up the four-inch platforms.

"All right," Brandy conceded. "Make-up, hair, and heels for one week. But you'll really have to work it with me. And don't even dream about being a pussy. I'm counting on you for after your ten o'clock set. Cool?"

"We're cool." Lillian quickly twisted her hair into a loose bun, barely securing it with a single hairpin all designed to fall out the minute she snapped her neck.

———————

Warren never looked forward to the weekends; especially the Saturdays' his daughter Amber spent with his ex. He usually managed to keep busy during the day, puttering around in the yard, working on his car, maybe even studying a few of his apprenticeship manuals, but the evenings were a whole other story.

Head buried in the refrigerator, he finally surfaced with a bowl of cooked spaghetti, one onion, half a green pepper, and two Italian sausages. Throwing the raw meat down into a Teflon pan, he set them to fry while taking a few minutes to chop the Spanish onion and pepper into bite-sized chunks. "Now the sauce," Martin continued to cook, pulling a can of diced, stewed tomatoes out of his pantry.

One hand encased in a padded oven mitt, he carefully removed the sizzling pan from the stove and unceremoniously dropped the two cooked sausages on a cutting board. Effortlessly moving the fry pan below the counter's edge, he brushed the raw vegetables into the hot fat with one quick swoop of his hand.

As Warren quickly stirred the vegetables with a wooden spoon in an attempt to coat them with fat, he watched them slowly began to turn translucent. Satisfied, he reduced the heat and turned his attention back to the cooked Italian sausages. Slicing them on an angle into manageable pieces, he threw the meat back in with the peppers and onions before pouring in the small can of stewed tomatoes. Snatching an open jar of pasta sauce from his refrigerator, he added a generous cupful.

A healthy tablespoon of red-hot chili sauce and two tablespoons of white sugar to counteract the tomato's acidity, and Warren was almost finished.

Pouring himself a glass of dry red wine, he sat it aside to breathe as he reached for the bowl of cold noodles and turned the spaghetti into the steaming sausage and peppers. Satisfied that it was thoroughly heated after only a couple of minutes, Warren poured the entire mixture into a large pasta bowl and made his way straight toward the living room.

Returning to his kitchen to grab his wine, a paper napkin, and the necessary cutlery, he returned to his favorite recliner and settled in for his late night. With his taste buds watering, Warren dove straight in, enjoying every bite of the spicy delights as he counted the seconds until his stomach began to protest against the heat-fueled sauce.

Suddenly forced to set down his half-eaten bowl of Italian sausage and peppers, Warren reluctantly snatched up his ringing telephone.

"Hello," he mumbled through a mouthful of food.

"Warren, its Jody calling. I need to talk to you about your daughter. She's becoming so obstinate, so…"

"Must be bad," he groaned aloud. "Otherwise she'd be *our* daughter."

"Listen!" his ex-wife barked. "I'm not some glorified babysitter who takes over every second weekend so you can enjoy your single life."

"Single life? What in the hell are you talking about now? I'm sitting here alone in front of my TV eating leftover pasta out of a bowl. Wow, I'm really whooping it up, aren't I?"

"Don't get sarcastic with me. I'm phoning about Amber," Jody hissed as if the mere mention of their daughter's name would be enough to snap him out of some self-imposed trance.

"So what's she done now?"

"It's her insolence. She looks at me as if I'm just some sort of annoyance she has to suffer through for forty-eight hours twice a month. I'm not an irritant, Warren. I'm her mother!"

"I know," he said as he closed his eyes and threw his head back into the softness of the recliner's headrest.

"She's, she's…"

"She's what?" he coaxed Jody to swallow her tears and finish her last statement.

"She's calling me… *Aunt Flo.*"

"Aunt Flo?" he repeated. "I don't get it. What does it mean?'

"She's calling me Aunt Flo because I remind her of her… of her menstrual period." His ex-wife's voice finally broke into another cascade of sobs.

Warren struggled to grasp the concept, suddenly realizing the intended insult behind the nickname.

"You know, her period," Jody repeated. "It comes four or five days a month. She can't do anything about it but suffer through, and wait until it goes away. She... she thinks I'm no different than her goddamn cramps," Jody howled across the phone lines.

"Oh." He raised his left hand up to rub the muscles tightening across his forehead. "I get it now."

"Isn't that just horrible," his ex continued to wail.

Creative was more the word that jumped to mind, but Warren figured he'd better keep that opinion to himself and just work on putting out the fire. "So what do you want me to do about it?"

"Well, where'd she get it from? Did you teach her that?"

"Hell, no." He sat up in his recliner. "I think our little darling figured that one out all on her own."

As Jody sobbed into her telephone, Warren reached for his satellite remote and began absentmindedly flipping through the movie guide. She didn't really want his help, she wanted his pity. *Poor, poor me,* had always been her favorite tune, and she'd probably just phoned so Warren could hum her a few bars.

"It's so awful being a weekend parent. You don't know what it's like to hear about my daughter's life after the fact. I feel as if I'm a spectator in Amber's world. I just don't know how long I'll be able to handle this kind of visitation arrangement," she continued to drone on.

"You're the one who chose to move out of the city to commune with nature," he curtly reminded his wife. "You want joint custody now, move back within bussing distance to Amber's school and we can talk about sharing her fifty-fifty."

"The city," she moaned. "You know I hate the city. The noise, the traffic, the..."

"Well then, its weekends." He finally chose a movie and pressed the enter button. "You know, what with her piano and dance lessons, you're lucky we're able to schedule in every second weekend, as it is."

"I'm lucky?" Her voice suddenly took on a tone of irritation. "I'm her mother, not some long lost grade school playmate. I deserve equal time with my daughter. Maybe if she saw me more than four days a month, she'd respect me more. Maybe we'd…"

"Shit," Warren mumbled to himself. He'd already seen this movie; he just hadn't recognized the title.

"This isn't getting us anywhere," Jody abruptly announced, hanging up the receiver without any warning.

"And you have a good night, too" he shook his head, dropping the cordless phone back into its cradle.

———————

The eight o'clock shift had been quiet; the bar still half-empty as the evening regulars only began to fill their usual seats sometime after nine.

"This is a really nice gold eye shadow," Lillian complimented Brandy as she touched up her make-up after finishing her ten o'clock set.

"It's got real 24 karat gold flakes in the powder. It should be fucking nice," she said, knowingly nodding her head.

"You got some really cool stuff." Lillian slowly returned the screw-on cap to the pot of powdered shadow.

"Everybody's got their thing," she chuckled. "Some spend it on shoes, others on dope. I got it bad for make-up. You know what I mean?"

Lillian just nodded; having spent the last half hour flipping through all the dancer's cases. "This must have cost you a small fortune," she picked up an unopened tube of concealer, shocked to see the fifty-nine dollar price tag still taped to the side.

"It's my hobby," Brandy took a second to check her own appearance in the brightly lit mirrors. "What you do for fun?"

"Fun? Fun?" she repeated as if the word was somehow foreign to her. "I've been kinda busy with work and everything. My ex-boyfriend's nephew, Tito, he'd been staying with us, and between bottles and diapers, there just hadn't been a lot of time for any fun."

"Fuck me if I'd raise somebody else's brats. I barely had time for my own." Brandy stood up and checked the clasp on her belly chain.

"You have kids?"

"Had," the senior dancer corrected her young protégé. "My youngest ran off from home with her friends when she was fourteen, and my son, he's up in juvey until his eighteenth birthday."

"Oh," Lillian muttered, turning her attention back to the make-up case.

"Don't worry. It don't bother me none that they turned out just like their fathers. Useless to the core," Brandy sighed, dropping down into any empty chair. "I did my best, but they were damned and determined to show me how it's done. Now I bet both them little shits are wishing they were back at home and safe in their beds."

"Probably," Lillian quietly agreed. "So how long you been dancing?"

Brandy took a second to do a little math. "About thirteen, fourteen years. Right after my second kid was born I guess."

"You been dancing for fourteen years?"

"Well, on and off." Brandy stood up to snatch a can of soda out of her duffle bag. "You want one?"

"Sure." Lillian accepted the lukewarm drink.

"In between, I had a couple of relationships and took a few years off, but each time they turned out to be total wastes of my time, and I eventually had to come back to work .You know what I mean?"

"Yeah," she nodded.

Carefully prying her soda can open with the tip of a nail file;

Brandy managed to open her drink without chipping any of her acrylic tips. "Hey, I heard you'd quit stripping to go make pornos. What's up with that?"

Flipping open her own soda, Lillian downed a good swallow before taking the time to answer the question. "The Giovanni's hired me, but I kinda messed up on the first film shoot."

"You froze?"

"No, worse." She hung her head in total embarrassment. "I got my rag right on the set and bled all over my costume and the male lead."

"No way?" Brandy howled. "You didn't?"

"I did," she began to snicker. "It was so unbelievably awful. You should have seen me. It was some kind of old Wild West project and we were wearing hand-beaded white leather costumes. Everything was stained with my blood. I think it was probably all ruined."

"Didn't you know it was coming?"

"That's the thing." Lillian jumped up to her feet to pace the club's dressing room. "I was a whole week early. I can't believe it came so hard and so fast."

"So you get fired?"

"No, they just put off the shoot for awhile 'til I finish my period. Then we're gonna try it again."

"So what you doing here?"

"Cash. I'm dead broke."

Brandy nodded. "I hear ya hon. Well," she asked, straightening her back and walking over to where the young girl was standing. "You ready for the lap dance?"

"Yep," she nervously smiled, knowing that the senior dancer was alluding to her period. "Don't worry. I cut the string off my tampon, so nobody will see, it no matter how close they look."

"Don't you just love fishing em' out?"

Giggling, Lillian raised her soda can back up to her lips for another sip. "I could sure use those two-hundred bucks. My tips will just pay my food and rent. I need extra for cabs and a few clothes."

"Then don't worry," Brandy patted her on the shoulder, "you'll make a few extra bucks tonight."

"Cherry, Tiger," a man's voice called out from the other side of the dressing room door. "Boss wants you guys on the floor."

"Sounds like we're up," Brandy winked at Lillian as they both began making their way out of the club's dressing room.

"Well, well," Big Daddy couldn't help but tease. "Can't believe you're finally gonna work my floor. So how'd you do it?" he turned his attention back toward Brandy. "Hear you're gonna use her in a double. That true?"

"It's true," Lillian nodded, nervously twisting her toes in the borrowed heels.

"Well then, you go make Big Daddy proud," he roared, slapping both girls on the ass as they turned and made their way toward the strip club's V.I.P room.

"Where you been, my little Tiger?" one of Brandy's regulars toasted their entrance the second the girls appeared through the slit in the drapery.

"I was just having a little girl talk with my friend," she lovingly slipped her arm around Lillian's waist and pulled her forward into the dimly lit room.

"Son of a bitch, that's nice," the client growled. "What's your name, sweetie?"

"Cherry Blossom," Lillian answered, her stage persona suddenly taking over the conversation. "I hear you gentlemen are interested in a little double action."

"Before we get going, I think Cherry and I would both like a drink to get us in the mood. How you boys feel about a couple shots of tequila and a few beers?" Brandy began working at prying open their wallets.

"I suppose you want Tequila Gold, hey Tiger?" the first man stood up and walked over to where the girls were standing.

Without any warning, Brandy suddenly turned and planted a full kiss on Lillian's mouth, even taking a second to dart her tongue in between her partner's unsuspecting lips.

"Gold it is," both men yelled in unison, instantly alerting the waitress that they were in immediate need of her services.

CHAPTER TWENTY

"Sometimes we don't do things we want to do, so that others won't know we want to do them."
— *The Village*, 2005

With a massive array of scrap-booking materials covering nearly every inch of her dining room table, Jody was still unable to find just the right borders for her latest collection of photographs.

"What's the mess all about?" her daughter Amber demanded from the adjoining doorway.

"Scrap booking. It's a new hobby of mine. I've been taking a class down at the resource center. Maybe you'd like to come with me and check it out tomorrow?"

"Why bother? It looks like a giant kindergarten class of cut and paste."

"Well," she took a second to formulate her answer. "I thought it would be nice to organize all our family photos into albums— keepsakes for you to show your children one day."

Amber never answered; she just sauntered up to the dining room table and pushed around a few of her mother's snapshots.

"I'm never getting married," she suddenly announced. "It's just a bullshit institution implemented by a male dominated society to force all females into subservience."

"Glad to see all your internet minutes haven't been wasted surfing for rock stars," Jody tried to temper her daughter's sarcasm with a little humor.

Leaning over to snatch up one of her parents' wedding photos, Amber dropped the glossy five by seven photograph directly in front of her mother's line of sight. "Why don't you tell me exactly what the institution of marriage has done for you, Mom?"

"It gave me you," she warmly smiled.

"Procreation has nothing to do with marriage. You could have just as easily gotten knocked up by a stranger in a bar."

"Amber. That's a horrible thing to say to your mother. Your father and I both love you with all our hearts. We desperately wanted to have a baby, to make a family."

"So what happened? What went wrong?" She folded her arms across her chest, instantly assuming a position of defiance. "You didn't like the outcome after your first try, so you decided to call it quits and run for the hills? What's the matter, Mom? I didn't turn out to be the child you wanted?" her voice began to take on a shrieking quality.

"Oh God, no. It's nothing like that. Your father and I have told you a hundred times that this had nothing to do with you."

"Oh, come on." Amber uncrossed her arms and angrily slapped them down to her sides. "How can you keep repeating that bullshit line? *It's not you, it's between your father and me,*" she mimicked her mother's voice. "How can you keep chanting that shit? Of course, it's about me," she said through sobs than began to catch in her throat.

"Why would you think something like that?" Jody slowly rose up from her seat to face the distraught young woman.

"Because I've heard a thousand times how happy you and dad were for the first couple years of your marriage. How your life was like a never-ending honeymoon. And then all of a sudden, whamo! You had a baby, and a year later, all the problems started. Things were never the same again. Right Mom?" Amber angrily demanded; her breathing coming in short gasps as she fought to control her outrage.

Speechless, Jody found herself desperately wringing her hands as her mind scrambled to try to rationalize her daughter's insecurities. "The decision to not have a second baby had nothing to do with you, sweetie, it was all mine. Your father would have loved another child."

"I don't understand." Amber slumped down into one of the oak dining room chairs. "It was...just you?"

Amber was only thirteen years, and although Jody had not planned to explain all her personal *life choices* until her daughter was much older, it didn't look like this teenager was about to wait.

"I don't understand," Amber muttered to herself. "I always thought it was dad who wanted to get divorced. Are you trying to tell me now that it was actually you?"

Moving over and pulling up a chair right beside her daughter's, Jody slowly took a deep breath and began to relate her side of the story. "I may have been the one who initially filed for divorce, but in all reality, it was your father who'd left the marriage years before."

"I don't understand."

"Well honey... you see... your father's been in love with someone else, ever since he was a teenager," Jody blurted out, wondering how her daughter would digest the impromptu revelation.

"But you guys got married?"

"After your dad couldn't be with his first love for whatever reason, he finally summoned the courage to move on and date me. During our college years, we did consummate our relationship and decided to marry. But after you were born, I finally realized that even though we were husband and wife and I'd given him a beautiful baby girl, his heart would always belong to that other woman, and he'd never totally be mine."

After wiping the tears from her eyes, Amber unconsciously allowed the fingers on her right hand to inch back up her chin and slip into the dark recess of her open mouth. "Who is she?" she whispered, between bites of her freshly painted nails.

"I don't know," Jody shook her head in dismay. "I've never been able to figure that one out, and no matter how many times I ask, your father won't give me a straight answer."

———————————

Sharing a round of beers at the empty bar, Lillian and Brandy unwound from their performances on and off the stage.

"How about another dance?" One of the club's last patrons teased as he stumbled past them waving a crumbled ten-dollar bill.

"Tomorrow night. Come back early baby, and I'll dance something really special for you," Brandy took another slug of beer without even shifting her eyes to see who she was promising.

"I'll be back," he vowed, suddenly propelled toward an exit by one of the club's bouncers as the hired muscle continued to sweep the building for stragglers.

"That lap dance wasn't as bad as I thought," Lillian set down her empty bottle. "Especially for my first," she admitted with a nervous chuckle.

Signaling the bartender to bring over two fresh bottles, Brandy couldn't help but shake her head in amazement. "I still can't believe how much cash you've pissed away not working the floor between your sets."

"I know," she sheepishly admitted, taking a second to snatch up her fresh drink. "But this was my first dancing job, and somehow, I always figured that if I stayed on the stage and didn't let any of the guys touch me, then… somehow…it was more respectable."

"Respectable?" Brandy howled. "Nothing says respect like having some loser jack-off on a single, and then try to stuff the slimy bill down the crack of your ass."

"Amen," Lillian agreed with the sentiment.

"Which one of your girls is Lillian Cardy… Cardinal?" the new coat check girl continued to stumble through the handwritten note.

"I'm Lillian. What's the matter?"

"Some nurse keeps calling for you. I think it's kinda urgent." The girl held out a handful of wrinkled messages as Lillian jumped up off her barstool and snatched them from her grasp.

"What'd she want?"

"Your kid is in emergency, down at County." The girl spun on her heels and sashayed back toward her post.

"You have a kid?" Brandy couldn't help but ask, positive that Lillian had told her earlier that she was childless.

"It's Tito." She quickly shuffled through the messages. "He's my nephew and…"

Brandy watched the color drain from the young girl's face as she continued to digest the limited information recorded on the scraps of paper.

"I gotta go!" Lillian reached back toward the bar and snatched her duffle bag off a neighboring stool.

"You wanna lift?"

"You got a car?"

"No, I'm gonna sprout wings and carry you on my back. Course I got a car. So you wanna ride or what?"

"Sure." Lillian leaned over and grabbed Brandy's bag. "Lead the way."

As Jody walked through her house, shutting off the lights, and securing all the doors and windows, she took a minute to stare at the collection of memories still scattered across her dining room table. Maybe her daughter Amber was right; her scrap-booking was little more than a creative waste of time and supplies. Maybe the memories she personally treasured were of little importance to anyone else but her? Was she only deluding herself? Was her latest project nothing more than an exercise in futility?

"Mom," Amber's voice called out from the kitchen. "I can't find the air popper."

"I'm coming," Jody answered back, thrilled that her daughter was addressing her by *Mom* instead of the sarcastic *Aunt Flo*.

"I couldn't sleep, so I got up to make popcorn, but I can't find the machine," Amber explained in a rush of breath, jumping up and down on her toes as she strained to see if it was hiding up on any of the pantry's top shelves.

"I moved it to the lower cupboard near the stove," Jody reached down and swung open the door. "I did a little reorganizing since you were last here."

"Obviously." Her daughter turned and dropped to her knees. "You wanna give me a heads up with the popcorn kernels before I start ripping the rest of this place apart?"

"Still in the refrigerator door."

As Amber set up her machine, Jody moved around the counter and took up residence on one of the kitchen stools.

"Are you gonna have some?" She looked to her mother before filling up the dispenser.

"No... well maybe," she shrugged, not really interested in popcorn but unwilling to brush off her daughter's offer in case it was actually a thinly veiled attempt to spend some time together.

"Yes or no?"

"Yes," Jody smiled, "with extra butter. So, do you want me to open us a big bottle of root beer?"

"I'd rather have a real beer," Amber answered without skipping a beat.

"Me too," Jody took a deep breath and walked over to pull two cans from the refrigerator door. "Can or glass?"

"Are you shitting me?"

"I don't *shit* anyone." Jody set the cans down on the counter and reached up for two glass mugs. "We'll use glasses. Ladies don't drink from cans."

"You're really gonna let me have a beer"

"Yes. One beer—in my house—with me present. We're not going to get drunk, and we're not going to make a habit of this, but I think one beer might actually be all right. At least you'll know how it tastes, and the effect it might have on your stomach, and your sense of judgment."

Amber knew exactly what beer tasted like, and how half a case erased all her inhibitions, never mind the minimal affects of one lousy can.

"Thanks Mom," she switched on the air popper, their conversation instantly drowned out by the roar of the whirling tumbler.

Moving their supplies into the living room, Amber plucked an old comedy from her mother's ancient collection of movies. "You wanna watch this, or you going to bed?"

"That's fine with me," Jody eagerly sunk into the couch, willing to sit through a showing of the Exorcist if her daughter was planning to stay in the living room with her.

"I've seen it a hundred times, but it's still kinda cute." She tossed her mother the plastic case while dropping the disc into the open tray. "You know," Amber rolled her eyes while waiting for coming attractions to play out, "DVD players are so last year. Why don't you step into the twenty-first century and get yourself a Blu-Ray player. I can't even bring any of my own stuff over here to watch."

"But, what about my old favorites?" Jody pointed to her shelved collection. "I don't want to have to buy them all again on some new format, I already have way too many boxes of VHS movies cluttering my storage."

Satisfied the movie was ready to start; Amber pressed play and returned to her seat on the couch. "All Blu-Rays are reverse compatible," she offered, diving straight into the center of the buttered popcorn. "They'll play all your old DVDs too."

"Oh, I didn't know that," she smiled, "but then, I just figured out last week where the USB port was on my computer."

Passing her mother the bowl, Amber stood up to adjust the television's volume. "And they also make universal remotes to replace any you've might have thrown out or accidentally trashed."

"I was going through a hard time back then," her mother offered with an apologetic smile.

"Obviously."

As the opening music began to fill the room, Amber turned her full attention to the television screen and settled in against the cushions.

Unable to concentrate on the disjointed plot line, Jody found her attention wandering back to the very night she'd lost her cool and smashed the remote.

She had still been still married to Warren, and he'd just blown most of their family weekend helping his twin sister move to a better apartment, after she took some kind of secretarial job with another new company.

"Can we take Amber to the carnival now?" Jody had demanded the minute her husband appeared through the house's back door.

"I need a shower," Warren had answered without even acknowledging her request.

"I'll go change Amber. You don't have to shave too, do you?"

"Shave for what?"

"For the carnival?" she'd angrily repeated. "Don't you ever listen to what I say Warren? It's as if I'm talking to a brick wall half the time. What in the hell is the matter with you, anyway?"

"I can't go to the carnival, I promised Wanda I'd help her move her office stuff over so she can get settled at her new desk. She wants to be all set up before work on Monday morning."

"That's bullshit and you know it! Your daughter and I have been waiting all day to go to the carnival. You know how she loves the kiddy rides and…"

"I told you to take her," Warren stripped off his clothes and threw everything but his under shorts down the basement stairs.

"She wants her daddy to come," Jody desperately tried to make her point.

"Well, Wanda needs me this afternoon. This is her career we're talking about, not a couple of spins on a plastic horse."

"This is *your daughter* we're talking about!"

"And this is *my sister* we're talking about, too!" he continued to retort back. "Family is family and I have to take care of them both. I've decided that playing at the carnival can wait. Wanda needs my help setting up for her new job, so this is my priority today."

Before Jody could mount any further arguments, Warren had disappeared behind the bathroom door, preparing to freshen up before heading back to help his sister.

"Fuck you and your family," Jody had spun around and grabbed the remote she'd absentmindedly carried to the kitchen counter. "I think you need to re-evaluate your priorities before you lose what's really important to you," she yelled at the top of her lungs, hurling the electronic control against the bathroom door with all her might.

As the plastic housing instantly shattered upon impact with

the wooden door, Warren suddenly re-emerged into the hallway a second after the final pieces had stopped skidding across the linoleum floor.

"Are you insane?" he demanded.

"No," Jody cried, suddenly thankful her daughter was still playing outside in the backyard sandbox. "We need to be the number one priority in your life. I won't be treated like... like a... like an inconvenience." The tears began to run down her face.

"You're my wife, and Amber is my daughter." Warren stepped forward, angrily making his point with an accusing finger. "You *are* number one! But being number one doesn't give you the right to run my goddamn life!"

"Run your life?" She spun away and grabbed a handful of tissue. "I don't want to run it Warren; I just want to share it." She shakily wiped at the fluid trickling down from both her nostrils.

"You're my wife," he repeated, as if the title gave her all the security she'd ever need.

"Yes, I'm your wife," she repeated. "So what? You spend every spare hour with anyone but me. It's like you look for projects to keep you away from us here at home. What's the matter, Warren? Why don't you wanna be married to me?"

"If I didn't want to be married to you Jody, I'd file for divorce."

"Is it someone else? Are you seeing some other woman every time you tell me that you're helping your sister? What's the matter? Why don't you want me anymore?" His wife begged in a defeated voice.

"It's not you." He lifted his hands to rub the building tension throughout the muscles in his forehead.

"Then who is it?"

"Nobody," he answered, as he would repeat for the remainder of their married lives.

CHAPTER TWENTY-ONE

"It is not our abilities that show what we truly are. It is our choices."
    —*Harry Potter and the Chamber of Secrets, 2002*

Repeatedly rubbing the wad of tissue back and forth across her face, Lillian attempted to remove as much of her stage make-up as possible.

"I can't go in looking like this," she proclaimed, suddenly flipping down the visor mirror to inspect her appearance.

"You think County's never seen a stripper before?"

She ignored the comment, intent on removing as much of the black eyeliner and glitter shadow as was humanly possible without the aid of make-up remover or soap and water.

"Here's Emergency," Brandy announced as she quickly pulled her car up to the sliding glass doors. "You run inside, check on your nephew, and I'll park this hunk of junk and join you."

"You don't have to…"

"Go inside!" Her co-worker suddenly took charge of the situation.

"I'll at least come inside and see what's going on. This might be some big mix-up and you'll be ready to leave."

"I doubt it," Lillian mumbled as she shoved the soiled tissue down into her jean pocket.

"Now get!" Brandy ordered, as the driver behind loudly tooted his horn to signal his impatience.

As soon as she passed through the emergency doors, Lillian was immediately inundated with the sounds and smells of a bustling hospital. Feeling herself propelled toward the admitting desk, she stumbled along, unaware that her feet were unconsciously following brightly painted arrows.

"Can I help you?" the uniformed woman inquired from behind the counter.

Still working on familiarizing herself with her surroundings, Lillian was too rattled even to formulate an answer.

"Excuse me, are you hurt?" The nurse's initial inquiry suddenly shifted to concern.

"No," she finally snapped back to reality. "My name is Lillian Cardinal. You've been trying to get a hold of me."

"Cardinal, Lillian," the nurse repeated, as she typed the name into her desktop computer. "Yes, we have your son, Tito here. He was admitted with a dislocated shoulder and some other minor complaints earlier this evening. Just take a seat please. I'll let the doctor know you're waiting to talk to him."

"Where's Tito now?" she demanded, not willing to admit she was only the ex-girlfriend of his biological uncle. The nurse ignored her, and turned to the next person in line.

"Miss Cardinal?" a young woman finally stepped forward and asked. "I was wondering if we could have a word?"

"Where's Tito?" she demanded for the second time.

"Please follow me," the hospital's social worker gently commanded, signaling for the security guard flanking her right side to step forward. "We'll be able to talk privately in my office."

"But Tito?"

"He's absolutely fine. From what I understand, he's been moved upstairs to the children's ward and he's sleeping comfortably."

Resigned to her fate, Lillian reluctantly followed the lady through a maze of corridors, finally accepting a chair, and a hot black cup of coffee.

Opening the file, the social worker got right down to the business at hand. "I assume you're the child's biological mother?" Her pen began marking notations within the file.

"Actually no, I'm not."

"You're not? Well then why was your name, and work number, inscribed all over the young boy's knapsack? It says *in case of emergency* to contact you."

"Tito was actually my boyfriend Ronnie's nephew. He was living with us for a while when his mother Gloria was taking care of some personal stuff. I had bought him the knapsack, so I marked it with my name just in case."

"And at present, is Tito still residing with his mother?"

"As far as I knew, he was still with his mother. You see," she nervously fiddled with the edge of her cup. "Ronnie and I split up, so I really haven't been in contact with either Gloria or Tito since the day I walked out of the apartment."

"Well, can you then tell me when you last saw the child in question?"

As Lillian took a second to count back the days, the social worker raised her head and silently dismissed the security guard, confident her visitor posed no physical threat.

"It's been about a week. Last Monday, when I was out, Gloria stopped by the apartment and picked up her son. I left Ronnie that night, so... well... I've been kinda busy and I didn't have time to check on Tito. Was he really hurt?"

"According to the admittance record, he was found wandering down the street near a McDonald's restaurant, dragging his knapsack. He was disheveled, dehydrated, and extremely hungry. Upon a closer examination up by the EMTs, it was determined that he had a dislocated right shoulder, and numerous fresh bruises to his arms, lower back, and buttocks."

Lillian wanted to puke, her stomach churning as her head began to pound. "Where was his mother?"

"At this exact moment, I'm unsure. Until a few minutes ago, I thought you were his mother."

"Aunty," she whispered.

"Do you know the mother's home number, or address?"

"No. They were staying with friends or something. I don't exactly know where."

"And your ex-boyfriend, Ronnie?" The lady looked down at her own notes. "Do you think he'd be able to help us locate his sister?"

"I don't know where Ronnie is right now, either. I can give you our old address, but I know he's not there, so I really don't have any idea. He's not exactly employed, so his days are kind of up in the air."

Grabbing a fresh piece of paper to make further notations, the social worker finally set down her pen and looked Lillian deep in the eye. "We suspect Tito had been physically abused either by a caregiver, or during his brief time on the street. Being that he is only around two years old, we don't expect to extract any further information from the child. I must say," the lady suddenly leaned back in her chair, "that I am very disappointed to find out that you are not a blood relative."

"Why?"

"Because now it looks as if the child will have to be remanded into the care of the courts."

"But..." she began to argue as the social worker stood up from behind her desk.

"Let's go see Tito," the woman said as she looked down at her watch. "Maybe we can talk a little bit more after you've had some time to visit. He'll probably welcome a friendly face."

"Good," Lillian jumped up to her feet. "I'd really like to see him and make sure he's alright."

"Two smokes for your plate?" one of the older men in line attempted to strike a deal with anyone in earshot.

"Piss off," Ronnie quickly turned his back on the smelly drunk.

"A whole pack," Jerome teased. "And if you want my desert, it's gonna cost you a lighter, too."

"You're crazy, just damn crazy." The homeless man shook his head while stamping his right foot. "A whole pack for a plate? A lighter for a desert? You're crazy boy, just plain crazy," he continued to rant.

"Don't sound like praying to me," one of the shelter's volunteers strolled down the line and reminded the men that their time could be better spent thanking the Lord for the bounty they were about to receive.

"I'm so fucking starved," Jerome continued to moan. "I'd even eat one of Lillian's overcooked macaroni and tomato casseroles."

"Fuck her," Ronnie hissed, still too pissed at the thought of his girlfriend's departure to even joke about her limited cooking skills.

"I can't believe we're fucking broke," Jerome slowly shuffled forward in the line. "It's like we was rolling in it on Thursday, and today we's all broke. Where'd it all go?"

"Is today Saturday or Sunday?" Ronnie muttered; his brain still scrambled from the myriad of drugs they'd been ingesting for the last seventy-two hours, coupled with their recent beatings.

In three days, not only had they managed to blow every penny of their cash from the sale of Lillian's belongings, but somewhere along the line, they'd even managed to lose their own bags of clothing and personnel items.

"It's Sunday morning," one of the women passing out plastic trays gleefully announced. "You've come to the house of the Lord to ask for his forgiveness and share in his blessings. Amen brothers."

"Amen, sister," a large percentage of the men chanted back.

"Fucking trained monkeys," Ronnie sneered under his breath as he accepted the empty tray before shuffling off toward the steam table.

Finally seated, both men dove into their plates, shrunken stomach forced to expand as they shoved in mouthfuls of powdered scrambled eggs and oil-soaked hash browns.

"Morning service at ten," a man's voice suddenly rang out from the front of the room. "We'd really like to see you all there."

"Amen, brother!" Jerome couldn't help but shout out.

"Shut the fuck up," Ronnie quickly kneed him under the table. "Finish eating and let's get the fuck out of here before some priest wants to take us up behind the altar and teach us both to pray… private style," he knowingly winked.

"Yeah, man." Jerome opened his mouth and simulated the actions of performing oral sex.

"Will you boys be joining us for worship?" the same woman inquired who'd originally passed them their meal trays.

"Sure," Jerome chirped up. "We wouldn't miss it for the world."

"Well good, then. I'll save you both a seat."

This time, when Ronnie kneed Jerome, their shins met in a clank of bone and both had to bite their tongues to stop from yelping in pain.

Back on the street, stomachs temporarily sated, Jerome dug in his pocket for his cigarette package. "I think we're kinda fucked here. I'm not exactly sure what we're gonna do for cash. We ain't even got enough left for a new pack of smokes, do we?" Jerome asked, never trusted to carry any of the available cash.

"No, so give me one of those," Ronnie demanded. "I ain't gonna stand here and watch you smoke up what we got left."

Slowly making their way down the empty streets, both found themselves wandering aimlessly through the Sunday morning crowds until Jerome suddenly decided that he needed to relieve his bladder.

Cutting back behind one of the buildings, Ronnie stood watch while Jerome slowly unzipped his pants and gingerly pulled out his penis.

"Fuck man," he winced, still bothered by the pinkish urine now pooling in the cardboard box at his feet."

"Guts still hurt?" Ronnie kicked an empty soda can across the alley.

"Only when I breathe or piss."

"How about you? How's your arm?"

"Ain't broke," Ronnie conceded, gingerly bending his elbow to make his point.

They were both the walking wounded, barely recovered from their last beating when Jerome suddenly had another one of his brainwaves. "You know, when I was a kid; I remember paying two bucks for a smoke. How about we walk over to some elementary school and sell the last half a pack. Should give us enough cash to buy two more packs, and that'll easily be enough smokes for the next couple of days."

"No bro. I got a better idea," Ronnie began to think aloud. "We sell the half pack, buy another, and just keep going. We do that three or four times, and we'll have enough cash for a small buy. Then we can get back to what we're good at, selling dope."

The idea sounded plausible, so with nothing else to do, they both began making their way toward the neighborhood schoolyard.

The paper shoved under the basement door clearly reminded Pete that it was only day six, but he knew his body was starting to smell as if he'd been sleeping under a bridge for at least a month. The baby wipes just weren't cutting it, and he was well aware that unless he stepped up his personal hygiene, he was probably going to start rotting.

"Fuck man. I'd give my left nut for a shower," he muttered to himself, leaning over the wall sink as it slowly filled with hot soapy water.

Dipping the cotton facecloth in and out of the sudsy liquid, Pete finally rung out the excess water and began vigorously rubbing at his naked chest. Repeating the same steps, over and over, within twenty minutes he managed to remove most of the original crust from his body.

Padding across the concrete floor in his bare feet, he tossed the soiled facecloth and damp bath towel across his impromptu clothesline. Unwilling to live with a month's worth of wet laundry molding in plastic bags; he continued to dry everything out every piece before bagging it.

Surprisingly, Pete's entire detox experience wasn't turning out to be as bad as he had originally imagined. Sure, he'd thrown his guts up for a day, fevers and cold sweats for another two, but it didn't seem like the physical cravings were gonna be his worst enemy. According to everything he had read while confined to the basement, it was going to be *the External Cues* or the *Triggers* that might trip him up.

During the last six days of his self-imposed exile, he realized he needed to establish what it was exactly that set him off. According to the books, he physically needed to transcribe a written list. This written list would help him identify the triggers and then change his life to remove the people and things that sent him running straight for the dope.

The development of these specific lists was usually accomplished in group therapy, but now it was up to Pete to tackle it alone. He jumped right in and started with the first category of *People*, names running through his head as he returned to his floor mat and grabbed a pad of paper.

"Well shit man, where do I start," he laughed aloud, random faces beginning to flash back and forth in front of his eyes. His drug dealers, his brother Boyd, and his cunt-faced wife Julia were definitely at the top of the list, but they weren't alone. There were all the guys down at Giovanni Films, the girls who starred in the movies, and of course, the boys from the old neighborhood. Drugs had become an integral part of every single one of his relationships. In retrospect, other than his mother, he'd shared drugs with every single person in his life. Consciously or unconsciously, he'd surrounded himself with only those who shared his lifestyle, and if expected to clear the slate, he'd have to start off totally alone.

Before Pete had a chance to fill in any information under the remaining four categories of *Places, Events, Objects,* and *Behaviors or Activities*, he was suddenly struck with the first of a string of debilitating headaches.

Dropping his pen, he lay back down on the mattress, covering his eyes with his upper arm as he attempted to shield his face from the light.

"Oh God," he moaned, his mind painfully scanning his own memory banks for any mention of migraines or tension headaches in the pages of literature. Unable to recall anything relevant, he began rocking his own hips back and forth in an attempt to soothe himself to sleep.

CHAPTER TWENTY-TWO

"Erotic films are when you use a feather. Porn films are when you use the whole chicken. Girl's been through a lot of chickens."

—Nip/Tuck, 2004

"Do you want anymore hollandaise sauce?" Julia questioned her husband as she accepted the sterling silver platter from their cook.

"No, go ahead," Boyd absentmindedly answered at his wife, continuing to shuffle papers as he attempted to make a little headway through his pile before driving into the office.

"Do you have a copy of the filming schedule for the Pocahontas shoot?" Julia set down the eggs Benedict and reached for the carafe.

"I thought we'd try it again later this week. I told Malcolm Friday," he looked toward his wife for her approval. "You think that'll be fine?"

"Don't ask me. Ask Lillian," she shook her head. "I don't know when her period is gonna be over."

"Well whatever, I'm confirming the shoot for Friday."

"Fine," Julia smiled to herself. "But you better check with Wanda and make sure those new costumes are going to be ready on time. A week isn't really that much time to work with leather, especially if the seamstress had to start each costume from scratch."

"I'll check," he agreed, holding out his cup for a refill. "Have you finished negotiating with that Frank guy?"

"Frank?" she set down the carafe, searching her short-term memory for any mention of a client named Frank.

"Frank, Francis, Francois," Boyd suddenly stumbled onto the appropriate pronunciation. "You nail down the particulars on that deal?"

"Almost. Francois Dubois was having a little trouble liquidating his paper for our cash payment, but I was able to help him work a deal with Jake. And as soon as Jake's cleared Francois's paper, he's gonna cut us back a point cross the board for the intro."

"Nice catch hon," Boyd couldn't help but admire his wife savvy business sense. "So now Francois is done?"

"Like I said, almost," she repeated for the second time. "I've had to convince him that I can find eighteen year olds that look no more than twelve or thirteen."

"Can you?"

Stirring in a packet of sweetener, Julia quickly ran a mental tally of the possible actors she'd be able to use. "I guess I could go back in the files and see if the twins from last fall are still interested in working."

"Fuck. I really hated those little assholes. Believe it or not, their egos were bigger than their dicks," Boyd sarcastically growled.

"I know," Julia wholeheartedly agreed. "But they looked really young and that's one of the specific requirements for Francois's film. That, and being uncircumcised of course."

Pushing his plate aside, Boyd stood up from the kitchen table and moved a stack of papers over to the settee. "Please tell me that little French fucker isn't some kind of pedophile? You know that's the one brand of asshole that I just can't stomach."

"He's not a pedophile," Julia reassured her husband. "He just has a very specific fantasy he'd like us to capture on film, and if we're going to pull it off, I'm going to have to find at least another three or four young guys who can pass for teenage boys. I guess if push came to shove, we could place a bunch of print ads and run an open call," she began to plan aloud. "But I'm already gonna be paying a lot of cash for all the special effects make-up on this film. I gotta curb the budget, and training new talent can be costly, and a real pain."

Standing up to snatch his coffee cup off the table, Boyd just shook his head in disgust. "I see you've conveniently forgotten what happened last time we advertized an open call? Well let me refresh your memory, my dear. We had guys from fifteen to fifty jacking off in our lobby, trying to prove that they were the next *Ron Jeremy*."

"Jeremy who?" Julia forced herself to tune back into the conversation.

"You know...Ron Jeremy," Boyd insisted. "*The Hedgehog, The King of Porn*...the actor with the most appearances in Adult Films... ever. You know who I'm talking about, don't you?"

"Well of course I do," she threw her hands up in exasperation.

"Well then tell me, where have all the old pros gone? You just don't find that caliber of male talent anymore. I'm sick of working with snot-nosed kids who're too busy tweeting on their fucking I-phones to even hit their mark and follow the goddamn storyboards."

"Fine," Julia conceded, rising from the table to join her husband on the settee. "Forget the open call. I'll just keep beating the bushes to find the right talent."

"Talent," he laughed. "That's kind of a joke."

"Talent!" She turned to glare at her husband. "Until *you've* had to strip down naked and fill sixty minutes of blank tape with sexually explicit and painfully acrobatic moves, you better damn well agree that it takes talent."

"Sorry honey," he started to backpedal. "I wasn't talking about you."

"Yes, you were." She stood up and slammed her china cup back down onto the breakfast table. "When you make fun of any porn actor, you're making fun of us all. You have no idea how hard it is to make a living in this industry, to hold on to your self-esteem while strangers are shooting cum all over your face. You have no…"

Boyd stood up and wrapped his arms tightly around Julia's shoulders, allowing her the brief opportunity to lose herself in his powerful embrace.

There were rarely any warnings, and it never happened on any schedule—but every now and then, Julia would find herself crippled by the haunting memories of her past. The reality of having offered up her body up to any director to toss around and manipulate at his will, had left her with immeasurable scars.

Ninety-nine percent of the time, Julia was able to push the memories back, forcing herself to mask the trauma inflicted by the physical torture. There were years and years of pain, caused by the men and women she barely knew who were paid to stuff her orifices full of foreign objects and rigid human flesh. But through strict mental discipline, Julia somehow managed to block out the choreographed gang rapes and the dehumanizing treatment. Still, every now and then, a small trickle from her memory banks filtered down through her defenses and momentarily brought her crashing to her knees.

"When you're br… broke," she sobbed, "you'll do just about anything to pay the bills. If the director tells you to lick shit off his toes, you'd do it. If they bring in a big harry dog and tell you to drop to all fours, you do that too."

"Julia, that was a lifetime ago." Boyd gently pulled her up and away from the table, waving off their cook as she returned to refill their coffee cups. "We left all that behind years ago. We treat *our talent*," he heavily stressed the word, "with respect and dignity. We pay three or four times the industry standard, and we don't allow any film projects that play out like snuff films. We have a strict *No Minors Policy,* and we…"

"Is that a cop-out or what?" She pulled back long enough to wipe her eyes. "Are we just kidding ourselves, Boyd? Sure we pay everyone big money, but it's still porn. We still expect our actors to strip buck-naked, perform the most intimate of sexual acts, and then record it all on film for some freak to watch at his leisure. We're still stripping them of their dignity, whether they're smart enough to realize it or not."

"Julia, you know our clients are some of the country's most influential citizens."

"Who the fuck cares," she shouted out. "Just because you're a successful businessman doesn't mean that you can't be some kind of sicko pervert!"

"Come on, baby. You think I don't know exactly what you mean? I came from the same streets you did. I was one of the scum." He wrung his hands in his lap. "No matter what I do now, I can't make up for all the shitty things I did when the girls ran to me, trying to make a few bucks to score a little dope. It actually sickens me too, whenever I remember." Boyd dropped his head down into his hands, taking a second to massage away the pressure headache beginning to build at his temples.

"Maybe we need to close shop? Maybe we need to quit making porn?"

"And do what?" He slowly lifted up his head, already mentally exhausted at nine in the morning.

"I don't know," Julia stood up and began pacing around the dining room table. "We have at least a couple hundred thousand dollars worth of film and editing equipment. We could make movies, the real kind they show in the theaters."

"You know how to direct a feature?" He threw the question up at her face. "You know how to buy a script, hire the stars, maybe solicit an extra ten million dollars worth of financing?"

"No!" she barked. "Do you?"

"Of course not," he retorted. "But then I'm not debating whether or not I should try and break into the business. I'm not trying to be the next boy wonder of indie prod."

"Sorry," she apologized in a defeated tone, sinking back down beside her husband. "I was just trying…"

"I know." He threw his right hand around his wife's shoulder. "I don't have any back-up skills either. I direct porn for a living, and you manage the company that markets it. We pay our talent top dollars, and we try our best not to scar them for life in the process. That's it, babe." He leaned over and planted a firm kiss on his wife's cheek. "We are what we are, and we're probably going to hell for it."

"Yeah, you're probably right." She turned back and kissed him before wiping away her one remaining tear. "But at least we'll be together."

Make-up and hair professionally set, Julia marched straight into her office and snatched a stack of files off her desk. Turning to leave without even bothering to check the personal note attached to a stunning arrangement of pale yellow calla lilies, she strolled right out of her office and over to her purchasing agent's door.

"Is Wanda in?" she stopped at the secretary's desk.

"Yes, she is, however she's down in receiving. Would you like me to call her up?"

"Not necessary," Wanda cheerfully called out from down the

hall. "I was just re-routing a shipment," she explained, motioning for the mailroom worker to wheel the trolley into her office. "Please, come inside," she graciously beckoned.

"You've done a nice job redecorating your office." Julia took a small stab at office pleasantries.

"Thank-you. I hope Boyd is also pleased with the changes."

"You know men…" her boss shrugged. "So, what's in the boxes?"

Carefully slicing both cardboard tops open with a razor sharp box cutter, Wanda reached into the first and carefully extracted the newly sewn Indian costumes.

"They're fabulous." Julia quickly stepped up to her side. "I can't believe the workmanship."

Holding up the white leather, both women leaned in for a closer inspection, taking a few minutes to marvel at the intricate beadwork adorning the bodice and both sets of leather moccasins.

Turning and reaching down into the second box, Wanda extracted yet another set of costumes.

"What's that?" her boss demanded.

"Looks like the originals." She ripped open the plastic bag and held up the bloodstained leather.

"Why in the hell did they send those back to us?"

"Well, they do belong to Giovanni Films. We did pay for them in full, the first time around."

"Send em' to storage," Julia shook her head. "You'll never know when they'll come in handy."

Closing up the box flaps, Wanda moved the trolley toward the far wall in her office. "Can I help you with something Julia?"

"Yes," she smiled, motioning for Wanda to join her on the office couch. "I've brought a stack of papers with me. I need your help sorting through these talent files."

"Are they mixed up?"

Setting half the pile in Wanda's lap, Julia held the remaining half back for herself.

"Here's my dilemma. I need another woman's eye to help me choose the right boys for our next film project."

"What exactly are we looking for?" Wanda nervously opened her first file.

"Youth," Julia summed up in one word. "I need eighteen year olds who look twelve or thirteen."

"Oh, I don't know." Wanda quickly slapped the file folder closed. "I don't know if I can do that."

"Why? I'm not asking you to have sex with the guys. I'm just asking you to help me pick out a few faces."

It was definitely beginning to happen, just as her brother Warren had warned her it would. The lines were becoming blurred as her original position of secretary had transformed into that of Purchasing Agent, and now was slowly transforming itself into that of Senior Assistant to Julia and Boyd Giovanni. Day by day, her position became more hands on, and if this present pattern continued, it wouldn't be long before she was directing a porn shoot of her very own.

"I don't know anything about this kind of stuff." Wanda quickly set the files down on the coffee table as if the mere touch of the paper were somehow caustic, burning the very palms of her hands. "Don't you think you'd be better off asking Boyd… or maybe… Martin down in editing?"

"Boyd?" Julia shrieked with laughter. "He's absolutely no help when it comes to finding male talent. He's strictly a T and A man. And Martin, you've got to be kidding me. He's all about the editing. All he's worried about is lighting, framing, and running time. He wouldn't know talent if it leaned over his computer and bit him on the balls."

"Well… I've, ah… I've gotta run back down to receiving," Wanda began to babble, ripping the waybill off the side of a cardboard box. "I have to cross reference this shipping order with my other supplies. Make sure we've received everything we've ordered, before I submit this bill to accounts payable."

As Julia watched her employee literally flee the room, she snatched up the files and found herself joining in on the chase.

"Wanda!" she called out as the young woman literally ran down the hall. "Wanda, wait up for me."

"Is something the matter?" Boyd suddenly poked his head out from around the corner.

"No, everything's fine," Julia brushed by, breaking into a full run as she made her way down the hall toward the office's rear stairwell.

Hand finally reaching the doorknob, Wanda stopped dead in her tracks. This was ridiculous; running away as if she was a six-year-old schoolgirl, scared of the playground bully.

"What in the hell is going on with you?" Julia demanded, her breath now heavy from the impromptu sprint in designer heels. "Are you all right?"

Flushed from embarrassment, Wanda forced herself to turn and face her boss. "I'm so sorry, Julia. I really just don't want to be involved in that end of the business. I hope I haven't offended you," she continued to blurt out her apology. "When Boyd promoted me to Purchasing Agent, I thought it was going to be mostly paperwork. I didn't know that…"

"Whoa, girl. Just slow down a second," Julia began to snicker. "I didn't ask you to give the guys a hand job and rate them on a scale of one to ten. I just asked you to sort through a few pictures, and help me pick out a couple of young faces."

Taking a moment to make sure no one was listening; Wanda took a giant breath and then forced herself to level with Julia, once and for all.

"I'm afraid that the more I help out, the more I'll be drawn into the world of pornography."

"You do know what kind of movies we make here, don't you, Wanda?"

"Of course I do," she admitted, slowly raising two fingers to fidget with her necklace. "And trust me—I'm not some kind of prude who was just released from a convent and has lived my entire life in a plastic bubble. It's just that I don't wanna get drawn into the middle of it, is all."

Julia was absolutely stunned. She didn't have a clue what to say. Here she stood, face to face with one of her company's most promising employees, and the girl was begging not to be promoted, never to rise above her mid-level position.

"Look honey," Julia's voice suddenly took on an authoritative tone. "Giovanni Films is the name on the bottom of your pay check, and Giovanni Films is a company that films and markets sexually explicit adult entertainment. If you can't handle those basic facts, I suggest you consider an immediate job search. Cuz to be honest with you, Wanda," she leaned forward and opened the stairwell door, "I don't have time to run after my purchasing agent and beg her for some basic office assistance."

Wanda stood absolutely motionless, unable to speak as Julia pushed the stairwell door wide open and motioned for her to continue on with her escape.

"Make a decision Wanda, and make it quick," she ordered as the young woman nervously stepped onto the concrete landing. "We have a hell of a busy week ahead of us, and I either need your cooperation or your resignation on my desk by noon. Have I made myself perfectly clear?" Julia demanded.

"Yes ma'am," Wanda nodded, the stairwell door slamming shut as if set to accentuate her boss's point.

CHAPTER TWENTY-THREE

"This is the way it goes. Sometimes you're flush and sometimes you're bust. And when you're up, it's never as good as it seems, and when you're down, you never think you're gonna be up again. But life goes on; remember that. Money isn't real—it doesn't matter. It only seems like it does."

—*Blow, 2001*

Folding and refolding the crumpled waybill, Wanda repeatedly heard Julia's departing words reverberate off the stairwell walls.

Your co-operation or your resignation! Your co-operation or your resignation! Your co-operation or your...

The statement hung in the air as she sat motionless on the concrete stairs, unaware of the time as the minutes clicked by and the hands of the clock slowly inched their way toward the noon hour.

———————

Back in her own office, Julia settled in behind her desk with a cup of coffee, two Tylenol tablets, and an ever-growing stack of messages.

"What in the hell was that about?" Boyd bounded through her door.

"Nothing." She threw back the painkillers and washed them down with a swig of freshly brewed coffee. "Just a little office politics is all."

"Well, it looked like hell from where I was standing. What, you two have some kind of bitch fight?"

"I don't *bitch fight* with company employees," she curtly reminded her husband. "And besides, when did you decide to get so involved with the little everyday stuff?"

"When it goes running up and down the hall."

"Yeah," Julia finally conceded with a smirk, "I guess we looked pretty stupid."

"Come on, level with me." Boyd picked up her cup and helped himself to a sip. "I feel like a junior partner who's been shut out of the big meeting."

"Well, our little Miss Wanda Finkel wants to continue playing her game of ostrich, is all. I guess her visit to the Pocahontas set was a little much for her, cuz ever since last Friday, she's suddenly decided she doesn't want to get any further involved in the company than her paper duties as purchasing agent."

"Oh, I see." He moved up toward his wife's desk and took a seat in one of her guest chairs. "She wants to keep her head in the sand and pretend she doesn't work for a company that makes porn, right?"

"Abso-fucking-lutely." Julia threw her head back and rubbed her temples.

"You know, she's not one of us," Boyd gently reminded his wife. "Wanda has no background in porn. Nothing! Zippo! Remember, she was just working the phones before Pete got the idea to promote her to his private secretary."

"Yeah, but she's so damned good at her purchasing job that I sometimes forget."

"Me, too," Boyd admitted. "And I'm sure her first screening of our lemon pudding video back in the editing room, while she watched our girls fuckin' and suckin' in the hot tub, was quite an eye opener. Then we drag her out to the set to experience it live. Poor kid." He shook his head, disappointed at his own insensitivity. "She was probably wondering what the hell's next. Shit, we probably scared the living fuck out of her. Bet she's worried that she's might be tied up and raped for the cameras, too."

"Maybe it's time for a new company policy? Everyone has to have worked in the porn industry in one form or another. What you think?" Julia suddenly sat up straight in her chair. "We could fire Wanda and replace her with that *fluffier* we used last year who kept pissing on the floor every time she watched a guy shoot his load. Remember her?" she began to giggle. "We'd have to pull out all the carpet and replace it all with tile, but think of what we'd save in coffee breaks. The woman would never have to leave her office to take a leak."

"And the kid with the ten inch cock, and the crossed eyes— remember him?" Boyd howled, joining in on the joke. "He could take over Martin's job down in editing. Think of the money he'd save us, too. That kid could watch the playback with one eye and keep the other on the sound levels without even breaking a sweat."

Tension released, Julia finally settled back down and took a long hard look at her husband. "It's getting to be a lot harder than we'd ever imagined. Isn't it?"

"It's definitely more complicated," he agreed. "When we lived hand to mouth, it seemed like our biggest worry was our next score. Now I stay up at night, worrying about re-shoots, client financing, and a whole bunch of other shit that has absolutely nothing to do with making good porn."

"I know. I agree. What happened to the plan to make classy little videos financed by the rich and famous, for a tidy little profit?"

"I don't have a fucking clue," Boyd walked over to his wife's bar cart. "I always thought that once the money started rolling in, we'd run more like big business and less like triple X."

"Oh no, not us," Julia joined her husband in a glass of port. "We've got all the problems of a growing Fortune-500 company, and all the bullshit of a backroom peep show. What in the hell are we going to do?" She returned to her desk before turning to look out her office window.

"You," Wanda interjected, "are going to let the people who know about running a corporation handle the business end, and you're going to let the people who know about filming sex handle the porn end. That's what you're going to do," she boldly stated from her position in Julia's doorway. "We all have different strengths and weaknesses, and what makes a good business really great is capitalizing on your employee's positive strengths, not focusing on their abject weaknesses."

Julia's gaze suddenly shifted from Wanda's face, to her husband's, and then back out her office window.

"You're absolutely right." She straightened a picture frame on her rear credenza before slowly turning her body back toward to her desk. "I definitely know how to find talent. Boyd knows how to direct, and you know how to organize and run the office. Together, we can fuckin' take this town by storm."

"I agree," Wanda smiled wholeheartedly. "As long as we capitalize on what we know and don't bang our heads against a wall, trying to understand what we don't, I believe we've got nowhere to go but up."

Boyd lifted his glass and toasted both women. "Amen," he smiled, as there was really nothing else left to add.

———————

It had taken Ronnie and Jerome a good hour to make their way to the neighborhood elementary school, only to realize it was Sunday afternoon and the playground gate was firmly locked. Frustrated and angered by their stupidity, the boys turned tail and headed down the block to a neighboring park, relieved to see the playground littered with small groups of children.

Within fifteen minutes, they'd managed to sell their half pack of cigarettes to a couple ten year olds for a grand total of nine dollars and twenty-five cents. Enough for little more than a second package, they hit the sidewalk and trudged back to the closest corner store to replenish their supply.

By the time they returned, word had spread throughout the playground and the minute they stepped onto the sand, they had the attention of the entire park. Unfortunately, a wary parent brandishing a cell phone was also watching them as she deliberately made her presence known, circling the playground on some kind of volunteer patrol.

"This isn't going to work," Ronnie sneered. "Anyone of these kids comes up and talks to us, that bitch is going to call it in. We gotta move." He shook his head in disgust.

"Ah, fuck me." Jerome grabbed his friend's arm. "I'm tired, I'm hungry, and this is bullshit! We're only selling smokes. What's the harm?"

"Don't rag on me," Ronnie hissed back. "I'm not the one itching to dial 911."

Cutting directly across a grassy field, they made their escape to the relief of the parent, and the disappointment of many of the children.

"Now what?" Jerome continued to rag on his best friend. "We gonna look for more kids?" he anxiously stroked the cellophane covered cigarette pack nestled deep within his right hand pocket.

Too disgusted to speak, Ronnie just picked up the pace, silently praying that the earth would open up, and swallow Jerome in one giant gulp.

"What about the mall? We's got enough change to grab a bus and head downtown. Mall's full of kids on a Sunday afternoon. We could sell the smokes there."

"Security's too tight," he barked. "We'll be busted for sure."

"Then what?"

"Just follow me," Ronnie turned to bark at his friend, also dying to rip open the pack and light up smoke.

As they continued to trudge down the street, the smell of freshly roasted chicken stopped them both dead in their tracks. The restaurant's departing lunch crowd carrying the lingering aromas back out onto the sidewalk after having consumed their fill.

"Fuck, that smells good," Jerome couldn't help but mutter. "I'm so goddamn hungry that my stomach thinks my throat's been slit. It's been hours and hours since breakfast. I gotta eat again."

"Don't think about it." Ronnie grabbed his friend and attempted to propel him down the sidewalk, fully aware that their bodies were desperately craving a lot of solid nutrition after three days of ingesting nothing more than draft beer and crystal meth.

"I can't go anymore," Jerome literally cried.

Barely enough strength to pull himself forward, Ronnie couldn't imagine where in the hell he was supposed to find the energy to take care of Jerome.

"Look bud," he turned to face him head on. "We ain't got the cash to eat right now, so standing around here and hoping and praying it was different ain't going to change shit. So let's keep moving and find a place to scalp these smokes. We do it a few more times, and we might have enough to buy a couple dime bags. We'll sell those, and then maybe we'll have enough for a few more. We keep doing it all night, and by tomorrow morning we'll have worked our way up to an eight ball of coke."

"An eight ball, really?" Jerome bobbed his head in agreement, having forgotten that the idea was originally his.

"We sell an eight ball or two, and then we're making some decent profit. We can think about getting something to eat and maybe looking for a place to crash. You with me?"

Following in Ronnie's footsteps as he had since he was a child, Jerome silently nodded in agreement, forcing his feet to slowly shuffle down the sidewalk.

By the time the clock struck noon on Monday, Ronnie has managed to sell his third eight ball and had already tucked away a hard-earned seventy-five dollar profit.

"Wake up," he roughly shook Jerome's shoulder.

"What time is it?" he struggled to extract himself from his impromptu hiding place behind a metal dumpster.

"Dinner time," Ronnie roughly yanked him to his feet. "We got enough profit, so let's go eat."

"Steak and eggs? I was dreaming about a T-bone with little potatoes and …"

"Burgers," he shook his head. "One a piece, and we're gonna share some fries."

"Gravy?" Jerome brushed some clinging garbage off his dirty jeans, unwilling to give up without a fight.

She wasn't exactly sure how the social worker from the hospital had managed to pull it off, but Lillian had found herself staying in Brandy's apartment with Tito happily playing at her feet.

"Guess we gotta go shopping," Brandy tossed the food stamps down on the kitchen table.

"I guess we should," Lillian agreed, closing the empty refrigerator door. "You got a pen and paper I can borrow? I wanna make a list before we head out."

Brandy tossed her a message pad and dug through her purse for something to write with.

"Diapers, milk, bread, and eggs. How you set for toilet paper and dish soap?" She stood up and walked over to peer under the sink."

"You better have a look around," Brandy shook her head. "I never really cooked much, and ever since my sister moved out; I ain't been much into cleaning.

"Holy shit?" Lillian gasped after accidentally opening what she assumed to be a broom closet.

"Told you I've been stripping for awhile." Brandy stepped over and lovingly stroked the closet stuffed full of glittery costumes. "I just don't have the heart to throw any of them out. They all got memories." She shrugged. "Some good, some bad, but they're all mine. You know what I mean?"

"I hear you," she nodded, heart sinking as she was suddenly reminded of all her lost belongings. "You know," Lillian forced herself to change the topic, "I still can't believe she let me keep Tito."

"Well, what in the fuck else was the woman gonna do? Take the kid home herself?"

Both Lillian and eventually Brandy had nervously sat in the hospital, quietly listening as the social worker contacted a handful of shelters and six prospective foster homes, finally coming to the realization that Tito was truly in need of *emergency housing*. Without any other options, she'd reluctantly helped Lillian fill out a handful of forms, and after a rushed home visit to Brandy's two bedroom apartment, they'd come to a workable agreement.

"He can stay with you on a temporary basis, as long as the lessee," she looked directly at Brandy, "is willing to provide shelter at a reasonable cost. We will provide food stamps, along with a clothing, and housing allowance."

Lillian had been thrilled with the development, still surprised that Brandy was willing to open her home to a near stranger and a two-year-old child.

"But I must warn you, Lillian," the social worker had sternly interjected. "This is a temporary situation, and I will be actively researching a more permanent residence for your nephew."

Lillian had quickly agreed, anxious to get on with it and settle into her new accommodations.

"I'll swing back after checking in with a few of your old neighbors and co-workers," the woman had promised her, handing each girl one of her business cards. "Please don't let me down," she almost begged. "I'm really going out on a limb here."

"We'll be fine," Brandy promised. "She's a good mama, and I don't mind her crashing for awhile. Trust me, they'll be all right."

Shaking hands for the last time, the social worker had departed, finally leaving the girls alone with Tito as he played in the middle of the living room rug.

"You're gonna have to drop me off at the club," Brandy had suddenly announced. "I'm working this afternoon, but you can keep the car and do whatever shopping you need to. All right?"

"No, I can't" she suddenly turned to carefully pluck Tito off the floor, conscious of his bruises and sore shoulder. "I can't drive your car."

"Why not?"

"Well, I can't drive nobody's car," Lillian sheepishly admitted. "I never learned to drive. Nobody in my family's ever had a car."

"Holy fuck, child. You raised in the jungle?" Brandy plopped down into a kitchen chair. "You never had a license?"

"Nope." She took a second to wipe Tito's face.

"Cookie," he muttered, one of the few words he'd been able to master.

"Well, guess we better get some grub before the kid's bellybutton rubs a blister on his backbone," Brandy conceded.

"What about your shift? Didn't you just say that you needed to head down to the club?"

"Fuck 'em. I could use a day off. Haven't had one in…" She stopped to flip through her mental calendar, "I don't know when," Brandy admitted. "Think they're gonna have to find someone else to fill up the holes in Big Daddy's schedule."

"Good for you," Lillian smiled. "Today we shop for diapers for Tito. Tomorrow we shop for a life for you. How's that sound?"

"Sounds good to me," Brandy agreed, grabbing her purse off the table.

By the time the women had spent their fistful of food stamps, the car was filled to the roof with diapers, three bags of groceries, and a handful of second-hand toys and outfits.

"If Tito could talk, he would definitely say thank you for all your help." Lillian bent over the car seat and worked to strap in the wiggling child.

"You know, none of us had car seats when we were kids," Brandy announced. "Do you think they really do any good?"

"I'm not sure. But the social worker was pretty definite about us taking this loaner from her office."

"Say, you mind if I stop by Cheeks on the way home? I should at least let Big Daddy know that I won't be coming in this afternoon."

"Good idea," Lillian agreed, realizing that two unemployed strippers wasn't exactly a good idea.

By the time they'd driven back to Brandy's apartment, the social worker was already waiting for them by the front door. "Mrs. Jones," Lillian said as she stepped out of the car, Tito attempting to follow by wiggling out of his restraints. "I didn't expect you back so soon. Did you get a chance to speak to my old landlord?"

"Let's go inside." The social worker helped carry in one of the grocery bags.

Brandy busied herself stuffing the food into her cupboards, barely paying attention to what went where.

"So what did my landlord say?" Lillian sat her nephew down in front of a small selection of Tupperware bowls.

"According to your neighbors, your ex-boyfriend brought over a couple friends a few nights ago, and within an hour, they'd loaded everything up in their trucks and moved it to an undisclosed location. The landlord has also confirmed that your rent wasn't paid and as far as he's concerned, you skipped out on your lease during a midnight move and he's within his rights to keep your cash deposit to help cover the cost of the used appliances.

"They weren't friends," Lillian mumbled, her heart breaking as the reality of the situation began to sink in. "He sold all my stuff."

"To who?" Brandy stepped back into the living room.

"To whoever," she said and wiped a single tear. "Whoever could load it up the quickest I guess."

"All your stuff," Brandy fought to get a handle on the situation. "Everything's gone?"

"Looks that way." Lillian grabbed a tissue and roughly swiped at her nose. "Oh well, easy come, easy go."

"But it wasn't easy, was it?" The social worker couldn't help but offer her sympathies. "You probably worked really hard for all your belongings, and now they've been stolen from you without warning. I bet you're devastated. Aren't you?"

"You sure it was everything?" Lillian dropped down into the

cushions on the couch. "He even took all my clothes and my dishes?" She was unsure what in the world he'd do with her skirts, tank tops, and cooking pots.

"Everything," the social worker confirmed.

"Don't worry about clothes," Brandy laughed, "I got more shit than I'll ever be able to wear in my lifetime."

"We're not just talking about clothes, are we?" Mrs. Jones walked across the living room and took a seat opposite Lillian. "I assume all your personal memories of your family and your past life was in your apartment, were they not?"

"Mostly," she choked out and dropped her face into her hands, the tears finally released.

"A fresh start," Brandy said in an attempt to look at the bright side.

"But I've lost everything," Lillian cried through her fingers, her sudden burst of emotion startling Tito as he began to whimper.

"Don't cry, baby," Brandy leaned down and scooped up the child to the social worker's delight, relieved to see both women exhibiting signs of maternal instincts.

"How about we all have a cup of coffee?" the social worker suggested in her most soothing voice.

Both girls nodded, strangely comforted by the looming mother figure suddenly in their midst.

CHAPTER TWENTY-FOUR

"I know I gotta keep breathing, because tomorrow the sun will rise, and you'll never know what the tide will bring."

—Castaway, 2000

W arren found it rather amusing as he watched his daughter struggle to cut her lasagna into bite-sized pieces without marking her freshly painted nails.

"You know we have supper at six. Why'd you paint them right before we ate?"

"Oh Dad. In your perfectly ordered little life, haven't you ever lost track of time and done something without checking your timetable first?"

Amber was sounding more and more like her mother with each passing day.

"No," he laughed, "So you want me to cut up your food for you?"

"I'm fine." She hooked her fork under the top layer of noodles and flipped the cheese-baked mouthful right past her gums.

"Well, that's one way to do it," Warren focused his attention back on his own plate. "So tell me," he asked between mouthfuls of Caesar salad, "how was your weekend?"

"Not that bad."

"Really?" he stopped chewing. "We talking about the same two days?"

"Saturday and Sunday, right?" She scraped up the white layer of ricotta cheese and began shoveling the filling directly into her mouth. "It was fine."

Slowly wiping his face with his dinner napkin, Warren carefully debated his next statement. "Your mother called me, complaining about you calling her *Aunt Flo*."

Amber giggled, amused at her own wordplay.

"You gotta cut that woman a little slack. She's really stressed, and every time you give her a hard time, she picks up the phone and passes it on to me."

"I'll cut her a little slack," Amber set down her fork, "but I want you to level with me first."

Pushing his plate aside, Warren looked across the table at his daughter, surprised to notice that his thirteen year old was somehow morphing into a young adult. The transformation was more than a little unsettling.

"Dad, tell me why you and Mom really got divorced."

Warren swallowed hard, unsure of where to start. "You know Mom and I hadn't been getting along for quite a few years. I guess… after awhile… we just decided that we'd be happier sharing custody, yet living apart."

"I know that," Amber groaned. "I've heard that speech a thousand times. I wanna know the real reason."

"The real reason?"

"Yeah, like what's her name, and are you guys still seeing each other in private?"

Rising from the table, Warren nervously began clearing off the dirty dishes.

"I'm not a child, Dad. You don't have to worry about shocking me. Just level with me," she coaxed. "Was she married too?"

"Amber," he suddenly returned to his seat at the table. "Your mother has been convinced for years that the reason our marriage failed was because I was in love with another woman."

"And..." she waved her hand to encourage him on.

"And she was wrong. I wasn't having an affair, and unfortunately, our marriage fell apart all on its own merit."

Amber contemplated her dad's last statement, unwilling to just throw in the towel and just give up. "Okay," she rose from her chair. "Let's just say I believe you, and you weren't having an affair. Why is Mom absolutely convinced that you were?"

"I don't know," he said and shook his head side to side. "She has no proof! I never strayed from our marriage bed. I was a hundred percent faithful, and to be honest, even though it's none of your business, my dear, I haven't even slept with another woman since our divorce."

"I know," Amber joked. "It's kinda like living in a monastery around here."

"What, you think I should date?"

"Yes... no..., I don't know, Dad. I guess I'm just telling you that I wouldn't freak out if you wanted to take some woman to the movies or for a pizza."

"Thank you," he graciously smiled. "I'm glad I have your permission, my dear."

Slowly pulling away from her father's impromptu embrace, Amber stopped dead in her own tracks and carefully spun around.

"Dad," her facial features suddenly softened to that of a trusting child. "Is there someone you would like to be with, but haven't found the guts to tell them yet?"

Wanda awoke with a yearning to attack her job with renewed vigor. The first to arrive at the office early Tuesday morning, she spent the first two hours reorganizing the message center, not a small feat when you considered five different sub-offices and three private secretaries dumped all their incoming into one area for distribution.

After she was finally satisfied with her first task, Wanda focused her attention on the company's shooting schedules. It was always a balancing act to keep the local businessmen happy. Car commercials and neighborhood restaurant openings were not feature presentations, but they were a solid piece of Giovanni's bottom line. And they too required film crews, supplies, and costuming that had to be ordered in conjunction with their personal timetables. It had been only two and a half years since Julia and Boyd had chosen to diversify, but for many a month since the decision, the advertising department had kept the financial wheels of Giovanni Films rolling.

By the time the office started to buzz, Wanda was already knee deep in a month's worth of supply lists, location shoots, and product release dates.

"Excuse me, Wanda," her secretary announced from the office door. "I know you asked me to hold all you incoming calls, but I have the Community Clinic on the line. They'd like to talk to you about one of our regulars who'd just come in for routine testing."

"About their health?"

"I guess so," she shrugged.

"Boyd or Julia in yet?"

"No. You're the highest ranking employee on the floor."

Taking a deep breath, Wanda turned to stare at her phone. "All right, put the call through."

"Hello, this is Nurse Borden, calling from the Community Clinic," a pleasant voice announced over the line.

"What can I do for you, ma'am?"

"Well, usually we just mail back your company's test results, but on this particular file, the doctor felt it prudent to contact your office as soon as the test results were verified."

"Is it HIV?"

"Oh no, nothing that serious," the nurse reassured her. "But NGU is highly contagious, and in your company's line of work, it's imperative that we act on these kinds of results as soon as possible."

"NGU?"

"Non-Gonococcal Urethritis—or in layman's terms, a bacterial infection of the throat."

"Is it like strep throat?"

"Not exactly," the nurse attempted to explain. "These kinds of infections are usually brought on   by unprotected oral sex, either with the patient directly, or with someone they've had direct contact with."

"What should we do about it?"

"Well, the patient is usually prescribed seven days worth of Doxycycline as a precaution and is normally able to return to work within a week. However, in your business, we'd more than likely suggest a two-week sick leave to ensure a full recovery and no further spread of the infection.

"I want to thank you for calling," Wanda grabbed her employee register file to record the name of the infected actress. "Is it Cassidy or Melanie," she randomly guessed aloud.

"Actually, it's not a female."

"Malcolm?"

"It's… let me see," the nurse flipped through the paper file. "It's Boyd Giovanni."

"Boyd?" Wanda repeated in utter shock.

"Yes," the nurse checked her file a third time. "Would you like me to schedule an appointment for Mr. Giovanni to come by and see the doctor for his prescription?"

"No, I don't think so," Wanda began unconsciously gnawing on her plastic pen. "I think I'll need to check with Mr. Giovanni first before scheduling any appointments."

"That's fine. Why don't you call us back at your convenience," the nurse said as she began to close her file.

"One more thing," Wanda stalled on the line. "Is it at all possible that your lab might have made a mistake and assigned the results from another patient to Mr. Giovanni's file?"

"Well, anything's possible, Miss Finkel, but to be honest, highly unlikely. All our lab work is double-tagged with file registration numbers and bar codes. Maybe you'd feel more comfortable if the doctor called you personally to verify the results?"

"No," she finally conceded. "And thank you for calling. I'll take it from here."

He couldn't be sure whether it was the boredom or the cravings that were starting to gnaw on his nerves, but Pete was beginning to climb the walls. He'd been stuck in his self-imposed cell for a whole week, and in retrospect, he was actually disappointed with his results.

In the first week of his stay, Pete expected to be so physically sick that he'd be consumed by his pain. Moaning and groaning, begging for relief as he thrashed about on his mattress, the days would somehow meld into one another.

The second phase would be a time of enlightenment, a time of spiritual and mental awakening as he came to understand his personal weaknesses and his unrealized potential. After twenty-eight days, he'd resurface a better man. Stronger for his time in exile with a deeper understanding of his addiction and the pain it had caused everyone around him.

That's what he had expected.

Instead, one week later, Pete had found himself relatively pain free and no closer to understanding his addiction than the day he'd first strolled down the basement stairs.

———————

"Is Boyd inside?" Wanda nervously stood outside his closed door, silently praying that he'd been inadvertently tied up outside the office.

"He's in with his wife," his secretary cheerfully announced. "Would you like me to let him know you're waiting?"

"Oh no, this can wait." She quickly spun on her heels and headed back to the privacy of her own office.

By the time Boyd appeared at her door, Wanda had managed to bury herself so deep in company paperwork that she never even heard him knock.

"Heard you were looking for me," he said as he swung open the door and casually made his way inside Wanda's inner sanctum.

"Oh, Boyd," she nearly jumped out of her chair. "I didn't hear you."

"Sorry." He set down his half-empty coffee cup. "My secretary said you stopped by, so I thought I'd return the favor and this time I'd make the trip."

Rising to her feet, Wanda slipped around her desk, and discreetly closed her office door.

"Oh, I see this is going to be a private moment," he started to tease, enjoying her slight discomfort as she began fidgeting with a lock of her curly hair.

"I... I uh..." she continued to stammer, unable to verbalize her thoughts.

"Is something the matter, Wanda?" her boss suddenly shifted his tone.

"I have something for you," she yanked the handwritten note out of her pocket and thrust the message toward her boss.

"NGU?" he repeated as if reading a coded message.

"Non-Gonococcal Urethritis," Wanda blurted out as if the words had been fighting to be freed.

"I take it this is from the Changeroom?"

"Community Clinic," she politely corrected him.

"Then what's Doxy... cycline?" He continued to decipher the wrinkled paper.

"It's the necessary prescription you need to clear up your bacterial throat infection."

Color draining from his face, Boyd stuffed the paper deep into the front pocket of his suit pants.

"Anything else?" he demanded in a sharp voice.

"No. Well, yes," Wanda stammered.

"Well what?"

"They said it was extremely contagious, and you should make an appointment to pick up your prescription as soon as possible."

"Is that all?"

"Yes sir," she obediently returned to her seat as if just dismissed by a grade school teacher.

"Then, thank you for your discretion." Boyd forced himself to look Wanda straight in the eye, leaving little doubt that the topic was never to be broached again.

Mindlessly tapping the shifter of his sapphire blue Corvette, Boyd sat in the underground parking lot and contemplated his next move.

His gut told him he could trust Wanda emphatically, but he'd still have to come up with a reasonable excuse for his wife. The doctor had been explicit about *no deep throat kissing* for two weeks until the infection had passed, and as for their nightly cocktail hour, that was also now *contraindicated*.

"Fuck me," he swore, reaching down into his pocket to retrieve one of the plastic pill bottles. "One tablet to be ingested every twenty-four hours with food or low fat milk for seven days," he read aloud. "One hundred milligrams per tablet. No refills."

Realizing it wasn't exactly the kind of prescription he wanted Julia to find in his possession; Boyd unlocked his glove box and tossed one of the bottles inside. Reluctantly plucking his cell phone out of his breast pocket, he sucked in a giant breath of air and dialed his wife.

"Julia Giovanni," she answered.

"It's me." Boyd pasted a smile on his face, praying his nervousness didn't translate over the phone. "Doesn't look like I'll be making it for supper tonight. Still got a shit load of stuff to take care of, so you go ahead and eat without me. Okay, hon?"

"Fine by me." Julia quickly changed hands with the receiver as she fought to right the huge pile of files threatening to spill over onto her office floor. "I'm still trying to figure out who we're going to hire for the Dubois shoot. It's taking a lot longer than I thought it would."

"Did you talk to those twin dicks from Houston?"

"Dallas," she absentmindedly corrected her husband.

"Whatever. You get a hold of those little pricks yet?"

"Yeah, but wouldn't you know that they've doubled their rates and won't even consider my offer unless we fly them both in first class and put them up in a five star hotel for two weeks."

"It's gonna take us two whole weeks to shoot this project?"

"Hell no," Julia laughed. "But they still want a fourteen day stay on the Giovanni tab."

"Fuck them," Boyd ordered, feeling more in control by the second. "You can't tell me that those two little assholes are the only *boy toys* on our books. Who else we got around twenty?"

"Being the right age isn't enough," Julia reminded him for the second time that day. "They've gotta have the right look, and be uncut. Remember?"

"I know, I know," he abruptly cut her off. "Twelve or thirteen max. Right?"

"Right. So what time you think you'll be done?" she switched the topic back to their original conversation. "Cuz I'm not that hungry. So if you want, I'll wait for you and we can grab a late bite."

"Three, maybe four hours," he said, taking a wild guess. "Don't wait, sweetie. I can't promise anything definite right now."

"All right. Then call me later." She prepared to hang up the phone.

"You know I love you, Julia."

"I love you, too," she answered back, his sudden declaration throwing her a little off guard.

Switching off his phone, Boyd tossed it down onto the passenger seat before slamming his six-speed into reverse. Racing out of the parking lot, he headed straight for the origin of his latest problem.

CHAPTER TWENTY-FIVE

"What do you know? There is life on this planet."
—What Women Want, 2000

It had taken little or no effort to acquaint Tito with his temporary lodgings in Brandy's two-bedroom apartment. Having already moved countless times in his young life, his roots were rather shallow and out of necessity, he'd already taught himself to adapt quickly to any new surroundings.

"Supper's ready," Lillian called out, carrying Tito over to the table while Brandy shook her head, still struggling to wrap up her telephone call.

"If she checks in, I promise I'll let you know," she solemnly vowed for the third time in the last five minutes.

Watching the ice cubes dissolve in Tito's bowl of soup, Lillian quickly cut up two pieces of sandwich meat and dropped the pieces into another plastic bowl.

"Here you go, sweetie," she said as she handed him the meat.

Snatching up a fistful and shoving it directly into his mouth, Tito took the opportunity to reach for a second helping, obviously not willing to take a chance that someone else might eat his food before he'd even a chance to swallow his first portion.

"Well, he don't waste no time, does he?" Brandy smirked as she slid into an empty chair at the table.

"No, he doesn't," Lillian gingerly handed her a steaming bowl of canned tomato soup. "I know what it's like," she suddenly offered in his defense. "Never really getting enough, you tend to shovel it in as fast as you can."

"But he's so young."

"Even little kids know what it's like to be hungry."

Before Brandy could swallow her first spoonful of soup, the phone began to ring again.

"Ignore it," she commanded, shaking her head in frustration as the ringing continued to interrupt their first meal together.

"Maybe I should get it?"

"No. It's just my sister's ex. He can't get it through his fucking head that she's moved out, and I don't have a new number for her yet. He keeps harassing me. He calls from the minute he gets home from work, 'til he falls asleep at night. That guy's driving me fuckin'nuts."

"So what should we do about it? I don't think I'll be able to put Tito down with the phone ringing off the hook all night?"

"Before we go to bed I'll unplug it, but right now, I'm kind of waiting for a call."

Doing their best to ignore the incessant ringing, both women busied themselves with making their own sandwiches.

"You think your sister will be back soon?" Lillian asked between bites.

"I doubt it. She found a new guy who'd just come into some kind of inheritance money, so realistically, I don't expect to see hide nor hair of her 'til the well runs dry."

"More," Tito pushed his empty bowl toward Lillian.

"First, eat some soup," she poured the cooked liquid into his sippy-cup and set it down within his reach.

Grabbing the plastic handle, Tito tipped it straight back and began sucking down mouthfuls of his soup, small rivulets escaping the corners of his mouth and splattering down the sides of the kitchen chair. "Sorry about the mess. I'll clean it up the second we're done."

Reaching for yet another piece of fresh white bread, Brandy quickly fixed herself a second sandwich while Lillian stood up to grab a wet cloth for Tito's face.

"What you gonna do with the kid when we both have to work?"

"Mrs. Jones said I could drop him at the hospital day care during the day, but they have a six hour maximum, so I'll have to make some other plans if shooting looks like it's going to run late."

Carrying her second sandwich to the kitchen counter, Brandy grabbed the plastic wrap and quickly rolled up her leftovers, planning to brown bag it for work.

"It's none of my business, mind you, but I was just wondering if you really think it's a good idea to try and raise that kid on your own."

"It's just temporary," Lillian quickly reminded her.

"I know that's what the social worker said, but I also know that nobody's lining up to adopt little homeless kids from the wrong side of the tracks. Trust me," she said, knowingly nodding her head. "I'm sure the kid's file is gonna read *junkie mother, and unknown father,* and when it gets right down to it, nobody wants a black crack baby."

"Tito's not a crack baby," Lillian quickly jumped to his defense. "Cause I don't think Gloria would use when she was pregnant," she stopped for a second to evaluate her proclamation "And besides, Tito's not just back, he's half Cree too. Remember?"

Brandy just sighed. "Look, it really don't matter what he is or what he ain't. It's how they got him labeled that really tells the story, and as far as I can tell, the poor kid's already been saddled with a bad tag."

Shoving the key into the apartment's deadbolt, Boyd slowly pushed open the door, mindful of the toys that would be scattered like trip mines all over the living room floor.

"Daddy," a voice called out the second his feet crossed the threshold.

"Ain't daddy, its uncle Boyd," he called back.

"Hey," a woman's voice answered from the kitchen. "You bring some beer? It's as hot as a fucking oven in here and I could sure use a cold one."

"No." He covered his mouth when he coughed, suddenly mindful of spreading his germs to the kids. "I forgot, but I'll leave you a few bucks before I go."

"Well, you hungry then?"

"Nah, I'm fine." He picked up his youngest nephew and wandered through the apartment, casually checking for any signs of another man.

"You hear anything from Pete lately?"

"Not a word." Boyd finally made his way into the kitchen. "Must be lying low, trying to dry out."

"Well, that's fucking great. Got me the electrical and the rent all past due, and that no good son of a bitch is nowhere to be found."

"Here you go." He handed Maxine a wad of twenty-dollar bills. "Should cover what you're short."

"What I'm short?" she began to cuss. "Well, I'm short my fucking man. You bring me that? You find me my man?" she continued to shout as her voice started to crack.

"No, just a little cash to help out 'til my brother comes back. So calm the fuck down."

"Sorry Boyd. I know it ain't your problem to cover your brother's bills," she mouthed the words, while stuffing the twenties down into the depths of her bra.

"He'll make good."

"Wanna shot?" she walked over and pulled a half bottle of vodka out of her fridge freezer.

"Sure," he said, setting down the child before rising to pluck two glasses from the drain board.

"I really didn't expect to see you 'til next week."

"Well, I needed to talk to you about something." He downed his initial drink, sucking in a deep breath of air as the vodka splashed down into his empty stomach, vaguely conscious of the fact that he was supposed to be abstaining from alcohol until his infection had cleared.

"Here's mud in your eye," Maxine offered the toast before draining her glass.

Stalling while he poured himself a second drink, Boyd finally set down the bottle and picked up his glass. "You remember that night a couple weeks ago when I stopped by to tell you Pete was in rehab and we both got real pissed?"

"Sure." Maxine winked, taking a second to move a strand of greasy hair back behind her right ear.

"Well, you kinda gave me a bad case of Chlamydia of the throat that night and…"

"What'd you say I gave you?"

"Doctors call it NGU. Non… gono… something or another." He waved his hands in the air. "It's a really, super bad, throat infection."

"You made a special trip downtown cuz I gave you a fucking cold when we were necking in the kitchen?" She laughed, actually amused that her brother-in-law suddenly took his health so seriously.

"It ain't just a cold," he tried to explain. "Without the right treatment, it can spread to your organs and you can get really, really, fuckin' sick."

"What makes you sure you got it from me?" She turned away to nervously clear her throat.

"Here's the thing," he said and set down his glass, waving off Maxine's attempt to fill it for a third time. "Other than Julia, you're the only person I've touched in a long time, and the doctor says it has to have been in the last thirty days. Well, since my wife ain't sick, I thought..."

"So!" She walked over and pulled her son away from the cat's water bowl. "You come here to yell at me or what?" Maxine struggled to stifle her nagging cough.

"No, I just come here to give you these," he pulled a bottle of pills out of his suit pocket. "You gotta take one a day for the next seven days or it won't get any better."

"But they've got your name on the bottle." She shoved it back in his face.

"Well, what the fuck was I supposed to do? Give Julia's doctor your name so he could type it up all neat and tidy on the bottle? I had to bullshit the guy as it was to get two prescriptions of the same shit. One for you, and one for me."

"I guess." She leaned over, setting the plastic bottle on top of her microwave.

"And for the next two weeks, try not to kiss your kids or anybody else. Don't want them getting sick, too."

"This don't sound like no cough I've ever had before."

"That's cuz it ain't," Boyd stepped over to the sink and set his dirty glass down amidst the other dishes.

"You ain't gonna tell Pete, are you?"

"Just take the pills," Boyd started walking toward the front door.

"If I gave it to you, someone else must'a gave it to me."

"Just worry about you and your kids for now. All right?" he asked before turning to make his way to the apartment door.

Maxine nodded, her fingers already reaching down into her bra to retrieve the wad and count out her cash.

―――――――

Phone unplugged, Tito fast asleep in the spare bed, Lillian and Brandy sat together on the couch and watched the 1962 version of *Lawrence of Arabia*.

"If they're out in the desert and it's like two hundred degrees," Brandy thought out loud, "why do they always wear so many fucking layers of robes?"

"I've always wondered about that, too."

"And what about those camels? I heard their humps are full of water and they don't have to drink anything for a month at a time. You think that's true?"

"I don't have a clue," Lillian twisted her head side to side, lifting her arms in an attempt to stretch out her tightened shoulders. "But I have to confess. I've always wondered what it would be like to be one of those Arabian princesses, someone who lies around on satin pillows all day, eating grapes and waiting for the King to come home and visit her tent."

"Does sound like fun," Brandy laughed. "But don't those kinds of Kings have like a hundred wives at the same time."

"Yeah, I think they do."

"Sounds to me like you'd end up spending most your time with a bunch of other wives."

"Fine by me," Lillian plucked a tissue off the end table and waved it seductively under her eyes, attempting to imitate a veil of silk

Brandy's next sentence caught in her throat, her excitement

suddenly rendering her speechless. Lillian was an absolutely gorgeous young woman, and as she continued with her playacting, Brandy could barely stop herself from reaching out to touch her.

"You think I should wear a veil too?" she teased.

"Uh... no," Brandy suddenly jumped up and made her way into the kitchen.

Nervously stuffing the unused tissue back into the box, Lillian jumped up and clicked off the television, wondering what she'd done to offend her hostess.

"Is something the matter?" she padded into the kitchen, accidentally banging her hip against the counter as she tried to negotiate her way in the semidarkness.

"No, it's cool," Brandy whispered back, bathed in the bluish glow of the city's streetlights.

"Why'd you leave then?"

Taking the small step necessary to bring their bodies face to face, Brandy surprised herself by reaching out and gently touching Lillian's left cheek.

"You're so beautiful," she purred, her beating heart instantly betraying her arousal.

"You're beautiful, too," Lillian responded, not sure if it was appropriate, yet suddenly willing to take the chance.

Slowly moving her hand from the young girl's cheek down to the nape of her neck, Brandy found her fingers gently tracing the delicate line of Lillian's collarbone.

"You can stop me anytime you want to," she announced in a husky whisper, fingers gently brushing Lillian's hair back behind her shoulder blades.

"I will," was Lillian's only reply.

———————

Since Giovanni Films demanded quarterly physicals and monthly blood tests for all their talent, Boyd and Julia had decided to set an example and follow the same regimen. These monthly screenings had done their job, catching Boyd's *little problem* and most likely saving him from spreading a serious bacterial infection to his wife. Still, the results and subsequent treatment had brought him little comfort.

"When are you gonna fucking grow up?" he began verbally berating himself, his sports car zipping in and out of the early evening traffic.

No matter how hard he tried to understand his own actions, he couldn't believe that he'd actually shared spit with a woman like Maxine. She was the epitome of white trash.

An alcoholic who just happened to pop out a kid or two after hooking up with his brother Pete, Maxine had little more than an eighth grade education and zero career aspirations. Abandoned by her first husband, she now lived off Pete's handouts, his cash feeding all her kids, even though only one of the brood appeared to carry any of Pete's DNA.

To date, Boyd still hadn't figured out how a woman like that had managed to hook up with someone like his brother. For reasons he couldn't understand, Pete obviously had chosen to ignore his penchant for twenty-year-old busty blondes and instead had consciously decided to spend his time with a haggard, street worn, thirty-five-year-old from the old neighborhood. This fact had always amazed him until one night, a fifth of vodka burning in his own belly; Boyd too had found one hand on Maxine's tit, another on her ass, and his tongue half way down her throat.

Some things were just unexplainable.

CHAPTER TWENTY-SIX

"My dreams were taken from me. Well, now... now I've stolen them from someone else."

—*Corpse Bride*, 2005

With the coffee slowly dripping out of the machine, Brandy leaned her hip up against the kitchen counter and nervously puffed on her cigarette, anxiously waiting for the level to rise high enough so she could yank out the pot and pour herself a cup.

"Hi," Lillian walked by, her greeting much too monosyllabic for Brandy to read. "Coffee ready?"

"Just about," she said, quickly snubbing out her smoke.

"I was gonna make Tito some scrambled eggs. You want?"

Brandy wanted more than scrambled eggs. She wanted to grab the young girl and kiss her so hard that that their lips would be sealed together forever. But she couldn't. Not now, not in the light of day.

Standing in the kitchen, Brandy began to feel more and more like a world-class letch. A total waste of skin who'd used her position of power to hit on this defenseless young girl. Shit, the kid had nowhere else to go. What in the hell had Brandy been thinking? She was disgusted with herself and could barely lift her face to reply.

"I usually put a few pieces of crumbled cheese in the bowl with the eggs. Gives it a little extra punch, if you know what I mean? But if you don't like cheese, I can always leave yours plain?"

"No, I like cheese," Brandy shook her head in an attempt to clear away her burning sexual fantasies and deal with the problem at hand.

"Good, then I'll make one big batch."

Brandy stepped out of the way, as Lillian began puttering around the kitchen, obviously at home playing the little woman.

"About last night," Brandy suddenly blurted out.

"Forget it."

"Well, I can't," she said and reached for the coffee pot, finally pouring herself a cup. "I didn't mean to freak you out, to make you feel like you had no choice."

"I'm not freaked." Lillian picked up a fork and vigorously began whipping a plastic bowl of raw egg and milk before adding a few dashes of salt and pepper.

Fuck! This was turning out to be a nightmare. Brandy felt like she owed the girl an apology for crossing the line and hitting on her, but the damned kid wouldn't stay still long enough to hear her out.

"Do you mind if I have a cup, too?" Lillian reached toward the pot.

"Sit," Brandy suddenly pointed to the kitchen table.

"But…"

"Just sit!"

Blindly obeying the order, Lillian quietly slid into the closest kitchen chair.

Brandy now had her undivided attention, but unfortunately, she wasn't quite sure what she was supposed to do with it.

Lillian took the guesswork out of the situation and spoke first. "The reason I stopped you last night was because I was on my *moon*, and my *cookum* always said that any woman who plays around on her *moon*, is an *oopisikwatiskwao*."

"What in the hell are you talking about?"

Rising from her chair, Lillian walked straight over to Brandy and gently stroked her cheek, imitating her own moves from the night before. "My *moon* is my menstrual period. I told you I was bleeding, and I didn't feel clean enough to share my body with you."

"Cuz you wanted to cook?"

"No," Lillian laughed. "*Cookum* is the Cree word for grandmother.

"And an oopa...?

"*Oopisikwatiskwao* means whore. You know, slutty woman?"

"Yeah, I kinda understand what you were trying to say now. Your grandma said you'd be a whore if you fooled around when you were on your rag."

"I'm glad you got it," Lillian gently closed her eyes and ever so slowly leaned in for a kiss, offering up her lips, and inadvertently her heart.

"I'm forty-one," Brandy suddenly blurted out as if vying for first prize on a game show.

Without a second's hesitation, Lillian moved forward and gently set her mouth on top of Brandy's, waiting to see if she'd respond to her offering.

"You don't have to do this," she reminded her young roommate, the vibrations and brushing movement caused by speaking with her lips pressed against Lillian's setting her entire body on fire.

By the time Tito wandered into the kitchen looking for his breakfast, both women were locked in a passionate embrace and it took a good tug on Lillian's pant leg to even get their attention.

_____

"Who'd you say sent those flowers?" Julia nodded toward the vase of calla lilies still adorning the corner of her desk.

Her secretary immediately stepped forward and plucked the card from its holder. "They're from a Mr. Dubois. They came by courier just before I left yesterday.

Accepting the envelope, Julia opened the card and read the handwritten note aloud.

"Thank you for your generosity. I greatly appreciate your..."

"What the fuck does that mean?"

"Boyd, I've been waiting hours for you. Where you been?"

"Out with it. Who's the flowers from?"

"Francois Dubois," she unceremoniously tossed the card down on top of her desk.

Dismissing his wife's secretary with one look, Boyd strolled up to his Julia's desk and reached for the card.

"What you doing?" she slammed her right hand down directly on top of her husband's, effectively pinning the note to her desk, underneath both their palms.

"What the fuck you hiding?"

"What the fuck you insinuating?"

Boyd slowly pulled his powerful fingers into a fist, effectively trapping the crumpled note in the middle of his palm.

"Maybe you'd like to go through all my mail?" Julia yanked back her hand.

"Personally, I don't give a shit about your fucking mail, but I got a bad feeling about that dick wad, and I don't like him sending you flowers."

Julia defiantly crossed her arms at her chest as her husband lifted his hand straight in the air and unceremoniously dropped the crumpled cardboard back down on top of her desk.

"He sent me flowers. He didn't come into my office and wave his dick in my face."

"But he probably would if you asked him, wouldn't he?"

"What in the fuck are you babbling about now?"

"He's got the hots for you. I can tell. Why do ya think he sent you a fucking vase full of goddamn flowers?"

Boyd's jealous streak was usually well contained, rarely flaring up at work, and hardly ever jeopardizing their professional relationship. But when it did, it was ugly, and it always managed to irritate Julia.

"You know how many fruit baskets and bouquets of flowers I get delivered here in a goddamn month?"

"No."

"Well, I'll tell you." She yanked open a desk drawers and pulled out a ledger. "See this?" She flipped open the book and began scrolling down a random page. "Line after fucking line of names and stupid little gifts," she shouted up at her husband's face. "And I gotta keep track of all this shit, cuz I got nothing better to do but send fucking thank you notes. And you know why?" she continued to yell. "Cuz that's the kind of shit you have to do when you're trying to run a legitimate business, and you have to deal with all kinds of other legitimate business people."

Boyd shrugged, suddenly feeling a little stupid for making such a big deal out of the delivery.

"You want me to save every fucking card and then run it by you so you can decide if the guys got a hard on for me, or he just told his secretary to send a fruit basket to say thanks for all the hard work?"

"Sorry," Boyd shook his head. "I guess I kinda lost my mind for a second. Been a little on edge this morning."

"Yeah, I noticed. What's eating you?"

"I don't know," he rubbed his right palm over his face, afraid that maybe the doctor's prescription might be inadvertently upsetting his stomach and aggravating his ulcer.

"Want a coffee?"

"No."

"Excuse me Julia," her secretary buzzed through and interrupted their conversation. "I have a call for you from a Miss Cardinal."

"Cardinal?" Boyd looked to his wife for clarification.

"Pocahontas," she whispered before clicking over to the line.

"Sorry for not staying in touch," Lillian immediately opened with an apology, "but I just finished moving and I finally have a home phone number."

"So how you feeling? You think you'll be ready to work by this Friday?"

"Friday? You mean tomorrow?"

"Yes, I guess so," Julia flipped open her Daytimer to confirm the date.

"I should be fine," she nervously giggled. "So you still want me to work for you?"

"Yes, we do."

"Well, then Friday will be fine. Do I come by the office first?"

"Be here at nine. We'll head out to the shoot together."

Lillian repeatedly thanked her boss before hanging up the line, promising that come hell or high water, she'd be at the office for nine a.m.

Finished with the call, Julia was just about ready to get up from behind her desk when her secretary buzzed through for a second time. "Excuse me Julia. You have a visitor by the name of Mr. Dubois here to see you."

Without saying a word, Boyd shot his wife a disapproving look.

"He doesn't have an appointment," she reminded her secretary.

"No ma'am, he doesn't, but he asked me to mention that he's

about to leave town on business and he wanted to drop something off for you before he left."

"Jewelry?" Boyd couldn't help himself.

"Send him in," Julia replied before turning to shoot her husband a warning glance.

"Julia," Francois strolled into her office, box tucked firmly underneath one arm. "I'm so glad you agreed to see me."

"What can we do for you?" Boyd abruptly demanded as he walked up past Francois's back and joined his wife behind her desk.

"Mr. Giovanni," Francois instantly thrust his hand out toward Boyd. "I'm very sorry to intrude on your morning; however, I just wanted to drop this piece of art off for you both to view."

"This ain't a gallery," he curtly reminded their visitor.

"I am aware of that," Francois bristled. "However, your wife had previously expressed a concern about not being unable to fully visualize my proposed film project."

Boyd turned his head sideways and shot his wife a questioning glance.

"It has been kind of difficult," she was suddenly forced to admit.

As the tension continued to build, Julia realized she'd have to intercede quickly or risk a full-scale blow out. "Since you made the trip all the way down to our office, do you think we could maybe see what you brought?"

This wasn't exactly how he planned to reveal his inner most sexual fantasy, but he had an inkling that if he didn't open the box at Julia's request; her pig-faced husband might actually lunge across the desk and rip it from his grasp.

"I purchased it from a local artist who hand-carved each figurine in painstaking detail," Francois explained as he set the box down on Julia's desk before gently lifting out his treasured art.

"In wood?" Julia cleared her throat before leaning in for a closer look.

"Red oak is his medium of choice."

"I don't get it," Boyd blurted out before he even had a chance to process his own thoughts.

"This is very helpful, Francois," Julia jumped to her feet and rushed around her desk. "You've managed to clear up any lingering questions I had about your vision. Thank you so much for dropping by."

"Well," he said, suddenly checking his watch, "I really must hurry if I'm going to make my flight. I'll be back in town next week, and I'll make an appointment to drop off the first half of my cash payment and also pick up my statue. So thank you again for your time." He bid them both farewell before spinning on his heels and marching straight out the office door.

———————

Their bellies were full and their bodies were rested. It was a dangerous time, and Ronnie was determined not to let their comfort derail any of his plans.

"Time to hit the pavement," he walked over and kicked the foot of Jerome's bed.

"In a bit," he slowly rolled over and grabbed for his pack of smokes. "What's your rush, bro? We gots' this room till two."

"Time to roll. Kids down at the high school be roaming around through their lunch hour, looking to score before heading back. Can't sell jack shit if we're lounging here watching *The Price Is Right*."

"Relax," Jerome's left hand groped for the remote control securely screwed down to the nightstand. "I just wanna see them spin, then we can roll." His fingers continued to search for the volume button.

"Get the fuck up!" Ronnie yelled at the top of his lungs. "You're fucking rolling now or you ain't rolling at all."

"Sorry," Jerome squeaked as he jumped to his feet. "You ain't gotta be so mad."

As Jerome scrambled to assemble his few belongings, Ronnie walked out of the motel room and lit up a smoke. They had blown way too much of their profits on fast food and motel rooms. They needed to find a place to crash where they'd be able to store up a change of clothes and maybe do some basic cooking, least breakfast or lunch. The way it stood right now, he was blowing three quarters of their take just on food and shelter, and they'd never get ahead on that kind of split.

"I'm ready," Jerome bounded out of the room, his shoelaces dragging on the concrete.

"Let's head over to Gloria's. Maybe she's got a room we can rent off her for a little cash, or maybe some dope. The bitch is always short. Might be able to work some kind of deal or something."

"You wanna stay with your sister?"

"Don't wanna, ain't got no choice."

"Fine," Jerome muttered, fully aware that his opinion carried little or no weight.

"Besides, maybe she's heard from Lilly." Ronnie crushed his cigarette under his boot. "And you know that I've got a couple words I'd really like to give that bitch."

"Me too," Jerome chimed in, clueless as to what Ronnie was alluding to, but positive that he'd follow suit no matter what happened.

CHAPTER TWENTY-SEVEN

"In my life it's always been the harmless stuff that hurts the most, whereas the things so horrible you can't even imagine it, is usually a lot easier than you think."
—Monster, 2003

His knuckles were sore from pounding, but Ronnie wasn't in the mood to give up and just walk away. He wanted to talk to his sister, and as far as he knew, this was her last known address.

"What the fuck is your problem?" a guy finally swung open the house's front door and shouted in their faces.

"Where's Gloria?" Ronnie demanded, trying to look around the guy's shoulders to see if he could recognize anyone inside.

"Who's Gloria?"

"She's my sister, man."

"Sister sister, or street sister?" the guy demanded, suddenly taking an interest in Ronnie's quest.

"Sister sister," he turned his attention back to the guy. "She's used to live here with her kid, Tito."

"Tito?"

"Yeah. You remember an Indian chick with a little black kid?"

"Don't member the chick, but I kinda member some kid."

Ronnie wanted inside. He needed to take a look around and check for any of his sister's stuff. If her shit were lying around, she'd probably be back. If she'd packed it all up and left, he'd just hit a dead end.

"Hey buddy," Ronnie leaned in a little closer. "You got a beer in there?"

"Why?"

"Cuz I got me some dope, and I always like a cold one when I smoke."

Ronnie's plan was a success. Within seconds, all three guys were squatting in the middle of the living room, sharing a small glass pipe as they heated the crystallized chunks of methamphetamine to a smoldering temperature, alternately inhaling the acrid white smoke.

"Brews in the fridge," their host announced, unwilling to walk away from his turn at the pipe. "So what's your names?" He turned his head toward Jerome for an introduction.

"I'm Jerome, and he's my best friend, Ronnie."

"I'm Freddy, and this here's my house."

Rising from his squatting position as the boys began to make small talk, Ronnie made his way into the kitchen, almost slipping and falling face first right into an open cupboard drawer.

His sneakers, greasy from walking over a rotting layer of garbage, skidded across the room, his movements virtually turning the small eight by ten space into a mini skating rink.

"Watch the garbage, man," Freddy yelled out. "Fucking neighbor's dog got in and ripped it all apart. Ain't got round to cleaning it up."

"I see that." Ronnie took a deep breath and carefully righted himself.

"Beer's in the fridge," their host repeated for the second time, his clouded memory a permanent side effect of amphetamine abuse.

Counting seven cans of beer, an open jar of dried mustard and an empty pizza box, Ronnie was almost ready to slam the door closed when he finally spotted a single glass baby bottle lying on its side. Having rolled to the back on the bottom shelf, the milk had remained untouched and undoubtedly unnoticed. The question was, for how long?

Reaching in to lift up the bottle, Ronnie instantly noticed that the liquid had began to separate, the milk curds gelling as a yellowy liquid pooled at the top. This bottle was at least a couple of weeks old, he guessed.

"You still here Ronnie?" Jerome shouted from the other room, always paranoid that he might be inadvertently separated from his best friend.

"Yeah," he grabbed two cans and very slowly made his way back through the disaster zone. "Here," he dropped them down on the floor, realizing that both Jerome and Freddy were suddenly far too stoned even to remember they'd originally wanted beers in the first place.

"Want some, bro?" Jerome offered up the ragged square of tin foil as Freddy busied himself with a patch of scabby sores adorning a large portion of his right cheek.

"No man. I gotta take a leak."

It was a two-bedroom house, or would have been, if someone had bothered to clear out the truckloads of garbage and broken down furniture piled up in every available corner. Wandering room to room, Ronnie wasn't able to spot anything that reminded him of his sister or his nephew. No girl's clothes, no children's toys. Nothing. Except…

"Hey Freddy, what you got down in the basement?" he called back toward the living room. "Doors locked up tight as a fucking drum."

"I dunno," he began to howl with laughter. Jerome joining in as something obviously struck both guys as extremely funny.

Testing the basement door with his shoulder, Ronnie decided to give it a little shove, surprised when it gave way and popped open like a cardboard cereal box.

"Come back," Jerome called out, trying to rise to his feet but unable to stabilize his stance.

Before Ronnie had a chance to reach out and hit a light switch, the stench of human decomposition flew straight up the stairs and hit him smack dab in the face.

"Oh fuck," he swore, staggering backwards as his arms wildly flailed in an attempt to block the oppressive wall of stink.

"Gloria?" he mumbled, clamping his right hand firmly over his mouth, not sure if he was trying to keep the stench out or his breakfast in.

———————

Having already plowed his way through at least half the self-help books he'd bought at the college bookstore; Pete still hadn't been able to locate that illusive passage, the exact cluster of words that would sum up his condition in one concise statement. That was, until now.

"Eight five percent of hardcore addicts are unable to maintain a state of clean sobriety and are doomed to re-offend for the remainder of their significantly shortened life spans."

Rereading the passage over and over as it burnt a permanent scar into his memory banks; Pete tried to comprehend the ramifications of the simple statement.

"Re-offend," he muttered to himself. "Unable to maintain. Significantly shortened life spans," he continued to chant the disheartening words.

Unsure of exactly what he was trying to accomplish, Pete suddenly jumped up to his feet and began frantically churning through his boxes of books, pulling out everything he'd carried down that even touched on the topic of addiction recovery.

"Unlikely, unrealistic," he repeatedly read aloud.

Frustrated, he changed books, skipping straight to the next index and looking up *Recovery Rates*. Flipping through the pages to the last chapter, Pete scanned the paragraphs, once again confronted with the dreary facts.

"Most recovering addicts live a life tempered with habitual relapses and occasional downward spirals into clinical bouts of depression."

Book after book, the information was exactly the same. Once addicted, the long-term prognosis was bleak. Most addicts were unable to totally severe the hold of their chemical addictions and found themselves a slave to their cravings for the rest of their lives.

Picking up the closest hard-covered volume he could reach, Pete pulled back his arm and violently threw the book across the room. He was angry with himself, pissed that he'd made a special trip all the way down to the college bookstore just to spend his hard-earned cash on a collection of their fuckin' garbage. He thought the eggheads down at the college would have all the answers with their fancy classes and big degrees. He'd never dreamed that his answer would come in the revelation that there was *no hope*.

As the research textbook landed with a thud on top of the paper marked with the words *Day 8*, Pete collapsed back on his bed. Eyes closed, tears beginning to stream down the side of his face, he pulled his knees up to his chest and sobbed.

It was the first time he'd cried aloud since he was a six-year-old boy and his mother had been burdened with the task of explaining to him that he'd failed grade one.

He still couldn't make the light switch work, and without a flashlight or some other source of illumination, Ronnie wasn't taking another step.

"Hey Freddy," he continued to cough, peeling off his coat as the stench seemed to somehow linger in the folds. "You got any candles, man? Anything like that?"

"You got candles?" Freddy repeated, his eyes twitching in their sockets as he continued to make a bloody pattern on the living room wall, repeatedly dabbing his thumb in his open facial wounds and alternately pressing his fingerprints up against the dirty wallpaper.

"Forget it," Ronnie stepped past him and looked down at Jerome. "Give me your lighter, bro."

Fiddling with the laces on his sneakers, Jerome barely heard the voice, mesmerized by the metal grommets attached to his shoe's leather.

"Fuck me," Ronnie reached down and snatched up the plastic Bic.

Returning to the top of the basement stairs, he couldn't be sure if he was becoming accustomed to the stench, or if the dank basement had somehow managed to air itself out a little. Either way, he flicked on the lighter and began slowly making his way down the old wooden stairs.

The small two-inch flame only allowed him minimal illumination, and without additional overhead lighting, he immediately realized that he was walking down into a deep, black pit.

"Hello," Ronnie called out as a precaution, not the least bit interested in surprising some *tweaker* hiding out in one of the basement's corners. "Anybody down here?" he continued to yell, his feet finally leaving the steps and planting themselves on the concrete floor.

With no verbal reply, he decided to take a chance, carefully stepping over the piles of garbage as he systematically searched the darkness for a body.

"What ya doing down there?" Freddy finally managed to stumble to the top of the basement stairs.

"Just looking around," Ronnie suddenly began to cough. "You gots a real nice house here," he spit out a giant ball of saliva before wiping his mouth with the back of his hand.

"Your buddy was wondering if you gots more ice we can smoke?"

"Tell Jerome I'll be right up and to just have another beer."

"Okay," Freddy nodded, staggering off toward the living room.

Almost ready to call it quits, Ronnie decided to just stick with his plan and check the last corner before heading back up the stairs. Forcing himself to wade through a pile of discarded clothing, he nearly jumped out of his skin when his right foot suddenly squeaked.

"What the fuck?" He bent down, yanking a rubber toy out from underneath his sneaker. It definitely belonged to some kid, he just couldn't be sure if it was Tito's. Tossing it aside, Ronnie continued on with his journey.

The stench was growing stronger, and even though he'd only smelled human decomp once before, Ronnie was pretty sure he was smelling it once again.

It was different from plain old rotting garbage, even somehow stronger than the stench of sewer from the portable construction toilets. Human decomp had a taste as well as a smell. It kind of locked itself around a person, and the only way he knew to shake it off was to burn the clothes and scrub one's hair with lemon juice.

Lighter dangerously low on butane, Ronnie slowly bent down and peered down into the small space between the basement's concrete wall, and the house's forced air furnace.

"Gloria?" he whispered. "You sleeping back there?"

When she never answered, he reached out and gently poked at the large lump with one finger, surprised to feel the coarse wool of an old blanket.

"It's me, Ronnie," he continued to whisper as if negotiating with a young child playing hide and seek. "I've come to help you."

Flame sputtering; he decided it was time to make his move.

Screwing up his courage, he thrust the light toward the wrapped form, nearly falling back in fright when his flame illuminated a rotting human face.

"Fuck me!" he yelped at the top of his lungs, the lighter falling from his left hand as the basement plunged into complete darkness.

"You all right?" Freddy called out for a second time from the top of the stairs.

"I can't see shit," Ronnie scrambled to locate his lighter, dropping it from his fingers it each time his hands touched the red hot metal.

"Well, then just turn on the lights," Freddy laughed as he leaned down the stairwell and yanked the hanging cord.

As the basement was instantly flooded with the cold white light of the naked ceiling bulb, Ronnie froze, body motionless, his brain fighting to assimilate the horrific image in front of his eyes.

———————

"What ya mean they ain't worth shit?" Maxine demanded. "It's full. Brand new and all."

"I don't give a rat's ass," her dealer moaned. "I ain't got no market for Dio… diox… whatever," he shoved the bottle back into her hand.

"Well, can you front me? Maybe just a quarter ounce? Come on baby," she tried her best smile, which might have been more effective if her teeth had been brushed and her lipstick had actually been applied with a steady hand.

"I look like a fucking bank? You wanna loan, talk to your man. I ain't eating it on any more shit for the likes of you."

"Eating what?" she began to argue, her youngest son now beginning to stir on the other end of the park bench.

"Eating your fucking debt! Now piss off, and quit following me. I got legit customers and you're scaring them away."

"I got cash," she reluctantly dipped her hand down the front of her tee shirt.

"Well, why the fuck you playing games?"

"I was just hoping to trade for it," she shrugged, debating just how far she'd be able to stretch the remaining fifteen dollars she had left after paying her rent and power bill.

As her dealer passed Maxine a small plastic bag filled with yellowish colored rocks, she alternately shoved her prescription bottle back into her pocket. "You know anyone else who'd buy the pills?" she asked as she leaned across the bench and shoved the dope down past the front waistband of her son's diaper.

"Try Antonio, down on Fourth. He might. Ya never know. I hear he's so fucked up lately that he even traded some chick an eight ball for a baggie of Aspirin."

"No fucking way?"

"Yeah, it's the fucking truth. He's that fucked up."

"Shit, Antonio used to be one hot piece of ass. I nearly fucked him once," Maxine reminisced aloud.

"I can see that," he mumbled without even raising his eyes.

"We were partying, and decided to share a cab home. Would a done him right then and there, but the cabbie was some kind of born again Christian."

"Worst kind," her dealer agreed.

"So he's on Fourth?"

"Down behind the movie theater. Can't miss him. Still wears that fucking ugly yellow wind breaker some coach gave him back when he was running track."

Nodding her head, Maxine stood up and stretched her legs, her circulation beginning to give her problems.

"See ya, man," she snatched her son up off the park bench and began making her way down to Fourth Street.

"Yellow wind breaker," he called out after her.

By the time Maxine had totted her youngest the five blocks to where Antonio was supposed to be hanging out, she was drenched in a cold sweat, and in dire need of a hit.

"Seen Antonio?" she asked the first kid who walked past her on the sidewalk.

He shook his head no and continued on his path.

"Anyone seen Antonio round here," Maxine interrupted a group of young kids lounging in front of a gas station.

"He's right there." They pointed to a dirty yellow lump leaning up against a light standard.

Making her way across the street, she came up behind him just as he bent down to zip up his pants.

"Antonio?" she called out, shifting her bleary eyed son from one hip to the other.

"Who's asking?" He slowly spun around.

"It's me, Maxine. Remember me? We used to party together at the afterhours club under the Pearl City Restaurant."

His smile widened to flash her a toothless grin, yet his eyes remained absolutely blank.

"We was gonna do it in a cab one night, but the driver kept threatening to make us walk. Member that? He was all religious and shit."

"I don't take cabs," he continued to smile.

Her dealer was right. Antonio was seriously fucked.

"You got a baby." He reached out as if he wanted to hold her son.

Pivoting on her heels, Maxine managed to sidestep his reach, effectively pulling her child out of harm's way.

"I got some pills to sell. You wanna trade me for them?" She struggled to pull the bottle out of her pocket.

"No." He turned his back and began shuffling down the street.

"But it's good shit," she yelled. "It'll get you off for the whole night. You'll be rocketing in and out of space for hours." She winked as if sharing a personal revelation.

Antonio never answered, he just continued on his path.

"Hey," Maxine yelled at his back. "I just walked five fucking blocks to come here and sell some shit. What the fucks' the matter? You ain't got nothing to trade?"

Without warning, Antonio suddenly jerked around and headed straight for her face, snatching the sleeping child from her arms and thrusting him straight up toward the sky.

"I got something to trade. I got something to trade," he chanted.

"Give him back!" Maxine began to screech, frantically beating her fists against Antonio's back.

By the time help arrived, not only was Maxine screaming, but her son had joined in with shrieks of his own.

"Get moving," the theater's security guard shouted in Antonio's face.

Cradling her child as if he suddenly was the most important thing in her life, Maxine continued to try to soothe her son.

"He'll be all right," the man leaned in and took a peek at the wailing boy. "I saw everything from inside. He never dropped the kid, or nothing."

"I know," she snarled. "You think I'm fucking blind?"

"Just trying to help." He shook his head and made his way back toward the theater's main entrance.

"Well, we're fine." Maxine cradled her son into her left arm as her right hand slipped under his waistband to check for her baggie of rocks. "We'll be *just fine*," she repeated with renewed confidence, suddenly debating whether she was better off buying diapers and a small bag of macaroni, or diapers and two loaves of bread.

"Bread," she finally announced to nobody in particular. She

could pan fry it with a little butter and sugar, and it'd feed em' all for days. Hell, her mama had raised them on it and she'd growed up just fine. Too bad she didn't have any money left for powdered milk though.

CHAPTER
TWENTY-EIGHT

*"Salvation… Damnation… got one thing in common.
You gotta die to find either one."*
                                        —The Legend of Zorro, 2005

He really didn't wanna call the cops, but Ronnie was pretty sure it was the only thing to do when you found a dead body in a house.

"Ronald," the detective handed him back his only tattered piece of I.D. "We're going to need you to come down to the station so we can take your statement."

"But you already got Freddy. What you need me for? It was his house."

"We need a full account of the events leading up to the moment you found the body."

"Can't we do it here?" he nervously shuffled his feet on the grass.

"And what in the hell am I supposed to write it down on? A goddamn gum wrapper?"

"Okay." Ronnie shoved his hands into his jeans. "But I was just wondering if you could tell me if that's my sister, Gloria?"

He pointed to the body bag being wheeled past them both on the coroner's gurney.

"Well kid, to be honest with ya, it's gonna be pretty hard without dental records or some other kind of family photos. Don't suppose you got any of those back at home."

"No." Ronnie shook his head.

"You know the name of her dentist?"

He shook it again.

"How about a doctor she visited in the last year or two? You know a doctor's name?"

"Nope," he folded his arms at his chest.

"Damn boy, you sure don't know much about the comings and goings of your own flesh and blood."

This time he agreed.

———————————

Driving up to the high school gym, Warren quickly found an available space and parked his car.

"Hey Finkel," one of the guys called from across the lot, "We're going for wings and beers after a little b-ball. You wanna come?"

"Maybe."

"Quit being such a pussy. You haven't bought a single pitcher yet. I'm ordering the first round and it's on you." The guy pointed straight toward his chest.

Duffle bag in hand, Warren walked into the men's locker room of the gymnasium, the sounds of bouncing basketballs already echoing through the empty halls.

"Nice shorts," one of the other players began to tease the man changing in the middle of the locker room.

"You like it, boys?" Arnold jumped up on the wooden bench and began grinding his hips.

"Looks like something my kid would wear," one man sounded off as another player from the pick-up team began to whistle.

"Shut the fuck up." He suddenly jumped off the bench. "My girlfriend gave them to me for my birthday last night. She says they make her hot."

"They make your boyfriend hot, too?" Warren snickered into his open locker.

"Fuck you." Arnold peeled off his silk boxers and threw them right in Warren's face.

Ninety minutes later, after they'd finished four full games of six on six, all the men were sweating buckets, ready to run through the showers and meet up in the pub.

"Now Finkel, you ain't going to run off and hide without buying us a round, are ya?"

Ready to call out across the locker room and give the guys another excuse, Warren suddenly stopped himself. "What the hell," he bunched his wet towel down into his duffle bag. "My daughters having a sleepover at the neighbors' so I guess I could blow off a little steam with you guys."

"Go Finkel, go Finkel…" his teammates began to chant.

"Hey, where exactly is this pub, anyway?"

"I'll ride with you," Arnold announced before whipping off his towel and strutting butt naked toward the showers.

"I guess I'd better hit the bank first," Warren announced half an hour later as he pulled his car up to the drive-through bank machine.

"Whatever, man." Arnold began digging through his bag.

"Ah shit. It's broken," he suddenly read the note taped to the screen. Tromping down on the gas, he whipped his car around so it faced the front of the bank. "I'll be right back," Warren promised, pulling the access card out of his wallet and running up to the front door.

Returning with a hundred dollars folded in half and neatly tucked into his back pocket, he slid into the driver's seat, surprised to see Arnold casually rolling a joint.

"It helps me relax after a game. I find that I don't cramp up if I smoke a little."

"I usually just stretch," Warren offered, starting his car and quickly backing away from the front of the building.

"Want some?" Arnold asked; holding out the joint as Warren circled the pub's lot for a space.

"Just let me park first." He waved it off, hoping that Arnold would finish his joint by the time he'd been able to find a spot.

"There," Arnold suddenly pointed. "She's pulling out."

Taking the woman's space, Warren put his car in park and shut off the engine.

"Come on, have a drag," Arnold waved the joint under his nose.

"No man. I gotta drive."

"Oh, come on. The beers will straighten you out and you won't have a single sore muscle. I promise."

Warren couldn't help but smirk.

"One drag isn't gonna bring down the unflappable Warren Finkel?"

"Throw it out, Arnold. Come on. The guys are waiting for us inside."

"This is Hawaiian Gold, baby. I ain't tossing anything out."

"Fine then," Warren reached over and grabbed the smoldering joint.

It was already extremely late, but Wanda still had a thousand things to do before Friday's shoot.

As it turned out, the Pocahontas story line had turned out to be one of their most ambitious productions to date, and after the lecture she'd given Julia and Boyd, she wasn't going to be the one to drop the ball in the eleventh hour.

Needing to confirm the crew's morning arrival with the landowner, Wanda flipped through the file to find the farmer's name and number. Dialing as she continued to shuffle papers, she finally reached the man and was able to check *location* off her list.

"Wanda, I'm heading home now unless you need me for anything else," her secretary announced when she poked her head in through the door.

"Thanks." Wanda waved without even taking the time to raise her own head.

Checking her master list, she realized that she had a good couple of hours of work before she'd be able to call it a night. But at least she didn't have to head down to the shoot tomorrow morning. That was now the domain of the filmmakers, and she was strictly administration.

Head buried in her papers, the hands on her clock continued to spin around the dial, and by the time Wanda had stepped out from behind her desk, it was nearly midnight.

Stopping to grab a fresh pita topped with shaved ham, grated Monterey Jack, and stuffed full of iceberg lettuce, Wanda couldn't wait to get home and just put her feet up. It had been another sixteen-hour day, and by the looks of all the wrinkled flyers stuffed through the grate in her mailbox, she'd been too busy of late to even haul up her own mail.

"Hey, baby," a man's voice purred from somewhere beneath the stairwell.

"Who's there?"

"It's me." A shadowy figure struggled to right itself.

"Warren," Wanda gasped, dropping her purse and sandwich to rush to her twin brother's aid. "What are you doing here?"

"I dunno," he chuckled, nearly falling flat on his face as Wanda fought to support his weight.

"Well, come up." She carefully leaned her brother against a wall while snatching her purse and sandwich off the lobby tiles.

With much effort, they finally managed to negotiate the thirteen steps to Wanda's floor, literally bouncing off the walls as they made their way to her condominium's front door.

"Home sweet home," he slurred.

Unlocking her door, Wanda literally let go and allowed Warren to fall inside. "Watch the coffee tab…"

Too late. He crashed directly into the oak and wrought iron table and fell sideways onto the couch, yelping like a puppy that had just caught his tail in a door.

Pulling off her jacket and setting her crushed sandwich and purse on the kitchen counter; Wanda reached into the refrigerator and pulled out a bottle of water.

"So you decided to do a little partying tonight?" she asked him.

"Don't worry, I'm fine," his words dripped with sarcasm.

Unscrewing the cap, Wanda downed a few quick gulps.

"You want some?" she offered him a drink.

"How about a beer?"

"I don't have any beer."

"Well then," he smiled. "How 'bout some wine?"

Wanda disappeared into the kitchen, and when she returned, her brother had somehow managed to pull his arms out of his coat and was now fighting to kick off his high tops.

"Here's your wine."

Suspiciously eyeing the glass, he reached out and grabbed the tumbler, sniffing the liquid before even taking a sip.

"This ain't wine. It's juice!"

"This ain't a bar. It's my condo," Wanda countered back, dropping down to her knees to help untie his sneakers.

"You're such a good girl." Warren clumsily patted the top of his sister's head.

"You gonna tell me why you drank so much?"

"I smoked a *big fattie,*" he proudly announced.

"A what?" She finally was able to pull both shoes off his feet.

"A big fat joint." He thrust his arms out in opposite directions.

"Great." Wanda suddenly stood up to fetch a pillow and a blanket.

"And I bought beers. And then... and then we smoked again," he laughed.

"Get some sleep." She threw the bedding down on the armchair.

"Don't leave me," her brother begged, reaching out to grab her hand. "Sit and talk to me. We never talk no more, do we?"

"Does Amber know you're here?" Wanda reluctantly took a seat at her brother's side.

"She's at Lucy's house. Lucy has a mommy and a daddy. Lucy has a dog, and a cage of little white bunnies, and Lucy has..."

"I get it," Wanda interrupted. "Lucy has everything."

"But Lucy doesn't have you," he suddenly threw his arm around his sister's shoulders. "She doesn't have a great mommy like you to watch over her."

"Aunty," she corrected him. "I'm Amber's aunty."

"*Aunty smanty,*" he laughed, pulling her tightly to his side. "I love you, my little Wanda bear."

"I love you too, but I gotta get some sleep. And so should you." She tried to extract herself from his grasp."

"Remember when you taught me how to kiss? We'd practice for hours and hours..." his voice trailed off as if lost in the flood of his own private memories.

"That was a hundred years ago." She finally managed to extricate herself and rise to her feet.

"I liked that."

"Good, now go to sleep. I'll see you in the morning."

Unexpectedly, he reached out with his hand and grabbed her wrist.

"I wanna talk for awhile. Sit with me." He pulled her back down onto the couch.

"Let me go, Warren. I'm serious." She struggled against his hold.

"You never liked Jody, did you?"

"Ah, come on. I gotta go to bed," she collapsed against the back of the couch. "I don't have time for this shit tonight."

"You didn't like my wife, did you?"

"What makes you say that?" She was finally able to release her wrist through a series of painful twists and turns.

"Cuz when Jody moved into my life, you just up and moved out."

"You were married. I had to go."

"But I wanted you to stay," his voice took on a whiny tone.

"Warren, we can talk about this in the morning. But right now, I've gotta crash. Okay?"

"Give me a kiss goodnight," he turned toward his sister.

Quickly pecking her brother on the cheek, Wanda once more tried to rise to her feet.

"Not that like. Like you used to." He grabbed both her shoulders and pulled their faces tightly together.

"Don't!" Wanda twisted her body away from her brother.

"Why not?"

"Cuz I said no." Her neck strained to pull backwards as her brother's lips locked down on top of her mouth for a second time.

"Warr..." Her muffled cries were muted by the pressure of his tongue raking itself back and forth across her teeth.

"Quit it!" She finally ripped her mouth away.

"I love you, Wanda."

"Stop it!" She continued to bark commands, hoping that any second, her brother would snap out of his delusional state.

"I need you." His breathing began to come in short, harsh gasps.

Before she realized exactly what was happening, Warren had managed to scoop her legs up onto the couch, positioning her body so she was lying flat on her back while he excitedly hovered right above her.

"I can't live without you." He bent down and began hungrily ravishing her neck.

"Stop it!" She pushed hard against his shoulders.

Quickly sliding his knees from their positions on either side of her waist down the full length of the couch, Warren's entire weight now lay directly on top of his sister's body.

"God, I love you," he moaned, oblivious to the tears streaming down his sister's cheeks as his hands began to roam freely up the sides of her blouse.

"Please don't do this again," she begged, her words carrying the same weight as paper confetti in a windstorm.

"I love you, Wanda bear," he panted in her ear, his erection grinding into her thigh as the fingers on his right hand finally pushed their way past the barrier of her under-wire bra.

CHAPTER TWENTY-NINE

"You're just like a duck on the pond. On the surface, everything looks great. Underneath, your little feet are just churning the water."

—*The Replacements, 2000*

Having crawled off the couch and stumbled straight to the bathroom the minute her brother had passed out beside her, Wanda turned the shower on full blast and quickly peeled off her tattered underwear.

Standing under the hot spray, she tried to cry but somehow was unable to summon any tears. This lack of emotion scared her, and without warning, Wanda began to panic. She needed to get out, to get away before Warren woke.

Barely taking a minute to dry herself off, she wrapped one towel around her hair and another tightly around her body. Slipping out of the bathroom and across the hall into her bedroom, she gently closed the door and locked it before taking a couple minutes to throw a few of her personal things into an overnight bag.

"Hair dryer," she muttered, having bent across her dresser

to unplug the appliance when she heard the first of her brother's footsteps.

Paralyzed by fear, Wanda froze, every nerve in her body poised to run, even if her only path of escape was through the double panes of the bedroom window.

She heard him begin to relieve himself and then immediately flush the toilet, still urinating while the tank drained into the bowl. Either too drunk or too tired to bother washing his hands, it sounded like Warren had turned and was walking back to his spot on the couch. Unfortunately, with the living room carpet padding his steps, she couldn't be absolutely positive without a visual check.

If Wanda was going to take a chance of opening her door, she was going to do it fully dressed with her bag in her hand. She might have only one chance to run before her brother was fully awake, and she wasn't going to waste it fiddling with the task of packing.

Dressed in faded jeans and an old sweatshirt, she brushed a quick swath of make-up and hair products off her dressing table straight into her open bag with her right hand while scanning the bedroom for her purse.

"Shit," she swore. Realizing she'd left it on the kitchen counter. Now she'd be forced to divert from her direct path toward the apartment door just to grab it.

"That's fine," she promised herself. It was only a little after two in the morning, and the alcohol and drugs should still have a firm hold on her brother's sense of balance. If he tried to jump up off the couch to chase her, he'd probably stumble, and if he stumbled, she'd have the seconds she needed to make it out her door.

Two deep breaths to summon her courage, and Wanda quietly stepped out into the hall, heart racing as she spotted Warren passed out, still face down on the living room couch.

Tiptoeing with her bag in hand, she moved through her living room, not even bothering to pick up her white cotton blouse and the shredded lace skirt that had been torn from her body during her brother's attack.

Forcing down the bile beginning to creep up the back of her throat, Wanda shook off the nausea and grabbed her handbag, one eye nervously trained on her twin brother's form.

"Ohh," he started to moan, the side effects of all the alcohol beginning to ravage his body and upset his stomach.

Bending down to snatch up a set of heels while she shoved her feet into a pair of brown leather boots, Wanda straightened her back and had one final look around. Forced to sneak out her very own condominium, she scurried down the building's rear stairwell to the anonymity of the night and the safety of her own locked car.

———————

Lillian had spent the night nestled in Brandy's arms, cuddled together in Brandy's bed, tucked safely away in Brandy's little two-bedroom apartment, and she couldn't have been happier.

It had taken most of her life, but she'd finally found a partner who cared about her feelings and her needs. Their lovemaking had been a sharing experience of giving and receiving. So different from the power struggle that usually ensued whenever Ronnie had felt like throwing her down and mounting her until his own urges were satisfied.

"I gotta go," Lillian gently stroked her lover's naked shoulder. "I'm gonna drop off Tito at the hospital daycare, but I'll call you later, on one of my breaks."

"I'm working tonight," Brandy moaned, early mornings her least favorite time of the day.

"Mommy," Tito began to cry, upset that a closed door had barred his entry into their bedroom.

"When he start calling you mommy?" Brandy pulled herself upright in bed.

"He's just a little confused," Lillian pulled on her tee shirt before jumping up to open the bedroom door.

"Hungry," Tito announced, dropping his empty juice bottle in the middle of the bedroom floor.

"Let's get you dressed," Lillian scooped him up into her arms and carried him into the spare room.

By the time she'd pulled off the store's tags, and dressed the child in his new sweatpants and tee shirt, Brandy had thrown on a robe and wandered into the room.

"What you gonna do if your movie shoot runs late this afternoon."

"Don't worry," she began pulling back the covers to make the bed. "As soon as I get to work, I'm gonna tell the Giovanni's that I have a child now and I have to leave at a decent hour."

"Like fuck you will!" Brandy barked. "Have you suddenly lost your mind?"

"No."

"Well then why in the hell are you going to sabotage a good thing?"

"Well, what do you think I should do?"

"You should shut the fuck up and keep our little arrangement to yourself. Nobody needs to know that you're staying with me, or that you're trying to raise somebody else's kid. As far as any of your co-workers are concerned, you're just crashing with a friend from the club and you absolutely *love, love, love,* your new job. Trust me baby," she walked up and tenderly kissed her on the lips. "The less people who know about your personal life, the better off you are. They'll only try and use it against you later."

"All right," Lillian reluctantly nodded her head in agreement.

"And I'll phone the club and tell them I'll be in by eight. That way I can pick up the kid at daycare if you're running late."

"Thank you," Lillian threw her arms around her girlfriend's neck. "I don't know what I'd do without you."

Brandy nodded; that very fact left her comforted and fearful, all at the same time.

———————

Sneaking back into her office hadn't been nearly as difficult as Wanda had initially thought. Instantly recognized by the security guard on duty, she'd only been forced to wave hello from a distance before stepping onto the elevator and making her way up to the executive's private floor.

Once entombed inside her office, Wanda had finally allowed herself a deep breath, a little surprised when the tears still never released. Curling up with one of her couch's decorative throws, she'd eventually passed out from sheer exhaustion, her eyes fluttering as her subconscious fought to sort out the night's events.

"Wanda," her secretary gently nudged her shoulder a few hours later. "Are you all right?"

"What is it?" she nearly jumped up off her couch, her wild hair only adding to her disheveled appearance. "I'm fine, I... I..."

"How about some coffee?"

"A coffee would be great," she muttered, finally able to wipe a small tear away from the corner of her eye.

After two cups and a glazed donut from the lunchroom, Wanda finally felt like she might be able to face the world.

"I'll be stepping out for a few minutes. Please take messages," she smiled at her secretary, grateful for her show of kindness.

Overnight bag spread out across the loveseat in the executive washroom, Wanda slowly started to brush the tangles out of her naturally curly hair, surveying her limited selection of clothing in the mirror.

Grabbing fresh underwear, a brown skirt, and sleeveless beige turtleneck, she stepped into a locked cubicle to change, not willing to be caught standing naked by either Julia or any of the other handful of female executives on the floor.

"Oh no," Wanda sighed, her blood stained panties a glaring reminder of the physical trauma her body had endured just seven short hours earlier. No matter how much she wanted to forget the nightmare, it was real, and the evidence was staring her straight in the face.

Soiled clothes stuffed in a side compartment of her bag, Wanda exited the washroom fully dressed for work with her hair pulled back in a tight ponytail and only a swipe of pink lipstick to try and distract from the darkened shadows under her eyes.

"Wanda, you're here bright and early," Boyd called out from somewhere behind her back.

Heart racing at the mere sound of a male voice, she forced herself to paste on a smile and slow her pace.

"It's a busy day for Giovanni Films. I wanted to make sure both you and Julia had everything in order for the Pocahontas the shoot, especially after Julia confirmed the date for this Friday.

"Thanks," he said when he finally caught up to her. "My god, girl. That has to be the biggest damn purse I've ever seen."

"You know us women," she joked. "The bigger the bag, the more stuff we can jam inside."

"Good morning!" Julia surprised them both by stepping out by the lunchroom.

"Good morning," Wanda returned the greeting, her forced smile almost becoming painful. "Is there anything I can help you with?"

"Damn, you're an angel," she said and motioned for her purchasing agent to follow.

By the time Lillian had arrived at the office, Julia was almost ready to go, her car loaded with a few of the last minute supplies Boyd had forgotten when he'd taken off an hour earlier.

"How do I look?" she discreetly whispered in Wanda's direction.

"Good. You look well rested and ready to work. How do you feel?"

"I feel good," Lillian nervously cracked her knuckles. "I just pray that I don't do anything to screw up the shoot this time."

"Don't worry, it'll be fine. You know what they say. Bad start, great finish."

"Well," Julia finally appeared in the hall. "I think I've got everything, even the megaphone," she lifted it up from her side. "Can you believe he forgot it? I had it sitting right on the corner of his desk."

"Now, don't forget this," Wanda turned to present Lillian with a full-length garment bag she had draped over her right arm.

"Aren't you coming?" Lillian's voice betrayed a hint of panic. "You were there last time."

"No, I have too much to handle here," she said as she made the transfer.

"But…"

"Don't worry." Wanda patted the young girl's shoulder. "You're going to be great. You know what you're doing, and I'm sure the shoot is going to be a fabulous success."

"All right, let's hit the bricks." Julia turned to make her way to the elevator.

"I'd really like it if you'd come with us," Lillian turned to beg, reaching out to the closest thing she had to a company friend.

Just as Wanda opened her mouth to make an excuse, her secretary walked up and interrupted her train of thought.

"I didn't know exactly what to say, since he never had an appointment, and you hadn't added him to your visitor list. But this guy down in the lobby claims to be your twin brother, and he's demanding that security let him up the elevator immediately. What should I tell them?"

"Tell security that I'm not here." Wanda reached over and lifted the garment bag off Lillian's arm. "Are we ready, ladies?"

Julia never said a word; she just spun on her heels and led the way toward the parking garage's rear elevator.

———————

"I really liked the beadwork on the old costume," Malcolm continued to mention to anyone who would listen.

"I believe it's exactly the same," Wanda mused, trying to deflate his escalating complaints. "Either way, it shouldn't matter, since I've been told we're not cutting in any of the old footage from the run through."

"The other chaps still looked better." He finally turned and sauntered off.

Suddenly making her debut, Lillian stepped out from behind her change screen to the applause of Julia and the surrounding crew.

"You really do pull off that look my dear," her boss couldn't help but compliment. "So how you feeling?" She gently pulled the girl aside.

Well aware that everyone was worried that she might suddenly start bleeding again, or maybe this time even puke up a lung, Lillian couldn't help but answer with a twinge of sarcasm. "I won't make a mess this time. I promise."

"I'm more concerned with here." Julia pointed to her forehead. "You gotta be in the right space to perform. You know what I'm trying to tell you?"

Lillian just shrugged her shoulders, not sure what her boss was attempting to infer.

"Okay." Julia suddenly glanced up at the sky as if looking for answers while she struggled to make herself understood. "You ever had sex with a guy when you weren't in the mood, but he walked away saying thanks, cuz it was the best he'd ever had?"

"Well, yeah."

"Well that's what I'm talking about," Julia tried to explain. "It's all about performing. About making everyone else around you feel like they've had the best of you, when really nobody's touched anything that matters." She now took a moment to point to Lillian's heart. "They can kiss you, and slobber on you, and even ram their shaft deep inside of you, but they really can't touch you." She moved a couple inches closer so they were staring directly into each other's eyes.

"They can't touch me," the young girl repeated as if hypnotized by her boss's words.

"That's right, so don't worry about here," she said and pointed down toward Lillian's crotch. "Cuz as long as your head's on straight, they can't even begin to touch you here," and she gently pressed the palm of her hand down over the young girl's heart.

"Are we ready?" Boyd shouted across the grassy field.

"Yes," Lillian yelled back. "And I'm ready to perform."

CHAPTER THIRTY

"If you can't fix it, you just gotta stand it."
—Jarhead, 2005

"I'd really like a chocolate bar. A big one with nuts and stuff," Jerome continued to babble. "Maybe one of 'em extra big ones that you're supposed to share, but I wouldn't have to. What you think about that?"

"Just keep walking," Ronnie grumbled, not the least bit impressed with his best friend since he'd sent him running from Freddy's house with their combined stashes of dope securely tucked down the front of his pants.

"But I would share it if you wanted half."

"Shut the fuck up!"

"What's the matter Ronnie? You still pissed at me about the dope?"

"Fucking right I'm pissed about the dope. You fucking smoked up all our profits, you piece of shit."

"Don't be mad at me, Ronnie. I didn't mean to. I... I just wanted one more hit on the pipe. I was scared cuz you found that body, and you made me run away from the house, and I just thought that..."

"Don't think. I told you never to think. Didn't I?" He continued to berate Jerome as if dealing with a disobedient child. "You're just supposed to do what I say. Right? What'd I say? What I'd say?" He repeatedly shouted at the top of his lungs.

"You said run. You said hide," he repeated the very commands Ronnie had chanted as Jerome had been sent fleeing minutes before the cops arrived.

"I didn't say smoke. I didn't say party. Did I?"

"No."

"Well then?" Ronnie threw his hands up in the air.

"I'm sorry, bro. I'll be real good from now on. I promise."

"Then just shut the fuck up," Ronnie barked for the last time. "I gots' to think and I can't think when you're jabbering."

"I'd still like a chocolate bar," Jerome continued to mutter.

"You're just craving sugar cuz you're coming off the ice," he reminded the kid. "You'll get over it, now walk."

Obeying as he had since they were children, Jerome fell in step.

Walking without talking, they managed to cover the twenty-seven blocks to the police station in under an hour.

"What we doing here?" Jerome suddenly backed away from the precinct's front steps.

"I gotta give a statement."

"Why?"

"Cuz unless I go inside, I ain't never gonna find out if that dead body was my sister's or not. That's why."

"I gotta go, too?"

Ronnie stopped for a second to debate the point.

"I promise I'll be good," Jerome continued to plead his case. "I won't go very far. Okay?"

He wasn't packing anymore dope and he definitely wasn't carrying any of the cash, so he'd probably be fine for a few minutes.

"All right, but I don't want you taking off. Cuz when I come out, I'm not spending another half a day looking for ya. This time I'll leave you. You understand me, bro?"

"Yep," Jerome spun around, already looking for a comfortable place to chill while Ronnie took care of his business inside the police station.

"Stay close," were the last words Jerome heard as he jogged across the street and headed straight for a neighboring park bench.

Once inside, Ronnie had to force himself to move, the mere sights and sounds of the police station nearly paralyzing him with fear.

"Can I help you?" an officer finally looked up and asked Ronnie after he'd been standing motionless at the front desk.

"I need to speak to a cop about my sister Gloria."

"Is she missing?" the man asked, reaching back around his chair to grab a well-worn clipboard.

"I found a dead body yesterday. I just wanna know if it was her."

"What's your name?"

"Ronald Bowers."

"And you said you reported the body?"

"Yeah. The cops came out and everything. I'm supposed to come in and make a statement."

"Well, why didn't you say so?" The cop turned his attention to his computer. "Detective Kuhnert is the man you want. Take a seat," he said, pointing to a small bank of chairs, "and I'll give him a call."

Within ten minutes, the detective suddenly appeared at the front desk.

"Ronald, I was worried you might be ditching your civic duty."

"What?"

"Come on, son." He motioned for the kid to follow him deeper inside the precinct's walls.

"So was it my sister?" Ronnie instantly jumped to the point, not the least bit interested in continuing with the small talk.

"We had a hell of a time." The detective grabbed a manila folder off the corner of his desk. "Was pretty hard, especially with no dental or medical records to match to."

Ronnie just nodded.

"But it seems that your sister Gloria Louise Bowers had a criminal record." He flipped through a couple pages before spinning the file so Ronnie could look at one of her mug shots. "Is that your sister?"

"Yeah," he said, reaching out to decipher the month and day on the bottom of the picture, shocked at just how emaciated his sister had looked in the black and white photo.

"Gloria had already been nabbed twice for solicitation, twice for possession with intent to sell, and most recently, she'd been charged with one count of theft under five thousand."

"She was a junkie." He pushed the file back toward the officer.

"It says here that she was also the sole provider for a minor child living under her care. You know anything about that?" The detective continued to scan the pages for more information.

"She had a little kid named Tito. He'd just finished staying with me and my girlfriend for about a month. But Gloria picked him up around a week ago or so. She gave me the address of Freddy's house—said she was going to be staying there for awhile."

"And you haven't seen or heard from her since then?"

"No." He shook his head.

"Well Ronald, my first concern right now is for your nephew. How old was he?"

"I dunno. One or two?"

"You don't have any children of your own?"

"Nope, dodged that bullet," he proudly smirked.

"Well, was the child still in diapers?"

"Yeah, he was. But he could say a few words and he walked pretty good."

"Probably closer to two, then." The detective began to compile a few notes. "Do you have any idea who the father was?"

"Nope, and I doubt that my sis did either. Tito was pretty dark though, with that kinky kind of afro hair, so I guess the guy was probably black."

"Do you have a picture of your nephew?"

"Nope."

"How about other relatives who Gloria might have left the child in the care of? Can you think of anyone she might have trusted with her son?"

"She only had me."

"No parents?"

"Nobody you could trust."

As detective Kuhnert continued to fill up his page, Ronnie nervously shifted in his seat.

"So, can you tell me what happened to Gloria? Why she's dead and all?"

Setting down his pen, the seasoned detective took a long hard look at the young man sitting across from him. Unfortunately, the kid had a fifty-fifty chance of ending up in the same city crematorium, ashes catalogued right behind his sister's. Living hard and dying young seemed to be the motto of this generation, and no matter what the cops did, they just couldn't seem to make any kind of measurable difference.

"Ronald, as far as I can tell from the county's preliminary autopsy, your sister died from a combination of malnutrition and dehydration, all coupled with a large overdose of methamphetamine."

"Like I said," he turned to look at the wall, "She was a stupid junkie."

"Well, it appears she had been hiding out behind the basement furnace by her own accord. We haven't found any signs of foul play. There were no ligature marks on the body. Nothing to make us believe she was being held there against her will. The basement door was locked as you know, but from inside the basement, so she could have easily opened the door and left at any time."

"She was a tweaker, man. Probably just hiding out cuz something scared her," Ronnie began to reason aloud. "Tweakers see all kinds of shit that's not really there."

"So, how well do you know Freddy?"

"I just met him yesterday when I went looking for Gloria."

"And what do you do to pay the bills?" The detective suddenly surprised Ronnie by changing the course of the conversation.

"Odd jobs. Painting…little bits of construction. Stuff like that."

He was lying. The detective knew it for a fact. There wasn't a fleck of paint on his skin or his hair, and his hands weren't the slightest bit nicked or bruised. His nails were long and dirty, and the boy's fingertips were stained with brown residue from the smoke and carbon of an addict's pipe.

"I ran your name, Ronald. You've somehow managed to fly under the radar, 'til now, and I wanna tell you, it's not too late for you to choose a different path. You finish high school?"

"Nope."

"Well, maybe you'd consider going back and getting your GED. Maybe some kind of Trade School or something? How about that?"

"Look man, I just came to check on my sister. I didn't come down here for a lecture."

"You're right," the detective said as he closed his file. "I've got no reason to detain you, so you're free to leave at any time. I was just giving you a little free advice."

"Thanks." Ronnie began to rise up from his chair, anxious to get out of the cop shop before their little meeting developed into anything more personal.

"One more thing. Do you know if anyone will be coming forward to claim your sister's body?"

Ronnie shook his head no.

"Well then, follow me." The detective rose from his chair. "I have a couple papers for you to sign and then you can be on your way."

Instantly rising to his feet, Ronnie shoved his hands in his pockets, anxious to sign whatever was necessary before making tracks and getting his ass back out on the street.

Protected by the walls of the portable changing room, Lillian continued to shiver in place while the make-up lady quickly washed the cum and ground-in dirt off her lower back and legs.

"Damn, its cold." She rubbed the goose bumps on her naked skin.

"You're just wet is all." The woman continued to sponge her skin with the tub of lukewarm water.

"How much longer," Boyd called out from across the field. "We able to go in five?"

Standing up to survey the first scene's damage, the elderly woman shook her head in disagreement. "I'm gonna need at least fifteen," she yelled back at the top of her lungs.

"You did really well, Lillian. I can't believe this is your first film." She tried to take the young girl's mind off her dampened skin.

"Thanks." Lillian reached up to pluck a blade of grass still clinging to one of her braids. "I'm sorry, but I don't know your name."

"Jeannie," the make-up woman said with a smile. "Now bend over and touch your toes, sweetie. You've got dirt all the way up the crack of your ass."

As Lillian was quickly prepped for the next scene, Wanda and Boyd poured over the *dailies*.

"She's quite the little performer, isn't she?" Julia smiled to herself.

"She makes Malcolm look like a *has-been*."

"He is a *has-been*."

"You're right," Boyd nodded his head in agreement. "We definitely need some new cock around here. He's getting stale and everybody's tired of looking at his sorry ass."

"I've got a lot of fresh faces on my desk. I think it's time we interviewed for some new *house cock*."

"Done." Boyd signaled the end of the conversation just as Wanda walked over to where they were standing.

"Coffee?" she offered.

"Surprised to see you." Boyd couldn't help but tease. "Aren't you *office?*"

"So what?" she bravely countered back. "Even office staff are allowed field trips now and then."

"Glad you came," he suddenly changed his tone, winking his silent apology as he accepted a steaming cup. "So Wanda, what you think? We capturing the whole Cowboy/Indian thing?"

"Authentic... no. Entertaining... yes."

"That's all we're looking for." Boyd returned his attention back to the monitor.

From across the set, one of the grips came barreling down the grassy field, panting as he fought to speak.

"We can't... we can't get the horse to stand... stand still," he finally blurted out, his breath coming in ragged gasps.

"So?" Julia looked toward her husband.

"So then we're hooped." Boyd stepped away from his monitor to stare back at the set. "One of the things the client really wanted was a shot of the Indian and the Cowboy sitting face to face. A couple of angles looking like they're really fucking on top of the horse. Can't do that if the horse is bucking off riders, now can I?"

"Boyd, did you even stop to ask Malcolm or Lillian if they've even been on a horse?"

"No, but how hard can it be? You just crawl up and sit on its fucking back."

———

The farmer continued to shake his head, stunned that with all the grown men they had running round and round his field, that they still couldn't control one damned horse.

"Maybe if you had a gentler horse Noah. Maybe something a little older," Julia politely suggested. "Maybe then…"

"Shit." He yanked the cowboy hat off his head to dust off the front of his denim pants. "I pick one any older; she's gonna be stone cold dead."

Malcolm decided it was time he added his two cents, since he was going to be the one expected to ride bareback.

"I ain't getting up on that unless it stands totally still. There's nothing in my contract about breaking bones to make a film."

"Don't be such a girl," Boyd hissed, walking up beside the farmer. "Is there some way we can stabilize your horse so she won't buck when my actors climb up on top of her back?"

"Guess we can tether her."

"Then let's tether her." Boyd threw up his arms.

With two men holding her reins, and another two squatting low in the grass holding the leather straps tethered to the mare's back legs, everyone anxiously waited for the actors to try and climb up on their mount.

"They're just gonna be in their birthday suits." The old farmer couldn't help but laugh. "You trying to tell me that they're gonna ride like that?"

"Not exactly ride," Boyd leaned over and gave him a little nudge.

As Malcolm started to make his way toward the horse, he stopped for a brief second to hand Jeannie his robe, proudly puffing out his chest as he forced himself to climb up the wooden steps and throw his left leg over the animal's bare back.

"Now just get comfortable," Boyd tried to keep his actor calm as Lillian appeared from behind one of the stationary cameras.

Also handing her robe to the make-up lady, she gracefully ascended the stairs and slowly swung her right leg high up and over the horse's neck, wiggling to bring herself face to face with Malcolm. Being careful not to move more than absolutely necessary, Lillian slowly set each leg on top of her co-stars, effectively bringing their bodies together, chest to chest.

"Okay, get comfortable, and try not to scream or fidget around." Boyd slowly made his way as close to the animal as he dared without encroaching on the shoot.

"Hold down that tether," the farmer barked at one of Boyd's grips as he struggled to steady the horse.

"I can't," the kid whined. "He's gonna kick me."

Trudging through the grass, the weathered old farmer leaned down and yanked the leather straps from the kid's hand, instantly shoving him out of the way while he gently pulled back to let the horse know it had even pressure.

Satisfied that a pending emergency had been diverted, Boyd turned his attention back to his stars, encouraging them to start getting into the scene.

"Now there's no dialog, so I'll cue up a little music and we'll just continue on. I'll dub in a few moans and groans later." He looked toward Julia, aware of how much she usually hated voiceovers.

"Fine," she nodded, bending down to cross check their storyboards. "Just don't forget that the client wants to see lots of nipple action. Him on her, and her on him."

"You heard the lady. Don't forget them nipples," Boyd firmly ordered his actors.

Hoping to help put Malcolm and Lillian in just the right mood, Julia bent down to start the CD player, unaware that during transport the volume had inadvertently been turned all the way up.

As the throbbing rock music began to pulsate through the speakers, the horse began to pull against the ropes, and even though Julia immediately hit the power button to stop the noise, the damage had already been done.

"Whoa girl." The farmer jumped to his feet, dropping his rear tether to run to the front and grab hold of the reins.

"What the fuck?" Malcolm began to yell. "Get me off this thing," he squealed as his voice began to take on an extremely excited pitch.

"Take it easy." Boyd rushed up, waving his arms but effectively accomplishing nothing.

"Just sit," Lillian attempted to coax her costar. "You're making the horse nervous with all your twisting around."

"Fuck you," Malcolm answered her in one simple statement, turning his body to try and slide sideways off the horse.

"Stop it." Lillian started to get mad, his grinding hips inadvertently pinching the tender skin on the underside of her bare buttocks. "Please stay still!"

With all his twisting, Malcolm had somehow managed to lean far enough to his right to lose his balance, effectively pulling himself and Lillian right off the horse, down on top of the unforgiving wooden steps.

As the farmer fought to bring his horse under control, Wanda rushed forward right past the cameras, stopping dead in her tracks when she spotted the blood beginning to pour from the side of Lillian's head.

CHAPTER THIRTY-ONE

"Sometimes it's just stopping—allowing the pain to come."
—Flightplan, 2005

"Is that really blood seeping out of that guy's hat?" Julia leaned over and quietly whispered in her husband's ear.

"I don't know." He continued to flip through one of the waiting room's magazines.

"Well, don't you think we should tell somebody?"

"He's sitting in a goddamn emergency room." Boyd finally raised his face to meet his wife's. "I think they already know."

"Fine," Julia sniffed, pivoting toward Wanda. "Did you notice that guy's hat? I think there's blood dripping down the side."

"I know," she whispered back. "I think we should tell somebody."

"I think you're right." Julia stood up and simultaneously shot Boyd a dirty look. "I'm going to get some help."

"Try to make it a doctor this time."

Mouthing the words *fuck off,* Julia turned and marched straight up to the intake desk.

"One second," the nurse said as she held up her finger, taking a brief minute to forward a few of her blinking lines.

Try to make it a doctor. Who in the hell did she think she was going to call this time?

Well, it wasn't her fault that everyone from the cleaning staff all the way up to the chief of surgery seemed to run around in drab cotton pantsuits. What happened to the good old days; when a nurse wore a little white dress, the doctor a lab coat, and the janitor had the name *Stan* embroidered over his left pocket?

Besides, the orderly she'd addressed as doctor had turned out to be so sweet. He'd practically tripped over himself running to find a fresh gurney for Lillian to lie down on.

"Mr. and Mrs. Giovanni." A doctor appeared in the waiting room.

"Yes," Julia rushed up to his side. "Is Lillian going to be fine?"

"It was just a one inch dermal laceration and I see no signs of a concussion. I've put two small stitches in her scalp to help control the bleeding and alleviate the chances of any opportunistic infection setting in while the wound naturally seals itself. When I left, the nurse was just about finished dressing her wound."

"Thank you, doctor." Julia smiled from ear to ear. "Can we go see her now?"

"Sure, but only two at a time." He nodded as Wanda and Boyd both crossed the floor to join him. "I hope you understand. It's pretty tight quarters back in our treatment area."

"We understand." Julia reached out to link her fingers through her husband's. "We'll only be a minute." She suddenly turned to face Wanda. "You don't mind?"

"No, go ahead. I'll just wait right here."

As both Julia and Boyd rushed off to check on their hurt employee, Wanda turned back toward her seat in the waiting room, nearly knocked off her feet by a young man dragging two very upset children.

"Please sit," he tried to plead with them.

"I want mommy," the smallest started to cry.

"Me too," the older brother joined in with his baby sister's sobs.

"They're inseparable," he turned to apologize. "One starts crying and it just sets the other right off."

Wanda nodded, not in the mood to make small talk with this stranger, no matter how needy he appeared to be.

"I've never knew kids could be that close. Did you?"

Wanda nearly dropped her purse; her fingers reaching out to grab the carved wooden handle at it began to slip toward the floor.

Growing up, she'd been that close with her brother. Hell, her mother used to say they actually shared a brain. The big family joke had been to speculate who'd get custody of the organ when they finally separated and went off to college.

As twin brother and sister, Warren and Wanda were even closer than most. Sharing the same classrooms through grade school and the same friends through junior high, they'd even weathered puberty hand in hand. But it wasn't until the summer of the eleventh grade, after they'd been forced to share genuine heartbreak, did they finally achieve their true level of symbiosis.

During the twin's seventeenth birthday dinner, Warren Finkel senior had dropped dead of a heart attack in the family kitchen, and in their wildest dreams, no one could have imagined just how much life was about to change. Within the blink of an eye, they'd been forced to rely on only each other, all external measures of support suddenly evaporating from their lives.

Within two months of their father's funeral, their mother had been forced to sell the family home and move her children out of the city to their Uncle Mike's farm. The move was traumatic, but the subsequent breakup of their uncle and aunt's marriage turned out to be even worse.

Without any hint of things to come, their mother suddenly moved from the spare room into their uncle's bed, and with the move, of course, came the blame. Their cousins would not let them forget how Warren and Wanda had wrecked their family, ensuring complete and total alienation at home, as well as at school.

It was nearly the end of senior year before Warren even considered dating, and when he fell, he fell hard. When the relationship eventually ended, he of course turned to his sister for the comfort he desperately needed.

One night, as they listened to their uncle's portable radio while hanging out in the barn's hayloft, Warren had begun unburdening his soul. He cried about the father he'd lost, their alienation at school, and the true love he believed he'd never experience.

Wanda had reached over to comfort him, and within a blink of any eye, found herself pinned down on the hay. What first appeared to be an emotional embrace soon turned into a physical struggle, as he began pawing and groping her tender young breasts.

"Please don't," she'd begged, shocked that he'd be so rough with her body after the practice time they'd spent tenderly kissing.

Warren relaxed; his hands slowing as he gently explained that his love, although unnatural, was truly the real thing.

Wanda's objections were silenced with hungry kisses, as her brother systemically stripped her body of all her clothes. Finally lying totally naked underneath his body, she had tried to reason with him that night, begging that he step back and try to see what he was doing, and why it was so totally wrong.

Warren couldn't understand his sister's objections. As his lips attempted to kiss away her tears, his right hand continued to pin her wrists high above her head while his left roamed freely up and down the length of her exposed body.

At first, he'd been satisfied to rub himself against her. But as his passion built, his need for satisfaction grew, and Warren found himself pressing his throbbing penis up between her legs.

"Please don't. It's going to hurt me," Wanda had continued to beg, her throat hoarse from crying, her mind whirling with the imminent loss of her virginity.

The initial thrust had been the worst, the sharp pain sending little white dots of light swirling in front of her eyes, but then the second and third hadn't really been that much better. Thankfully, he'd been quick, and by the time Warren had eventually released her wrists and rolled over on the hay next to her, Wanda had suddenly stopped crying.

"I love you," he continued to chant.

She answered by rising to her feet and attempting to dress, mindful of her lost buttons and broken zipper.

Wanda had never told a soul, and Warren had never tried anything like it again. Luckily, she hadn't become pregnant that night, so as the years passed, it had almost been possible to pretend it never happened at all.

Tonight, Wanda prayed her luck would hold one more time, because she didn't have a clue what she'd do if her very own twin brother had somehow managed to impregnate her.

Dragging over his pad of paper, Pete began scratching out a written list of the special times in his life where he'd seemed to escape death. Like the time he crashed head on into the telephone pole doing sixty, and the cop had told him that he was just damned lucky to be alive and in one piece.

Or the time he'd found himself at a party with a bunch of Hell's Angels. He had matched the guys, line for line, drink for drink, until noon the next day, when one of their own supporters just stood up from the table and then suddenly crumpled to the floor, dead as a door knob.

Pete knew he was kind of special. Maybe he could be one of the fifteen percent of addicts who managed to kick their habit. It was a big *if* to count on so early in the game, but he definitely needed something to hold onto.

Rejuvenated by the idea, Pete slowly rose from his blankets to relieve his bladder, his knees stiff from lying motionless on his mattress for the last twenty-four hours. Feeling sorry for himself, he'd spent most of the previous night wallowing in his own sorrow, afraid that he was doomed to a pitiful life with little or no foreseeable future.

Now a faint ray of hope seemed to shine through the darkness. It was definitely faint, but it was there, and he could feel it as he returned to his literature.

According to what he read, Pete had a long struggle ahead of him. For a successful recovery and treatment, he'd need to make his way through the first stages of detox and that could range anywhere from four to six weeks.

"Done," he mentally checked the first step off in his head, surprised to suddenly read that physical cravings for meth could last up to a year, often intensifying at three-month intervals. "Great," Pete continued to study, a little disheartened to find that a strong psychological addiction triggered by common sights, conversations, and thoughts, could easily lead to a quick relapse if not kept under control.

"Methamphetamine users are considered the hardest type of addicts to treat," he read aloud. *"Most do not suffer significant physical or psychological symptoms until they are firmly addicted, and then they try to deny they have a problem for as long as they can, because they do not want to give up something that makes them feel so good."*

Dropping the book back down on his mattress, Pete rose again and began anxiously pacing the small eight by ten foot room.

"Doesn't anybody have anything good to say?" he shouted out at no one in particular, pissed off that it was already the second week of his self-imposed isolation and he felt no measurable change.

In an attempt to shake off his sense of doom, he decided to have something to eat and maybe try to lay down for an afternoon nap. Walking over, he evaluated his cache of supplies. Choosing a juice box and two granola bars, he strolled back to his mattress and plopped down amongst the sleeping bags, surprised at how the exhaustion seem to encompass his body.

Every time he closed his eyes, the nightmares had been horrible. But he was just so damned tired, his body fighting to rid itself of the dangerous pollutants trapped in each and every one of his cells.

Damned if he did and damned if he didn't, he laid his head back on the pillow, closing his eyes as he waited for sleep to overtake him and the nightmares to follow right behind.

"I guess we can't just put her in a cab." Boyd looked at his wife Julia, as Lillian busied herself signing multiple copies of the hospital's release forms.

"Well, I could drive her home," Julia suggested.

"With what? All we have is the hummer and we have to head back to the shoot and make sure everything was packed and properly dismantled."

"I'll take her home." Wanda quietly stepped out of the background. "I don't have my car with me, but I can ride with her in a cab and make sure she gets home in one piece."

"Good idea." Julia fumbled to find her cell phone.

"And make sure to bill the office," Boyd yelled across the floor.

Settled in the taxicab, Lillian and Wanda both continued to wave until they'd cleared the hospital's parking lot.

"How's your head feeling?" Wanda gently inquired.

"It hurts, but I'll be fine. I got these," Lillian held up a small white envelope. "I'm supposed to take two when I get home and then another two before I go to sleep."

"T-3's?"

"Yeah, I think so." She quickly peeked down into the paper folds.

"Well, watch out," Wanda felt compelled to warn. "I had them once for a sprained ankle and they bunged me up so bad I had to go back and get a prescription for suppositories."

"What are suppositories?"

Sometimes she forgot just how young Lillian was. She may have been a quick study, picking up on the unwritten rules of the porn business in record time, but she was still an uneducated young woman, struggling to make her way in the big city.

"Just make sure to eat a lot of fresh fruit and vegetables when you're taking the pills," Wanda warned. "They can actually do a number on your stomach."

Digging down in her knapsack, Lillian finally found the exact address of Brandy's apartment, having given the driver only basic instruction to bring him to the right corner of town.

"You just moved into a new place?"

"Actually, it's not my place, it's…"

"Your boyfriend's?" Wanda took a guess.

"Actually," Lillian swallowed hard. "My girlfriend's."

Wanda wasn't shocked, she'd actually found the information strangely comforting. The idea of two women living together sounded peaceful, a simpler life without conflicts or worry. A life different from the one she'd lived, where the men had been anything but a source of comfort.

"How long have you two been living together?"

"Only a few days," Lillian excitedly turned to face Wanda, "and

I'm loving every minute of it. But it's busy, especially with the diapers and balancing the day care schedule and all."

"I didn't know you had a child together?"

"Oh no," she adamantly shook her head. "We don't. I'm just babysitting my nephew Tito until the social worker can either find his mother or some other suitable home. It's just temporary. You ever live with anyone, Wanda?"

"Just family when I was growing up."

"Really? That sounds so lonely, don't you think?"

"Right now, I'm more interested in my career than finding the right guy. I prefer to spend all my spare time working. But I do have a niece who's very special to me, too."

"That's cool," Lillian turned to look out the cab window. "Hey Wanda, can I ask you a personal question?"

"Shoot."

"Well Brandy, that's my girlfriend's name," she suddenly blushed. "Well, Brandy said that I'd be just asking for it if I told anyone about our living arrangements. Do you think she's right?"

"It's really no one's business what you do after hours, and to tell you the truth, I don't think anyone at Giovanni Films would really be that shocked to find out that one of their employees is gay and sleeping with someone of the same sex. You know what I mean?"

"Well, we do make pornos, don't we?" She couldn't help but laugh. "And Julia did tell me herself that *girl on girl* is one of the most common fantasies in our business."

"See, you understand," Wanda took a second to read the passing street signs. "But…" She suddenly felt compelled to share a last thought with the girl, "Brandy might have a point about keeping your personal life under wraps for awhile."

"Why?"

"Because sometimes our personal lives are much too painful when they're exposed to the light of day. What seems normal, or maybe even acceptable to us, may appear seedy or possibly evil in the eyes of many others. People don't always understand the choices we've made, or the secrets we've been forced to keep. They're too… critical. They're too…" she searched for another word, "judgmental."

"Are you gay, too?" Lillian blurted out the question without taking a minute to ponder the inappropriateness of her request.

"No," Wanda shook her head."

"Husband? Boyfriend?" she continued, unwilling to back off without at least a few pieces of the puzzle.

Shaking her head no, Wanda couldn't help but smirk. How could she possibly explain to this young girl that she'd never been seriously in love, especially not with her last boyfriend, Pete Giovanni? If you could even call what they had a relationship, because looking back now, she only felt disgust. She was about as experienced in long-term committed relationships as a catholic nun, and just about as interested.

"It's all about the career," she repeated.

"Sounds so lonely."

"Maybe, but it's a choice I've made, and right now in my life, it suits me just fine."

"So you wanna come up and meet Brandy?"

"No, I'd better get home and…" Wanda stopped dead. Her brother Warren had more than likely staked out her house and her office. He'd be making the rounds, dying to speak to her. Not the type to give up until he'd made his point, Wanda realized that heading home was definitely asking for trouble.

"Actually, I'll come up and say hi. I'd like to meet your nephew."

"Good. Then let's go," Lillian swung open the cab door while Wanda reached over the seat to sign the driver's payment stub.

CHAPTER THIRTY-TWO

"I know things can get a little scary, but courage isn't the absence of fear. It is the presence of fear, yet the will to go on."

—*Black Knight, 2002*

Watching Brandy and Lillian interact with Tito was slowly breaking Wanda's heart. She couldn't exactly put her finger on it, but seeing a couple who had no biological link or binding marriage contract still do such a good job parenting a toddler together somehow felt like a slap in the face.

Why were they able to handle it when even her own mother hadn't been able to do a decent job? What kind of special parenting gene did these two women have that had obviously eluded her own family?

"Mama," Tito reached up to Lillian for another sip from his juice cup.

"Aunty," she repeated for the tenth time that night before handing him his drink.

"Kid can't get it through his head." Brandy bent down and

snatched the child off the living room floor. "He thinks anybody with tits who hands him food has to be his mama. Well, I ain't your mama." She shook her head, the sudden attention sending Tito into a fit of laughter. "See?" She held him by his waist, still mindful of his sore shoulder. "He ain't right in the head."

Wanda watched Brandy tuck the little boy in at her side and start walking down the hall toward the bedroom.

"He stinks to high heaven. I'm gonna check what kind of load he's dropped."

"Thanks," Lillian called out.

"Well, I think it's time I called a cab and headed out too. You're gonna need to rest, and I should get back to the office and pick up my car."

"So, what you think?" Lillian excitedly danced on the tip of her toes.

"I think you have a good thing going on here."

"I know. It feels good to me too."

Wanda rose up from her seat and reluctantly started to move toward the apartment's door.

"You going?" Brandy suddenly reappeared.

"Yeah. I still gotta head back to the office and clear up a few things before I can call it a day."

"Well, thanks for bringing her home," Brandy threaded her arm around Lillian's waist.

"You're welcome," she said with a smile, dialing the number of the cab company that Julia had called earlier, while slowly making her way down the building's front stairs.

"Where to?" the cabbie asked, right hand poised on his computerized meter, as Wanda wearily crawled into his backseat.

"I'm not sure," she admitted, with a shake of her head.

"Well, I can't help you, lady. You're gonna have to figure that one out for yourself. But I gotta be honest," he engaged the meter. "The clock's ticking as of right now."

Laughing, Wanda finally pulled herself together and recited the address to Giovanni Films, taking a second to dig through her purse for her parking badge since she planned on bringing the cab straight down into the underground garage.

"You like movies, lady?"

"I like movies."

"That building you're going to. I hear they make special movies up in there. That true?"

It was dark outside and Wanda realized she was traveling down deserted side streets in the back of a car with a man she didn't know.

"I'm just a receptionist who answers the phone. I really don't know what goes on upstairs." She felt her heart began to race inside the confines of her chest.

He didn't immediately answer, and even in the minimal light afforded by the oncoming traffic, Wanda could still feel him checking her out in his rear-view mirror.

"You look like you could be an actress."

"Well, I'm not," she snapped back.

"So you say." He slowly shrugged his shoulders.

"I think I've changed my mind," she nervously began to fidget with her purse. "You can just drop me up there at the donut shop. I think I'll get a coffee before I go back to work."

"Sounds good. How about we have two coffees to go? I'll run in and grab us a couple and maybe we can just drink them in the car? How much you think your coffee is gonna cost?"

"What?" She watched the cabbie suddenly cancel the meter's running tally.

"What you think a large is worth? Forty, fifty bucks?"

The picture was becoming clear. He'd somehow mistaken her for a hooker who obviously worked in the film industry making pornography, and he had the gall to try to negotiate a cash price for sexual favors.

"You're going to stop this car and I'm going to get out." Wanda calmly laid out her plan. "You're not going to follow me inside the donut shop, or hang around in the parking lot. I'm not a hooker, I'm a secretary. And if you don't believe me, maybe you'd like to explain your suspicions to the cops?"

He never said another word as Wanda jumped out of the back seat and ran straight toward the safety of the public restaurant.

"Anywhere you want," the waitress shouted as she rung up a patron's order.

Wanda chose a small table in the corner and immediately ordered a coffee, hoping the steaming liquid would calm her nerves and the break would somehow change the course of her evening.

"Here you go." The waitress quickly returned, cup and saucer in one hand, and the coffee pot in the other.

"Sorry, but I changed my mind. I think I'll just take it to go."

As the waitress made her way back to the counter, Wanda followed her, purse still tightly clasped in her fingers. As Wanda's eyes casually scanned the pegboard that hung directly behind the till; she couldn't help but comment on the collection of taxicab business cards.

"You know any of those driver's personally?"

"George is real good. But if you're looking to trade, better call an independent."

"Trade?" she repeated without thinking.

"Yeah. Independents aren't usually hooked up by computer to their dispatch. They can trade their fares for a few miles on your ass, if you know what I mean. But any of the big four, they'd have to explain why their fare didn't clock on their meter."

"I think I was just in an independent." Wanda took a deep breath and confided in the waitress.

"Take a seat," the waitress pointed to one of the counter's front stools. "I'm gonna give George a call and you can fix up your coffee while you wait."

"Can I ask you one more question?" Wanda called out as the waitress picked up the phone and prepared to dial.

"Sure child. Ask away?"

"Do I look like the kind of woman who would trade sex for a free cab ride?"

"Do I?" she fired back.

"No, absolutely not," Wanda sat straight up on her stool.

"Well, there you go." She finished dialing the cab's number. "You can't tell shit just by looking."

He had to get home before his daughter started to panic. Last thing Warren needed was for Amber to call his ex-wife and get her all riled up, too. He'd just had the day from hell, and there was no way he had the patience to deal with his ex. She'd have gone ballistic if she knew that he'd just used some of his precious holiday time to stalk his own sister. His salary and any paid leave were stretched thin enough for a third-year electrician without unscheduled days off, obviously his fault for changing career paths in midlife.

Grabbing a bucket of take-out chicken, Warren reluctantly abandoned his well-worn route and turned the car towards home. Over the last eight hours, he'd clocked at least a hundred miles driving back and forth between his sister's apartment, the two neighboring motels, and her office building downtown. No matter how many times he checked, she still was nowhere to be found. Wanda was hiding, and she obviously wasn't ready to surface yet.

Checking his cell phone for *the call* that never arrived, Warren decided that everything else would have to wait until tomorrow. Tonight, he'd have to return home and play father.

He'd eat, listen while Amber talked about her day, then excuse himself early and head straight up to bed. After a long hot shower, he'd try to make sense of what he'd done; it would be a struggle to put all the scrambled pieces back together, but come morning, he was sure they'd somehow fit.

For a night that had started out so innocently, Warren now found himself carefully replaying the hours, trying to pinpoint the exact minute when everything suddenly turned to shit.

"Basketball, then beers," he began literally retracing his own footsteps. He remembered sharing one joint with Arnold in the car before heading inside and drinking his first pint. But it wasn't just the beers, if Warren's memory served him right. The guys had moved from draft, to shooters, and the taste of limes and salt suddenly returned to upset his stomach.

"Fuck," he groaned, his bouts of early morning nausea now beginning to make sense. Good thing he'd been able to make the bathroom. Wanda would be mad enough without the stink of vomit contaminating her living room rug.

He couldn't exactly remember the initial cab ride over from the local pub, but he could remember waiting for his sister at the bottom of her stairs. Unsure if he'd sat for ten minutes or ten hours, Warren figured he must have sobered up somewhat during his wait, his memory finally beginning to register his version of the night's events once he reached his sister's condominium.

She'd offered him something to drink, and they'd sat down to talk. Warren was pretty sure he had wanted to talk to Wanda about his relationship failures from the past and the present, but he just couldn't recall anything they'd said.

Then the mood had suddenly changed. His sister had turned to him with her puppy-dog eyes and looked at him as she had when he was a teenager. That needing look, the one that said *nobody else understands me but you.*

He tried to resist her, fought the urge to touch her, but once again Wanda had gotten her way. She was a beautiful woman, and no man in his right mind would have been able to deny her. He knew it, and so did she.

Still, he was fighting the nagging feeling that he might have used her. Enjoyed her body for his own personal pleasure. He needed to talk with her, to make sure he hadn't treated her like a sexual object. Wanda was better than that; she was a woman of class.

All Warren could do was pray that his sister would understand that if he had rushed, if his touch had been hurried, it was not his fault. It had been so long since he'd made love, he might have acted a little like an animal.

She'd understand, because she loved him, too. This he knew for a fact, because she'd told him.

And that's exactly how Warren remembered it.

———————

Boyd watched Julia frantically dig to the bottom of her clutch purse, desperately searching for any kind of spark.

"You aren't planning on smoking those in here, are you?" he nodded toward the hand-rolled joints she'd managed to pull out of some secret compartment.

"I've had a fuck of a day, and yes, I plan to smoke those in here. Actually, I plan to smoke until I can't remember a goddamn thing."

Boyd hadn't seen his wife so stressed for a long time, and for some strange reason, he was finding it slightly amusing.

"So maybe I should stop and grab you a six pack and a bag of Cheetos, too?"

"Piss off."

Pulling his hummer off the main road, Boyd was finally able to spot a deserted side street and immediately parked under a clump of over-hanging trees.

"Come on, let's go," he grabbed Julia's hand seconds before she lit up her first joint.

"Where?"

"For a walk."

"Fine. But I'm taking my shit," she shoved everything back into her purse before reluctantly stepping out the passenger's door.

Gently guiding her toward a solitary tree, its hanging branches offering them some semblance of privacy, Boyd reached for his wife's hand and gently pulled her toward a clean patch near the base of the trunk.

"Are we done now, or you wanna dig us a foxhole before I spark this shit up?"

"Go ahead," he chuckled, lying back in the grass, shifting his shoulder blades to find the most comfortable position against the tree trunk.

"We were lucky," Julia announced as she held back her last breath, attempting to trap the smoke in her lungs as long as humanly possible.

"Yeah, I guess we were."

"That girl," she exclaimed in one large gush of air, "could have easily broken her neck. We gotta get some kind of insurance. Something to cover our asses."

"I hear ya, and I'm on it." Boyd accepted the joint from his wife's outstretched hand and brought it straight up to his lips.

"And we gotta talk about going digital. Martin's been nagging me ever since that sploshing film. Claims he could have really worked miracles with a digital editing program. Guess our video filming equipment is ready for the archives. Some shit about manipulating pixels...blah, blah, blah," Julia waved off the remainder of her own explanation.

"I hear," Boyd reluctantly agreed. "We're dinosaurs, and if we don't adapt, we're gonna go extinct."

"Speak for yourself," Julia smirked, her shoulders beginning to relax with the ingestion of the marijuana.

"Hey, you notice our little purchasing agent out at the shoot?" Boyd began to replay the day's highlights.

"Yeah, bit of surprise. Wasn't it?"

"What was that all about?" Boyd passed back the smoldering grass. "You handcuff her and then throw the poor girl in the back of your car?"

"No," Julia took another giant drag. "Believe it or not, she almost ran out of the building when she got word that her brother was hanging around down in the lobby."

"Really?"

"Really," Julia flicked the roach across the grass before cuddling in at her husband's side. "And you notice her wrists?"

Boyd had, but he thought he might have been the only one. "Brother related?"

"Fucked if I know, but whoever made those bruises, they scared her shitless.

Both lay back contemplating the information while enjoying the pot buzz beginning to wash down over their bodies.

"You know what else?"

"What, baby?" Boyd reached over, bravely sneaking his left hand up under his wife's tailored blouse as he mischievously attempted to free one of her concealed nipples.

"I heard some of the staff gossiping in the lunch room this morning, and they were saying that Wanda had spent the night on her couch."

"Her office couch?" he repeated, suddenly more concerned with his own *search and rescue mission* than his staff's personal problems.

"Yeah, but I thought she lived alone?"

"Now I have to keep track of our staff's living arrangements, too?"

"No," Julia sat back up and reached for her purse.

"We smoke anymore of that shit, and neither of us will be able to drive."

"Then we'll call for the car," she reasoned, sparking up the second joint.

"And leave my new Hummer here?"

"Hummer, Hummer, Hummer. That's all you fucking think about." She passed the joint to her husband.

"I love that Hummer."

"I love hummers, too." With that, Julia dropped her head and began nuzzling into the warmth of her husband's crotch.

CHAPTER THIRTY-THREE

"What is it that makes a man, a man? Is it his origins, the way things start? Or is it something else, something harder to describe."

—*Hellboy, 2004*

Ronnie sat back and watched Jerome tear into his second chocolate Easter bunny, positive that within an hour, he'd more than likely just be puking his guts up all over the street.

"You sure you don't want none?" Jerome held up the headless figure. "Cuz I gots' lots."

"No, I'm good. Fill your boots bro."

"It's got something in the middle!" He excitedly dropped the bunny down on top of its cardboard box. Smashing the hollow body into a hundred chocolate shards with one fatal blow from his fist, Jerome was finally able to expose the cellophane packet of candy.

"Good, more sugar," Ronnie moaned.

"Gummi Bears. I love Gummi Bears," Jerome excitedly reported, ripping open the package and pouring the rainbow colored candy down into his mouth.

Ronnie sat quietly on the broken fence, watching his best friend continue to gorge himself, surprised that they'd been able to find the old Easter stock at a liquidation store for pennies on the dollar.

"They're... they're... really hard," he barely was able to move his jaw.

"Just swallow. We gotta get moving."

Jerome struggled to comply, forcing the dried *soft chews* down the back of his throat. "So what we gonna do now?" He grabbed a can of cola and swished the liquid back and forth across his teeth.

"Well, I was just thinking about that," Ronnie said as he lit another smoke. "The way I see it, we're back to square one. We's got no more profit left, since you and Freddy managed to smoke most of that."

"Sorry."

"Whatever." Ronnie carefully tucked his smokes back into his jacket pocket. "So we're gonna have to hit the streets again and try to sell the couple rocks we got left for a little higher price than usual. Make some profit real fast, cuz right now, we got nowhere to sleep, and no money for real food. Know what I mean?"

"Where we gonna sell them?"

"Only one place I know of."

Jerome suddenly lost interest in his treats, jumping to his feet to try to change his best friend's plan. "You don't really wanna do that, do you?"

"We're outta options, man."

"But if we get caught up there again, this time they'll beat us 'til we're dead," he alluded to the strip of uptown nightclubs favored by mostly university and college students.

"But that's where the bucks are. You know it, and I know it. Those trust fund babies don't give a fuck how much they pay, as long as it's there when they want it."

"But if we get caught..."

"We ain't gonna get caught!"

Jerome suddenly didn't know what to do. He'd walk barefoot over broken glass for Ronnie, but this was a suicide mission. You didn't just waltz into Triad territory, pedal your dope, and then think you were going to waltz out untouched.

"I uh... I uh... I don't know bro." He nervously shuffled his feet. "There's only two of us, and hundreds of them fuckers. And... and... and they're mean. Really, really mean," he said as his voice suddenly began to quiver. "I don't wanna get beat again. Please?" he actually begged. "Please think of something else we can do."

Ronnie had never seen Jerome so scared; his face turning a funny grayish white at the mere mention of a trip into Asian gang territory.

"We sell all this," Ronnie explained, pulling the dope out of his pocket, "and we only got an extra ten bucks after we re-buy. Shit man, that's just enough for two burgers and two pops. That ain't living, that's just fucking surviving. That'll mean another night on the street. Another night in this stinky fucking underwear, and a whole other night with no place to lie down. I'm tired bro, I'm really fucking tired. I don't wanna have to walk my way through another twenty-four hours."

"Me neither," Jerome reluctantly nodded his head in agreement.

"So, I've got a new plan."

"Really?"

"Yeah." Ronnie stood up and ground his cigarette butt into the asphalt. "You know how you usually watch my back, making sure that nobody's coming 'round to jump me when I'm making a sale?"

"Oh yeah. Like when I whistle if any cars look like they're gonna turn down the alley?"

"Exactly. But this time, I think it'll work better if I go alone."

"Why?"

"Cuz I don't think the two of us blend in that well. We don't look like we go to college, so I think it's best if there's just one of us. But I'll take your jacket," he pointed to Jerome's navy windbreaker, "and you take mine. And your hat," Ronnie said as he started to think aloud. "I'll take your hat, too."

Reluctantly, Jerome handed over his belongings.

"And your cell phone," he added by pointing to Jerome's front pocket.

"But it don't even work no more."

"So? Nobody knows that, and it just looks good."

"How long you gonna be gone?" He watched Ronnie slick his hair back behind his ears, hiding his remaining waves underneath the peak of his cap.

"I walk up there, sell my shit, and then maybe take a bus back." He stopped to figure. "Three or four hours, tops."

Jerome wanted to say something smart, something to make his best friend feel like everything was going to work out fine. Unfortunately, he couldn't think of anything worth saying, so as usual, he just kept his mouth shut.

"We'll meet right here at midnight." Ronnie pointed at the broken fence that cordoned off the back alley. "Midnight, that's when they shut the lights off in the big grocery store across the street."

"Midnight," Jerome repeated, planning to never lose sight of the grocery store's front window.

"I have a little money for ya." Ronnie handed Jerome every last piece of change from the bottom of his pockets. "Should be enough for another pop, maybe a handful of licorice. But that's all," he warned, "so make it last."

'Til midnight?" Jerome confirmed.

'Til midnight."

———————

Julia crossed Lillian's name off her *to do list* the second after she hung up the phone, satisfied the girl was taking it easy during her recovery.

"You want something before I run?" Boyd waited for his wife to answer.

"Nah. I might just order a pizza later. Looks like I'm gonna be stuck here for a while.

"Really, what's the hold up?"

"Our Mr. Francois Dubois."

"I gotta tell you, Julia; even that guy's name rubs me the wrong way. I don't know why, but the hairs on the back of my neck stand up the minute I know you're even thinking about that asshole."

"Well, I don't hate the man like you do, but I gotta tell ya Boyd, he's becoming a real pain in my ass."

"Long as he ain't a pain in your pussy."

"Come here, you big jerk." Julia shook her head as she motioned her husband over toward her desk. "See all this shit. I've made a giant pile of possible guys that fit Dubois's specific little profile. Unfortunately, eighteen and nineteen year olds flit in and out of this business at the drop of a hat. By the time I finally make a decision and call one of their contact numbers, the little fuckers have either taken a union job down at the manufacturing plant, or they're doing a nickel for possession with intent to traffic. I can't seem to win."

"Don't take this the wrong way, but I gotta ask you something."

"Shoot," Julia stood up to refill her wine glass.

"You really think this one film is worth it. I mean, don't you think maybe we gotta draw the line somewhere?"

"You're right, we do. But if we pass on this film, I want it to be because it hit one of our top three absolutes. Not because the client just rubs us the wrong way."

"Then let's review," Boyd joined his wife at the bar cart and finished off the remainder of her bottle. "First off. Can we bring it in on budget? You quoted that guy a price and I was wondering, with all the extra time and money spent dealing with a whole whack of independents, are we still gonna be in the black when this project's in the can?"

"Yes," she nodded her head. "But to be honest, when it comes to budgets, I'm more concerned with our Pocahontas film right now. We've got to schedule a third shoot, and I still can't guarantee when we're finally gonna have that project ready for delivery."

"Okay fine, whatever. We're probably on budget then. But how about our *No Minors* policy? You gonna be able to pull in enough young talent that'll pass for thirteen year old boys?"

Downing her third glass, Julia absentmindedly began flipping through the stack of files occupying most of her desk space.

"I can't tell you right this second, but I'll know for sure by tonight."

"Well, that's two out of three, but what about the third?"

Julia hated the third. She always had, even though she'd originally been the one to put the last absolute in place.

"Are you vetoing this project Boyd?" she demanded in one simple question. "Cuz I need to know, and I need to know right now. If you're gonna pull the rug out from underneath my feet, I wanna know tonight. I ain't putting in another minute's work on this fucking film if you're vetoing it anyway. Alright?"

"I didn't say I was using my veto."

"Enough bullshitting. Yes or no?"

In the history of Giovanni Films, Boyd had only been prepared to veto one other project, and in retrospect, it would have been a good move.

Their prospective client had ordered a *mock snuff*, and even before Julia had been able to sketch out some of the basic details that would be necessary for faking their actress's death, the client had been yanked from his very own home in the middle of the night and arrested for second-degree murder.

Only by the grace of God, had Giovanni Films escaped all the negative publicity associated with the case, but to this day, Boyd still wondered how much of their private business had been captured on the cop's surveillance tapes.

Having finally made his decision, Boyd walked up to his wife and gently closed her open file. "I got a bad feeling about this project, and to protect us, and our company, I am going to use my veto."

Julia dropped down into her chair. "You're gonna veto it now? After all my hours of fucking research, you gonna fucking veto it tonight?" she angrily repeated.

"Yeah, I am."

"Well, look who's got the biggest balls now." She spun her chair around to face the rear wall.

"You can be as pissed at me as you want, but this is the right decision," Boyd set his glass down with an audible thud.

"For you?"

"For us."

Spinning her chair back toward her desk, Julia jumped up and walked over to where her husband was standing his ground. "I meet with the client; I negotiate the deal, I even spend my days locating the necessary talent. Then without warning, you waltz into my office and announce you're activating your veto and blowing off the project. Did I get that right?"

"He's a freak," Boyd shouted, tired of trying to reason with his wife.

"Everybody's a freak. We make fucking porn. You think we're dealing with the cream of the crop?"

"I... don't... like... him," Boyd growled through clenched teeth.

"So?"

"So I'm vetoing the project. End of topic!"

"Julia Giovanni," a young man suddenly appeared at her door. "Sorry to barge in, but nobody is sitting at that desk out there, and..."

"Who the fuck are you?" Boyd glared at the kid, heart pounding as he tried to control his impending outburst.

"I'm Justin Carrera. Your office called me in for an interview and told me to bring any samples of my work. Here they are." He offered up a paper folder.

"I'm outta here." Boyd turned on his heels and started to walk out Julia's door.

"Oh no you don't." She started to run after her husband. "You're the one who exercised your veto. You're the one who can clean up the mess."

Justin stood his ground in the middle of the office, wondering what in the hell was shaking loose around him.

"I told you, I gotta go. Dinner at ma's."

"Boyd, don't you dare leave me with this."

"Sorry, but I gotta run." He turned and walked straight to the waiting elevator.

Julia was vibrating in her shoes, so incensed that if she had a gun in her hand, she probably would have blown a hole right in the center of her husband's back.

The kid didn't know what to do, but he was damn sure that he'd just walked into the middle of something pretty big. "I think I'll go," he said, tucking his folder in at his side.

"What?" Julia turned toward him, her focus finally ripped from Boyd's disappearing form.

"Now's not a good time. Is it?"

"It couldn't be a fucking worse time," Julia hissed through clenched teeth.

"Maybe I should just leave you this." He pulled a page out from the middle of his papers. "It's kind of like a resume." The young man shrugged his shoulders. "It's got my numbers if you wanna call."

"How old are you?" She started barking orders.

"Twenty-five."

"Right, and I'm Mary fuckin' Poppins. Now tell me exactly how old you are and don't bother opening your mouth if you're just gonna lie, cuz I ain't got the time or the patience for it right now."

"I'm only nineteen," he said and looked at the floor.

"So why'd you say twenty-five. You're legal?"

"I got a record." He shook his head side to side. "I was using my brother's ID, and it says he's twenty-five."

"What kind of record?"

Justin stopped speaking, his eyes darting around the room as he evaluated his surroundings and quickly debated his willingness to share.

"I got popped for solicitation. Three counts. But that was over a year ago. I'm not doing that no more. Really," his eyes begged for her approval.

"Have a seat." Julia suddenly motioned to one of her guest chairs. "I want to talk to you about this little movie that I've just decided to make."

"Really?"

"You want a glass of wine?" Julia walked over to her bar cart and began uncorking a fresh bottle of merlot.

CHAPTER THIRTY-FOUR

"When a person dies in extreme sorrow or rage, the emotion remains, becoming a stain upon that place."
—The Grudge, 2004

"How about a pipe?" The kid shoved the packet of rocks deep inside the front pocket of his jeans. "And a lighter. You got lighters too?" He reopened his wallet and pulled out an extra five-dollar bill.

"Just the dope, man." Ronnie shook his head and turned to walk away, still amazed at how these stupid little college boys would open a wallet and flash their cash without even thinking twice about what they were doing.

"You wanna tell me how in the hell I'm supposed to smoke this shit?"

"You can fuckin' shove it up your ass, for all I care."

"Up my ass," the kid pondered the idea for a second. "That'll work?"

Ronnie never answered; he just turned and kept on walking, eyes always peeled for anyone loitering around the back door of a club.

"Hey kid?" A voice beckoned him from across the alley.

"Hi." Ronnie waved back.

"What you doing, hanging around here?"

"Just waiting for some friends," he nodded his head toward one of the club's flashing lights.

"Really. You don't look like the type." The guy continued to make his way across the asphalt.

There was just enough room for Ronnie to push past him, but if he did make his move, he knew he wouldn't be able to turn back. He'd have to keep running until he was totally out of sight, and with his pocket still holding half his rocks, the night would be a total failure.

"Well, I was actually just passing through. This a good place to stop for a beer?"

"You said you're a queer?" The guy started to laugh.

Ronnie swallowed hard, the approaching footsteps sending shivers up and down the length of his spine.

"Hey, I found a couple bags of rock here on the ground. You want it bro?" he desperately offered to trade the dope for his freedom.

"You don't like hoes?"

He was scared. The guy was taunting him, egging him on in the hope that he'd maybe be stupid enough to take the first swing.

Not sure what was expected of him, Ronnie did what he'd been trained to do all his life. When seriously outnumbered and obviously out gunned, he handed over the spoils to the victor and prayed that he'd survive his attack.

"I think he likes you Ty," one of the surrounding gang members laughed as Ronnie stripped off his windbreaker and set it on the ground with Jerome's brand new hat.

"I'm packing five dime bags," Ronnie announced, also setting them all down on top of his coat. "And another eighty bucks in cash."

As all six of the guys began to approach him from opposing angles, he took a deep breath and looked down at his wad of rolled bills—silently praying that if he lived, he wouldn't be a cripple.

———————

Stomach growling, Jerome continued to pace outside the grocery store, eyes still glued to the overhead lights burning through the early evening.

"Where are you, Ronnie?" he called out to the air as he looked up and down the busy street, each simple step forward draining his limited reserves as he attempted to shake off his fear of impending doom.

———————

"Skinny glasses," Ronnie's mother had shouted at Gloria. "Set the table with the skinny glasses or I'm gonna give you a swat."

Ronnie's mind alternately flashed to his sister pulling down the small juice glasses and his mother always standing guard to make sure Gloria did just that. Because the moment she used the tumblers, each of her brothers and sisters would dip their cookies in the milk and pollute it with their crumbs. Later, pushing their glasses away from their plates, all the kids would complain their milk was too dirty to drink.

"Small spoons," she also chanted, but he couldn't exactly remember why.

He was numb now, the pain finally receding to another place. Totally unaware that he lay naked in a congealing pool of his own blood, Ronnie continued to fade in and out of consciousness.

Small bursts of light suddenly illuminated his entire field of vision, the neurons in his brain randomly firing as they systematically began to shut down in no discernable pattern.

Breathing shallow, his lungs now fought to nourish the starving tissue of his brain, unfortunately hindered by the multitude of fractured ribs and the frothy blood beginning to pool in its cavities.

"Don't... don't... touch thaaaa," Ronnie incoherently muttered as he tried to stop Jerome; his last breath spent warning his best friend of one final imagined danger.

The sun would be coming up soon and Jerome hadn't seen Ronnie since late afternoon the day before. He was shivering now, his feet pinched and aching inside his worn sneakers, and he was starting to get really scared.

Desperate for memories of comfort, Jerome delved back into his past, searching for something pleasant to make him feel warm.

He couldn't remember the exact day he'd met Ronnie, but he always assumed it had been as babies in the neighborhood, since they'd walked side by side across the school's playground for their first day of kindergarten.

Ronnie, in turn, had accepted their friendship as a gift and a burden, always conscious of the fact that Jerome's mind could be easily swayed, yet never doubting the convictions of his loyalty.

Jerome had acknowledged their friendship as the ultimate bond. He'd have even been prepared to die for Ronnie, and without him, he knew he probably would.

The first time Ronnie had saved his life felt like a thousand years ago, the night his drunken parents had accidentally set their own house on fire.

Candles burning in lieu of the electricity bill that hadn't been paid, Jerome and Ronnie had eaten cold hot dogs and canned beans, wondering if they were going to get a crack at the half pail of ice cream slowly melting in the kitchen freezer.

"Go to the corner and get me a bag of ice," Jerome's father had barked, dropping two dollars in change on the worn surface of the kitchen table. "And no lollygagging about it, ya hear? You boys may be eleven, but I can still throw both you over my knee."

Upon stepping out of the grocer, Ronnie had been the first to pick up on the smell of smoke, his ears suddenly alerted to the wail of the oncoming sirens.

"What's the matter?" Jerome had asked, too much excitement usually rendering him useless.

"Come on, follow me," Ronnie reached out and forcefully dragged him by the sleeve.

As both boys ran toward Jerome's house, the city's emergency vehicles circled the burning structure as if zeroing in on wounded prey.

"Mom," Jerome had muttered, his feet frozen to the ground as his widened pupils reflected the burning flames.

"Get back, kids." A fireman had physically pushed them both behind the wooden barriers.

"That's my house," Jerome cried, fingers still clenched around the plastic handles of his grocery bag.

The flames didn't care that the firemen were trying to drown them with their water hoses or suffocate them with their little axes and fallen timbers. The flames just turned their faces up to the sky and roared in absolute defiance.

Ronnie had to pry the plastic bag from Jerome's shaking fingers, the ice cubes long melted and running freely into a puddle at the base of their feet.

By the time the police had started canvassing the crowd for close neighbors or reluctant family members, the boys had snuck past the barricades and were making their way toward the smoldering remnants of the family yard.

"Where you think they're hiding?" Jerome leaned in for a closer look, trying to figure out where his mom, dad, and baby sister would have gone to escape the searing flames.

As Ronnie watched the fireman remove the first black body bag from deep in the house's basement, he realized right then and there that Jerome was suddenly all alone.

"Let's go to my house."

"But my dad. He'll whup me bad if I don't stay by the yard."

Ronnie walked toward the crowd and borrowed a scrap of paper and a pen from one of the women behind the barricade.

"We'll leave him a note. When he's ready, he'll come get ya."

Jerome had agreed, watching Ronnie roll up the lined paper and stuff it between two of the remaining boards on the neighbor's wooden fence.

"Now follow me," Ronnie had ordered.

Jerome had turned and followed him for the next eleven years.

By the time some passerby had finally noticed that the lump in the back alley was human and called the police, all life had drained from Ronnie's body; his limbs in a full state of rigor mortis.

"John Doe," the EMT proclaimed, after having scouted the perimeter for any signs of a discarded wallet or loose identification.

"Blunt force trauma?" his partner guessed from the gaping wounds on the back of the victim's head.

"Maybe, but I'm not ready to discount internal hemorrhaging," he motioned toward the bloody broom handle still protruding from the body's rectum.

"Load them up, boys," one of the policemen stepped forward to announce.

"What about forensics? Aren't they going to want to take a look around before we move the body?"

"Not tonight. That was the coroner I just talked to, and he's backed up for another five to six hours. Now, if we don't collect what we can and move this body before last call, we're gonna have a thousand drunken kids leaving the clubs and trampling over our crime scene, looking for souvenirs."

Decision made, the two EMTs pulled a gurney from their ambulance and began sizing up their situation. With the body lying on its right side, the left leg jutting backwards with the both arms sprawling forward as if begging for help, they knew a zippered body bag was out of the question.

"Let's just wrap and load. The county morgue can always re-bag him once rigor loosens."

"Yeah, you're right," the second EMT agreed as he unfolded two sterile blankets and laid them flat on the ground. "Now, on the count of three," he bent down, grabbing both ankles. "One, two, three…"

———

When they arrived at the morgue, the ambulance backed up to the loading bay, the electronic back-up beeper sounding off with the steady rhythm of a heartbeat.

"John Doe." The ambulance driver handed the morgue attendant his clipboard, patiently standing by as he waited for a signature.

"You forgot the coroner's name," the attendant said and turned to hand back the board.

"No coroner. He's running behind so we just wrapped and loaded. Crime scene was in serious jeopardy of contamination anyway."

Shrugging his shoulders, the attendant looked up at the clock and scribbled his signature and the time on the bottom of the page before ripping off the top copy for his own records.

"All right, I'll throw him in cold storage," the attendant conceded, turning to pull up one of the county's metal gurneys.

The body finally transferred from the ambulance to the morgue's cold room, the attendant slowly plugged the gurney into an empty spot along on the far wall, forced to twist the metal wheels to accommodate its unusually wide girth.

"John Doe," he muttered to himself, cross checking the file number off the paperwork before recording it on the body's toe tag.

With the room's airtight door now firmly secured, the attendant turned to extinguish the lights, unaware that the corner of blanket covering Ronnie's left hand had unexpectedly slid off towards the floor.

Suddenly exposed, the outstretched fingers of his hand now reached toward the sheet covering his sister Gloria as she quietly lay ahead of him, patiently waiting for her turn in the county's crematorium.

Jerome remembered the burning smell of the fire, and he remembered returning with Ronnie the next day to rummage through the charred debris, but he really couldn't remember much else of his life before that night.

The social worker who came to his school the next day, promptly took him to some big building with rows and rows of beds, all lined up against both walls. He was given two blankets, a set of clean clothes, and a small bag with soap, toothpaste, and a stubby black comb. His bed was number fourteen, and the minute he sat down on the saggy mattress, he knew he wasn't going to stay.

None of the other boys spoke to him, but he didn't care. He wasn't looking to make new friends; he had Ronnie. And as soon as they shut off the lights, he planned to run.

Seven hours later, when Jerome crawled through the basement window and fell the four feet straight down onto Ronnie's bed, he instantly felt better. Ronnie never asked Jerome what he was doing or why he'd ran away from the orphanage. He just rolled closer toward the edge and made sure his best friend had enough room to sleep.

Ronnie's mother never said a word either when she saw two boys slurping down cold cereal at her kitchen-counter the following morning. She just set the record straight, reminding them both that she wasn't their slave, and now that they were both in sixth grade, they'd be expected to get paper routes or dog walking jobs and help out with the groceries. Twenty dollars each a week would be fair, and she wanted it in her hands come Monday morning. No excuses, and if they didn't like the arrangement, they could both go live in the county orphanage.

They immediately agreed to her terms and it had worked out fine for quite a few years, until Ronnie's mom finally latched onto a boyfriend who wanted her to move into his own place.

"Here's fifty bucks each." She'd handed the boys some cash. "Gloria said you can stay with her for a month or two until you get yourselves on your feet. Be good, and mind your sister," she ordered, shaking her finger at Ronnie's face. "We gotta be outta the house by noon tomorrow, so you both better go pack up your shit."

———————————

Life without Ronnie was an impossibility, something that Jerome couldn't even imagine. With nowhere to go, and nothing to do when he got there, he found himself wandering aimlessly, moving through the neighborhood in a state of total and utter exhaustion.

Something told Jerome not to cross the freeway, to stay in the same neighborhood so Ronnie could easily find him whenever he returned. The only problem with that plan was that the only soup kitchen he knew of was clear across town, and without a dime in his pocket, he'd need a little of that charity just to fill his belly.

"Hey, you looking to buy something?" A dealer finally approached him after Jerome had aimlessly trudged past his doorway for the third time in half an hour.

"No," He never even bothered to raise his head.

"Don't even wanna look at any of my *powders or pills?*"

He wanted—he wanted bad—but he also knew that no one was going to give him jack shit on credit.

"Come on, little man," the guy continued to taunt him. "I got everything you need."

Stopping dead in his tracks, Jerome turned to look the dealer straight in the eye. "I ain't got no money, so unless you wanna give me something for free, you gotta stop bugging me."

"Nothing? You got nothing, little man?"

"I got nothing."

"Well, then fuck off and quit wasting my time," he yelled, waving his arms as if Jerome was little more than a pesky fly.

Continuing his trek up and down the streets, no path in mind and no plan of attack, he began to clock the miles. Sweat beading on his forehead, the moisture beginning to collect in the small of his back; Jerome's tee shirt and pant legs were soaked with perspiration.

Ronnie would have made him sit and rest. Ronnie would have made him drink some water. But Ronnie wasn't there, so Jerome just kept walking.

When the headache first hit, he thought it was because he was hungry, so Jerome just kept moving, forcing himself to finally start walking toward the soup kitchen, unaware that he was making his twenty-first trip around a giant, ten-block loop.

When the headache and cold sweats turned to shivers and muscle tremors, Jerome finally stumbled into a park and collapsed on all fours behind a tree. By the time a patrolling policeman found his body later that night, his internal organs had already succumbed to dehydration and exposure.

With his leathery skin framing his cracked lips, and his dried tears gluing his eyelids securely shut, Jerome patiently lay on the park grass, waiting for *his* free ride to the county morgue.

CHAPTER THIRTY-FIVE

"Sometime we're forced into actions we ought to have found for ourselves."
— *Maid in Manhattan, 2002*

It was Sunday morning, but instead of a full brunch with crispy bacon, fresh waffles, and a pot of steaming coffee, Pete chewed on a handful of dried fruit and sipped room temperature bottled water.

"Day eleven," he firmly announced. And after a long sleepless night, he decided that today was definitely going to be the big day.

Closing up the reusable bag, he shoved the food to his side and stood, gingerly stretching his legs. "Eleven days," he continued to chant as if the number somehow carried a magical connotation.

Beginning to prepare, Pete dug down in the bottom of one box and methodically laid out his necessary supplies. Starting with his favorite gold lighter, he added a brand new glass pipe and a swatch of folded tin foil to his pile.

The feeling beginning to churn through his guts was indescribable, a combination of fear and anticipation somehow rolled into one giant ball.

Without the background noise of a radio or a television set, he could hear Rico's footsteps the minute they hit the very top stair. Hair bristling on the back of his neck, he anxiously waited to see if his old friend was going to follow through with the plan.

As Rico's eyes suddenly appeared in the small window at the top of the door, Pete raised his face to offer him a weak smile, even allowing himself a small accompanying wave.

"You sure?" Rico yelled through the door.

"Yep," he nodded, able to feel his buddy's uncertainty through the locked barrier.

"I don't know man."

"I explained it in yesterday's letter," Pete took a deep breath and tried to hold his temper. "So, shove the envelope under the door and get the fuck out of here."

"Good luck man," Rico reached in his pocket and pulled out a packet of crystal meth. "You want me to stick around for awhile?" he offered, dropping the packet into a paper envelope.

"No man. I gotta do this all on my own."

"But maybe if we talk, then you'll be able to resist."

"Maybe, but that ain't a real test then. Is it?"

Rico reluctantly nodded in agreement.

"Just push it under the door and hit the bricks, man. I gotta deal with this shit myself."

Following his orders, Rico slid the dope underneath the door and then brushed two fingers across his forehead in a mock salute.

"Thanks man." Pete returned the sentiment.

As his friend trudged up the basement stairs, he slowly bent down and plucked the white envelope off the concrete floor. Unconsciously raising it to his nose for a quick sniff, his lips turned upward in a knowing smile. Barely aware of his own ritualistic behavior, Pete swallowed the saliva beginning to pool in his mouth as his body began anticipating the chemical high.

Carefully setting the dope down beside his assembled tools, he returned to his mattress to wait.

Pete needed to know which was stronger—his resolve not to touch the meth—or his crippling addiction to indulge. One would eventually win over. And locked in the basement with no way out, he was prepared to just sit and wait, a mere spectator as his past cravings battled his future sobriety.

———————————

Sundays were usually reserved for sleeping in late, indulging in French crepes, and surrendering to an afternoon of bad television. Except this Sunday, Julia found herself alone.

"Just coffee and some fruit," she called down to alert their weekend cook before she began preparing any of the usual fare.

"And toast," Boyd announced as he strolled through the bedroom door.

"Where you been?"

"I drove around for a couple of hours, and then I spent the night crashed on my office couch."

Julia tended to believe him, especially since they both knew how quickly she'd be able to either confirm or deny his story with the building's security desk.

"Did you get any sleep?"

"I survived." He peeled off his clothes and headed straight for the shower.

Debating whether she should join her husband for a second shower and take the opportunity to soothe any of his ruffled feathers, Julia's attention was suddenly diverted by the ringing of her cell phone.

"Hello Julia?" a young man's voice suddenly chirped.

"Yes, it's Julia. Who is this?"

"It's Justin. You said to call you first thing so we could make Sunday a productive day. Remember?"

She remembered two bottles of wine, a couple joints, and…"

"I'm kinda busy today Justin," she quickly blurted out her answer. "My husband just hit the shower, and I think we might head out together for brunch."

"Well, that's cool," he nonchalantly answered. "I wanted to shoot a few hoops with my boys first."

Julia closed her eyes for just a split second, remembering the softness of his lips and the taut muscles of his sculpted abs.

"But I might be able to make it to the office by one o'clock if you wanted to meet me there later."

"That'd be great," she hung up the phone before she had a chance to change her mind.

"I hate that fucking showerhead." Boyd appeared, towel wrapped loosely around his waist. "That damn thing barely pisses down enough water to drown a rat. How's a grown man supposed to take a goddamn shower?"

"It's economizes on water by restricting the spray's pressure," she crossed her arms, tired of explaining herself every time he stepped out of their bathroom. "If you hate it so much, why don't you take a goddamn bath?"

"Why don't you just put the old one back?"

"I'm going out," Julia announced, sitting down at her dressing table to blow dry her hair.

"It's Sunday. You're going shopping? You know the stores will be jammed."

She never answered. Her only reply was the roar of the blow dryer as her fingers wrapped around the handle of her brush and began pulling her blonde locks into compliance.

"But I've got an appointment," Justin continued to argue with the building's security. "Julia Giovanni is expecting me at one. I'm supposed to meet her upstairs in her office."

"It's Sunday, kid. Nobody gets past me until I can confirm it with one of the senior employees."

"I'm not some kid. I'm an actor, and I have an appointment."

"Good for you," the guard smirked. "But until I confirm it, you aren't taking one step near that elevator. You hear me?"

"So..." Justin looked at the guard. "Keep dialing."

Julia parked her car and rode up the rear elevator, half-expecting to see Justin's smile the minute she stepped out into the hall. Unfortunately, she remembered too late that there was no way he'd be able to make it past security without a pass, her ringing landline serving to remind her of that very fact.

"Julia Giovanni," she called out toward her speakerphone.

"Mrs. Giovanni, this is main floor security calling. We have a kid down here by the name of Justin... ah, Justin Carrera," he read the last name off the high school identification card. "He claims to have an appointment with you."

"He does. But can you give me fifteen minutes, and then send him up?"

"Yes ma'am," he confirmed before hanging up the phone and turning his attention back toward the cocky young kid. "Might as well take a seat. The boss lady won't be able to see you for another fifteen minutes."

"That's fine," Justin sauntered over to pick-up his student ID. "Just call me when she's ready, okay?"

The guard handed the laminated card back, warily eyeing him as he unceremoniously plopped down into the nearest chair.

Upstairs, Julia found herself pacing back and forth across her office floor.

"This is bullshit," she nodded, dropping down into one of her guest chairs as she fought to make sense of her own intentions.

She'd never actually planned to start any film projects without her husband's input—in actuality, it had been the farthest thing from Julia's mind. Together, as husband and wife, they'd done well with Giovanni Films, and until present, neither had ever branched out on their own. All projects had been joint collaborations; even the local advertising gigs had only been booked after mutual consideration. Some projects were memorable, some not worth a ten-dollar tape, but each and every one had been a joint effort.

However, Julia hated nothing more than being told what to do by anyone, especially someone as close to her as her husband. Besides, Francois Dubois was an account that they really needed, and no matter how much he rubbed Boyd the wrong way, he was still willing to pay big bucks for his film. From experience, she knew that guys like Dubois rarely paid up and disappeared off the face of the earth. The Francois Dubois's of the world couldn't get enough to fulfill their twisted fantasies, and they usually came back time and time again, with more and more requests for depraved vignettes from their own warped imaginations.

"Julia." A young man's voice suddenly jolted her back to reality.

"Justin, come in," she motioned, quickly rising to her feet and moving back around to the safety of her own chair.

As he walked into her office and reacquainted himself with his surroundings, Justin took a chance and moved straight toward the couch.

"Coffee?" she offered before realizing that with no secretarial staff working on a Sunday afternoon, more than likely, the machine would be powered off and bone dry.

"I don't drink coffee."

"Fine, then let's get down to business."

"Sounds good to me," he said, slowly leaning back as he stretched his arms out along the top of the couch.

Fighting the urge to go over and join the young man, Julia busied herself with locating her original copy of the Dubois file.

"You look lonely over there," he purred.

Raising her head, she couldn't help but smile at Justin as he continued to offer up his body for her pleasure.

He was nearly twenty years her junior, with about as much experience as any young guy his age. However, he definitely deserved an *A for Enthusiasm*. Whether Justin had actually been that turned on by making out with a forty year old woman, or just truly deserved and Oscar for his award winning performance...Julia really didn't care. That kind of talent she could harvest, she could mold him into the newest and brightest adult film star this city had ever seen. Justin Carrera could be a financial goldmine for Giovanni Films, and Francois Dubois's sick little fantasy was going to be just the steppingstone she needed to prove her point.

"Maybe we should have some wine?" he suggested with a smirk and a wink.

"Maybe" Julia answered. "But first, I think we need to clear up a little misunderstanding before we commence with any more alcohol."

"What's the matter?"

"Justin, what happened last night between us was a small indiscretion that I do not wish to repeat. Do you understand what I'm saying?"

He did, and he'd heard it before.

"I'm a happily married woman who had a little too much to drink and then I let myself get caught up in the moment. Nothing more."

"I know." He sat up on the couch and straightened the shirt buttons on his J. Crew knockoff. "So what'll we do now?"

"We talk about making a film."

"You really want me to act in one of your films?"

"Well, that's why you came here, wasn't it?"

Justin stood up and quickly rushed over to the front of Julia's desk. "I can act you know. You wouldn't believe just how convincing I can be."

"I believe you," she knowingly smiled to herself, the fullness of his bottom lip still taunting her with its pleasurable softness.

"What kind of film is it?"

"You ever do gay?" She grabbed a pen in preparation for her note taking.

It was truth or dare time, unfortunately, Justin wasn't quite sure he was ready to play.

"A little," he cautiously answered, leaving his experience open for interpretation.

"Well, I'll lay it out for you, Justin. My client is rather particular with the actors he wants in his film. They all have to be young, as young as legally possible, and they have to be able to perform in conjunction with other young males. You interested?"

"What's it paying?"

"A lot. But, first off, you're going to need to do a screen test. You see, just because you have a beautiful young face and a muscular body, it doesn't mean that it'll translate to the screen. Sometimes, even the most beautiful people come across as little more than wooden stick men. You understand what I'm trying to tell you?"

"You think I'm hot, but you're not sure if when the camera's rolling I'll freeze up or not."

"Right." She picked up her phone and dialed from memory.

Justin sat back in the guest chair and listened as Julia quickly arranged for a screen test with two of the company's veteran actors.

"Three o'clock?" she pulled the receiver away from her mouth, waiting for a silent confirmation from Justin.

He quickly nodded in agreement.

"Then we'll meet you there," she abruptly ended the call.

———

By the time Boyd had woken from a nap, dressed, and grabbed a bite to eat, he still hadn't heard one word from his wife.

Sundays were usually spent together, the one day of the week where they could ignore the phones and just kick back and relax without the distractions of their work. It was their alone time, and Julia's absence was really starting to piss him off.

"Fine," he growled. "Might as well get some fucking work done."

Just as Boyd grabbed his coat and headed into the office, Julia decided to invite Justin out for a bite to eat and a few drinks in an attempt to loosen him up before his big screen test. A minute later, as she pulled her car out of the building's underground lot and turned onto the busy street, her husband's Hummer came bounding down the entrance's main ramp.

Expecting to find the entire floor vacant on a Sunday afternoon, Boyd was shocked to hear a small crew rummaging around in the video supply room, picking out tripods and loading their bags with the necessary lighting equipment.

"What about these?" one of the guys asked before pointing to a collection of light standards.

Martin just shook his head. "When Julia called, she said it was just going to be a simple screen test and we wouldn't need a lot of extra lighting. Our usual flash mounts should be enough."

One of the company grips stopped loading the equipment into duffle bags long enough to catch his breath and ask, "where we running this?"

"We're just using a place on the outskirts of the city. Some local roach motel where we can move in and out and without being questioned. You got it?"

"Got it." He leaned down and zipped up his bag, not bothering to unload any of the discarded tapes from the original Pocahontas run through.

Boyd hung back in the shadows, never announcing his presence, just soaking up the information and making his own plans to follow.

CHAPTER THIRTY-SIX

"I see now why you like sumo. You can never judge a man's power by his appearance alone."
                                                    —Memoirs of a Geisha, 2005

Boyd may have dressed in designer suits and sported a genuine Rolex on his wrist as he tooled around town in loader Hummer, but he never ever forgot where he came from. Even after he'd rented the mansion, hired the staff, and leased the cars, Boyd still couldn't shake the memory of what it was like to have lived *hand to mouth*. He'd fought his way out of the grips of poverty, and he'd never let himself forget that with just a couple steps backwards, he could have easily been right back from where he'd started.

Although Boyd no longer felt it was necessary to protect himself by carrying a knife or by packing a thirty-eight in his jeans, he still never doubted for a second that if things got ugly, he could still *take care of business*. A man didn't forget that kind of training, regardless of whether you picked up the techniques in a trendy gym or a darkened back alley.

Growing up on the streets, Boyd had been forced to fine-tune his survival skills. Since grade school, he'd had a sixth sense for trouble, personal radar that alerted him whenever something was going wrong in his world. And something was definitely going on with his wife Julia. He could feel it all the way down in his bones, and before the day was through, he would damn well know what it was.

———————

"This is really good," Justin continued to devour his pasta Alfredo.

"Sure, why wouldn't it be," Julia teased. "Half cream, half butter. What's not to love?"

"I'll work it off," he winked.

"So, we're gonna have to get a little creative with your screen test."

"Why?" he muttered through a mouthful of garlic toast, washing it down with a quick gulp of the chilled Pinot Grigio.

"Because I haven't had a chance to send you to the Community Clinic, I don't have a clue about your medical history, and without a history, I'm not about to risk any of my other employee's personal health just because we're in a bit of a rush."

"I'm clean. I get tested regularly."

"Good, but until my doctor tests you, *your word* means shit. Nothing personal."

He liked her. She was total class with no bullshit. And man, could she give good head. Too bad she was married, though. A woman like Julia Giovanni could have been a great hook-up for a guy like him. Maybe a place to stay, maybe a pocket full of spending cash, maybe even the keys to a car if he played her right? Too bad though, it sounded like her bed was already full.

"So if we ain't gonna fuck, then what are we gonna do for the screen test? Play checkers?"

"Be patient," she motioned for the waiter to bring them each one final glass of wine. "There are ways to try you out without swapping bodily fluids."

"This I gotta see." Justin wiped his mouth before dropping the linen napkin down into his empty pasta bowl.

As usual, Martin was either yapping on his cell phone, or too busy pissing around with the stereo to even notice that Boyd had been tailing him every since they'd pulled out of the office's underground parking lot.

"Going left?" Boyd guessed, just as Martin hit his signal lights before turning the company van off the main street and heading into the motel's parking lot.

Continuing past the entrance way, Boyd finally pulled off the street into a secondary driveway, moving to the very end of the block before tucking his Hummer around the back of a storage garage. Just before hopping out on foot, he threw off his sports jacket and grabbed a ball cap, pulling the peak as low as possible in an attempt to conceal his identity.

"You want two beds?" Martin asked Julia; the remainder of his conversation lost as he turned and made his way on foot toward the motel's check-in desk.

As Martin rented the room, Clayton opened up the back door of the van and began pulling out equipment, not the least bit concerned that someone might walk by and snatch up one of the bags he was casually piling up on the asphalt.

"Sorry about the stain." Justin continued to rub at the drop of Alfredo sauce stubbornly clinging to the front of his shirt.

"You're not trying out for GQ," Julia laughingly reminded him. "This is adult entertainment. Besides, we have our own costume department. You won't be expected to furnish any of your own wardrobe."

"First class," he nodded his head in agreement.

"Here we are," she pulled into the parking lot, her face flushed from the three quick glasses of wine she'd consumed on an empty stomach.

As Justin piled out of the passenger's seat, Boyd found himself quietly sneaking in for a closer look.

"Room nine," Martin called out on his way back toward the van. "Two doubles, air, and white sheets. Sound good?" He looked toward his boss for her approval.

"Sounds good," she answered while he unlocked the door.

Watching his wife prepare to shoot some kind of footage in the sleazy fucking motel room was sending Boyd's temperature through the roof. He was pissed, and he wanted to know what the fuck was going on. But as much as he wanted immediate answers, he also wanted to know exactly how far this was going to go and who in the hell the bitch was filming.

Busting in right now would definitely put a stop to the shoot, but then he'd never really know exactly what was supposed to happen. He'd only have her word for an explanation, and Boyd was beginning to feel that Julia's word was suddenly worth shit.

"The crew I get, but the little *wanna be* surfer boy... who the hell are you?" He hissed between clenched teeth.

As everyone filed into the motel room, Julia anxiously wrung her hands, more than ready to get this test over and done with.

"Okay boys," she immediately took control of the situation once everyone was sequestered behind closed doors. "I want you to set up both pods at the foot of the far bed, but remember to leave a little wiggle room. I've got Melody and Blaine coming down and they're gonna need to be able to move in and out of the action."

As they set up the cameras, Julia quickly dialed Melody's number and passed on the hotel's room number.

Pacing outside the door, Boyd had worked himself into a lather and was about five seconds away from kicking down the door; when he heard Melody roar into the parking lot with her bright red Mustang. Rubber squealing, she pulled up beside the company van and finally killed her supercharged engine just as Boyd forced himself to reluctantly pull back into shadows.

"Fuck me. This place looks like shit, man," Blaine complained as he threw open his passenger door, slowly extracted himself out of the leather seat. "I can't believe we're filming here."

"Like I give a fuck." Melody adjusted her bikini top before pulling down the stretch knit of her miniskirt. "Five-hundred bucks for an hour's work—Julia can film my ass in a garbage dump."

Banging his fists on the wooden door, Blaine gave a small wave to Martin as he pulled back the heavy drapery to check who was knocking.

With the impromptu cast finally gathered inside, Julia took control of the shoot, wasting little time getting the screen test rolling.

"Now Justin, we're gonna open with some basic massage play. Melody is going to help you undress, and then when you're naked, Blaine will take over the massage. I want you to get hard, but I don't want you to cum. You understand me?"

"Sure," he nodded, attempting to act like he'd been filming porn for years.

"And Blaine," Julia turned her attention back to her contract player. "Take it easy on the kid. I don't want him blowing his load all over this place. He's medically untested. You got me?"

Blaine nodded, beginning to strip off his clothes without even being asked.

Within ten minutes, Martin had finished setting up the cameras and all three actors were ready to take their positions.

"We're just going to shoot this in one take," Julia pulled up a padded chair. "I wanna see how Justin looks on film and how he performs in an ad lib situation. Everyone understand what we're trying to accomplish here?"

"You want me to cum?" Blaine leaned over toward the wall-mounted mirror to check his hair.

"No," Julia replied with a quick shake of her head. "Hold onto your load. This is all about Justin. Nobody loses control; they just work themselves up into a frenzy. Think of this as a good hour of foreplay. No insertions, no climaxes."

Everyone agreed and waited for Julia's call to action.

Listening through the door, Boyd continued to boil, the fury steadily growing inside him.

She was betraying him. Julia had blatantly ignored his veto and was preparing to make a film for Dubois. How in the hell could she choose that sick fuck over him?

"Bitch," Boyd cursed his wife, absolutely pissed that she'd chosen to be his rival instead of his partner. "Fuck!" They hadn't even been married for four years and she was already looking over the fence and getting ready to move on. Boyd couldn't fuckin' believe that he hadn't seen it coming. "Fucking whore," he sneered, the realization of her betrayal instantly manifesting itself into white-hot anger. The longer he continued to seethe outside the motel room door, the darker his intentions grew.

"Everyone ready?" the lead detective quietly whispered into the hidden microphone carefully mounted in the lining of his leather jacket.

The entire team took turns verbally responding, each decisively positioned around the motel's parking lot for maximum deployment during the raid.

"All right," Norman Sanders pulled his badge out of his pocket. "Doug and I are gonna grab the lookout and the second he's secure, I want the Alpha-team to rush the room. The Bravo-team will stay put, guard the exits, and secure the suspects' vehicles. Rock and roll, boys!" He whipped out his police issued revolver and quickly motioned for Doug to rush up to where Boyd was standing.

———————

"JULIA..." Boyd somehow managed to shout out the simple warning as a set of powerful arms roughly pulled him to the ground, away from the motel room's door, effectively smothering any further chances to warn his wife.

"Vice!" Detective Norman Sanders shouted at the motel room door as all three members of his Alpha Team began to rush up from their flanking positions.

———————

"Giovanni Films has been completely shut down and locked up, and I suspect by tomorrow morning, your bank will have been served with a court order to freeze each and every one of your accounts."

"Personal accounts, too? They can do that?" Boyd demanded answers from their lawyer as he and Julia sat side by side surrounded by the stark white of the interrogation room.

"Actually, not only will the DA freeze your personal and business accounts for review; all safety deposit boxes, stocks, and personal assets purchased with funds from Giovanni Films will also be untouchable until the investigation is complete."

"Why untouchable?" Julia struggled to be heard, her voice hoarse from sitting overnight in a drafty holding cell.

"Simple," their lawyer said before closing his briefcase. "Everything you and your husband have accumulated during your relationship can be deemed proceeds of crime by the DA's office, and until your innocence or guilt is proven, it will all be untouchable."

"Well how the fuck are we supposed to live? Pay our bills? Pay you?" Boyd demanded, his limited goodwill evaporating by the second.

"I can't answer those kinds of questions for you Mr. and Mrs. Giovanni, but I guess this is as good a time as any to address my fees."

"We're good for it," Boyd nodded, reaching over to squeeze his wife's hand.

"Well, unless I have a fifty thousand dollar retainer in my office before the closing of business tomorrow, you're going to have to find yourself another firm, and another attorney."

"How the hell am I supposed to do that from here?" Boyd jumped to his feet.

"You had better sit," the lawyer motioned toward the guard standing watch on the opposite side of the locked door.

"Forgive my husband, he's really stressed," Julia continued to pick at the broken thumbnail she'd sustained in the raid. "I just can't believe how hard they're coming down on us. You'd think we'd been filming snuff."

"Child pornography is one of vice's top priorities," the lawyer bluntly stated.

"How many times I gotta tell you, we don't shoot fucking minors?" Boyd yelled across the table.

"Well," the attorney said, reluctantly reopening his briefcase and pulling out his top file. "Your charges speak otherwise. And according to the DA, Justin Tyler Carrera was only sixteen years old."

"Sixteen?" Julia's stomach began to churn. "He told me he was nineteen."

"Didn't you fucking check him out? You know you gotta check him out," Boyd continued to berate his wife. "What'd his ID say?"

"It was fake. It… it said he was twenty-five. Justin admitted it was fake, but he said he was nineteen."

"He said? He said? You know better than to trust some street hustler looking for a quick payoff. I can't believe you were putting the little fucker on tape without checking him out first. What in the hell were you thinking Julia?" Boyd collapsed against the back of his plastic chair. "What in the hell were you fuckin' thinking?"

"I'm sorry," she cried. "This is all my fault."

"Not totally," the lawyer's hands slowly pushed a set of photographs across the paint-chipped table. "Here are photos of a young Native American girl losing her virginity right on the set of one of your movies—blood dripping down her legs, tears running down her face."

"That's Lillian Cardinal," Julia snatched up one of the pictures. "She's not a minor. She's old enough. I know. I had her checked, I did," she turned to her husband for his approval.

"Well, when the DA contacted Miss Cardinal for a statement, she came forward with a young boy that she is desperately trying to adopt. It looks like they are working out some kind of a deal as we speak, or so I hear."

Boyd and Julia felt their world slipping out of their hands, the bars of the city jail slowly closing in on their lives.

"Mr. and Mrs. Giovanni, I feel that we should all take the opportunity to be honest and forthcoming with each other. Your legal defense is going to be extremely expensive. We are dealing with sexual child abuse, and child endangerment for the purpose of distributing pornography. Those are two very, very, serious charges."

"You think we don't fucking know that?" Boyd growled his response.

"All right," the lawyer took a second to clear his throat. "We can agree that everyone here understands what you're both up against. So, before I spend my entire weekend preparing briefs and running up your legal bill, I need to know if you are able to raise that retainer."

"Fine then. I'll sign over my goddamn Hummer to ya," Boyd took a deep breath. "You can drive her 'til we finish with this court shit and I can pay your bill in full. But be careful," he nervously chuckled. "That baby's worth a hell of a lot more than fifty thousand bucks."

"Your SUV was impounded at the time of the raid."

"My Hummer?"

"Everything, Mr. Giovanni. Maybe you have a friend or a family member who could financially assist you temporarily?"

With Boyd's brother Pete still missing in action, and his mother surviving on little more than her monthly pension, they were totally on their own.

"How are we supposed to raise fifty thousand dollars when we're stuck in city lock-up? You think the judge will consider giving us bail tomorrow?" Boyd tentatively asked.

"I'm afraid it's not looking good," he shook his head, reaching into his briefcase for a second file. "Especially with the mountain of evidence they have accumulated during their last six months of surveillance. And, as you know, you both have prior criminal records. I'm sure the DA is going to paint you both as flight risks, and ask that you be held either without bail, or with at least a half a million dollar cash bond…each."

Both Boyd and Julia audibly groaned.

"You wanna tell me how I'm supposed to raise a million for bail if everything I own is fucking tied up in a goddamned police lock down?"

"Like I said Mr. Giovanni, your bail hearing does not look very promising, so I wouldn't waste too much time or energy even attempting to raise bail funds right now. I'd personally be much more concerned with retaining appropriate counsel."

As the lawyer carefully tucked his files back into his briefcase, Boyd and Julia sat motionless, their heads whirling as they fought to make sense of their shattered world.

"I appreciate the predicament you have both found yourselves in, so I'm going put a call into legal aid myself. I'll see if I can find you someone competent." With that, the senior partner of Reid and Quail rose to his feet. "I wish you both luck," he turned to leave the interrogation room.

"Is that all?" Julia turned her tear-filled eyes up toward the departing lawyer.

"No. I suggest you instruct legal aid to make a deal with the DA, attempt to reduce the charge to contributing to the delinquency of a minor, and maybe pleading guilty to a couple of counts of tax evasion. You will both have to do some time, but neither of you want to be labeled as child sex offenders, and then be thrown into the general population at the penitentiary. Well anyway," he shrugged his shoulders, "that's what I would do."

Boyd and Julia were absolutely speechless.

Good luck." Theodore Quail politely offered, knocking on the glass window as he signaled the guard the completion of their meeting.

CHAPTER THIRTY-SEVEN

"You never really know until you're the one standing there."
—Monster, 2003

"Just personal items," the court appointed sheriff reminded Wanda for the second time that morning. "No company documents or office equipment will be allowed to leave these premises without the prior written consent of the court."

"I know, I know," she yanked open the top drawer of her desk and extracted a leather-bound Daytimer.

"I don't think so." The sheriff stepped over and plucked the book right out of her hands.

"But it has a lot of my personal phone numbers in it."

"Then I suggest you grab a pen and copy them down." He handed her back the leather bound book.

In her allotted hour, Wanda managed to pack two cardboard boxes of personal items, all under the watchful eyes of the court officer. A picture of her niece Amber, one Boston fern, and a handful of trinkets filled the first box. The second, much larger, held a collection of ornaments, and the one picture she'd actually lugged up the freight elevator that hung over her office couch.

"What about the personal files I had on my computer?" Wanda motioned toward the empty space on the corner of her desk.

"You'll have to fill this out and send it in to the District Attorney's office," he ripped a page off his clipboard and handed Wanda the legal form. "Make sure to quote the file number that I've circled on all your correspondence."

"Well then, I guess this is it," she said, turning to look around her office one last time.

"After you." The sheriff stood back and waited for her to lead the way.

Stepping out of her office into the bustling hall, Wanda jumped out of the way in the nick of time as two movers began wheeling a trolley of equipment from the editing suite toward the rear freight elevator.

"What are they doing with all of Martin's computers and monitors?" she turned back toward the sheriff.

"Just your basic search and seizure," he announced. "We're cataloguing every piece of equipment and scrap of paper from Giovanni Films."

"Why?'

"Because as of Monday morning, it all became evidence in conjunction with the criminal charges filed against your boss Boyd Giovanni, and his wife, Julia Giovanni."

Wanda hung her head and slowly began the long walk down the back hall, knowing that her feet would never cross the building's threshold again.

"Hey guys, come look at this," a second sheriff casually called out to anyone within earshot as Wanda slowly stepped onto the elevator. "You gotta look at this shit, man. It's really sick."

As the room began to fill with court officers, everyone jostled for a position around Julia's private desk, starring down at the freshly discovered piece of art.

"What in the hell is that?" a voice called out from the back of the crowd.

"Looks like some kind of a circle jerk," one of the men laughed.

"I don't think so," another woman stepped forward and began to mutter in a disgusted tone. "It's, it's… a self-circumcision. Look really close." She bent her head and pointed toward one of the young boys, apparently stretching out his own penis between his fingers. "He's got a knife in his hand. He's cutting off his own foreskin while all the other boys are standing around, watching him."

"And that must be pools of blood," another man pointed to the bottom of the sculpture. "I thought it was cum, but it's gotta be blood. Right?" He turned to face the woman.

"I guess," she replied, shaking her head and swallowing the bile suddenly rising up from the depths her stomach.

"Now you know why we're shutting this place down."

The crowd murmured its agreement and slowly dispersed from the office, leaving the statue to be packed up for evidence in the Federal case against Boyd and Julia Giovanni.

———————

As Wanda sat in her car, she debated just what she was going to say with only seconds to prepare as her brother Warren rapidly approached her car's rear bumper.

"I need to talk to you," he plainly stated.

Still locked inside, Wanda took a moment to debate whether or not she was even prepared to face her brother before taking a chance and stepping out of the security of her car.

"Please unlock the door," he begged, motioning for her to come outside and talk in person.

Reluctantly, she moved against her better judgment, sliding her hand down to release the power lock.

"I've been trying to get a hold of you since Thursday morning," Warren began to explain, his face betraying no signs or alcohol or drug consumption as he reached forward to hold open the driver's door. "Why've you been hiding from me?"

"It's been hell," she muttered, slowly extracting herself from the car's bucket seat. "The cops raided Giovanni Films, threw Boyd and Julia in jail, and then locked down the entire company until further notice."

"I already heard on the news. And I didn't wanna say *I told you so*," Warren shook his head. "But you know what I thought about your career choice in the first place."

"I know." She moved toward the hood, mindful to keep a safe distance between herself and her brother. "But it's gonna be hard to find another job that paid that kind of money, you know?" She fidgeted with the panic button on her key fob.

"So... I was thinking we should maybe talk about the other night." He bowed his head. "I wanted to ask you if..."

"Don't," Wanda warned. "There's nothing you can say that's gonna make me feel any better. You hurt me," she said through tears, stuffing her keys into her jeans pocket as she scrambled for a tissue to blow her nose.

"What are you talking about?" Warren stepped closer. "I was just gonna ask you if you wanted to move in with me and Amber for a couple months, until you were able to find a new job and get back on your feet."

"What?"

"Well, Amber could really use a little mothering, and since you've lost your job, I thought you might be interested in bunking in with your brother before you ate up all your savings."

"Brother...my brother?" She began to laugh hysterically. "You sure don't act much like my brother." Wanda's voice began to crack, her laughter slowly drowned out by a second bout of tears.

"You saying we aren't family anymore?" he suddenly barked; the pain of his sister's insinuation evident in his voice.

"We are family, Warren. That's the problem." She took a second to swipe her right hand across the tears running down both her cheeks. "You're my brother, and we can't have sex and pretend like we're some kind of normal couple."

"I know," he mumbled and shuffled his feet, suddenly unwilling to raise his head and look his sister square in the eye.

"Cuz it's incest. You know that, don't you?"

Warren never answered; he just continued to stare down at the asphalt.

"And you can't keep raping me. Cuz the next time it happens, I'm going to call the police, and they'll throw you in jail."

"But I love you, Wanda," he muttered.

"I love you too," she continued to cry. "But you still can't do that…ever again."

"No," he shouted, suddenly lunging forward and grabbing both her arms. "I LOVE YOU!"

"But I'm your sister," she whimpered, the strength of his grasp surely bruising her tender skin.

"I know," he argued back. "But I've loved you since we were kids and you taught me how to kiss."

"That wasn't real. That was just a childhood game we played because you needed a little practice. It didn't mean anything," she desperately attempted to reason with him.

Unfortunately, Warren was beyond reasoning, and the flash of anger in his eyes made it suddenly apparent that he had another plan in mind.

"Please let me go," Wanda pleaded. "You're hurting me."

"I hurt too! You think I don't hurt every night, sitting at home, wondering where you are or who you're with? I love you Wanda," he repeated the words, his hot breath hanging like a cloud over her face.

"You gotta get some help. You're my brother and you can't love me like that. It's just plain wrong."

"But I do. I love you. I've always loved you." He suddenly wrapped his arms around his sister and pulled her firmly toward his chest.

Wanda allowed him to hold her for one last time, tilting her head sideways to accommodate her brother as he nestled his face in toward her neck and released an anguished sob.

"I just wanted to be with you. I know it's wrong," he moaned, "but I do love you."

Wanda silently counted to ten and gently began pushing her brother away.

"Please don't leave me," he begged.

"You have to get some help," she firmly demanded, unsure exactly where she was summoning the personal strength from. "And until you do, I don't want you anywhere near me. Do you understand what I'm saying?"

"No. I don't."

Wanda stepped around her brother and reached for the driver's door, seconds away from the safety of her car.

"Come home with me," he continued to beg, simultaneously reaching out to grab her left arm. "I need to talk to you," Warren began to propel his sister toward his own car.

"No!"

"Come on." The pressure on her arm became more insistent as he started to literally drag her across the lot.

"Warren, I gotta go," Wanda begged, heart beating wildly as she scanned the underground parking garage for any of the police officers who been monitoring the search and seizure.

Warren was unable to hear her. His mind was set on the single act of loading his sister into his car.

"Not again," she began to cry.

"Hey," a voice called out from inside the stairwell doors. "What's going on?"

"Get in the car," Warren ordered, attempting to shove Wanda into his passenger seat without causing any more of a ruckus.

"Let her go, or I'm calling 911."

"Fuck off," he yelled, resorting to brute force as his hands clamped down on her narrow shoulders and pushed.

"I need a cop really fast," the passerby began to shout into his cell phone. "A lady's being kidnapped right in front of my eyes."

———————

Pete woke up some time on Monday afternoon to the banging of Rico's fists as they rained down on the basement's metal door.

"I'm fine," he said and waved off the concern, dismissing his friend as he painfully forced himself to rise up off the mattress and take stock of his surroundings.

"How'd ya do, bro?" Rico's muffled voice reverberated through the locked barrier.

"It's all gone," Pete simply answered. He'd obviously smoked every last rock of the crystal meth in a hazy chain of events the night before.

Struggling to stay upright on his feet, Pete dug past the torn plastic into an open flat and extracted a fresh bottle of water. Hands shaking, he slowly twisted off the top and began forcing himself to ingest the lukewarm fluid as Rico disappointingly shook his head before pushing the day twelve marker underneath the door.

"Need anything before I leave?"

Pete just shook his head no as he returned to his mattress

and rested from the simple exertion of standing, his body already beginning to crave another hit of meth since the previous night's indulgence.

"Later bro," Rico called out, turning to trudge up the basement steps.

"I'm a failure," Pete called out in response, the verbalization of his simple statement resounding off the basement's empty walls. "But I know what I gotta do."

Without a moment's delay, he turned and retrieved the 9mm Glock he'd carried down with him, carefully taking his time to load the chamber with a single bullet from his cache of ammunition.

Suddenly stopping mid-task, Pete slowly laid the gun back down on the mattress, debating whether or not he should write a note. Deciding against it, unsure of whom he'd even write to, or for that matter, what he'd even say, he continued on with his preparations.

Raising the 9mm toward his face, he carefully set the gun directly in front of his right eye, deliberately resting the tip of the barrel on the lower orbital bone of his socket. The metal felt ice cold, the barrel's proximity to his lashes making his eye blink and subsequently water. But Pete chose to ignore the discomfort, squeezing both eyelids shut and simultaneously shoving the barrel's tip even closer, the gun now firmly pressing inward against his eyeball.

Pete had grown listening to horror stories of junkies who tried to blow their heads off by swallowing a gun only to have the bullet glance off their skull plate and mistakenly peel off a corner of their face. Effectively leaving the junkies still alive, permanently disfigured, and still horribly addicted to their usual shit.

Pete had a better plan. He'd mistakenly heard somewhere that the human eye was the most direct passageway leading straight through to the brain. He believed the path wasn't protected by any thick layers of bone. Hell, he didn't even think he needed a gun. A wooden pencil would have done the trick. One forceful shove;

and he'd have been able to push the sharpened writing tool straight through the fluid in his eyeball and directly into his brain matter. But he was going to use the 9mm anyway. It would probably be a lot quicker and hopefully less painful. Pete had been wrong on so many counts.

Taking one last breath before his resolve began to fade; Pete adjusted the barrel, making sure the gun tip pointed straight toward the back of his head, not twisted off in some cock-eyed angle toward his ear. Then without over-thinking his plan, the thumb on his right hand somehow managed to push the trigger and release the fatal bullet.

His last thoughts could have been of his kids, or maybe even of his mother. A fleeting memory of his brother Boyd wouldn't have been out of the realm. But in the last millisecond of Pete's life, his only thought was of his addiction, and whether or not the cravings would follow him all the way straight to hell?

"We need you to come down to the station to press charges Miss Finkel," the officer gently coaxed her. "Is there anyone you'd like us to call? Someone who could possibly meet you there?"

"No," she quietly shook her head.

"I've always... always loved you," Warren's anguished cries escaped the confines of the police car, his voice almost hoarse as he continued to profess his devotion.

Without warning, Wanda collapsed, simultaneously dropping to her knees as the sobs wracked her body.

"Hey, hey there little lady," the senior detective quickly followed her to the ground. "It's over. We've got him now, you're absolutely safe."

She couldn't be comforted, even though the officer said all the right words and spoke slowly in a soft and even tone.

The single blast, of course, was fatal—Pete's body immediately slumping down onto the soiled mattress as the blood splatter and brain material began to trickle down the concrete wall. He'd been wrong about his choice of entry; the ear actually being the softest and least protected point of access for a foreign object. Still, the orbital bone surrounding his eye socket had instantly shattered on impact, the bullet easily making its way straight through to the soft tissue of his brain.

He'd lost his battle with drugs, and the choice to end his life had been the one final act Pete had felt he'd been able to orchestrate in a world that held him captive.

As pools of fluid began to gel on the porous concrete, his body began to enter the first stages of rigor, his right hand still firmly clenched around the handle of his most valuable possession.

And in the very end, Peter Giovanni had done the only thing he could think of to escape the debilitating hold of crystal methamphetamine, even if he had to blow a hole in the middle of his head to do so.

EPILOGUE

"We saw something in each other neither of us liked.
Or maybe we were just looking in the mirror"
—Lord of War, 2005

L egal aid hadn't been of much assistance to either Boyd or Julia
with their actual trial wrapping up in less than a week, both
being sentenced to eight and ten years respectively. After serving
their time, they would be forced to register for the remainder of their
lives as sex offenders in whatever community they chose to reside,
effectively sentenced to a life of scorn and ridicule.

"Don't want your desert honey?" a two-hundred and fifty pound
woman chuckled as she leaned over Julia's shoulder and grabbed the
instant pudding cup off her plastic tray.

"No, help yourself," she muttered, still no appetite since she'd
been moved from the city's remand center to the Correctional Center
for Women.

"Hey, Giovanni," another woman called out from across the
mess table. "It true that you once blew a fucking football team and
had to have your stomach pumped cuz it was too full of cum?

Julia just glanced at the wall clock, praying for the mealtime to be over so she could retreat to the confines of her personal cell. At least there she'd only have to deal with the taunts of one cellmate instead of an entire mess hall full of angry and suspicious women.

"Still lookin' for a new wife," one of the other inmates called out, roughly brushing against Julia's back as she strolled past, en-route to her regular table.

Julia never acknowledged the offer. She just closed her eyes and silently screamed for the hundredth time that day.

———————————

"Mansbridge, Rodrigues, Pao, and Smanski to visiting," the guard's voice boomed out over the floor. "You got five minutes," he warned through the intercom.

Boyd raised his head from the tattered paperback long enough to notice a handful of men making their way toward the guard's bubble, turning to face the wall as they waited to be patted down, cuffed, and then shackled before being led off the *range*.

"No visitors again?" a young kid slid into an empty seat across the metal table.

"No. How about you?" Boyd closed the book and reluctantly turned his attention toward the pimply-faced inmate.

"Nah. I'm from Texas. Nobody's gonna get on no bus to come and see little ole' me. But I heard you's rich and famous. How come nobody's coming to see you?"

"I'm not rich anymore, and the only thing that makes me a little famous is the fact that my trial got a little publicity in the newspapers."

"*King and queen of porn get locked away in city dungeons,*" the kid eagerly repeated from memory "Hey Boyd, level with me man. It true you and your wife tested out every single piece of ass you ever filmed? You really get that much pussy?"

Boyd was tired of the questions, bored with the perverts and pedophiles who wanted play by plays of every sexual encounter he'd ever filmed.

"How's your wife? Julia...ain't it?"

Boyd had no idea. Since his wife was also his co-accused, neither he nor Julia was allowed to write to the other, institution-to-institution correspondence strictly prohibited.

"I've applied for special permission from the warden to send Julia a simple little letter. But it's been weeks, and I still haven't heard anything back."

"Don't worry," the kid laughed. "He'll get to your request one of these days. And besides, you got the time to wait. What the fuck else you got to do?"

———————

Lillian and Brandy took Tito to the bakery and let him pick out a birthday cake, deciding that today would be as good as any day to celebrate. His exact date of birth was a mystery, the court having deemed his second birthday to be the twenty-ninth of September. An estimated date picked by the court's family judge in an attempt to approximate the child's age.

"Maybe we should get some ice cream?" Brandy suggested, watching Lillian shift Tito from her right hip to her left.

"Don't you think the cake's got enough sugar already?"

Brandy nodded, amazed at the depth of Lillian's maternal instincts. "But we should get some milk. I used the last for coffee this morning."

"Between the three of us, we'd be better off buying a goddamn cow."

Handing Brandy the child, Lillian pulled her purse off her shoulder and paid the baker for the cake.

"Well, instead of a bigger apartment, maybe we should think about renting a farm?"

Brandy liked it when Lillian used the word *we*. It left her with a warm, comforted feeling. Being part of a couple was definitely more desirable than standing alone against the world.

"I'll take him back," Lillian motioned toward the child.

"I was thinking about the apartments we were looking at," Brandy leaned across the counter to pick up the cake. "I think we should take the two bedroom in the west end. What you think?"

"The two bedrooms was nice, but why that one? It's a good half hour longer to work, and you said the neighborhood was *infested* with kids."

Brandy cleared her throat, amazed at what she was about to say. "It's closer to a good school. I know—my kids went there when they were little."

Lillian just nodded, the words suddenly catching in her throat.

"And besides, we ain't gonna be strippers forever. Might be time to think about doing something else, now that we got a kid to raise."

Slowing in her own tracks, Lillian planted a warm kiss on Tito's cheek, surprising the young boy as he turned to return the affection.

"Your mommies are going to take good care of you," she grinned, reaching out with her left hand to link fingers with her girlfriend.

"Warren, you've gotta take your meds or you won't be allowed any time in the rec room," the nurse repeatedly reminded him.

Grabbing the plastic pill cup, he downed both tablets, not the least bit concerned with what the doctor has prescribed, his attention totally focused on maintaining his status of *good behavior.*

"Did the doctor say if I can use the phone today?"

"Warren, you know the rules. No phone calls for the first ninety days."

"Fine," he sulked, moving away from the dispensary window so one of the guards could check his open mouth to make sure he wasn't *cheeking* any of his medication.

"But she could phone me, right?"

"Yes, Warren," the nurse called out over another patient's head. "If your sister Wanda did phone, her message would be recorded and passed to you after the initial ninety day waiting period."

"I'm gonna have a shit load of messages come day ninety-one," he confidently nodded. "You just wait and see. The phone's probably ringing off the hook."

"You think he'd ask about his daughter," one of the nurses muttered as she shook her head. "All that man has babbled about since the day he was brought in was his sister, Wanda. You'd think the whole world revolved around her."

"To him, it probably does," the pharmacist nodded, firmly sliding down the dispensary window before making sure it was securely locked.

———————

"Six weeks and four days left," Amber laughed.

"I thought you liked school?" Wanda helped her niece dish out two generous bowls of pasta marinara.

"I do, but I *love* summer holidays more. And besides, Dad should be out of the hospital and feeling better by the time I start ninth grade in fall. Right?"

"Well, we'll see," Wanda's hands began to tremble, still unable to explain to her niece that her father would probably be locked up for at least another year, if not longer.

"I wish I could see him," Amber mused, lifting both bowls off the counter and carrying them straight to the kitchen table.

"Schizophrenia is a funny disease, my dear. Some people need a lot of special attention and must be isolated for their treatment."

"I suppose," she said and filled her mouth with pasta. "So," Amber reached for the pitcher of fruit juice. "Dad's sure gonna be surprised when he comes home and finds out that you're pregnant. We didn't even know that you had a boyfriend."

Wanda nodded, slowly shoveling her own mouth full of pasta as she consciously willed her teeth to chew her supper before forcing the tomato-covered noodles down her throat.

"Dad's gonna be so happy. He always said that if you had a baby, it would almost be like a brother or sister to me."

"Almost," Wanda forced herself to smile as her eyes darted to the red check marks adorning the kitchen calendar. Glaringly obvious, they stood to signal the half way point of her brother's initial ninety-day evaluation period.

"Is it too soon to know if it's a boy or a girl, because I know the hospital can do a sonogram test and see pictures of the fetus? We saw examples in a science class."

"It's too soon," Wanda patted her niece's hand. "And you know, I don't really care," she stood up to scrap her uneaten portion into the garbage. "I just pray every night with my heart and soul that it's a normal, healthy baby. I truly do."

Amber smiled back, thrilled that her growing family was now living together under one communal roof.

———————

It had taken over two months and dozens of phone calls, but Francois Dubois had finally tracked down another company willing to shoot his video. Gratefully, they'd been picking up most of the slack since

Giovanni Films had been closed down, and after his initial meeting, Francois was surprised to learn that they'd probably even be able to provide a superior product. Much more explicit, the new company was somehow not hampered with the minimum age requirements that always seemed to plague the Giovanni's.

"So it's a twenty-five thousand deposit, and another fifty on delivery," the filmmaker confirmed over his cell phone.

"And you can guarantee the actors will be age appropriate?"

"Absolutely, Mr. Dubois. Your cash payment guarantees that all our action will be authentic. No smeared ketchup or twenty year olds trying to act like teenagers. You've got my word on it. We deliver exactly what you order, or your money back. We only film first class *bloodsport*. Nothing phony or staged about our work. I can promise you that."

Francois was thrilled, especially after all his disappointment when he'd heard the news that not only had Giovanni Films been shut down, but that his precious statue had more than likely been confiscated in the process.

"One more thing," he suddenly remembered. "I'm not sure if I mentioned it, but I don't want any African-American boys in my movie."

"Don't like dark meat, eh Mr. Dubois?"

"No, it's not a racial issue," he reassured the caller. "I just don't believe that you'll be able to capture as good a close up on a black penis as you would if the skin were that of a white, Caucasian male."

"Good point. I'll make a note of that."

Francois said his goodbyes and dropped his phone back into his breast pocket before returning to his seat at the table.

"You're back," a young girl smiled up at Francois's face. "Mama said we couldn't order desert until you came back to your seat. May we order now?"

"Go ahead," he nodded toward Monique's daughter.

"I want a Baked Alaska," she announced.

"And what about you, my dear?" his girlfriend asked, casually scanning the restaurant's gold embossed desert menu.

"The usual," he returned her smile.

"Mr. Dubois and I will each have a crème brûllee," she said, looking up at the waiter, "and one child-sized Baked Alaska."

"Anything else?" He looked to Francois for permission to leave the table.

"Thank you," Francois politely dismissed him. "Everything will be just fine now."

The End

About the Author

LYNNE MARTIN is an advocate of women's rights and a staunch supporter of sexual education. She currently resides in Alberta, Canada, with her husband and their large extended family.

To learn more about LYNNE MARTIN, she can be reached through her Website and Blog @ www.lynnemartinbooks.com